ANNA
The Witch of Mull

A Scottish Saga of
Spirit and Survival

To Betty -
A special friend,
former librarian +
a great reader.

Virginia L. Altmann

BY VIRGINIA L. ALTMANN

Anna, The Witch of Mull

Copyright © 2019, by Virginia Altmann
Layout by Luna Lake Graphic Design

ISBN 978-1-54398-373-9

Special Thanks

Kim Altmann, who with immense patience
and thoughtfulness edited my first novel.

Chris Altmann, my son and publisher, who spent considerable
time laying out my book and getting it ready for the printer.

Nancy Tourkantonis, who did my grammatical editing,
even while she was in the process of selling her home.

Beth Grzegorzewski, who was able to create an image of
a 18th Century Anna on the moor of Scotland for my cover.

**Karen Faler, Sheila Geehan, Nanette Dolan
and the members of Circle 4 from
First Congregation Church in Melrose**
for reading the first draft of my novel and
were my inspiration and encouragement to
make this novel into a reality.

TABLE OF CONTENTS

PART I
The Macleans

1

Introduction

On the Isle of Mull in the Western Highlands of Scotland it is a dismal day. The bitter cold coming off the nearby ocean does not stop snaking its way through the cracks in the walls of his *bothie* (a black house). Lachlann Maclean is outside mulling over his situation on this dreary day in February. He observes his home, a rustic rectangular thatched stone building. While overlooking his home a despair enters his spirit which is more present in him lately. Life in his glen has become more and more difficult and this has been a particularly bad year brought on by a poor summer for farming.

Lach, as he is called by his family, is then brought back to what he came out for and yells out to Seathan, his *mac* (son), who has joined him, "Come help me gather some peat for our fire. Your *mathair* (mother) needs your help." The wind carries his words away and Seathan, although he hears his voice, cannot understand his words.

Seathan moves closer to his *athair* (father), "What did you say?" Lach repeats his request. Seathan knows that obeying orders is a matter of life and death on the rugged landscape of their Isle. He gathers some peat to bring into their dwelling. Quickly he disappears into the *bothie*, leaving Lach alone with his thoughts.

Alone and still troubled, Lach nervously rubs the large red scar on his right cheek. The bitter cold wind of February causes his scar to ache almost as if it was a fresh wound. Lach recalls that day when he was 20. It was an early spring morning when he and his *brathairs* (brothers), Seumus and Tomas, set out into the forest to hunt hares. Lach remembers the urgency that he and his *brathairs* felt to spend some time out of doors after the long cold and dark winter. He recalls that they were full of hope to bring back some fresh meat. Generally, their *athair* would accompany them on the hunt. But today he was not feeling well.

They had set off to the forest, located at a distance from their *bothie*. Each *brathair* carried his *dirk* (dagger) in the pocket of a long woolen cloak. On their trek Lach remembers leading the way. All the Maclean men were experienced hunters, having been trained by their *athair,* Angus. Once in the forest they walked silently and concentrated on finding signs of their prey. Lach pushed ahead while Seumus and Tomas lagged behind. After they had been in the woods for an hour, they become discouraged for as yet they had not sighted any hares.

Suddenly from out of the trees appeared several youths with *dirks* in hand who surprised Lach by lunging at him. Lach recalls that he screamed loudly, to let his *brathairs* know about the danger and his need for their help. Seumus and Tomas, although out of sight were not far behind and they frantically ran to rescue Lach. Unfortunately, it was too late to prevent one of the attackers from slashing the right cheek of Lach. The scar never let Lach forget about the dangers of living in the Highlands.

Now 25 years after the encounter of the rogue villains in the forest which Lach later found out were from the Campbell clan, he is standing in front of his *bothie* awaiting the birth of another *bairn* (baby). Lach anxiously remembers that Catherine, his *bean* (wife), had already born six *bairns* but only three are alive now; Seathan (13), Iain (7) and Caitriona (5). Three wee ones had died, 2 *macs* and a *nighean* (daughter), before reaching the age of 5. The boys died from small pox and the girl, always with a bad cough, finally just wasted away. Somehow his eldest, Seathan, had made it through his childhood and now he is entering manhood.

Seathan returns to be with his *athair.* "How is your *mathair?*" questions Lach.

"I have no news," replies Seathan.

The bitter cold prompts Lach to return inside to the warmth of the peat fire. "Let's go back inside where it is warmer and we can assist your *mathair.* The animals should also be looked after," reminds Lach.

Inside Catherine is making sure that all is ready for the imminent arrival of a new *bairn.* The door opens and a blast of wind accompanies the entry of Lach and Seathan. She speaks to them after they enter, "I think the time is near. Be ready to fetch my *mathair* and *siuir* (sister)."

"Aye, Catherine," Lach agrees. Lach then sits at the center fire and takes the moment to watch his *clanns* (children). He remarks to himself, "Seathan looks a lot like his *mathair* with her more delicate features. His nose is straighter and narrower, similar to Catherine's." Lach then brings to his mind that he has a broad nose with wide nostrils, a low brow and thick full lips. He has dark skin, made even darker by his constant exposure to the peat fires and the rugged weather of the Highlands. Although Seathan is also exposed to soot and the weather, it is easy to see that his skin is fairer and ruddier. Caitriona and Iain take after their *athair* with their darker complexion and broader facial features. Like himself all of his *clanns* resemble the Macleans with their dark curly hair and dark eyes.

Seathan now warmed by the fire gets up and heads to the *byre* (animal shed). In the cold months this extension of their *bothie* houses the family's animals and although it shelters the livestock from the harsh winter of the Isle, it is still quite cold. Seathan leaves on his warm cloak to tend the animals.

As he leaves the room Seathan assures Catherine, "*Mathair*, I am with the animals if you need my help." Seathan knows how much his assistance is needed in the care of the family and in the managing the chores of their croft farm. The farm and the animals are their major source of food. The cows and goats provide them with milk, butter-milk and cheese and several chickens are good egg producers. The family shares a small herd of sheep with other family members which gives them wool for their tartans and clothes. The rest of their needs are supplied by the moor and forests; nettles, sorrel and garlic to spice up their meals and deer, hare and fish to supplement their diet of home-grown vegetables. Seathan is aware that the family has very little of their fall harvest of cabbage, potatoes, turnips, kale, barley and oats left. He will be joining his *athair* as soon as their glen gives them a good day to hunt and fish in order for the family to survive.

While waiting for Catherine's time, Lach is feeling anger and resent-ment as he remembers how it used to be for his ancestors on their Highland island. In the past, before the great battle of Culloden when everything changed, the chiefs of the clans let their clansmen cultivate their farms as a reward to them for being their warriors. Now the chiefs and lairds are forcing the clansmen to make payments through annual leases. There are no laws or government control to protect the farmers from all the injustices such as annual rent increases. Sometimes the farmers face a worse fate of being evicted from the farms and homes that their ancestors had lived on for centuries.

3

Lach does not trouble Catherine with all his bleak thoughts and instead keeps them inside, making him feel more helpless and enraged. He remarks to himself more about the situation that he faces each day; the constant struggle of living on an island that is not very fertile. Through the centuries his ancestors have been able to make the best of the soil and climate by planting crops that are suited to the conditions. There are years, however, when the harvest is scarcer and this is one of them, leading Lach and his oldest *mac* to eat less, saving the larger and better portions for *torrach* (pregnant) Catherine and the younger *clanns*. Lach worries about his animals whose food supply of hay and oats is nearly depleted. The animals are becoming very thin and as in other lean years, the weak cows will probably have to be carried out to the pasture in the spring. Lach is engrossed in his misgivings about his life when he hears an urgent call from Catherine.

2

A *Bairn* is Born

It is late morning now when Catherine calls out to Lach who is sitting around the fire with his two youngest *clanns*. Catherine's water has come, signaling the beginning of her labour. "Lach, I do believe the time is coming. Send Seathan to fetch my *mathair* and *siuir*. Bring the young-uns to Molly. She will watch them and feed them while I bring forth this new addition to our family."

Lach anxiously calls to Catherine, "Aye, I will bring the young-uns to Molly and Seathan will fetch Jannet and Marta to help you with the birthing. I have great wishes that this will be easier for you than some of our other *bairns'* birthing which caused you so much pain. Whatever happens will be God's will, but it makes me suffer as I listen and watch the pain you must bear."

Catherine replies, "Now, now, this is the burden of women and I will try my best not to cause you so much distress. Now quickly bring our youngest *clanns* to Molly because the time is getting closer." Catherine then takes a moment to instruct Seathan, "When you come back you can go into the *byre* and finish feeding the animals and milking the cows and goats. Take up the eggs also," warns Catherine. "We don't want them to stop laying because of your neglect." Seathan knows these things and wonders why his *mathair* is reminding him. He keeps silent, however, and rushes off to fetch his *seanmhair* (grandmother) and his *piuthar-mathar* (aunt). Catherine is feeling short-tempered and impatient during her time of growing pain. She wants it all to go away.

While waiting for Jannet and Marta, Catherine continues to grow in her anxiety and she questions the amount of time it is taking them to come to her. She silently wonders what could be detaining them. She feels alone and frightened without her kin to give her comfort. There is nothing she can do but wait. The darkness of her *bothie* adds to her feelings of despair. Catherine thinks, "My *bothie* lit only by the fire has been well named. As she has done many times she notices the many layers of black soot on the walls, making them dark and smoky all year round. Calming herself, she watches the smoke escape through a center hole in the thatched roof. Catching a glimpse of gray sky through the only opening in the house, she tries not to feel threatened by the darkness.

Catherine has given birth during the winter months before. Iain and two of her deceased *bairns* had been born in the winter. The warmer months are the easiest. Seathan and Caitriona were born in the summer months and the warmth and light from the door of the *bothie* had brought comfort to her. From her birthing bed during her time of early labour, she was able to look out at the landscape of the moor with its amazing purples, yellows and reds. She watched as the Isle's abundant butterflies and birds flew by. The briny smell of the ocean nearby filled the *bothie*, eliminating much of the odor of smoke and waste.

Now without these summer advantages of nature, Catherine reminds herself that at least it is midday. The additional light penetrating from the hole at the roof top will help Jannet and Marta. Just as Catherine is contemplating all these thoughts Jannet and Marta, breathless, open the door. "Sorry we were delayed, Catherine, but we wanted to make sure that we took the 3 spoonfuls of oatmeal and water before we came, so that your newborn would have strength and luck," reassures Jannet. Catherine feels relief at their arrival and forgets that she was feeling so vulnerable just a few moments before.

Seathan appears soon after and rushes into the *byre* without a word to do his chores. He knows enough not to speak and interfere with the task at hand. They would not hear him anyway. Lach has not yet returned from delivering the young-uns to Molly; probably stopping for a brew of ale, a good distraction from hearing the pain of Catherine. Although his *athair* is still a brave warrior, through the years he has become worried and weak at home. Seathan has learned to fill in for Lach on many fronts.

Catherine lays on her straw mat in her birthing bed, moaning, as Jannet and Marta try to quell her discomfort by rubbing her back and whispering comforting and reassuring words. The pain is still minimal compared to how it will be shortly. Still fairly coherent and able to express herself, Catherine complains loudly, "Why did God will this pain upon me and other *mathairs*?" Finally, both Jannet and Marta strongly urge her to get up and walk around the small room to encourage the birthing and provide a distraction.

Jannet begins talking "Will it be a wee *mac* or *nighean*? I'm in favor of another *nighean*. She will help you with cooking, gathering peat and picking plants in the fields. Then reminded of her own advancing years, she adds, "And she will be such a comfort to you in your older age."

Catherine responds, "Perhaps." She doesn't know what it is, but she has a feeling about this *bairn*. Somehow and in some way this one will be very different from her others. Catherine is a God-fearing and devout parishioner, but she also believes in omens and the messages that she sometimes receives from a spirit outside herself. She has given up on sharing this with others, especially Lach, because he is too busy farming and responding to other needs of his clan to pay much attention to anything else. Catherine also discovered early in their relationship that Lach was fearful. When Catherine mentioned some of her premonitions, he would ignore her or worse become suspicious of such outlandish thoughts. Catherine knows that Lach is wary of her predictions of the future. She remembers how many times Lach looked over his shoulder to make sure that *Black Donald* (devil) or the *Clootie* (devil) was not following him, ready to bring him under their evil spell.

Catherine soon casts aside her thoughts because her pain is worsening and the contractions have become closer together. Suddenly a severe contraction causes her to emit a loud moan, almost a scream. Marta holds Catherine's hand and continues to walk with her.

Marta comforts her, "Catherine, you are doing well and soon you will have a wee *bairn* in your arms, suckling you and smelling so sweet."

Off in the *byre* Seathan is a silent witness to all the commotion of the birthing. He is not a novice when it comes to the realities of life. Living in one room with his family and the bed areas being within earshot of conversations, nightmarish dreams, the restlessness of his younger siblings and lovemaking have grown him up pretty quickly. Right now he tries to use the chores and the animals to distract him from all the gruesome sounds of humanity. He dreams that when he is old enough, he will leave this desolate and barren life and join his clan's warrior forces.

Seathan is then startled by very loud screaming coming from his *mathair* in the next room. He knows that this is all a part of the birthing. When his younger siblings were born, he had been taken to

Molly's. This time he was told that there was nothing to be afraid of. He was given the choice to once again leave and join his younger siblings at Molly's, but he chose to stay. After all he is almost a man and if his *mathair* needs his help; he wants to be there. Nonetheless, the screaming and groaning more than startle him. He wonders how his *mathair* can go through this a seventh time.

Seathan, to distract himself, begins to talk to the animals. Seathan has his favorite, a female, who is the most docile of all of the four cows, one bull and three females. His favorite is now pregnant and will be giving birth in May or June. Suddenly Seathan is torn from his reverie by more curdling screaming from his *mathair*. He now wishes he had stayed with Molly and the rest of his family. He believes that he is much the warrior, but listening to his *mathair's* screaming is quite another thing. Perhaps he is not quite the warrior that he thinks he is.

Meanwhile Catherine is now on her hands and knees, crawling in a circle around the fire in the middle of the room. It has been over three hours since her water had come cascading down her legs. Since this is her seventh birth, Catherine hopes that her time in labour will be shorter. Jannet and Marta have put down some woolen cloths to protect her hands and knees as she crawls along the surface of the floor. To provide some support and comfort they crawl along the floor with her. Then they feel her belly and know that the baby has descended further down. Jannet reassures Catherine, "The *bairn* is closer to being born. It won't be long now."

Catherine knows this but keeps silent. "*Mathair* bring me the chair. I feel the need of its support." Jannet and Marta once again examine Catherine's opening and realize that the *bairn's* head has begun to appear. Jannet, in between Catherine's painful contractions, asks her to push while Marta holds her *siuir's* hand. Skillfully Jannet guides the *bairn* through the enlarged opening. Jannet is well-seasoned for this role. She has assisted in the birth of all her *oghas* (grandchildren) and those of others. Her skills at midwifery are well-known in the glen and the village.

When the *bairn* has fully emerged, Jannet joyfully exclaims, "It is a wee *nighean.*"

Marta makes sure that the water in the kettle above the fire is warm but not too hot. Catherine, having given birth many times, has made sure that a supply of clean rags, washed several days before, is ready. A collection of special clothes left over from her other *clanns* and a brand-new woven cloth in the pile of birth objects are visible to Marta. The newborn emits her first vocalizations, the volume of which fill the small room. At that Jannet cuts the cord, wets some of the cloths and cleans the newborn while Marta gathers the rowan berry herbal mixture, prepared by Jannet in preparation of the birth.

"Here Catherine," offers Jannet. "Drink this mixture of rowan berries. It will protect you from the Evil Eye and the faeries." Catherine sips the herbal berry mixture and she scowls as the bitterness touches her tongue.

"Ugh," she wails and then remembering the powers of the fruit and the tree which bear the fruit, she swallows the rest of the potion without complaint.

In the pocket of her petticoat Marta produces a silver coin. "Here wee one," Marta announces as she places the coin in the newborn's hand. "Hold onto it long but not too long. It will give you great wealth when you are older." The little newborn grasps the coin in her small red hand and then soon after drops it. Jannet and Marta who have been carefully watching the newborn simultaneously declare, "I believe that your wee *nighean* held onto the coin just long enough to have riches when she is older.

Soon happiness turns to confusion and Jannet and Marta become silent. The light from the sun shining on the thatched roof at midday has penetrated through the open hole above and is reflecting on the newborn. The light highlights the outstanding feature of the little *bairn*. Marta, the first to speak, shouts with great concern, "She has a mass of flaming red hair!" None of them have ever seen a red-head in their lifetime. Catherine looks away, now understanding why this one is going to be different. All the old suspicions passed on through many generations, about red-heads and witches will mark her *bairn* as a witch. Right now she cannot accept this and trusts that this red-head is going to have special gifts. She refuses to be afraid.

While contemplating the destiny of her *nighean*, she begins to have more contractions. This is nature's way of expelling the mass of birthing waste from her body. As soon as she is done, Jannet takes it outside and buries it in a specially prepared hole, dug in the warmer months and marked by a large stick. In the spring a tree will be planted on the spot to reflect the child's life as she grows. Jannet knows that this tree will need to have special care so that it will grow straight and tall and fully leafed which will mean that the *bairn* will

9

always be healthy and strong.

Marta, after her initial shock of the birth of a red-head, knows that it is more important than ever to administer one more protective rite to this wee one. And so, as is the custom and belief of her ancestors and family, Marta places some whisky into the newborn's mouth to ward off the Evil Eye. All the women are hoping that the little red-headed *bairn* will now be protected from evil. Together they all invoke to the unknown spirits, "Please protect this little one from evil and misfortunes."

Before she returns to the birthing bed, Jannet and Marta remove all the signs of Catherine's recent birthing. Then they dress Catherine in a clean garment and place her wrapped *nighean* in her arms. At that Catherine, with her *clann* in her arms, returns to her bed.

When Catherine is settled, Jannet asks Catherine, "What do you intend to name her?"

Catherine, long before the birth, had settled on the name of Anna if it was a *nighean*, and now that she sees her wee one, she knows that this will be a good name for her. No sooner has Catherine responded to Jannet than Lach comes through the door, eager to see what was happening with the birthing.

He is surprised that the *bairn* is already born and settled in the arms of Catherine. He goes over to the bed where they both lie and at first, because the *bairn* is covered in cloth, he does not notice the red hair. "Let me see my wee one," pleads Lach. Catherine gently and slowly opens the cloth, revealing both the sex and hair of the little *bairn*. Marta and Jannet know that no one can miss the red hair. It is a bright red with plenty of it. Lach looks startled at his first viewing. This is not something he has expected. He is glad it is a *nighean* to fill out his family, but the red hair!" Annoyed and startled he cannot contain himself. "Now where has she come from? I can't believe that she is my *bairn*! Is she a witch or maybe she has been switched by the faeries?" The red-raised scar on his right cheek appears to become larger, more inflamed and rawer. His annoyance quickly turns into anger. His face, previously sporting a broad grin, is now contorted with a purple hue while his broad nose is made more conspicuous as heavy breathing cause his nostrils to flare as if emitting fire. His dark brown eyes are wide and enlarged. He looks as if he is going into battle.

Catherine does not like this mood of Lach, but she knows that Lach will not harm her or their new *nighean*. Observing this, Jannet and Marta know it is their time to leave. Catherine and Lach will be left to sort out this situation on their own. They are, themselves, fearful of Lach's outcries and that what he says might be true of the fate of the red-headed Anna. Catherine remains calm and is determined to protect her special *nighean*.

Jannet and Marta, as they leave, remind Lach, "Today is Sunday, the day of Anna's birth and a child born on the Sabbath Day is blithe, bonnie, good and gay." And thus it is that Anna Maclean is born on February 24, 1785. Jannet and Marta return to their *bothie*s with many misgivings about little Anna, but they keep their thoughts to themselves. They will keep a watchful eye, however, on her and Catherine and hope that Lach will learn to accept his new *clann*.

Catherine is too exhausted to talk to Lach about Anna. She takes Anna to her breast and she suckles gently with closed eyes. Catherine looks down on the top of her head. Her red hair is soft and wispy, although abundant. Catherine takes in the sweet smell of her newborn. Her eyes are closed but Catherine knows that they will be bright blue because the blue is showing through her delicate eyelids. She is also fair of skin. Catherine does not know how such a *bairn* has been given to her, but she does know that she is the offspring of Lach and herself. She hopes that soon Lach will accept this fact.

3

A New Day

Later that evening after Lach returned, Molly brought Iain and Caitriona back. Both *clanns* rush through the front door to see their new *siuir*. They run to Catherine lying in her bed with the newborn and they greet their *mathair* with a hug and then they lay eyes on their *siuir*. The first thing they both notice is her red hair. Molly had not prepared them for this unusual feature of their *siuir* because she did not know. When Jannet had come by Molly's *bothie*, she had only announced that a *bairn* had been born and that the *clanns* could be brought back.

Thankfully, Catherine had nothing to fear about their reaction because her two youngest were excited and happy to see their young *siuir* and had nothing but praise for her. They admired her beautiful wispy red hair and her sweet soft body. Then they both asked together, "What shall we call her?"

"Anna, her name is Anna," replied Catherine.

"Hello Anna," whispered the two. It was a lovely endearing moment watching them greet Anna and Catherine hopes that this will continue to be the reaction of others.

Meanwhile, Lach had gone inside the *byre* to see how Seathan was doing with chores. He was delighted to see that he had everything under control. The animals were fed and had been milked. The collected milk was resting in a few containers on the side of the *byre*. The hens had given them almost a dozen eggs. These along with their porridge will give them several hearty meals. Lach then approaches Seathan about his new *siuir*. "Seathan, have you seen your new *siuir*, Anna?"

"Yes, athair, I saw her soon after she was born."

"She has red hair!" Lach exclaims emphatically to his oldest. Seathan can see that his *athair* feels disturbed about the newborn, but he knows enough not to add to these concerns. He has learned the importance of quiet lips, needed so much when the head of the

13

family yields so much power over his family.

The rest of the night was uneventful. Anna lay next to her *mathair* in her wooden cradle, crying several times during the night to be nursed and cleaned. Catherine knew that keeping the *bairn* warm and dry in the drafty *bothie* during one of the coldest months of the year would be a feat of constant vigilance. Catherine constantly reminds herself that for all of the Highlanders life on the Isle of Mull is rugged. Many newborns do not survive the first year of their life, particularly the ones having the misfortune of being born in the winter months. Catherine recognizes that this could be the fate of her Anna, but she tries not to show her fear. Almost speaking the words aloud, "I will do everything I can to keep my wee *bairn* healthy and alive."

Catherine, upon awakening, feels the effects of her recent birthing. The first night had been difficult as she worried about Lach's reaction to Anna. She is very tired and before rising gives her body a quick look over, aware that that she is old for bearing a child. Her large pendulous breasts are filled with her first milk, ready for her little Anna. She feels satisfied that despite her age she has good proof that she will be able to nurse her *bairn*. She touches her face which is no longer smooth and soft as it was in her youth. Her face has more wrinkles and sagging skin than many others of her age. Her long curly hair, once brown and shiny, has become dull with many strands of gray. Catherine's age, however, is not reflected in her stout body that remains strong and muscular, a result of the demanding work of Highland living.

Lying in bed watching her *clanns,* Catherine is reminded that she will soon need to get back to keeping her family provided with the essentials of life: warmth, food and water. Her two youngest already help with the inside chores and once the weather turns warmer, they will help outside. However, they are still too young to fetch water in the heavy wood containers, but they can keep the fire going, fetch items needed for feeding the family and help in the *byre* with the animals. When they awoke that morning, after putting on some warm clothes, Iain and Caitriona head to the *byre*. Seathan is already there milking the cows. He stops to watch his *brathair* and *siuir* feed the animals. Later they will all clean the *byre* as best they can by pushing the dung into the ditch in the floor. Seathan thinks to himself that as much as the family tries, it is difficult to keep their dwelling clean. In the winter it is impossible to get away from the stench of waste and peat smoke. He cannot wait for spring and its sweet smells.

As her newborn finishes her suckling, Catherine is also thinking about unpleasant smells. To herself she says, "The sweet *bairn* smells are reminding me of spring and soon the animals will be far away in the fields. I will finally be able to open the front door and have fresh air. There is no time right now, however, to think of the warmer months." Catherine, with little time to waste, rises from her bed in order to begin the morning chores. With a sturdiness of thought she remarks to herself, "The women on the Isle and in our clan are rugged and I, like all those before me, must get right back into taking care of my family." The first thing that she notices is an urgent need for more water. Perhaps Seathan or Lach will help her with that chore this time.

She calls out to Seathan, "Seathan, will you go to the spring and fill the buckets? The water which I got yesterday has run out and we need more in haste."

Seathan, who is in the *byre*, hears his *mathair* and knowing the importance of water to the family replies, "I will go at once. The animals can be left for a short while." Seathan quickly appears and dons his warm cloak. Outside it is cold and windy and snow covers much of the ground. Seathan remarks to himself, "My ancestors chose this location well with a spring nearby that flows constantly, providing us with all the water we need year-round."

After checking on Seathan, Lach spent the early morning collecting peat for a fire that needs to be fed often. Catherine begins to gather the ingredients for the porridge and looks up when Lach opens the door and enters, looking agitated. Catherine learned long ago not to challenge him when he is in a mood. Lach begins the conversation, "I still do not know where little Anna comes from with all that red hair. We do not have red-heads in our family!"

Catherine replies, "It is God's will, Lach, and we must make the best of it! Others will accept her as God's gift if you accept her. She will need your protection and watchful eye as well as mine and the rest of the family." Catherine knows that the Maclean clan is closely knit and support one another throughout life. Still worried and angry, Lach is silent.

Just as the conversation ends, Seathan returns with the buckets of water. He has met his *seanmhair* outside on the well-worn path of trodden snow. Catherine is glad to be distracted from her thoughts

15

by the appearance of her *mathair* bringing freshly made porridge for the family. Jannet, upon entering, first goes over to the cradle of Anna to check on her newest *ban-ogha* (granddaughter). The *bairn* is sleeping peacefully. Jannet looks lovingly at Anna and although filled with trepidation regarding the red hair, she remarks to herself at the beauty of this wee one. Her skin is as fair as fair can be and she also has rosy cheeks. She does not utter these thoughts aloud, however, because she does not want the faeries to know of her observations of little Anna. If they are aware of Anna's attractiveness, they would want to switch her for one of their own sickly children. Jannet takes a moment to pray that God will protect this unusual little one.

With the hot porridge casting its hearty earthy aroma, the family members quickly get their wooden bowls and spoons from the cupboard and sit around the fire. Catherine brings out the freshly drawn milk for the family. Jannet joins them as they quietly eat. Catherine places some eggs in the hot water by the fire and before they are finished with the porridge, she spoons the eggs into a big bowl. This is an important meal for today because after the stress of Anna's birth, none of them had the usual evening meal.

Jannet interrupts the silence, "Little Anna needs to be baptized next Sunday. I will go to the *kirk* tomorrow and talk to the Pastor about a baptism." Although the reason is not uttered, Catherine knows the haste needed in baptizing a newborn. Jannet reflects on the urgency of a rapid protection needed for little Anna. It has already been suggested by Lach that this red-headed *clann* of his might have been switched at birth by the faeries and remains in danger until she is baptized.

Catherine consults with Lach, "I would like Molly to carry Anna into the *kirk*. She is the youngest *siuir* in the family and would serve the purpose well. Do you agree with that choice?" Although he is fearful of other folks and their reaction to red-headed little Anna, he is in full agreement. He likes the way Molly cares for his young-uns and she will carry little Anna with great care. "So, it is decided," Catherine states, "Anna will be baptized on Sunday." Although angry with the birth of a red-head, Lach will not give up on one of his own. Catherine assures him that there was no opportunity for the faeries to come into their *bothie* and make a switch.

Wanting to avoid tension, Jannet speaks up, "I have some cheese and bread to give Molly so that she can offer it to the first male stranger she meets on the way to the *kirk*." This was the custom of their clan, but it is at some risk. If the stranger accepts it the *bairn* would have some good luck, but if he rejects it the *bairn* will suffer a misfortune. Thankfully, the weather would still be windy and cold, giving the practice a greater chance that the gift would be accepted. Most on the Isle know about this ancient custom of offering food to a stranger, giving the newborn a chance at good luck in life.

4
The Decision

During the next few days ominous thoughts constantly fill the minds of Catherine and Lach as they try to adjust to the reality of their red-headed *bairn*. Would the pastor and the congregation accept their newborn, or would they be fearful and treat Anna and the family suspiciously? When some of their kin had visited them, as was the custom to welcome a new member, some had remarked on Anna's red hair with surprise and dismay.

Catherine kept quiet lips and presented Anna to them in a positive and accepting manner. Right from the beginning she had known that she would have to be an example of love and acceptance to quell the fears of her clansmen. However, the terror which surrounds a child born with red hair is so strong in the minds of her kinfolk that she knows it will be an ongoing struggle. She is not afraid that her little Anna might be a witch because she understands things that others do not.

Meanwhile Catherine keeps busy with the chores and activities of caring for a newborn along with the rest of her family. Her *siuirs* and the *beans* (wives) of Lach's *brathairs* (brothers) brought gifts of food to honor the birth. Life for a *mathair* of a newborn has never been easy in the Highlands, especially in the winter months. Catherine's and Lach's kin are very aware of the needs of family. Catherine is grateful for the closeness and support of their kin.

Soon all the clan members will be busy with spring chores. Catherine and her family will be on their own when the clan begins preparing the soil and then planting. Winter has caused some damage on all the thatched roofs of the *bothies* and the men in the glen will be harvesting heather to dry and repair them. The work never stops and now with a newborn Catherine is feeling overwhelmed. She thinks to herself, "I have managed many times before and I must again forget about myself."

The next day Jannet visits her *nigheans*, Molly and Lili. As the matriarch of the clan she is the organizer of social and religious events such as weddings and baptisms. She wants to talk to them about the plans of the baptism. At Molly's house she tells her, "Catherine and Lach have decided to have you carry young Anna into the *kirk*." Then she shares, "Molly, I do not know how the *kirk* will view this newborn with red hair. I fear they might reject us. If this is the case, we will act in the courage of our ancestors and not panic." Then with a determined spirit she asks, "Do you understand?"

"Yes, *Mathair*, I understand," Molly reassures her.

Then Jannet continues "I will bring some cheese and bread for you to give to the first stranger you meet so little Anna will have some good luck, which she certainly needs."

"Right *Mathair*, I will do what is our custom and put my trust in a good outcome," Molly agrees.

Jannet replies, "The weather is still windy and cold and a stranger will probably be appreciative of the nourishment."

Jannet then travels down the lane to the dwelling of Lili, her third *nighean*. Lili is expecting her and has some bread and cheese ready. They sit around the fire with Lili's young *clanns*. Lili's *fear* (husband), Brian, is in the *byre* with his animals and two older *clanns* are with him. "Lili, as you know it is important for a newborn to be baptized on the first Sunday following the birth or as close to it as possible," Jannet begins. "Catherine has chosen Molly to carry young Anna into the *kirk*, because she is the youngest in the family. I have not made a visit to the pastor yet to tell him about the newborn and the need for a baptism on Sunday. I am anxious to learn if the parishioners will accept a red-head into the congregation."

Lili, who always has proven herself to be very resourceful, says, "*Mathair*, I have been thinking about a plan since I went to visit my new *banta* (niece) earlier today. I have considered other ways to handle the baptism so that our little Anna will not be labelled as a witch or a changeling. I do not want Anna to wear the clothing of either of these unfortunate spirits. My thoughts have considered two solutions."

Jannet interrupts with great concern, "What are you thinking of my Lili? I am not sure that it will be good."

Lili then reassures her, "Of course, we will need to share my ideas with Catherine and Lach first and then if they agree, a clan *coinneamh* (meeting) of our closest kin should be called. Anna will need the support of all the clan in order to thrive."

"Go on, Lili, what are you thinking?" asks Jannet.

20

Lili cautiously shares her thoughts, "As you know *Mathair*, many newborns are born without hair. Anna's hair could be shaven before she is baptized, and a bonnet will cover her bare head until it is taken off to receive the baptismal water. If that plan is not acceptable, Catherine could use the brown dye which colors the wool of our tartans to change the color of Anna's hair."

Jannet interrupts "I don't know if those solutions would work, Lili."

"*Mathair*," responds Lili, "what other choice do we have to protect little Anna?"

"You are right. I have thought of none other. Let's go to Catherine and Lach right away and I will delay my visit to the pastor," Jannet responds. Lili calls to Brian and tells him that she is leaving briefly to visit Catherine and Lach.

It is late afternoon when Jannet and Lili appear at Catherine and Lach's. Lach is outside looking at the thatch on his *bothie*. He wants to see how much damage the winter and dampness has done. He reminds himself that no matter how much labour and time it takes, repairing the roof thatch has to be done whenever it is needed. This is a skill that is handed from *athair* to *mac* and soon he will be teaching it to his own *macs*. If the thatch is left unattended even for a short time, it will decay and cave in, leaving his family as victims to the harsh winds and weather of the Highlands.

Jannet and Lili notice that Lach is in deep thought when they approach him. They hesitate to disturb him, but knowing the seriousness of the matter at hand, they do so cautiously. Jannet speaks first, "Lach, Lili and I have come to you and Catherine to discuss an important matter."

"I will finish what I am doing and then I will be ready to hear what you have to say," responds Lach. "Meanwhile, go inside. Catherine will be glad to see you."

Catherine stops what she is doing when Jannet and Lili appear at the door. She is surprised because it is nearing the time to eat and she is just beginning to get food ready for her family. "We've come to talk with you and Lach, regarding the baptism of little Anna," Jannet announces.

"Come and sit here around the fire and we will wait for Lach," motions Catherine. There is silence around the fire with Catherine wondering what Jannet and Lili are about to share regarding her wee *bairn*.

While they wait for Lach, Catherine observes her *mathair* in a way she has never done before. The wind on the Isle has made her face dry and wrinkled. Her *mathair* is now in her sixth decade and her face is deeply furrowed. A once attractive woman is now looking like an old woman. Her hair has turned a silvery white. Her body, once strong and muscular, is showing her age caused by years of hard labour and caring for a family on the rugged landscape of the Highlands. However, Catherine reminds herself that her *mathair* still has quite a bit of strength and vitality as well as a quick mind. Catherine, herself, feeling very vulnerable with the birth and circumstance of her little *bairn*, wants her *mathair* more than ever to be strong and around for quite a while.

Just as the silence is becoming unbearable for Jannet and Lili, Lach opens the door and heads toward the warm fire. He sits down with the others. Lach, as the patriarch of the family, begins the conversation, "So Jannet and Lili what brings you here at this late hour?"

"Lach," Jannet begins, "we honor you as the head of your family and with this in mind we have a few ideas regarding the protection of young Anna. As all of us know some of the pastors of our Church of Scotland have great suspiciousness towards our Gaelic clan. Our language and customs are foreign to them," continues Jannet. "I believe that our kinfolk, who have seen the condition of little Anna, are fearful of what the reactions of the pastor and the parishioners will be towards Anna and our family."

Lach responds, "I have the same concerns as you. I have begun to accept little Anna and I also want to protect her from harm. What are your thoughts?" pressures Lach.

"Lili thinks that we can find a way to hide Anna's red hair either by shaving her scalp or dyeing her hair," shares Jannet. Both Catherine and Lach quietly take some time to assess these solutions.

Catherine speaks first, "I believe that we could dye Anna's hair by using the dyes I use for the wool of our tartans. But I do not support the idea of shaving her head because as a newborn her scalp is tender and sensitive. I feel that it is too dangerous."

Lach also weighs in, "Something does need to be done with haste and I agree that shaving Anna's head is not a good recommendation. Dyeing her hair makes more sense to me and I think it would work. I know that a baptism should take place as soon as possible, but we need to test out our dye solution first and share our thoughts with our kin." And so, it is decided that Lach will gather a *coinneamh* of all of the closest kin.

5

Plans for a *Coinneamh*

The morning once again is misty and cold. It is late and Lach decides to make a visit to his kinfolk. It is the first days of March and he knows that the soil in the glen will not be soft enough for planting until later Spring. This year Spring could not come soon enough for him. "It has been a difficult winter and our food is running scarce," Lach thinks. "Our vegetables from the fall harvest are mostly consumed. Our beef is gone. When I return I will draw some cow's blood and mix it with our porridge for the evening meal."

Lach then walks to the *bothie* of his oldest *brathair*, Seumus, and his *bean*, Moire. From the distance he spots Seumus gathering some stored peat to bring inside. Two of his *clanns*, Calum and Bride, are helping him. When he arrives Lach picks up a couple of roughly cut squares of peat, just large enough to lay on the fire inside, and motions Seumus to the door. "Seumus, I have something to ask of you and Moire." Seumus lets Lach and himself in, while his *clanns* stay outside to finish collecting. Moire is busy poking the fire and talking to her oldest *nighean*, Barabla. Barabla looks up and when she sees her *athair* and *brathair-athar* (uncle) enter, she dismisses herself by going to the *byre* to attend the animals. Her *brathair-athar* did not visit very often in the winter and she knows that he probably has something important to discuss.

Moire then invites everyone to sit around the fire. "Come here and sit, Lach. The misty and cold air might give both of you a chill," admonishes Moire. While she is inviting the men to the fire, she takes a few pieces of peat and places them on it. The black smoke from the fire finds its way around the room; eventually circling up to the center hole and then outside. It leaves its blackening marks on their *bothie*'s walls. Moire offers Lach and Seumus a vessel of ale. While she goes to fetch the ale, the *brathairs* gather themselves around the fire welcoming its warmth and the light it casts.

Seumus, the older *brathair,* begins the conversation, "Lach, what brings you here on this late morning in winter? Do you not have chores to do that are more important than visiting?" Both Seumus and Moire are in their mid-forties. Like the other members of their clan they have dark unruly curly hair. They are short of stature but quite robust. The hard labour of the Highlands gives them a rugged and somewhat wild appearance. Lach is observing these features which are not much different from his own. He also contrasts it to his own delicate, pale red-headed *bairn* that Catherine just gave birth to.

Lach begins, "I am here on a mission which I believe is very important, so important that it has taken me away from my chores. You both, I am sure, could not have missed when you visited, the unusual features of my new *bairn*, Anna."

Seumus and Moire both nod, "Of course we saw that she has very red hair. We were startled but were waiting for you to say something. We have the concern that your red-head might be a witch. The presence of red hair in our glen is just about nonexistent," continues Seumus. "However, when I have visited other glens on our Isle, I have occasionally seen other red-heads."

"Catherine and I believe that we might have a solution to the red hair dilemma and we would like to share it with our closest kin before she is baptized," proposes Lach. "We are inviting all our closest kin to come to a *coinneamh* so that we can share our ideas. Will both of you come to it? Lili and Jannet already know about this plan."

Seumus and Moire are very aware of the need for family members to stick together in their rough and somewhat inhospitable land. All of the kin have required help from one another at some time in their lives. Both Seumus and Moire are reminded of the time when Seumus was very ill and they called upon Lach and the clansmen to help with the thatching of their roof. Moire had thought that Seumus would not pull through his illness. She took care of him as best she could, but her children were small and needed her. It was then that the other female kinfolk came to her dwelling and shared in the care of her young *clanns*. They also brought food and helped prepare the meals for the family. The animals in the *byre* were taken care of by the male kinfolk. Moire and Seumus believe that the other kin will remember the times when the family came together to help them out during difficult times. Seumus and Moire agree to come to the *coinneamh* at their clan's *aite cruinneachaidh* (meeting place) tomorrow, when the sun was at its highest.

Now that the time and *coinneamh* are arranged with Seumus and Moire, Lach opens the door and proceeds on his way to talk to his other close kin. He will next go to Tomas, the youngest *brathair* and his *bean,* Rut. Then he will move on to Jannet's family: Marta and Micheal, Molly and Roibeart and Lili and Brian. It will be a long day visiting everyone. As he leaves he bids farewell to Calum and Bride who are still collecting squares of peat for the fire. As soon as Lach is gone Moire calls her *clanns* into their *bothie*.

Lach makes the visits and each time he leaves with a heavy heart. All his kin appear supportive and yet he also detects a lot of suspiciousness. Rut, the new *bean* of Tomas, does not say much. Lach has some bad feelings about her. She is the last one to offer aid to kin when help is clearly needed. And worst of all she makes up false tales of others in the clan, particularly other women. His youngest *brathair* does not seem to have much control over his *bean*. He will share this concern with Catherine before the meeting.

6
A Talk with Seathan

Wearily, Lach travels back to his *bothie* in the late afternoon. The sun is setting and the overcast sky looks ominous, reflecting Lach's mood. Lach loves the beauty of the glen and moor and would never want to leave his Isle. However, sometimes he is filled with apprehension. He does not completely understand from whence it comes, but knows at the end of the day, the shadows and sounds of the moor surround him not only on the outside but also in his heart. He has an eerie feeling of the unknown in his surroundings and when he is alone and unsure, he fears what is going to happen in his life.

Before he enters his *bothie* he picks up several squares of peat, which he will add to the fire, so it can burn through the night. When he goes in, Catherine is already preparing their meal of the day; blood pudding, potatoes, turnips, cheese, boiled eggs, butter and milk. This is the meager nourishment that they will have in this time of hardship. If the cattle get too weak to supply them with milk he might have to kill some of the chickens for food, although this will be his last choice. He is counting on spring coming soon so that he and Seathan, along with some of his other kin, can hunt rabbit.

Lach sits down by the fire and begins to share his concerns, "Catherine, after visiting with our kin I am filled with some apprehensions. I am most fearful of Rut. She kept quiet lips but I did not like how she looked. In the past she has not been loyal to our kinfolk. I have seen her create rumors about others, especially the womenfolk. I know this to be true because later her accusations proved to be false."

Catherine then interrupts Lach's train of thought, "Lach, I am also suspicious about Rut's motives. She was raised as a Campbell, a clan that traditionally had been supportive of the English, and our enemy. Now, however, with all the clans threatened by the changes happening in our Highlands, they are not warring with each other as in the past. Nevertheless, Rut probably has not been able to totally erase

27

the attitudes of her own clan's past loyalties. There is nothing we can do about Tomas' choice of his *bean*. We will just have to keep a watchful eye on her and maybe time will change her feelings."

Lach thinks and replies, "That could be Catherine but I still mistrust Rut's intentions which could pose as a danger to our little Anna." Catherine and Lach end their conversation about Rut and the Campbells and sit down to their meal.

Seathan and Lach, after eating, go into the *byre* to examine the conditions of their animals. The cows, except for the pregnant one, look thin and weak. They both feed and milk the animals and then collect some eggs. There is not the dozen that are usually collected but enough to feed the family members at their next meal. Lach who treats Seathan as his best friend and helper speaks to him, "Seathan, you have heard the conversation tonight and as you venture out more and more into our glen you will see and hear a lot. I know that I have told you some things about our history, but it is time for you to know and understand more. Now that our chores are done, let's go and sit in front of the fire while I share our clan's story."

Iain and Caitriona have been bedded down and Catherine is nursing Anna in her bed when Seathan and Lach move out of the *byre* to the stools. Lach speaks, "Seathan, tonight you heard your *mathair* and I talking about Rut and the Campbells. We have many Campbells living in our glen now, sharing our *kirk*, the farmland and the common ground for raising our animals. But before you and I were born, it was not always so with the Highland clans. As is our custom," continues Lach, "when we come together at our *ceilidhs* (social gatherings), the bards of our clan tell our history and traditional tales. These have been told and retold for many generations, so it is what we believe."

Lach continues, "For hundreds and hundreds of years there have always been feuds and warfare between the different Highland clans, each one loyal to their own chiefs. Often these chiefs would rally their clan members to go into a battle with another clan. It was not always clear to the clan members why they were warring with another clan. The clans had an obedience to their chiefs who took care of them in other ways. Sometimes the feuds were due to the stealing of cattle. These were usually minor skirmishes. The battles became more serious, however, when it involved disputes over boundaries of land ownership, religion and alliances with the English and their kings. Through the centuries many clans wanted Scotland to be independent of the English with a religion of their own choice. Other clans, however, were loyal to the English, believing that they needed the protection and economic advantages of a larger country. The Campbells were loyal protectors of English rule; whereas, the Macleans wanted Scotland to be independent with their own monarchy and government. These ongoing feuds eventually became more serious and led to the Battle of Culloden in 1746. I am sure you have heard the name and some of the details of the conflict between the clans as told by our Bard at our *ceilidhs*. However, you probably do not understand how all this is connected to Rut."

Seathan responds, "*Athair*, I have heard you and my *mathair* say that Rut is a Campbell and that because of that she might hold some long-seated grudges against the Macleans."

"That is true, Seathan and the story about the battle and the bitterness between the clans is a sad and complicated one. At another time I will tell you more about our clan's history, but I am too tired to continue. I need to rest. Tomorrow I will be talking at a clan *coinneamh* about plans for Anna."

Seathan then interjects, "*Athair* shall I come to the *coinneamh*? I am nearing manhood and would like to join in."

Lach responds to Seathan, "Not this time, Seathan. I will tell you what happened there later."

7
Getting Ready

The next morning does not come soon enough for Lach and Catherine. Catherine has arranged for one of her kin, Maighread, to care for her youngest *clanns*, while she is at the *coinneamh*. Although it is not an easy time to leave little Anna, Catherine feels it is important to go. She will nurse Anna just before she leaves. She will also arrange with Seathan to come fetch her if Anna cries excessively.

Catherine tells Lach that she is going to the spring to collect fresh water for the family. After filling several wooden buckets and lugging them back to the *bothie*, she decides that she wants to take advantage of a sunny day to wash clothes. She looks across the room at the pile of dirty laundry in the corner and sighs.

She bundles the wash into a large cloth satchel and with her washing stick traipses over the rough terrain of rocks and muddy grass to the river. The river is flowing rapidly when she comes to the location she always uses to wash her soiled items. It slopes gently down and at the end she is able to sit on a rock which protrudes into the river, providing both the water and the rough surface for scrubbing her items. This morning the swift movement of the river makes Catherine hesitate, knowing that a false step could send her plunging into the rapids. Through many winters she has faced the dangers of the river and with careful footing she finds her safe spot. Once the task is done she will hurry back, put the cloths out for drying, nurse Anna and then dress herself for the *coinneamh*.

It is mid-morning when Catherine rushes back with her bundle of wet clothes. She hangs them on the trees to dry. When she walks into the *bothie*, as she expected, Lach is waiting with a troubled expression. It is not surprising that Lach, who is already dressed in his cleanest *plaid* (men's garment blanket) is impatiently waiting for her. With a quick glance she rushes past him to nurse little Anna. Usually Catherine loves her time of nursing and snuggling with her, but she is well aware that right now there is no time. She picks up

31

Anna from her cradle and the *bairn,* drowsy from her recent sleep, is somewhat hesitant to nurse. Once she begins, however, Catherine is grateful that she nurses quickly and easily. When Anna finishes her nursing, Maighread, who has been waiting, takes Anna into her arms. She cleans Anna and wraps her in warm blankets. After a while of cuddling she will then put her back into her cradle to sleep.

Meanwhile Catherine realizes that in trying to complete her household chores, she has pushed the limits on the time needed to ready herself for this important *coinneamh.* She quickly gathers her cleanest clothes from her wooden chest and proceeds to her bed to take off her wet and soiled clothes. First, she puts on her linen shift and wool stockings which are held up by knitted garters. She groans at the need for the uncomfortable stay she must wear to support her nursing breasts. Over her stay and shift she throws on her gown. Four petticoats will keep her warm in the damp and drafty *aite cruinneachaidh* (gathering place). After she dons her cape and her *kertch* (cap of a married woman) she taps the shoulder of Lach, indicating her readiness to depart. Lach, who is bending over securing his breeches with the cloth ties, finishes the job and then looks up at her. As they head to the door Catherine gives final instructions to Maighread and Seathan.

8
The *Coinneamh*

Before they head on the path, Lach and Catherine pick up several squares of peat to add to the center fire in the *aite cruinneachaidh*. The sun is not quite at its highest, but the early start will give them time to add the peat which will take the chill off the room so that everyone will be able to focus on the difficult situation at hand. The snow has begun to melt, making the walk slippery. Catherine takes the arm of Lach. Due to the direction of the wind off the ocean they are able to smell and feel the ocean air. As they continue along these briny scents of the sea are generally welcomed treasures to them. Catherine is reminded, however, that their lives have also been negatively impacted by the sea. Harsh winds, coming from the ocean, pass unforgivingly over the moor as well as the little settlements of the Macleans. The weather of Mull is often unpredictable and often affects their crops. Unplanned frosts brought by this weather frequently kill their most vulnerable crops, resulting in winters of scarcity.

Inside the large circular stone and thatched *aite cruinneachaidh*, crude wooden benches have been placed next to the stone wall which is a distance from the large center fire. However, for this smaller gathering the clansmen will each bring one of the stools, scattered around the room, closer to the fire.

Catherine and Lach add their own peat to the fire, still smoldering from its last use. It lights up quickly and warmth begins to penetrate the room. With that done Catherine and Lach sit in silence. Catherine will wait until Lach speaks, if indeed he decides to talk.

Catherine glances around the room. It is a familiar space for her because it was here that she first met Lachlann. The year was 1763 and she was 20 and Lachlann was 23—a mighty attractive Maclean youth. They had both come on a cold February evening to the *ceilidh* which was a traditional event of the clans in the winter months.

As Catherine now sits in the almost empty room, she reflects, "At the *ceilidh* the room took on a life and vitality that is missing right now. The room would have been warm and cozy from a fire that had been burning for hours. Men, women and children would be sitting on the benches, eagerly waiting for the activities of the night. The evening would begin with the music of the fiddle and the melodeon playing the ancient Highland folk tunes that all knew and felt in their souls. After hours of dancing and singing, the bard would narrate poems, legendary stories and sing more ballads for the clans. These recitations were their favorite part of the *ceilidh*"

"Clans, long settled on Mull, would join the Macleans to socialize and mingle with the opposite sex. It was often the way the males and females met to find a mate. Catherine, a MacKinnon, liked the idea of meeting a Maclean. They were the most powerful clan on the Isle besides the Campbells and she felt that it would be a good match if she were to marry a Maclean."

Suddenly Catherine is awakened from her reverie when the door opens and Moire and Seumus enter. Like Catherine and Lach they have changed from their dirty soiled working clothes into an attire that is generally saved for special occasions. Lach speaks to Seumus, "I am glad to see you both. Get your stools and sit near the fire. It will take the chill away."

As they move to the fire, Seumus reports, "On our way I saw Tomas and Rut headed here. They should arrive shortly."

Although Lach and Catherine are pleased to hear that Tomas and Rut took the time to come, they still harbor some apprehension concerning Rut. Due to the clan hierarchy she will probably be silent during the *coinneamh*, but her silence does not mean that she will be supportive of little Anna. "After all," Lach silently considers, "Rut has made up falsehoods about other women and I am not sure of Rut's beliefs regarding red-heads." Lach remembers that last year Rut had made a big deal about a widowed young woman who was accused of being a witch. Rut had spread the rumor of the young woman's guilt among the villagers.

From then on the poor widow carried a stigma of being a witch. Although burning at the stake was no longer an option, she is avoided. She no longer attends the *ceilidhs* and very few folks help her in her times of need. This is a difficult and lonely life for a widow with two *bairns*. Rut and others base their suspicions on the unexplained deaths of some cattle owned by the farmer who lived in the *bothie* next to the widow. It never took Rut much time to accuse other women of witchery when sudden storms upset the boats of fishermen who died in the turbulent seas off their Isle.

Soon Tomas and Rut come in. They remark on the warmth of the *aite cruinneachaidh* while moving their stools close to the fire. The smoke from the burning peat has begun to fill the room. The blackened walls are reminders of the years of fires which have kept the clans warm as they gathered during their celebrations. Catherine watches the firelight dance on the roughly chiseled stones of the ancient walls of the room. She is reminded of century-old conspiracies hidden in the walls; evil plots and *bairns* illegitimately conceived were some of its secrets.

Catherine's eyes move to the faces of her family. The light from the fire casts shadows on each face, changing their appearances. She watches Lach rub his scar, a habit of his when he is unsure or anxious. Seumus sits silently but his countenance does not deceive; he is restless and apprehensive. Tomas and Rut, on the other hand, do not reveal any tensions about the unexpected request from Lach. Catherine remarks to herself, "Rut could have been an attractive woman but her evil nature has given her a hardened demeanor."

Catherine, not wanting to dwell on the peculiarities of the kinfolk now sitting in the room, gets up. She reaches the door and opens it to observe the sun at its highest point. She scans the landscape and in the distance she spots the rest of the family. Marta and Micheal are walking with Jannet. Jannet's arms are enveloped in theirs as they steady her over the slippery path. Catherine watches the approaching travelers for a few minutes and then she closes the door. She does not want to let the cold air of the glen take away the beginnings of warmth in the room. She sits down once more in the circle around the fire and updates everyone letting them know that it will be a few minutes before the rest will arrive. Catherine becomes more and more nervous as the moment nears to discuss the issues of her little *nighean*. She glances over at Lach who continues to look tense.

Finally the door opens and the folks gathered around the fire push back to make more room. There is some stirring in the room as each family member finds a stool, brings it to the fire and takes a moment to greet their kinfolk. Lach then opens the conversation, "Catherine and I are happy that you were all able to make it to this *coinneamh*.

The issue at hand affects our clan greatly and we are seeking your support in making the best decision. As you all know by now our newest *bairn*, Anna, was born as a red-head. Most folks in our glen have not seen a red-head and we are very troubled. We do not want our Anna to be labelled and persecuted as a witch."

Micheal speaks up first. Besides Jannet, he is the oldest of the kinfolk. In a loud controlling voice he utters, "How do we know that your *bairn*, Anna, is not a witch? Do you believe that we should take that chance? The witches of our clan have caused many misfortunes for us. I can remember and tell you of many." Some of the clan members appear to be stunned by Micheal's outburst, including Marta who had helped deliver little Anna and already has a fondness for her. She is completely surprised because Micheal had not expressed these misgivings when they talked yesterday after Lach's visit. She wonders to herself what has happened to change Micheal's thinking.

Lach is worried that Micheal will poison the attitudes of the rest. Lach is just about to interject when Seumus comments, "Micheal, I believe that we can think the situation through and come to some other conclusions about the little *bairn*, Anna. In my experiences of traveling throughout the Highlands, I have seen other red-headed folks. We also need to remember that all the folks who were witches in our glen were not red-heads, but in fact looked very much like we do with dark curly hair and dark eyes. No longer are we blaming witches for all the tragedies in our glen. Perhaps as little Anna grows we will witness other things about her."

There was silence for several minutes giving everyone time to think about the comments of Micheal and Seumus. In the quiet Lach reflects to himself, "This silence is worse than my kin bringing their thoughts into the open." Finally, Lach makes a statement, "I realize that many of you might be concerned about Anna's presence in our clan. However, I want you to think more about Seumus's comments. He makes a good point that none of those reported as witches have been red-heads. Why do we judge that just because our Anna was born with red hair that she is a witch? How can a tiny *bairn* be made guilty when she has not even lived more than two weeks of her life? Can we instead choose the action of just keeping our eye on her as she grows? Not all witches are bad witches who cause misfortunes and tragedies. There are white witches who are healers and know all about the power of herbs and other healing traditions."

He continues, "Micheal, I understand your concern. You were faced with many difficulties and tragedies in your life when your *athair* returned from battle. It is easy to believe that witches might have caused all of those calamities. But we must remember that no witch has ever been found guilty of causing your misfortunes. I do not want our little *bairn* to carry the burden of your difficulties. We all must give her a chance in life and give her support to deal with the challenges of possibly being labelled a witch."

Marta adds, speaking to Micheal, "I helped deliver Anna into our world. Although she is less than two weeks old, I already have very fond feelings for her. As she was born she was administered all the traditional rituals to give her good luck, strength and protection from the Evil Eye and faeries. Now it is up to all our kinfolk to continue to nurture and protect her through her life in the same way that we protect and guide all our *clanns*. I am sure that Catherine and Lach want to be assured that this is something all of you are committed to do. All of you have grown up in the tradition of being a warrior with great courage and strength. You have proved this time and time again. Now it is time to protect the little *nighean* of Catherine and Lach." Marta concludes with a plea, "Do we all agree that we will take care of little Anna?"

Roibeart, Molly's *fear* and usually a quiet member of the family, then states, "I must add my thoughts regarding the situation. I agree that Anna is a little *bairn* and we do not know her future. But the belief in red-heads and witches has existed for generations. I also have some worry about Anna and the curse of her red hair. I don't quite understand how a red-head is born in our clan of dark curly haired folks. But I also recognize the fact that there are many other different looking folks on our Isle. The greatest conflict about Anna I have is between our long-time beliefs and those of God and our religion."

Roibeart then shares, "This is what Pastor Douglas has read from the Bible 'A false witness will not go unpunished, and he who breathes out lies will perish.' Our religion teaches us that we should not judge others for wrongs and that this should be the judgement of our God. We are learning things that contradict our old beliefs. Which creed shall we follow? I, like you, am torn but on the other hand I do not want to judge little Anna before we have proof of wrong doing."

Brian then adds, "Roibeart has made some good points. I believe that we are all torn by our old ways which are challenged by our beliefs in our God. We are lectured to every Sunday that we should love others. This is often difficult here in Inivea when so many are suspicious and distrusting. Should we let this affect the way we treat Anna? What choice do we have but to accept our little *bairn* and watch her as she grows? We also need to love her as we love the others."

Brian continues, "If we can agree to watch over Anna, there remains the problem of how can we protect her from all the other clans on our isle? When Anna is baptized and as she grows, they will certainly notice her red hair. She cannot be kept in her *bothie* all her life. Other clans may despise her and ostracize her in the community. How can we shield her every moment of her life? We do not have time for that."

The discussion has at last arrived at the place where Lach can finally present a possible solution. It is now that Lach rises to present the solution of Lili. "My kinfolk, Lili and Jannet, visited us yesterday with a possible solution for Anna's red hair. As you know the women of our clan dye wool to make our tartans with a dye from the bark of the trees and other vegetation. I have consulted with Catherine as to whether she thinks that the dye will work on Anna's red hair. She believes that it might work but would like to test it on Anna first. If it works we could then move forward to Anna's baptism with Mollie, the youngest *siuir*, carrying Anna into the *kirk*. With her red hair as a dark brown, Anna can be administered the rites of her baptism and hopefully no one will be suspicious of the natural color.

With that proposal the kinfolk talk among themselves for several minutes while Lach and Catherine wait for the outcome. They overhear the continued distrust of Micheal and the remaining conflict of Roibeart. They know that their kinfolk need this time of debate to sort things out before they come to a decision.

Seumus finally speaks up, "Everyone has agreed that your plan should be tried." "Aye," shout all the clansmen, including the women. Seumus continues, "As Anna grows we will watch over her." Once again all agree, "Aye." And with that spoken promise the *coinneamh* ends. The kinfolk rise and quickly depart. As they leave Lach and Catherine can hear their whispers, still puzzled about this strange occurrence in their clan.

Lach and Catherine linger a few moments longer checking on the peat fire. It continues to smolder but can safely be left for the next use by the clan. They then begin the return hike to their *bothie*. While walking Lach confesses, "I am feeling a sense of relief after meeting with our kin but I am also heavy-hearted. I am confused as to why I have these strange feelings. I only know that when our future is uncertain I am left with ominous feelings about our wellbeing. There is something in the air, in our glen and in our clan that portends changes and they may not be positive."

Catherine is surprised. It is unusual for her brave warrior to share such fearful feelings. She answers him, "Lach, I have noticed a certain darkness about you in the last few years that is not connected to our Anna. Perhaps her unusual characteristic of red hair has increased your dark spirit, but there is something else. But look, we are nearing our *bothie* and we must not alarm our *clanns*. We will talk about this later when we cannot be overheard. Perhaps when we are readying the soil for our spring planting. I believe that right now we can just assure Seathan and the younger ones that the *coinneamh* went well and we are going to begin the dyeing of Anna's hair."

9
The Storm

Catherine proceeds into the *bothie* while Lach lingers outside to survey his farm. Much work lies ahead of him and the rest of the family with the approach of spring in a few weeks. Already today's sun and warmer temperature have melted much of the snow which had been covering the land around them. He has always looked forward to saying goodbye to winter and welcoming in spring, complete with all the chores of spring. To him the moor and the beauty of the glen gave him hope for rebirth and new beginnings. However, his dark spirit of late takes away some of this hope. Knowing that Catherine has already noticed his gloom, he will try harder to hide his hopeless feelings. Before they have their talk, he will pray for clearer sight. He is aware that Catherine needs all her energy to care for their newborn *bairn* and family. Lach is counting on the arrival of spring to brighten his spirits. It has been a long and difficult winter.

When he enters the *bothie* Catherine is settling down to nurse little Anna who has just begun to cry. The two little *clanns*, Iain and Caitriona, huddle close to her around the fire. Maighread, who is no longer needed, heads to the door and leaves. Seathan is busy in the *byre* finishing the last milking of the day. Since this last pregnancy he has taken over this chore from his *mathair*. Lach goes into the *byre* to check on his oldest *mac*. Lach wants to take this time when they are alone to share some things about the recent *coinneamh*. Lach begins, "Seathan, how are things? I am concerned about our cows."

Seathan responds, "There is not much hay and oats left and they are getting very thin. If they survive this winter we will have to carry them out to the pasture so that they can begin to get nourishment from the fresh growth on the moor."

Lach then comments, "We must remember that they are hardy animals who have been through this before. Spring will soon be here. Already the snow is melting and I have begun seeing some fresh growth peeking up through it."

"What happened at the *coinneamh*?" inquires Seathan. Lach cautiously responds, "The kinfolk voiced some apprehensions about Anna and her red hair. However, they agreed to be supportive of the dyeing proposal. Of course we haven't tried it yet, but your *mathair* feels confident that it will work."

"When will that happen?" questions Seathan.

"I believe there is some dye left over from the summer. If not your *mathair* will get some from her family. The dyeing will be done, hopefully, by the next Sabbath day and we can have her baptized," adds Lach.

Lach then leaves, passing through the room which houses his family and heads to get some peat for the fire. Due to strong winds he has a difficult time pushing open the door outside. As often happens on his Isle a furious storm has suddenly arisen. Dark clouds have formed overhead and the light, once bright and sunny, takes on an eerie darkness. It has not begun to rain yet, but thunder and lightning soon appear. Lach knows that he should not stay out too long, but he has a fascination and at the same time a fear of the storm. He believes it is the work of the *Black Donald* who makes the life of the Highlander so treacherous.

The salt air of the ocean fills his nostrils and large pieces of hail begin to barrage him. Soon his land and the whole moor is filled with large stone-like crystal objects of ice. Lach quickly grabs several squares of peat and heads back in. Just as he opens the door a large lightning bolt pierces the sky close by him. He doesn't wait for the thunder and quickly closes the door behind him.

As he enters his young *clanns* run to him. "Come *athair* over here. Our meal is ready. We have brought you your bowl and spoon," they exclaim with relief. Catherine calls to Seathan and they all gather around the fire to eat their meal. The only light is from the fire and it casts shadows on all of them. They are all relieved to have this warm fire and food. Lach looks at his two young *clanns*. Their dark unruly hair frames their tan grubby faces, made darker from the smoky peat fire. Their brown eyes are large and often give the impression of being haunted. They are impish in appearance but solidly built. He cannot help contrasting the tough solid bodies of his older *clanns* to the more delicate and fairer Anna.

Before they all begin to eat, Lach offers a mealtime blessing. This is a tradition that the family expects from the patriarch and will not start a meal without it:

"Some hae meat and cannae eat.
Some nae meat but want it.
We hae meat and we can eat and
Sae the Lord be thankit."

Little Anna has slept through the meal and the raging storm outside. The other *clanns* remain huddled near the fire while Catherine recounts ancient stories of their ancestors. They sit with wide open eyes listening to their *mathair*, distracted from the howling wind, thunder and pelting rain.

When the storm subsides, Lach goes outside. The storm was mighty close and he wants to make sure that it left his thatched roof intact. He checks for loose thatch as well as any smoldering that would indicate that their dwelling was hit by lightning. He is reminded of instances when *bothies* in the glen caught fire after lightning strikes. The stone foundations always remain solid, able to withstand the assaults of storms and all kinds of weather. The thatch, however, is another story and can be damaged by fire or even high winds. Lach climbs the walkway around the roof, examining it very carefully he sees no bad signs.

Lach then looks across the landscape from the perch of his roof and in the distance he sees the flickering light of fire on one of his clansmen's roofs. The fire illuminates a small group of clansmen with water buckets. Lach knows the routine. The men will hand the filled buckets from man to man. The last man closest to the *bothie* will pour the water on the fire until it is out. Lach hangs around to watch the progress. The clansmen would wave from afar if more help is needed and Lach will be ready for the call. After several minutes it appears that the fire is under control. He observes no more flames and instead there are clouds of smoke from the smoldering roof fire. These events are frequent and Lach is grateful that the clansmen on his Isle help each other in times of need.

10
The Dyeing

The next morning Catherine and Lach awaken to realize that it is Sunday. It has been a week since Anna was born. It is also the day when everyone goes to the *kirk* for Sabbath services. Catherine and Lach discuss whether they will attend. They do not want to be faced with questions about Anna from the Pastor and the parishioners. They decide today they will stay home. Catherine will go to the spring before the clansmen make their way to the *kirk*. She will need water to wash her young *clanns*. Sunday was usually their washday so that they will be clean for their Sunday clothes.

Iain and Caitriona are restless today. They are aching to get outside and enjoy the sunshine and fresh air. At this time of year they like to play in the remaining snow, making balls of snow and throwing them at each other. In the summer they like to go to the moorland, especially in early summer when the animals are grazing. Sometimes they go to the river and throw stones and watch the swift current of the river pass by them. Not far from them are the woodlands and their greatest joy is to hike there with Seathan. They have been warned enough times not to venture there alone. The threat of the *Black Donald* or the *shellycoat* (bogeyman) causing dreadful harm or stealing them is enough for the Maclean *clanns* to stay away.

Today Catherine's mind is swirling with many thoughts. The Sabbath is supposed to be a day of rest, but Catherine believes this practice is unrealistic. She uses the time for chores and the ongoing needs of her family. All the clansmen find that they also must work every day, including the Sabbath, to survive. Today with the precious free time created by not attending the Sabbath services, Catherine gathers her dyed wool and using her spindle she will spin her wool into yarn. When she has enough yarn she will take it to the weaver in her village so that it can be woven into cloth.

Before spinning her wool Catherine checks on the dye that she will use for Anna's hair. It appears that there is enough for the first dyeing.

45

However, realizing that she might have to dye her hair two times, she will ask her *siuirs* to share theirs. As soon as spring arrives she will take her young *clanns* into the moor and woods to gather the best lichens, roots and barks for more dye.

The time-consuming task of spinning wool takes up most of Catherine's morning. Often she dreams and longs for the modern spinning wheels that she has seen at Flora's. She would like one but she knows that Lach and she are too poor for such a luxury. She remarks to herself, "We are having a hard-enough time keeping the family fed and clothed. The annual rent increases don't help our situation. Oh, but I can dream, can't I?" In her reverie she fantasizes, "Perhaps Lach can find a way to earn more money." She knows, however, that the one way to get more money in the past was stealing and selling cattle. Now that the clans are not supported by their chiefs it has become very difficult. Her final thoughts are somewhat ominous, "Survival has become brutal. I pray that we will find a way. No wonder Lach is troubled."

Finally, with most of her other chores done, she has time to dye. Anna had been napping most of the day and had not stirred. Catherine then goes over to the fire, stokes it and places some peat on it. Then she realizes that she must go outside again to refill the water buckets. She opens the heavy wooden door and the bitter cold of the season remind her that she should have put on her warm shawl. She shivers as she treks on the pathway's trodden snow to the spring. After several trips she is finally back at her *bothie* with enough water for the family's needs. She takes a wooden ladle and spoons the icy water into the kettle. Anna's sleep is disrupted by her *mathair's* movement around the room and she wakes up. She cries and Catherine takes her into her arms so that she can nurse her. She is thankful for this lovely quiet time with Anna. As soon as Anna finishes nursing, the other *clanns* stop what they are doing and come to their *mathair* near the fire. Iain and Caitriona excitedly speak at once, "*Mathair*, when will you be dyeing Anna's hair?"

"Soon my little *clanns*, but first I need to wash Anna and her hair. Now go into the *byre* and help Seathan with the animals. I will call you when I am ready." The *clanns* rush to their *brathair*. Catherine goes to the cupboard and gathers dry cloths and soap. She places them near a large wooden bowl. She goes over to Anna's cradle and lifts her carefully. Once in her arms she cannot help but glance at

Anna's red hair. She sighs because she knows that she will miss it.

Before washing her Catherine sticks her elbow into the bowl of warm water. It is just right. After she washes Anna's pale body, she wets another cloth and drips the water onto Anna's head. She takes the soap and gently massages her head. It doesn't take long to wash and rinse her *nighean's* hair. After wrapping Anna in a clean cloth to keep her warm she calls "Iain and Caitriona, I am ready to dye your *siuir's* hair." They hurry to their *mathair,* filled with curiosity. They sit next to Anna as Catherine takes a clean cloth and places it in the dye. She then rubs Anna's hair, covering all of it evenly with the dye. After several minutes to let the dye work, she takes some water to rinse out the excess dye. She holds Anna in her arms waiting for the little *bairn's* hair and scalp to dry. She then announces, "That's all there is to it. You can now go outside and see what your *athair* is doing. Tell him that Anna's hair has been dyed. He might want to see how she looks."

11
Anxiety

Anna's fine hair dries quickly but it is not the color that Catherine expected. Instead of being a dark brown it is still red—a duller red with some brown but more like the hue of a late setting sun behind the clouds. She has seen this color many times at twilight, but it will not fool anyone. Catherine is troubled. Lach soon opens the door and joins Catherine and Anna. He notices that Anna's hair is not the dark brown that he was expecting.

"Catherine, her hair is still red, a different shade of red. "What are we to do?" exclaims Lach.

"Perhaps red hair does not take dye as easily as the gray wool of our sheep," replies Catherine. "I will give Anna a day to rest and then will try the dye again. And this time I will leave the dye on longer."

That day anxiety and uneasiness penetrate the *bothie*. Iain and Caitriona, who usually chatted, asking their *mathair* a lot of questions, instead are silent. They sense the distress of their *parantans (parents)*. As they sit around the fire they make braids and ties with leftover dyed wool which will later be used to hold up stockings. Caitriona shares with Iain, "I like to rub the soft braids against my face." Much more serious and older, Iain reminds her to keep at the job.

There is a knock on the door and Jannet and Marta enter, eager to see the results of the hair dying. Glancing at Catherine they can sense a disquieting mood in the room. Lach, who is prone to jump to conclusions, is pacing around the fire. His face is distraught and puzzled. Both Jannet and Marta go over to the cradle where Anna is lying. Jannet remarks, "Anna's hair definitely has some brown color in it. It will not be enough to fool the rest of our clan, but I believe another dyeing will change the hue from red to brown. I do remember times when I have had to dye our wool a couple of times in order to get the color I wanted for our tartans. Jannet then questions: Will you have enough dye for the second dyeing?"

49

"Aye. I have already told Lach that tomorrow I will give Anna a second dyeing," explains Catherine. Lach, hearing Catherine's comment, stops pacing and feeling overwhelmed leaves and goes into the *byre*. He is not always soothed by the hope and confidence of the womenfolk. It makes him feel weak and ineffective.

Seathan is in the *byre* milking the cows. It is getting harder because as the cows become thinner, their milk supply also diminishes. The pregnant cow will be giving birth in a few months and it is time to stop milking her. Seathan knows enough not to further worry his *athair*. However, Lach is well attuned to the status of the animals. "How much milk today?" he asks.

Seathan responds, "*Athair*, half the amount that our cows usually give us. I have stopped milking the pregnant one."

"And the eggs?" queries Lach. "Only six," shares Seathan.

"Our food supply is getting low. I believe that the time is near for us to go into the woods and hunt some wild rabbits," responds, Lach.

After her *mathair* and *siuir* leave, Catherine is left alone in the dark silence with her thoughts. A sadness penetrates her being as she thinks of the last few days. She reminds herself that she, as the *mathair* of the family, needs to be stoic and courageous. This has always been the role of women in the clan. It has always been the accepted practice for the men of the clan to arise by dawn, frequently leaving their *beans* and *clanns* to cope with the rugged life of the Isle while they go off to battle, cattle raids or hunting expeditions. They can be gone for days, weeks or months. Although brave warriors, the men have escaped many of the day to day worries of surviving the Highlands. It is up to the women to bear the *bairns*, keep them safe and nurse them back to health when they are ill.

12
Baptism Plans

The next morning Anna wakes up with a start. Catherine, already up preparing for the day, rushes to her cradle. She checks Anna over and realizes that she is quite wet and soiled. She asks Caitriona to fetch some dry cloths, while she pours some warm water from the iron kettle overhead into the wooden bowl. Once Anna is made more comfortable Catherine nurses her. While nursing her *nighean* she thinks about the dyeing, hoping it will turn Anna's hair brown.

It is a blustery morning as early spring often is on their Isle. Seathan and Lach head to the door and a blast of wind almost pushes them back inside. Holding onto each other they manage to stay erect and move outside. Peering across the landscape of their glen, the thick dense fog of early morning blocks them from seeing beyond a few feet. Unable to see through the moist clouds of whiteness, they return to the *bothie*. They will go out later.

Catherine looks up as the men come back in. She tells Lach that she is ready to dye Anna's hair. As this is woman's work, Lach and Seathan quickly head to the *byre*. Taking a clean cloth Catherine dips it in the brown dye. Carefully she passes the drenched cloth over Anna's scalp. Several times she does this, gently rubbing Anna's head with it. This time she will make sure that she gives the dye enough time to do its job. Anna, not liking wetness on her scalp, begins to cry. "Shhh, shhh little un," soothes Catherine. "It is all over now. I will just rinse your hair in the water and then get you warm and dry."

Anxiously watching Anna as her hair dries, the fear of having a red-head quickly vanishes. Her hair is a dark wispy brown! There will be no suspicions of Anna having red hair. "Iain run into the *byre* and ask your *athair* to come," excitedly shouts Catherine. "Seathan can come too," she adds. Soon they cautiously join Catherine. "Look," shares Catherine. "We now have a brown-haired *nighean*." Both Lach and Seathan are filled with a relief beyond words. The many days of tension has now diminished considerably. "Seathan, now run and invite your *seanmhair* and *piuthar-mathar* to see," Catherine hastily requests.

In short time Jannet and Marta appear. Gleeful about the news of the *bairn*. Jannet, upon the viewing, exclaims, "Now I can go to Pastor Douglas and make arrangements for Anna's baptism. You might have to dye Anna's hair one more time before the baptism, depending on how soon it can be scheduled. But now we know the formula of success. When winter is over, Iain and Caitriona will be busy keeping you well supplied with the vegetation needed for the dye."

Then in harmony Jannet and Marta add, "This task will be lifelong." With decreased anxiety both Jannet and Marta leave.

Jannet, adding as she goes out the door, "Tomorrow I will visit the Pastor."

Lach and Seathan follow Jannet and Marta out the door. It is now early afternoon and the fog has lifted and although still windy, the weather remains clear enough for them to begin making some spring plans. As they stand chatting about preparing the soil and harvesting the heather for their thatched roof, their laird's tacksman appears on his roan steed. "I've come to collect the rent that you owe," declares the tacksman. The tacksman is prepared for the response and shows no sympathy or compassion. Lach explains, "Mr. Johnson, I have not managed to save enough rent money this year. It has been a lean year due to the weather and this raise in our rent does not help. I need more time to give you what the laird demands," pleads Lach.

"This is not good," Mr. Johnson adds. "If you do not come soon with your rent money you will lose your farm," threatens Mr. Johnson. At that threat he gallops away on his roan, looking haughty and aloof.

That afternoon Jannet, as promised, starts out on the four-mile trek to the village to call on the Pastor. She is hoping the baptism can be set up for the very next Sunday. She fears that if Anna is not baptized quickly, she is in danger of being switched by the faeries. When she finally reaches the village, she momentarily compares it to the scattered settlement of farmers on the outskirts of the village. In the village the main building is a stone *kirk* with the graveyard beside it. It is the most important structure for the village residents and the surrounding farmers. The *kirk* has a small tower with a bell used to alert residents to important events such as funerals and celebrations. Beside the *kirk* is the Manor, the home of the Pastor. Other structures are the *bothies* of the village weaver, the blacksmith, the midwife, a healer and an assortment of poor folk with their small gardens and livestock.

Jannet has made this trek many times in her life but today her steps carry a heavy heart. As she proceeds to the home of Pastor Douglas, she wonders "Is the secret of Anna's red hair causing her such dread? She is not one to deceive folks, especially her Pastor. The Pastor has always preached that God knows all, even our deepest and darkest secrets. Will her face and manner betray her? Surely God would understand that she and her kin are hiding the truth to protect little Anna." With resolution she will keep this in mind when she makes her request to the Pastor.

Not usually tired from her four-mile walk, Jannet is fatigued today. Before she opens the gate she scans the Pastor's house in a way that she never has before. It is a stone building with a shingled roof, adorned with real glass windows and a heavy wooden door. The door is nicely made with an iron handle and knocker. In her mind she contrasts it to the crude structures of her clans folk. In the past she was able to overlook the difference but now she no longer can. Her kin live such a rugged and difficult life with little to show for it. "Why would such a powerful and righteous God allow this to happen," Jannet wonders. Entering the gate she notices the well-groomed area in the front of the house. Bushes create an exterior outline of the house and in the summer there will be flowers growing on either side of the pathway. "What a waste of tillable land," she thinks silently. Then she reminds herself that the Pastor's job is to serve God and his congregation and not to farm his property.

She reaches the door and knocks. A housekeeper answers the door and although Jannet's red face and her heavy breathing is evidence of the long journey in the cold, the housekeeper keeps Jannet waiting at the open door while she inquires as to the purpose of her visit. As Jannet explains her mission, she observes the woman at the door. Immediately she recognizes that this is a woman who has not had an easy life. Her face is drawn and wrinkled. Her shoulders are stooped as if carrying the weight of the world and although she is generally the first person that visitors meet when coming to make a call on the Pastor, her clothes, worn and drab, hang loosely on a figure that at one time filled them out more completely. Gray hair creeps out from her head covering. The housekeeper is unaware of Jannet's thoughts and is mainly interested in whether this is an appropriate visitor for a busy pastor. Her decision is finally made and she invites Jannet into the waiting room. "I will let Pastor Douglas know that you are here," she informs Jannet.

While waiting, she looks around the room. The worn wood-planked floor is covered by several faded rugs. On the edges of the room there are several large chests. Each chest is covered with a white cloth and some religious statues of Christ, St. Francis of Assisi and the Virgin Mary. Several chairs are placed around a roughly hewn wooden rectangular table. Jannet, tired from her hike to the village, decides to sit in one of the chairs. She hopes that the Pastor won't think her too bold. It is damp and cool in the room because the fire is merely one of dying embers now. To Jannet the room looks as if it is rarely used, but perhaps a morning fire is lit to take off the chill for the occasional guest that knocks on the door. There are two front windows with glass letting the light of late morning into an otherwise dark and somber room. A few scattered small tables support candle holders with their tallow candles.

She suddenly hears the Pastor's booming voice which interrupts her observations. "Mrs. MacKinnon, I didn't expect you to call today. What brings such an unexpected visit?" Jannet, taken off guard, is slow to respond. The Pastor, continuing on his way to the seated Jannet, speaks again, "Come, come Mrs. MacKinnon, I do not have all day."

Jannet then musters up her response but does not share her true disgust of this man, "I am very sorry Pastor Douglas. I guess I am still catching up from my trek from the glen."

Without bothering to sit down and join Jannet at the table he demands, "Go on, go on, what is it?"

"Catherine, my second *nighean*, just bore a little *bairn* and we would like her baptized at your earliest convenience. We were hoping that it could be this Sunday. We observe her to be strong enough to be carried to the *kirk* and the tradition of baptism requires that she have its protection as soon as it is possible." responds Jannet. "We would like her to be baptized as Anna Maclean."

Pastor Douglas takes a few minutes to respond and while Jannet waits, she looks the man over. He is a stout middle-aged fellow who bears a big pot belly. He is short in stature but nevertheless commands an imposing presence. His face is ruddy and full, and he often looks to Jannet as if he is going to explode. His complexion, although ruddy, is fairer than the clansmen of her glen. He has lost a lot of the hair of his youth and what is left is gray. Though not the most handsome of men, it does not interfere with his role as pastor. Jannet is aware of some of his history before he came to Inivea's *kirk*. After he completed studies at the University of Edinburgh, he pastored in that city for several years. Going on ten years in this village, he strictly follows his parochial training and expects all his congregation to do likewise. So that the parishioners will be obedient, he frequently preaches a fear of God's power over them.

Jannet is interrupted from her thoughts by the loud voice of Pastor Douglas. "Yes, it is important for the little *bairn* to be baptized as soon as possible. As you request I will baptize her on Sunday," the Pastor agrees. "Make sure that you get her to the *kirk* on time. I do not want her to arrive late and interrupt my Sunday preaching," the Pastor emphatically announces. "The housekeeper will show you out." Jannet rises after he leaves. As Jannet nears the door the housekeeper appears and opens it for her.

On her way home Jannet is glad that the dreaded task is done. Her mood is brighter but not without some anxiety about the future of Anna. She stops on her way to visit her kin and tell them that Anna's hair is now brown and the baptism will be next Sunday. Everyone was curious about Jannet's visit to the Pastor. Although she told them that all went well, inwardly she believed that the pastor treated her as a poor ignorant peasant. Jannet was well aware that some Christian Pastors regard the clan's folk as wild, lazy and superstitious with a reputation of being ferocious warriors. Many pastors, however, were unsympathetic to the fact that they had lost their way of life. Now no longer warriors, they were existing only as poor destitute farmers. Jannet knew that she could not change the Pastor's opinion of her kinfolk but, nonetheless, she did not like his disdain. She kept her feelings silent, however, because right now she did not want to open raw wounds. Instead everyone is relieved to hear the news of the agreed upon baptism of a brown-haired Anna.

13
The Baptism

After visiting all her kinfolk Jannet tiredly made her way back home. It has been a long day and she was indignant towards the Pastor's remarks. She had to remind herself that not every pastor had looked down upon the clan's folk. The previous pastor had been held in high esteem. Although confused about Gaelic traditions and beliefs, Pastor Buchanan had tried to understand them. This was easier for Pastor Buchanan because he had some ability in the Gaelic language. Pastor Douglas's knowledge of Gaelic, on the other hand, was limited. Nonetheless, he had developed enough vocabulary to preach on what he regarded as important doctrines of the Church of Scotland. In contrast, Pastor Buchanan had made it his practice to support his parishioners when they faced tragedies of death, illness, sick animals and failed crops. He took time in his preaching to pray for a grieving family, comforting them and showing much compassion for their pain.

Although the practices of Christianity have been followed for as far back as her history went, Jannet understood that old superstitions lingered among the clans of Mull. The kin did not speak of it, but Jannet knew in her heart that they still have a deep apprehension about the destiny of Anna. Will the clan continue to support and protect her? Will Anna prove wrong the old belief that a *bairn* who is born with red hair will become a witch able to cause great harm to her kin?

Sunday came soon enough and it is a decent spring day in the glen with the sun out and shining for a baptism, a good omen for the little *bairn*. In each *bothie* Catherine and Lach's kinfolk don their best clothes in preparation for the baptism service. Everyone, pacing outside their *bothies*, wait for the arrival of Lach and his family. They are anxious and curious at the same time, wondering about Anna's hair color. Once Anna arrives, they realize that they will have to wait to check it out, because a snug cap covers her head. The last kin on the way are Molly and Roibeart.

Catherine hands Anna over to Molly while Roibeart supports Molly and Anna on one side and Lach on the other as they make their way down the rough pathway to the *kirk*. Catherine, who has been rushing all morning, stops for a moment to take in the early spring air. She breathes in the fresh cold air while at the same time trying to relinquish her own unspoken dread of the baptism. She is still fearful that the dark secret she is harboring will be discovered. With this in her troubled heart she glances behind her and sees the imposing mountains of her Isle. Crevices in the mountains still carry some evidence of the winter's snow. These mountains, always symbolic of the rugged existence in their glen and Isle, are juxtaposed with the awe and beauty of their peaks.

Jannet, catching up to the group of her kin, hands Molly the bread and cheese. Molly places the food into the wide pocket of her cloak. Catherine and Jannet stride cautiously behind them. Soon all Catherine's kin are walking together in a somber and subdued mood. All are aware of the significance of this particular Sabbath Day for the little *bairn*, Anna.

As the group makes its way down the path Molly scans the landscape in a desperate search for a stranger. The only visible folks are the regular parishioners. Molly feels a lot of responsibility for doing this right. Success will be good luck for little Anna and failure will mean misfortune. After an hour they near the stone *kirk* in the little village of Inivea. They are early but clansmen from other glens have already gathered outside, exchanging hellos and catching up with the latest news from around the Isle.

Molly still has not encountered a stranger and is worried that it is almost too late to carry out the old tradition. Then she spots a small group of folks that she has never seen or met before. They have a definite look of being from the Highlands so they might know of the clan's tradition. Shyly and cautiously she approaches a young man among the group and hands him the bread and cheese. She mentions to him quietly that she is carrying young Anna who is to be baptized today. Molly further adds, "I hope that you will find nourishment in the cheese and bread." Molly does not hang around to see what the young man does with her offering. Instead she quickly returns to her own kinfolk, believing that it would be rude to watch the young man any further.

Catherine and Lach, along with Molly and Anna, enter the *kirk* first followed by the rest of their kinfolk. They proceed to the front of the sanctuary which has been saved for them by the Pastor. While waiting they watch as Pastor Douglas fills the baptismal font in the front of the sanctuary. The kinfolk are so plentiful today that they fill up the first three pews. Generally, they would wait outside until the Pastor's assistant ushered them in. But today was special and they want to be ready and not disturb the Pastor's routine.

Catherine, now sitting in the front pew, removes Anna's bonnet. She decides to put young Anna to her breast so that she can suckle and take some nourishment. This will also serve the function of keeping Anna calm and relaxed. While Anna is nursing Catherine silently studies the features of the sanctuary. There is not much to observe. It is a barren cold space of stone devoid of any color or statues. The glens serviced by this *kirk* are too poor to afford any special spiritual adornments. The pews are arranged on two sides. On the left of the pews is a high pulpit. The pulpit is the most prominent feature of the room and its height forces the parishioners to look up when the Pastor preaches God's Word. It symbolically enforces his authority over the congregation as well as showing his distinct closeness to God.

Before the service begins the pastor exits by the back door to give time for all the congregants to enter and settle into their pews. Usually there are some laggards, so he waits until ten past the hour to enter the sanctuary and climb the stairs to the pulpit. He starts with an introductory reading of a scripture. Catherine listens in her pew with the rest of her kin, waiting for the moment of the baptism. Anna is handed back to Molly who will bring her to the Pastor. Finally, the Pastor descends from the pulpit and begins the baptismal ritual. Catherine, Lach and Roibeart come to the front and join Molly and Anna.

The Pastor reads in Gaelic the designated written service for the baptism. He then addresses Catherine and Lach, "What do you wish to name your new *nighean*?"

Catherine responds, "Anna Maclean."

"You may hand Anna over to me for her baptismal waters and sacrament," requests Pastor Douglas. Molly gently hands Anna over to the Pastor. He cradles her in one of his arms while he takes a large pitcher and fills it with water from the stone font. Holding Anna's head backwards over the font, he uses his other hand to pour the water over her head. As soon as the water hits Anna's head, she lets out loud screaming which fills the small *kirk*. Everyone knows the reason for Anna's boisterous rebellion. The Pastor is prepared for Anna's outburst. He had filled the stone font with very cold water in hopes that she would cry. In the Pastor's eyes Anna's crying is a good sign. After a few chosen Gaelic ritual words, Anna's head is wiped with a clean dry cloth. She is then handed back to Catherine. Catherine is greatly relieved because Anna's christening insures that she is a member of the *kirk*, making her safe from the faeries. She is also thankful that the dye job has sufficiently covered Anna's red hair.

As Catherine and Lach hike home the mood of dread has been temporarily lifted. It is early afternoon and although the sun is hidden behind a multitude of clouds, they and their closest kinfolk walk with a lightened step. They are all silent, however, because they don't want outsiders to overhear their dark secret. Whatever happens in the future will be met and handled with guile and courage, but for now they can be pleased with their own cunning thanks to Lilli. Then all meet at Catherine and Lach's, crowding into the small space to partake of a cup of ale in celebration of Anna's baptismal success.

Iain and Caitriona follow everyone outside as they leave. The weather, although cold and brisk, is still warm enough for them to hike to the moor. The moor, clear of winter snows, shows evidence of autumn's garb of dried brown-colored grass. The *clanns,* having been pent up inside almost every day during the winter months, love getting outside and breathing in the fresh cold air. Today, as often happens in their glen, a thick mist is quietly rolling over the fields and the mountains behind them. A strange atmosphere starts to fill in around them. The mountains, masquerading like forbidding giants, remind them of the fearful folk who dwell in its caves, crevices and woods; witches, hobgoblins, and ghosts of the past. Iain and Caitriona are filled with anxiety as they begin to imagine these fearful creatures coming to life.

They hold hands and venture further afield into the moor. Right now the need for fresh air and daylight press them forward. Soon they will not be able to see their little *bothie* due to the heavy mist and fog rolling into their glen. But they know their way because they are on a familiar path, one they travel on frequently during warmer months to gather herbs and vegetation for their *mathair's* dye. They also love to hike further out into the fields so that they can watch the animals in the pasture. But right now there are no animals and no fresh grass for the animals, just old brown soggy hay. Iain then says to Caitriona, "Caty, the fog is getting denser and we do not want to be taken by surprise by a stranger. Let's turn around and return to our *bothie*. It is near our time to eat and *mathair* will be looking for us." Caitriona agrees and they carefully feel their way through the thick fog. The eerie sounds of the owls and other wildlife fill their ears as they cautiously move forward. Iain is afraid, but being the big *brathair*, he does not want to alarm Caty.

Suddenly Caty slips and falls. She begins to cry more out of fear than hurt. Iain quickly pulls her up and comforts her, "Now, now Caty, you are fine. Hold my hand and we will soon be at our *bothie*." Caty whimpers but is comforted by Iain's reassurance. She holds Iain's hand and quickly they trek down the path. The walk back seems much longer than the walk into the moor, but they finally reach their *bothie* and open the wooden door. Their *mathair* is indeed waiting for them, getting a little alarmed. Iain explained, "*Mathair*, the fog was thick, and it took us longer to get back home. I took care of Caty, and although she fell, she is not hurt."

"That is good, Iain, and thank you for watching over Caty."

14
A Battle Story

The fog has hidden the setting sun from their glen and their *bothie*. Their room is lit only by the fire and the *bairns*, after eating, are ready to sleep. Catherine is nursing Anna. Meanwhile Seathan and Lach are in the *byre* taking care of the livestock. Lach interrupts the silence, "Seathan, tonight is a good night to continue with the Maclean clan history. As soon as we finish our chores with the animals, we can go sit by the fire and I will share more of the story." Seathan is always eager to hear his *athair's* story about his ancestors, the Macleans.

They finish the chores and then head to the fire. Lach begins the story, "In 1715 the Macleans were involved in a battle to regain the Stuart throne. Many of the Highland clans supported James VII of England, also known as James II in Scotland. Despite the valiant efforts of the fighting clans, this Jacobite Rising was unsuccessful. The English won and kept their rule over Scotland."

"Thirty-one years later when I was only 5 years old, there was another uprising. Bonnie Prince Charles, the grandson of James, once again set out to have the Stuart House returned as the true monarchy of England, Scotland and Ireland. Your *seanair* (grandfather) and many of our kin joined the Jacobite cause and fought in the battle of Culloden in 1746."

"However, those clans that supported Bonnie Prince Charles lost the battle. Many of our warriors died. Even though they were armed with their *dirks* and swords, they were unable to defend themselves against the cannons and muskets of the English Calvary."

"Many from the Maclean clan were slaughtered. When they left to join the Jacobite Army, it was the last time their families saw them. Our elders recounted many stories of the massacre and many never recovered from witnessing the horror of this conflict. About two thousand of our Highland clansmen lost their lives. We lost our clan chief, Maclean of Drimmin, in that battle and that, combined with the retributions of the English, destroyed our clans and our way of life."

"But it is late now, Seathan, and I will tell you of the changes my *athair* and the other clansmen witnessed at a later time." At that Lach and Seathan add more peat to the fire and head to their beds. Catherine is already in bed after feeding Anna. She had overheard Lach's sharing the Highland story with Seathan. She senses that the story has stirred something in Lach and as he lays there she holds him close to her. Lach sighs deeply and returns her affection with a squeeze and a kiss.

Lach has trouble falling asleep as he thinks about what he didn't share with Seathan. His *athair,* Angus, had told him that following their victory, the English government wanted there to be no chance of any further rebellion. Charles, fleeing the country, went into hiding. The government sent its army across Scotland, punishing anyone suspected of having Jacobite sympathies. He also remembered his *athair* saying, "The English wanted to get rid of the Highland lifestyle and the clan allegiance to their chiefs with a policy of *pacification*. Clansmen could no longer legally use their weapons. Many of the estates of the chiefs and lairds were seized and tartans and kilts were banned. Angus then told Lach, "The biggest harm was the elimination of many chiefs. The chiefs and their clansmen for as long as it was known always had an abiding relationship. The chiefs would allow the clansmen to farm the land for free, while he could count on them to be his warriors in battles to protect his territory and power." Lach finally drifts off to sleep with all this on his mind, knowing that he and Catherine needed to have an important discussion soon.

After his talk with Seathan, Lach's fears about his future and that of his family almost put him in a state of panic. He knew that he did not have enough rent money and he did not know what he was going to do. In the past he and his kinfolk would hold cattle raids and stolen cattle would be sold to bring in additional money. This had been an annual rite of the clansmen who did not consider it stealing, but merely taking what was theirs. Soon he must talk with Catherine about this ongoing problem.

15
Lach Faces Reality

In the morning Lach awakens with a heavy heart. He had hoped that sleep would erase his troubles from his mind, but it did not. Several weeks have passed since Anna's birth and it is the beginning of spring. He goes outside and feels the warmer weather. The moor is turning from dull brown to a lime green. Dotting the meadows and hills are beautiful bluebells. All this usually fills Lach with the hope and promise of better weather and new beginnings. The azure carpets are an early harbinger of life's annual cycle of rebirth and is a beauty that normally takes Lach's breath away. This year, however, he is unable to summon his usual spirit of renewal.

Lach returns inside to eat. Sitting at the fire with his bowl of porridge and with a worried mind, he summons Catherine to his side, "Catherine, is this a good time to have our long-needed talk?" Catherine looks around the room. Seathan is in the *byre* tending the animals and Anna, whom she nursed recently, has fallen asleep. The two younger *clanns* are out hiking on the moor.

She calls to Seathan, "Your *athair* and I are going out to the spring to fill the buckets with water. Will you listen for Anna and get me if she begins to cry?"

Seathan comes out of the *byre*, "Aye, *mathair*, I will do that."

Both Catherine and Lach pick up a bucket and head to the spring. Once they are out of ear shot of the family, Lach begins the conversation, "Catherine, now that we are alone, I want to discuss what has been troubling me for some time now. You always help me find the answers and I need your ideas now."

Lach shares his thoughts, "In March, not long after Anna's birth, the tacksman came by as I was teaching Seathan how to repair the thatch on our roof. He demanded that I pay him our rent. I am not sure, if I told you this, but the laird has increased the rent on our farm," continues Lach. "This has been a tough year for us. The cow that I sold did not bring enough cash. It is getting more and more difficult to come up with the rent. I am at a loss as to how to make money on our farm unless I make some changes."

Although focused on her family and home, Catherine has been aware for some time of the difficulties of farming and surviving in their glen. She has been keeping her eyes and ears open for opportunities in this part of Mull. It is time now for her to speak up. "Lach, I wish that life could continue as it has always been without being as difficult. However, I see that times for us and the clans are changing. The old way of life that our ancestors knew is gone forever."

Catherine continues, "Although Seathan is only 13 years old, he is a strong and capable young person. I believe that he can manage more responsibilities of the farm, if the need arises. I have heard of several labours which many from our clan are using to add to their farming income. It will be up to you to judge which one will work."

Lach responds, "Catherine, what do you have in mind?"

"The government has been asking for labour to repair the roads of Mull. They do not pay much money, but it would add to any that our cows will bring us this year," replies Catherine. "Or perhaps the tacksman would accept oats and barley from our farm in exchange for some of our rent money," she adds almost as an afterthought.

"Do you have any other ideas, Catherine?" queries Lach.

"Some of our clansmen work as labourers for our laird," responds Catherine a little apprehensively. "You could ask the laird if he has work that you can do for him." Thinking a little she then states, "Besides these there are three other jobs which I can think of. Of course, all of them would create hardship for all of the family. There is the harvesting of kelp for one, fishing or the quarrying of granite. All these labours will be tough on your body and it will mean that you will have to be away for about 5 or 6 months of the year," adds Catherine.

"I have thought of all these, Catherine," responds Lach in a troubled voice. "Any of these choices will greatly affect our family. I think the one which will cause the least suffering is to ask the laird for work.

Catherine responds, "I don't like that you will be working for our laird. It feels as if you are betraying our kinfolk, but I also agree it will be less stressful for you and us."

"I will ask him the next time I see him," and with that they walk

66

back to the *bothie*; their buckets filled with the day's water.

Arriving back at the *bothie*, Lach calls to Seathan, "It is a good spring day to go into the woods and hunt. It is still early enough in the day and I think we will find the hares plentiful." Seathan agrees and they set out. Once in the forest they are silent and walk stealthily so they will not alert the hares. The woodland floor is covered with the wildflowers of the Highlands; wood anemone, violet, primrose, wood sorrel and damsons. Pinks, whites, purples and yellows dot the forest. Lach remarks to himself, "There is no sweeter season on this island."

After several hours Lach and Seathan return to the *bothie* with three hares. This is a successful hunt and will provide a couple of weeks of meat. Handing them over to Catherine, they go into the *byre* to complete their chores. Meanwhile Catherine, grateful for this addition to the food supply, goes outside to hang them upside down on a tree. Jannet had taught her when she was a child how to use all parts of the hare. When ready the hides and fur will be sewn into warm items and the meat will feed them for several days. Catherine has decided to use some of the tanned hide for a little fur muff for Anna just like the one she had made for Caitriona several years ago.

Later in the day, while the family is sitting together around the fire, Lach shares with the rest of the family that he will be making a visit to the laird. "I will be asking him if he has a need for an extra hand to work around his estate. I am hoping that this work will help pay our rent for the farm." He continues, "Seathan, if the laird gives me this labour, I will be gone for most of the day. I will be relying on you to help more on the farm. You will go with the animals to the meadows when it is time. Iain and Caitriona, you are to help your *mathair* in the *bothie* and on the farm. There will not be much time for play or for hiking on the moor, except to gather vegetation. These things must be done if we are going to survive and continue to live here," asserts Lach in a sad but demanding voice. The next day Lach goes to his laird who agrees to hire him.

PART II
The Campbells

16
The Blacksmith

The little village of Inivea needs a blacksmith and 33-year-old Iain Campbell has been taught to do this work. In his village, Ballygown, where his *athair* had been the blacksmith for many years, there is no longer enough work for two blacksmiths. Iain has been considering a move for a few years now. News of a need for a blacksmith in another village came to him through the gossip of recent travelers. Iain decides it is now time to check out these rumors and he will borrow his *athair's* horse to investigate. The village of Inivea is a two-hour journey for him by horseback and it would take at least a day of travel to move a family there. This would be a big decision for his family; Isobel, his *bean* and his two *clanns*, Roderick (7) and Donald (2). At least it would be close enough to visit his *athair* and *mathair*.

The next morning Iain announces, "Isobel, I am going to travel to Inivea to see if they have a need of a blacksmith."

Isobel responds, "Be careful, it is still a difficult time of year to travel. Snow still covers the ground."

"Of this I am well aware and I am counting on the sure-footedness of my horse," Iain reassures Isobel.

"Nonetheless, be careful, Iain. We will be awaiting your safe return," answers Isobel who is not very confident of her *fear's* safe travels, but she also knows it is important and he is determined.

Outside his *bothie*, the sky is overcast and foggy. Iain mounts his steed and quickly rides through the village of Ballygown. He passes by the blacksmith's shop where his *athair* is outside talking to one of the clansmen. He interrupts the chat to wave goodbye to his *mac*. Iain has traveled many times in his youth through the rough terrain of his Isle, so he knows the best way to reach Inivea.

Iain is always astounded by the desolate beauty of the Highlands in winter. The trees are bare and spring flora has not yet appeared.

The mountains beside him are haunting and their snow-covered cliffs make them appear more unattainable. During this time of scarcity, he hopes he might catch a glimpse of the magnificent red deer, venturing out into the open, seeking food wherever they can find it. The unadorned trees of the woods will not be hiding them as they do later in the spring. The path underneath the horse's hoofs is rough and snow-covered. Iain, despite his experience, is uneasy and having second thoughts about his choice to travel now. "Clop, clop, clop, clop" echo the hoofs of his horse. "Thus far my horse is steady and obedient to my commands," silently reflects Iain. The wind is turning bitterly cold and has begun making his travel more dangerous. Suddenly without hesitation Iain decides to hike the rest of the way. "Steady boy," Iain admonishes his horse as he lifts himself off his back. It will take him longer, but Iain feels more secure with his own booted feet on the ground. They have at least another two hours of travel. Iain is careful to lead his horse so that he will not fall and break a leg or worse yet, lose his balance and pull both of them down a ravine.

Even though weather in the Highlands is unpredictable and a storm can erupt at any moment, Iain continues along to his destination. He cannot dwell on these thoughts, but he will be relieved when he reaches Inivea. Suddenly, as he was hoping, he spots a group of red deer several yards ahead of him in a snow-covered clearing. Despite their somewhat gaunt appearance from a winter of sparse vegetation, this small herd is an impressive sight to Iain. Iain watches them as they scatter when they catch sight of him and his horse. As quickly as these great animals appeared in his view, they disappear into the landscape, invisible in the foggy and misty surroundings. Becoming anxious to reach his destination, Iain carefully picks up his pace.

17
The Search for a New Home

While Iain is traveling, Isobel Campbell has been left to worry. It is cold and overcast in their small village and she wonders how Iain is finding the trek to Inivea. She and Iain with their two *macs* living in Ballygown have a small garden beside their *bothie*. They keep several cows, goats and chickens to help feed the family. However, it is becoming more and more difficult for Iain to support his family on the limited income from blacksmithing. Many clansmen have moved out of the village and farms, seeking employment in other parts of Scotland. Isobel is sad; she does not want to leave her village, but she knows that eventually she must.

Donald is whining, not quite crying but needing her attention. "Ma, ma," he calls out to his *mathair*. At two his words are few, but Isobel knows his needs. Roderick is out in the *byre*, feeding the animals and collecting eggs from the chickens. Isobel tends to Donald who is wet and soiled. She looks at him noting his tawny brown hair and hazel eyes. Much like her own coloring he is fairer than that of her other son, Roderick. Donald looks more like her clan of Paterson. While Roderick, darker with brown hair and eyes, resembles the Campbells. Isobel takes a moment to further examine herself. Her hair, once of a light brown color is turning gray. Although slight in figure and stature, she is not weak. Years of labour on a farm in her youth and now as a married woman maintaining a household of feeding, clothing, sheltering and bearing her *bairns*, have left her with a sturdy able body.

While Isobel treasures her two *macs*, she wishes that her two *nigheans* were still alive. Her first *nighean*, born before Roderick, died at birth. It had been a difficult pregnancy with lots of nausea and vomiting. She was born perfect in every way except she was a still born. Her second *nighean*, born after Roderick, was sweet with a lot of eagerness for life, but she contracted small pox and at 3 years old was unable to fight off the illness.

Isobel with Donald at her side enters the *byre*. Roderick wants to milk the cows and goats himself, but Isobel cautions him that he is not old enough. He will do more when he is older, but right now he is just beginning to learn. Isobel milks the animals and then pauses, "Roderick, after I am done here I am going to the blacksmith shop to talk with your *seanair* (grandfather). You can take your *brathair* and visit with your *seanmhair* (grandmother). Maybe she will give you something to eat."

Isobel quickly walks over to her *ann an laghs'* (in-laws') *bothie* with her *clanns*. The two *clanns* disappear into the dwelling of their *seanmhair* as Isobel continues on the snow-covered rough path to the shop of Duncan Campbell. The shop is small and poorly lit and her eye first catches Duncan sitting on a large stone near his forge. He is a large man in his mid 50s with gigantic hands and muscular arms, made larger than normal by his years of hammering at the anvil. Isobel creates quite a contrast to this man of brawn and strength. Duncan speaks first, "What brings you here today, Isobel?"

"*Seanair*, I am worried about Iain," trembles Isobel. "He has taken off to Inivea and the passage is sure to be rough, icy and snow-covered. I fear for his horse and his ability to remain steady on a path, made slippery by snow."

"I understand your fears and I am not without them. However, Iain is well acquainted with traveling on rough winter terrain," Duncan reassures Isobel with hope. He knows that it is too late to tell of his own misgivings. "I am sure that if Iain believes that the terrain is too rough for the horse to carry him safely, he will dismount and lead the way himself. It will take him longer and perhaps he will need to seek shelter with someone in Inivea. So, if Iain does not return this evening it might well be that he has stayed overnight."

"Duncan, I will try not to worry," replies Isobel. With that Isobel leaves and rounds up her two *clanns*."

18
The Negotiation

After several hours Iain is finally nearing the village. It has been a hazardous journey and he had averted two near calamities when his horse stumbled on the rough path. Iain, with his powerful blacksmithing body, tightly held onto the reins with all his strength so his horse could regain its balance. Despite all the difficulty of this journey, Iain has a hopeful optimism that he will find new opportunities in Inivea.

Ahead of him Iain sights a clearing and then the first *bothie* of Inivea. Now that the fear of falling has vanished he lets out a sigh of relief. He is able to hear migrating birds and see smaller animals darting out of their underground chambers onto the decayed brush of the forest, ready to explore their changing world for food. Iain has been to this village before in his younger years and he knows several of the village clansmen. This is the end of winter, too early for most of the men to be outdoors. He will probably need to knock on the door of a *bothie* for his inquiries. First, he will try to find the shop of the former blacksmith to see if it is still vacant.

As luck would have it, when Iain enters the village, Dughall Campbell, a distant cousin, is outside his *bothie* looking over his peat pile. Iain calls out, "Dughall, how are you?" Dughall, not knowing at first who calls to him, stops what he is doing, looks up and peers into the distance. He does not respond immediately and waits until Iain gets close enough to recognize him. Dughall has not seen Iain for several years so he is not sure who is calling his name. Villagers, although generally hospitable, have an initial suspicion of strangers. Iain gets close enough to speak again, "Dughall, it is me, Iain Campbell, from the village of Ballygown." Iain then adds more evidence to his identity, "I am the oldest son of Duncan, the village blacksmith. When I was a youth I visited Inivea several times with my family to join in *ceilidh* gatherings. As you probably remember I am one of your distant cousins," continues Iain, hoping to make the familial connection.

"Aye," answers Dughall. "You have changed since your youth and the last time we were together. How are your *parantans* (parents)?" inquires Dughall.

"They are well but glad that our spring will soon be here." Iain continues, "Dughall, I have made the long trek here from my village to inquire about a rumor that some travelers recently shared with my *athair*. As you know many folks have been moving away from our village. Our village no longer has enough work for two blacksmiths. I have heard that the village of Inivea recently lost its blacksmith."

"Aye, this is true," Dughall responds. "Our blacksmith here was getting old; blacksmithing work was becoming difficult for him, but he kept on with it. However, in October he was found dead in his shop. Everyone was sad. He was the only blacksmith that most of them had known."

"It sounds as if your blacksmith was admired by your villagers," adds Iain.

"Aye," replies Dughall. "A good blacksmith and a good man are well valued."

"Dughall, has a new blacksmith been found for your community?" inquires Iain.

Dughall responds, "Nay, the villagers and farmers need someone to do that work for them."

Iain replies, "I have worked as a blacksmith for many years with my *athair*, Duncan, and he has trained me well. My *athair* has many more years of work in him. I would like to move my family here and be Inivea's blacksmith. May I take a look at the blacksmith's shop?"

Dughall advises, "Aye, let's us go a little further into my village. The blacksmith's shop is in the center."

Iain soon sees the shop and hurries toward it. He opens the wooden door and sees the tools of the trade from the doorway. They have been carefully taken care of through the years. The forge and bellows are waiting to be used again; along with an anvil, some hammers and a small selection of files and tongs. All these are sufficient for a blacksmith to do his work. Iain remarks to Dughall, "The tools that your blacksmith left are good. I am more convinced that I would like to move here and be your blacksmith," continues Iain. "Is there an empty *bothie* that my family and I could use?" queries Iain.

Dughall replies, "The widow of the blacksmith has left here to live with her *nighean* some distance from here. I am sure that she will not return. She was not in good health which is why she moved. Her *bothie* is next door to the shop. The stone is in good condition, but the roof will need to be repaired. Would you like see it?"

Iain replies, "Aye, but I first must ask for some hay and water for my horse."

"Of course, Iain, let's make our way back to my *bothie* and I will feed your animal."

Once the horse is fed, Dughall and Iain make their way back to the blacksmith's old *bothie*. Iain opens its door and notices that it appears to be in living condition. It is dark and cold inside, having been abandoned several months ago. The widow has left several items of furniture, some chests and boxed beds, which will make it easier for his small family to move in. Iain ventures inside, the open door casting enough light for Iain to discern other supplies. There are several large wooden bowls and a large iron kettle which hangs from an iron chain over the center hearth. In the cabinet are more wooden bowls for eating along with wooden spoons.

Then Iain ventures inside the *byre*. Dughall shares, "The blacksmith's animals were distributed to other clansmen in the village." Alongside the wall, neatly placed, were several milk and watering buckets. Iain is feeling hopeful about relocating his business and family to this small village.

Iain then speaks: "Dughall, this looks good for my family. I would like to spend the day here meeting the clansmen and tell them of my plans. I will need a place to stay overnight. Do you think we could get some dry peat to light this fire and round up some bedding to keep me warm?"

Dughall replies, "That is a good idea and I will ask around for some peat. The widow has probably left some clean coverings for one of the beds."

It is late afternoon and several of the clansmen are outside their *bothies*. Dughall is the first one to speak to each, "This is Iain Campbell, a distant cousin of several of the Campbells in our village. Iain is the *mac* of a blacksmith in the nearby village of Ballygown. He has been well taught by his *athair,* but there is not enough work there for two blacksmiths. Iain has agreed to move his trade and his family here. He will take over the shop and the *bothie* of the old blacksmith."

The villagers who have missed having the services of a blacksmith in their village for several months are very pleased. They agree to pass the word on to the other clansmen at their upcoming *ceilidh*.

Iain has a restless night in the new surroundings with so many thoughts keeping him half awake. Before he retired he had briefed the clan of his plan to return to his village and prepare his family for the move to Inivea. It might be several days before the family is ready for this big move.

He wakes up at early dawn and although there is morning fog, the weather is slightly warmer. Gathering his horse he makes his way out of the village, waving goodbye to those who are already out and about.

19
The Campbells' Plan to Move to Inivea

Iain Campbell's trek back to his village and *bothie* is easier than his journey the previous day. He is able to ride his horse and returns in three hours. He opens the door to his *bothie* and Isobel greets him, "Iain, your safe return is a welcoming sight. My thoughts and heart have imagined the very worst since you did not return yesterday."

"Isobel, it was a successful journey to Inivea. They desperately need a new blacksmith and gave me positive news. The blacksmith shop is ready for a new tenant and the blacksmith's *bothie* is vacant and available for our new life."

"Your news eases me and I will begin to prepare for our move in the morning," Isobel supportively responds. At that Isobel moves closer to Iain, takes his hand, squeezes it and then they hug each other, thankful for a new beginning.

Iain, ending the embrace, moves toward the door telling Isobel, "I am going to my *athair's* to tell him the news." The air outside is still crisp and cold but there is sunshine in the air and also in the step of Iain. He has more hope now for the wellbeing of his family than he has had in a long time. He arrives at the blacksmith shop of his *athair* and opens the door. "*Athair*, it is Iain. I have returned from my visit to Inivea and have good news. The villagers and farmers of Inivea do indeed need a blacksmith. There is a blacksmith's shop ready for a new worker and the *bothie* of the former blacksmith is available. The roof needs repair but otherwise the structure is good and ready for my family."

Duncan shows his pleasure at his *mac's* safe return and news. "Iain, this sounds good to me. I am sure that your kinfolk will help you in this move to Inivea."

"*Athair*, please do not share the news with my *mathair*. I want to tell her myself with my family in the morning."

"Aye, Iain, I will save the surprise for you," agrees Duncan.

In the morning Iain and Isobel share the news with their *clanns*, even though Donald is too young to understand. Roderick goes over to his *parantans* to gain some reassurance. They give them a hug and let him know that it will be a good move for the family.

Iain and Isobel plan on several trips, considering the unpredictably of the Highland weather at this time of year. Iain's *athair* has a cart which will help them to move their goods. Their animals will wait to be moved as soon as the weather is clear enough. When the time is right, several kinfolk will help Iain herd his animals across the rough terrain.

After breakfast Iain and his small family walk to his *mathair*, Beitris. As they enter she is sitting beside her fire. Beitris, in her 50s, is a quiet woman who has handled the challenges of her life with much determination and courage. She is the backbone of her family. The two *clanns* run to her and hug her. They are very fond of their *seanmhair*. Beitris greets her family, "Iain and Isobel, what brings all of you here?"

Iain speaks first, "*Mathair*, I have found a new opportunity to be a blacksmith in the village of Inivea. Depending on the weather it will take several days through the month to move my family and animals to our new home."

Beitris, a woman of few words, speaks matter-of-factly and without emotion, "Iain and Isobel, this is good news for your family." Beitris does not stir and Iain often wonders why she does not express more of her feelings. He knows life for his *mathair* has not been easy. Her *athair* died in a clan battle and her *brathair* died from smallpox. Two of her *clanns*, a boy and a girl, died young from illness. Two other *macs* and a *nighean* had survived. After they married they had moved to more distant villages.

The family sits awhile by the fire. Beitris brings them some tea and bread. The *clanns* stay with their *seanmhair* while Iain and Isobel visit their kin in the village.

20
A Difficult Journey

Iain and Isobel wake up the next morning, excitedly thinking about the journey ahead of them. However, it will not be an easy move. Weather at this time of year is unpredictable and transporting a family and their household goods over rough terrain would be an insurmountable task for lesser folk. Highlanders are tough and tenacious though and they will make it happen. Iain speaks first, "Isobel, while you gather our goods here, I am going to make another trip to Inivea so that our new *bothie* will be ready for our family. I will bring much of our peat and leave just enough to keep us warm until we move. I must also bring some hay and oats for the horse along with the food that you will pack for me and my helpers on our journey."

Iain adds as an afterthought, "I will fill one of our iron kettles with some smoldering peat. We can use this to light a fire if we run into bad weather on our journey. The rest of this load will be some bedding, straw mats and clothing."

"Isobel, depending on the weather that we encounter, we may not return until two or three days have passed so do not suspect that the *Black Donald* has caused harm to us," reassures Iain. The fact that Iain has prepared for the journey so well consoles Isobel. Iain further cheers her, "Thankfully, the move will be easier because the widow of the blacksmith left many items which we can use instead of taking many of our own. It is also fortunate for us that the blacksmith left his tools. I will use my *athair's* horse and cart for this job and two of our Campbell cousins will assist me. It is good that the warmer weather is not yet here because this task would have kept them from their spring chores."

Isobel is beginning to feel the reality of their move and the changes in her life and family. No longer will her *clanns* have the daily comforting arms of their seantuismitheoiris (grandparents), *piuthar-*

mathairs and *brathair-athairs* or be able to play with their *co-oghs* (cousins). However, she takes heart that in good weather it will not be a difficult walk from Inivea to Ballygown. Aye, the terrain is rough and uneven, but they are used to that and as her *clanns* grow they will acquire the sturdiness to make visits. Isobel responds to her *fear,* "Iain, while you are gone I will be busy getting our family ready for the move."

Iain then moves out the door to gather his *co-oghas,* Artur and Uilleam. They return to his *bothie*, ready to assist him with the move. They also realize that this might be their fate someday. Before they load the cart they stand together praying to their God that they will have a safe journey and protection from the *Black Donald*. Despite their courage and strength, they are also filled with a knowledge of their unstable environment, especially in winter. Immediately Iain and Artur and Uilleam pack the goods onto the cart, secure the them with rope and hitch the horse. Iain will stay in the front guiding the horse. His *co-oghas* will stay beside the cart, making sure that it remains upright and balanced during their journey. They wave goodbye to their *beans*, their *clanns* and other kinfolk who have come outside of their *bothies* to wish them a safe passage. Having asked God for his protection, they let go of their trepidations and press on to the village of Inivea.

The journey starts off on a good note. They have the morning mist with them. Thus far the horse is able to handle the load behind him. While they are traveling Iain, Artur and Uilleam observe the world around them. They do not want to miss one unexpected hazard or a rush of the wind which might cause a disastrous fall. They listen to the occasional flocks of snow bunting, ravens and hooded crows. Occasionally they observe the mountain hares in their partially white coats. They listen also mostly to the silence of the glen. Beside them the mountains loom with their austere winter makeup.

The travelers feel all is well with them and that they are making good time. They share with each other their good fortune. Soon after their remarks of confidence, they notice that the sky is filling up with dark clouds. They know that this is warning them of an upcoming storm. They press on, taking advantage of weather which has not yet released its cruelty on them. Soon they begin to feel the first flakes of snow as they quickly cover the uneven path under their feet. Knowing what an abundant snowfall could mean to their travels, they begin to worry.

Hastily they begin to make plans, shattering the silence of their travel of just a few moments before. Iain speaks first, "I am worried about this snow. Many times these gentle snowfalls erupt into blizzards. We need to plan for the worst."

Uilleam joins the discussion, "I think that we need to push ahead as much as we can for now until we find an adequate cliff overhang to shelter us."

"Aye, I agree," adds Artur.

As they trudge on the wind and snow begin to pick up. Iain, who is in the front guiding the horse, is the first to spot a low cliff which could provide some protection from the storm. Iain yells out to the others, "Over there on our right, what do you think about that overhang? The snow and winds are increasing. We want to settle into a shelter before we find ourselves in a very dangerous situation." Both Artur and Uilleam quickly agree to Iain's choice. Iain looks for level ground and when he does, he carefully halts the horse so that neither of them will slip on a pathway that has become snowy and icy. The horse makes a whinny, perhaps grateful for Iain's decision.

The snow is forceful as it gusts from the ocean on the west. They all hope in their hearts that this storm will be short-lived, but meanwhile they need to ready themselves. They lead the horse through a weedy, snow-covered field; not much fodder for the horse. Fortunately Iain's past experience led him to pack food for both the travelers and his faithful companion. They near the shelter that nature has provided for the worried travelers and they unhitch the horse. He will have to stand outside the shelter, but Iain and his cousins will cover him with some of the bedding to keep him warm.

Iain and his *co-oghas* push the cart close to the overhang. Gathering several squares of fresh peat, they place them in the iron kettle filled with the smoldering peat. The rocky surface is damp and cold so they lay several of the straw sleeping mats. Next they don a few of the clothes, keeping others to refresh used wet ones if the need arises. All of this is done in silence, because living in this rugged terrain there is no question of what each must do. They work together as they always have in their village, able to read each other's minds in a cooperation of survival. Iain feeds his horse with some oats and hay, leaving their own meal as the last detail before settling in. As they gather their food they put out a bucket to collect the snow which will be used to quench thirst. Gathered under the cliff the three travelers are grateful for all that nature and man has provided for them as they sit out the storm. They carefully eat their food, leaving some for later. Meanwhile the winds howl around them as the snow comes down thick and dense. Highlanders are not folks to complain. They accept whatever comes their way and deal with it. Their resilience has served them well through the centuries.

The minutes and then hours seem to drag on. Every several minutes they take turns to check on the status of the horse, brushing off the snow and making sure he is not shivering. They have the horse facing away from the storm's winds and towards the shelter near the fire, hoping that this will provide enough protection. They do not want to lose such a faithful animal. Thus far the horse is surviving the storm. It feels like forever since the storm began, but they are unable to judge the exact amount of time. The sun, their usual timepiece, is shielded by the clouds and snow. Even when the snow stops they will probably have to hunker down until morning.

Back in Ballygown Isobel is aware of the storm. She puts more peat on the fire and huddles with her *clanns* around it. She does not want to show her anxiety to them so she begins to tell them the story of Loch Lomond. The story is mainly for Roderick, but Donald is mesmerized by his *mathair's* soothing tones and falls asleep nestled in her arms. Isobel begins, "Once a very long time ago there was a young warrior, Donald MacDonald, and his beautiful bride-to-be, Moira. They were so very much in love and eager for their wedding day to happen. Many preparations for such a joyous event were being made. However, as fate would have it, Donald was called into battle. Despite his love for Moira he knew that he had to leave her. When he was departing to join his clan in battle, he promised his dear Moira that he would soon return and that she should come every day to the banks of Loch Lomond to await his return. Before he left he donned his bonnet, his jacket and belted *plaid*. Moira sadly thought to herself that her Donald was the most handsome of warriors. They gave each other a prolonged kiss with arms entwined and said goodbye."

"Donald travelled with the other warriors through the Highlands armed with his basket-hilt sword, handed down to him by his *athair* as his *athair* did before him. With his sword, bayonet and *dirk* by his side, he felt ready to be in battle. The battle was fierce with many of his clansmen killed, while Donald was captured by the English. With the threat of death in front of him, Donald wrote his last love letter to his beloved Moira."

Isobel continues the tale, "Donald is killed by hanging. Wanting to keep his promise of returning to his Moira, his spirit takes the low road, chosen because it is a quicker route than the high road to the banks of Loch Lomond. Moira is there waiting for him. Donald's spirit wraps around Moira in a final embrace. Moira knows that it is Donald's spirit and that Donald is no more and that she will never see him again."

Roderick half asleep shares, "*Mathair*, that is a beautiful story but oh so sad."

"Aye, Roderick, it is a sad story," agrees his *mathair*.

21
The Rescue

After a fitful night, Isobel Campbell is awakened by a loud banging on her door. As this is an occurrence that seldom happens, she is fearful. She arises up from her bed to see who is there. She opens the door to Iain's *athair*. As she greets him she also looks beyond into the landscape of drifting snow, probably three feet or more. Duncan speaks first in a soft gentle voice so as not to cause her more foreboding. "Isobel, I am gathering some clan folk to travel on the trail to Inivea. They are bringing their shovels in order to rescue and dig out Iain, Uilleam and Artur and the horse as well, if needed."

"We all believe that with the amount of snowfall that occurred overnight, they will need our help. We are also ready to shovel a path for them so that they can proceed with their horse and cart to Inivea. I don't want you to worry about your *fear* and the others. They are clever and have probably found refuge in a shelter. We are starting out very early. All the available clansmen are assembled now with extra clothing, food, water, picks and shovels. It will be slow going through the snow. However, we also know that it will be even slower for Iain and his kinfolk as they try to make their way through the deep drifting snow of last night." At that Duncan, with all the clansmen behind him, bid Isobel a farewell. Before they leave they pause for a moment to pray to God for safe travels and the well-being of Iain and his *co-oghas*. Isobel waves timidly, trying to appear full of hope and confidence. The clansmen then set off on their trek through the accumulated snow.

Isobel's *clanns* are wakened by the commotion at their door. They arise to see what is going on. Once their *mathair* comes back into the *bothie*, Roderick questions her, "*Mathair*, what is going on? Has our *athair* come back?"

"No, Roderick, your *athair* is still traveling to Inivea. There was a snowstorm last night and your *seanair* has gathered a group of

87

clansmen to help your *athair* and his *co-oghas* for the rest of their travels. They will help shovel a pathway so that the travelers and the horse and cart will be able to travel safely to our new home.

"*Mathair,* I am afraid," responds Roderick to her reassurances.

Although troubled herself, Isobel does not let the *clanns* know of her own misgivings, "Roderick, your *athair* will be fine. He knows how to travel through the rugged trails of our Isle in all kinds of weather. With the help of your *seanair* and the others, their travels will be easier. Now, while I prepare your food, get dressed and then dress Donald. By then your meal will be ready."

Isobel then busies herself cooking the porridge and gathering the rest of the meal; eggs, milk, cheese and bread. She thinks to herself, "I hope that I have reassured Roderick so that he will not worry about his *athair."*

Soon Roderick and Donald gather around the fire. "It is strange not to have our *athair* with us for our meal," Roderick comments as the family gathers.

"He will be back soon," responds Isobel. "While we are waiting for him we will keep busy with our chores as well as collecting the items we will need in our new home," Isobel adds.

"I don't want to leave Ballygown," Roderick brings up for the first time now that the move has become more real to him. "I will miss my *co-oghas* and other kinfolk," Roderick continues to make his feelings known.

Isobel tries to comfort him, "Aye, it will be hard to leave all our kinfolk, especially your *seanair* and *seanmhair*. However, Inivea is not that far away from Ballygown and when the weather is good we will return to Ballygown and visit everyone." Roderick remains silent at this promise. The day is then spent tending to the animals and beginning to collect the items which will be brought to their new home.

Roderick wants to make sure that his favorite cloak and tartan are packed, "*Mathair,* here is the cloak and tartan that I want to bring to Inivea. Will we be bringing our animals?"

"Aye, Roderick, your *athair* will lead them to Inivea when the weather is good," reassures Isobel.

Isobel worries but tries to stay positive for her *clanns*. She will have to wait patiently for the condition of Iain and his *co-oghas* and whether the rescuers were successful in their mission.

This is the story Duncan told her later. "The snow was deep and the travel was grueling. The journey felt endless. At one point one of the leaders suddenly stopped and shouted out that there was a large disturbance in the snow. It was too far away to see if it was Iain."

"I reminded the men that the disturbances might have been caused by red deer or other animals." Nonetheless, the men's spirits brightened. We persistently continued to plod through the snow. Sunshine reflected on the snow crystals and made looking in the distance difficult. When we finally reached the disturbance we were disappointed. It was recent animal activity."

Isobel was attentive as Duncan continued, "After what seemed like an eternity, we noticed an odd amount of snow against an outcrop that looked like a cart wheel sticking out. We surmise that surely it must be a shelter. We now believed that we were getting near the travelers. We all began shouting to let Iain and his *co-oghas* know that we had come to help them out. It took a while for Iain and the others to look in our direction." This ended Duncan's recounting of the rescue.

Before they had become aware of their rescuers, Iain and his cousins were discussing what they should do now that it was daylight. Iain spoke first, "If we are going to make it to Inivea before nightfall, we need to start as soon as possible. The way will be difficult and exhausting."

Uilleam and Artur agree, "It is going to be a difficult journey, but we must start out immediately."

Just as they are prepared to set out on the rest of their journey, they hear the shouts from Duncan and the rescuers. Iain hears the call of Duncan, "Iain, it's me, your *athair.*"

After the rescuers reach the stranded travelers, they take time to exchange hugs and greetings. There was an observable show of relief on the faces of those who had spent a frigid and harsh night in the storm. Duncan first inquires, "How are you?"

"We made it through a very difficult and frightening night," Iain answers his *athair.* He continues, "While huddled here we had no idea of our future, but we did not let our fears dominate our conversation. We kept busy sharing stories about well-known Campbell battles and clan folktales.

Duncan assures his *mac*, "Several clansmen have traveled with me to help you with the rest of your journey. We have brought supplies of dry clothes, water and food."

Iain gratefully responds, "We will change into dry clothes and then all of us can eat before we start our trip to Inivea."

After they finish their meal the small group of dedicated rescuers set off ahead of Iain. Artur and Uilleam walk on each side of the cart. Clearing the way, it takes the group another two hours of committed resolve and labour to reach the village of Inivea. It is early afternoon and many of the villagers, out and about, see the travelers and greet them with whoops and hollers, shouting with abandon for their safe arrival. The rescuers must leave Inivea immediately in order to make it back before dark. Iain and his cousins say goodbye to their rescuers. Duncan calls out to Iain as they are leaving, "I will give the good news of your safe arrival to Isobel and the other *beans*."

Now at last in Inivea, Iain shows his *co-oghas* to his new *bothie*, "This is where my family will live when we move here. The blacksmith shop is next door. We will stay here tonight and you can help me unpack. We will return to Ballygown tomorrow. Let's first unpack my tools."

Artur suddenly protests Iain's decision to return home in the morn, "Iain, we need one more day to rest before we return home. It was a horrific night and difficult trip here to Inivea. I am weary."

Iain is surprised by Artur's complaint, "Artur, I believe that we need to return as soon as possible. We don't know if the weather is going to turn again and give us more trouble. We can make our final decision in the morning when we look at the sky."

Uilleam agrees with Iain, "It does seem like a good idea to get back to Ballygown as soon as possible. Our family is expecting us and I would rather rest in my own bed."

Artur, not pleased with the response, is angry. "I believe that we need an extra day of rest so that we will be ready for any challenges that we might encounter on our trip." Artur realizes that he has no power in the situation and remains silent for the rest of the night.

The rest of the evening is spent with Iain and his *co-oghas* first unloading the tools for Iain's new shop. Then they unpack the peat, bedding, straw mats and clothing. Iain uses the smoldering peat in the kettle and starts another fire. The fire will keep them warm through the night. Artur, still looking for excuses to stay an extra day and night, informs Iain, "Iain, our clothes and bedding are still wet from our travels. It will take them a day to dry out."

"We will leave them near the fire through the night and, hopefully, they will dry out," replies Iain. Before settling into their beds Iain heats up some porridge, and hot water. After Iain gives the blessing, they sit quietly around the fire with a meal of porridge, cheese, bread and hot tea. Unlike the chatter and stories that they had shared, huddled together in the overhang shelter, they are now quiet. Iain silently remembers that he did warn Isobel that he might not return for several days and not to worry, but he is anxious to return home as soon as he can. The next morning Iain and his *co-oghas* awaken to clear spring-like weather. Iain remains convinced that it is important for them to stick to the plan of returning back to Ballygown. "Artur might not be happy with this decision, but perhaps a good sleep and the good weather will put him in a better mood," Iain ruminates silently. After a small meal they ready the horse and cart for the trip back to Ballygown.

Iain and his *co-oghas* look over the *bothie* before they leave. Iain comments to his *co-oghas*, "The fire is smoldering but will soon burn itself out. I will ask Dughall to check on my new home while I am back in Ballygown getting my family ready to move." He then adds, "It looks as if nature is going to be in our favor for our trip back." Artur quietly goes along with the plan and does not bring up his concerns of yesterday.

Outside there are several villagers chatting with each other. Among them is Dughall. Iain calls to Dughall. Dughall comes to the travelers. "You are ready to leave," comments Dughall matter of factly.

Iain responds, "Dughall, we are leaving today so that I can get my family ready to move here. Can you keep an eye on my new home and shop while I am gone? I am eager to begin my new life so I do not think it will be more than several weeks, maybe a month."

"I will watch over your *bothie* and shop," reassures Dughall.

Several villagers soon join Dughall to wish Iain and his *co-oghas* safe travels. Iain knows that they are eager for Iain and his family's quick return back to Inivea because they miss the work of the village blacksmith.

The trip back to Ballygown is an arduous one for the travelers. The travelers now faced knee-deep mounds of snow on the trail, caused by the fierce winds of the night before. If it was only Iain, Artur and Uilleam that had to face these difficult conditions of their return, it would have been manageable. However, the horse and cart add a great burden to the three clansmen. Pushing the cart from behind and pulling the horse in front, the travelers soon face exhaustion. After an hour of travel Artur is the first to speak out, "Iain, we cannot continue this way. We will soon collapse from exhaustion and our horse looks as if he is about ready to fall."

Iain knows that Artur is right and at that moment makes a monumental decision. "Artur you are right. We will unhitch the horse and leave the cart in the field behind a rock or a tree," he announces. All knew that this was a big but necessary choice for Iain to make. The cart was not his and it could be stolen. They also knew how useful the cart was as a way to transport his family and their goods to their new home. At that the travelers slow down and peer ahead and, on each side, look for a good spot to stash the cart. They slowly plod through the drifting snow.

Artur is getting discouraged, "Let's just pick the open field beside us. We will never find the perfect spot to hide the cart."

"No, Artur, we must find the best spot here to hide the cart. Be patient," responds Iain abruptly.

After several more minutes of travel the landscape changes. On one side is a more rugged landscape with trees and some larger boulders. Iain calls out, "There, over there, is a large boulder where we can hide the cart."

Silently the travelers stop. They do not waste any of their remaining energy by shouting or cheering. The horse is led into the field with the cart still behind him. Once they reach the large boulder, the horse is unhitched and guided back to the path by Iain. The cart is well-hidden behind the boulder. The travelers take a few items out of the cart which they will carry with them; cheese, bread and water, some dry clothes and cloths. Each traveler stuffs his goods into a sack made from a spare shawl. The rest of the cart's contents they will leave behind in the cart, covered by a large blanket which is weighted down by the rocks they gather from the ground around them.

The brief pause has renewed their spirit and energies. Iain shares his observation, "We are now ready to go."

"Aye," Artur and Uilleam in unison agree, eager to begin.

The trip back to Ballygown is strenuous but eased by no longer having the cart to push and pull through the mounds of drifting snow. The horse snorts frequently throughout the trip which the travelers believe show his approval of his lightened load. After several hours of travel, Iain, who is in the front leading the horse, spots a clearing with the *bothies* and *kirk* of Ballygown appearing. "Look, ahead of us is Ballygown at last," Iain shouts to his cousins. Artur and Uilleam emit sighs of relief.

When they finally reach the village, each head to his own *bothie*. Iain leads the horse to the shop of his *athair*. He tethers the horse and then knocks on the door of Duncan's shop. When Duncan sees Iain, he embraces him in a rare show of affection. His arms, sinewy and strong, surround Iain and almost knock the breath out of him. They sit at the fire. While Iain warms himself, Duncan probes his *mac* about the trip back. Iain responds to his *athair's* inquiries, "Drifting mounds of snow covered the road. We were often knee-deep in these snow mounds. Trekking was grueling and especially difficult for our horse pulling the cart. When it became apparent that we could no longer travel this way, I decided that it was best to leave the cart behind a large boulder. We hope that it will not be spotted by other travelers."

Duncan was not surprised by his *mac's* experience on the road to Ballygown. "Iain, I think you made a wise decision to leave the cart and travel the rest of the way without it. We can go out sometime soon and retrieve it. How are your *co-oghas*?" questions Duncan, out of concern that the trip would not cause any sour feelings in the clan.

"Artur was not happy that we left today," responds Iain. "He made a big fuss initially, but I held my ground, believing that it was better to take advantage of today's bright sunshine and spring-like day. Artur did suggest, however, that we unhitch the horse and leave the cart behind. I followed his advice. Once we traveled without the cart Artur appeared to be in a better humor."

"I must go to Isobel. I am sure that she is uneasy waiting for my safe return."

22

The Campbells Move

Iain opens the door to his *bothie*. Isobel, who was tending to Donald looks up when she sees Iain. She lets out a gasp, indicating both her relief and happiness. She puts Donald down and rushes to the door, puts her arms around her *fear* and plants a kiss on his cheek. Iain returns Isobel's embrace by hugging her and twirling her around. Neither can put their relief into words. Uncertainty and fear have been penetrating their lives recently. After their initial joyful snuggle they remain silent. Each is aware of the challenges that lay ahead of them.

Iain speaks first, "It was a very difficult trip both to and from Inivea. It was good that my *athair* and other clansmen came to our rescue."

Isobel replies, "Aye, Duncan told me about the rescue and that you had made it to Inivea safely. That eased my mind, but I was still worried about your return back to Ballygown."

"We couldn't travel with the cart. The mounds of drifting snow made it very difficult for the horse to pull it. He would have died from exhaustion if we hadn't unhitched it and left it behind," explained Iain. "I have told my *athair* and we will retrieve it when the weather is better. Although we hid it behind a large boulder, I am concerned that it might be stolen."

Roderick, who had been waiting patiently, finally runs to his *athair*. He hugs him and cries out, "*Athair,* it is so good to have you home. I have missed you."

"Aye, Roderick, as I have also missed you," Iain fondly responds to his oldest *mac*. Donald runs over to his athair and hugs his legs. "Our new home in Inivea is ready for us to move in," says Iain to his family.

The remainder of February is spent saying *tioraidh* (goodbye) to the kin. Although Isobel's *mathair* and *athair* have died, the rest of the Paterson clan have remained in Ballygown, farming their small plots of land while they pay rent to the laird. Isobel has two *brathairs* and their *beans* living in Ballygown as well as one *siuir* and her *fear.*

95

These kin will stay in Ballygown. When they were together and alone Isobel's *siuir,* Euphemia, shared with Isobel, "I envy your chance to leave Ballygown and start a new life. It is so difficult here in Ballygown making ends meet and paying increasing amounts of rent to our laird."

Isobel empathizes with Euphemia's situation, "I know that it is difficult for you and Archibald. Archibald is a smart man and he will find a way to help his family. Meanwhile, when the weather improves you can trek to Inivea and visit us in our new home."

Euphemia is silent, knowing that taking time from the chores of their farm in the good weather will probably not happen. Roderick and Donald have seven *co-oghas.* Roderick is especially sad. He will miss his *co-oghas* greatly, especially his closest *co-oghas,* Malcolm and Hector, the *macs* of Isobel's *brathair,* Niel. The day of the move finally arrives and in their favor, it is a good one. The whole village step out of their *bothies* to say *tioraidh.* Stoically the Campbells push back their tears and begin their journey to Inivea, trying to show confidence with their smiles.

Isobel climbs into the cart which Iain had retrieved from its hiding place several weeks before. Iain hands a sleepy Donald to her and with Donald nestled in her lap, she settles among the blankets and clothes. Rapidly, as to not waste any precious time, Iain grabs the reins of the impatient horse. Roderick finds his place beside the cart behind his *athair.* Roderick, who has not traveled far from his home in Ballygown, is amazed at all the sights around him. In the several weeks since Iain's last trip with his *athair* to retrieve the abandoned cart, the snow, except on the highest mountains, has practically disappeared. "Look *mathair,* the trees are so tall here," exclaims Roderick. Roderick continues to look around him. He notices the hills and then the snow-covered mountains hovering in the distance.

Although buoyant and excited initially, Roderick is letting the unfamiliar sounds and darkness of the forest penetrate his fragile nature. After an hour of travel he becomes uncertain in his step and begins to tremble with fear. "Ma Ma," using the language of a younger *clann,* he cries out to his *Mathair. "I* see the Black Donald following us in the woods. He is going to steal me and take me far away from you," Roderick continues.

Isobel does not let Roderick's fear be without her comfort for long. She calls to Iain to stop so that he can raise him into the cart. Once in the comfort of her arms Roderick stops trembling but continues to express his fear of Black Donald and the goblins and faeries he believes that are lurking in the dark woods around them. He whimpers as Isobel comforts and tries to silence him, not only to relieve him of his fears, but also so as not to disturb the sleeping Donald. It is a vain attempt, however, because Donald soon wakens. He reaches immediately for his mother's breast and soon relaxes in the warm nurture of his mother's milk.

Both *clanns* remain restless as the cart travels over the bumpy path to Inivea. It is difficult to contain a two-year-old in the confined space of a cart. Roderick continues to whine about his fear of the Black Donald and his anxiety only increases Donald's inability to remain still. Isobel, a wonderful story teller and songstress, calms herself and uses her talents to distract her two *clanns*. She bursts into song singing, "*Oh Rowan Tree.*" The melody has a sweet catchy lilt and the words, which Isobel sings so gently, sooth her young *clanns*.

"Oh, rowan tree, oh rowan tree,
Thoul't aye be dear to me,
Entwind' thou art wi' mony ties,
O' hame and infancy.
Thy leaves were aye the first o spring,
Thy flowr's the simmer's pride:
There was na sic a bonnie tree,
In all the country side.
Oh, rowan tree.
How fair wert thou in simmer time
Wi' all they clusters white.
How rich and gay the autumn dress,
Wi' berries red and bright.
Oh thy fair stem were mony names
Which now nah mair I see,
But there engraved on my heart,
Forgot they ne'er can be.
Oh rowan tree. "

Isobel finishes the four verses of the song she loves so well and stops. "Oh, *mathair*, sing the Rowan tree song again," pleads Roderick. "I'm not so afraid." At that Isobel sings it again and follows up with several more songs. By the time she stops it is time for the family to eat their packed meal.

Isobel calls out to Iain, seeing a clearing in the woods, just right for putting down a blanket and spread their food, "Iain, look on the other side of our cart. There is a clearing, just right, to stop and eat."

After lunch they continue on their trek to their new home. They have travelled more than half the trip and should be there in a couple of hours. Roderick, beckoned by Iain to join him again on the path, is feeling less frightened and wants to show his *mathair* and *athair* that he is indeed a brave clansman. The rest of the trip to their new home is without incident.

Once they reach Inivea they are greeted warmly by the townsfolk who have been waiting many months for a new blacksmith. Dughall and some of the other villagers quickly come to Iain and Isobel's aid as they unpack their goods, light the peat fire and feed the horse. A few women come by with some bread and cheese and oatmeal to help the family feel nourished through the night and the next morning. The next day while Isobel is transforming her new home for residence, Iain sets up his new shop.

Although the family has been busy with the settling in their new home and shop, the next Sunday they are determined to attend services at Inivea's *kirk*. They are thankful to God for giving them this opportunity and for their safe passage from Ballygown to Inivea. It is a sunny spring morning on this March day in 1785 when Iain with his family don their best clothes and leave for the *kirk*. The *kirk* is fairly close to their *bothie* in the village. As they are nearing it, a young woman with a *bairn* in her arms rushes up to Iain and hands him a gift of bread and cheese. Iain, being a Highlander, knows the significance of this gesture and accepts the gift without hesitation.

PART III
Inivea—1790

23
Spring and Summer in Inivea

Spring and summer chores on the Isle of Mull are endless. In April Seathan and his *mathair* prepare the soil for planting. Seathan is then ready to make the long trek to the ocean to harvest seaweed for fertilizer. While there he notices some of the farmers from Inivea harvesting kelp to sell for additional income. Curious, he asks a few of the farmers about their experience and whether it has helped them out financially. From what he can gather, it is extremely difficult work and the meagre income does not take one out of poverty. Additionally, this work kept the farmers away from their families for 5 to 6 months out of the year. Of course the family left behind did their best, but without the men tending the soil and crops their farms suffer. At the time of the harvest these families especially feel the effect of their absence. Even though the extra income was small, most feel that they have no other choice.

Heavy-hearted Seathan returns to his farm. With his help the soil is soon prepared for planting and soon he and Catherine will turn to the community chore of cutting peat for their fires. They listen to for the cry which is heard throughout the glen, 'Going to the peats,' signaling all that it was time to gather together and begin the arduous task of cutting the peat. Strong men are the cutters while the women and their clans will lay the wet slabs of peat on the moor to dry. When dry, the clan's folk will work together and stack the peat. Each family will then cart the peat to their *bothie* and stack it for use later. Seathan is the first to hear the cry and he signals, "*Mathair*, it is time to go gather the *clanns*. They will help with the stacking.

Catherine reminds Seathan, "Anna is not strong enough to carry the wet peat, but she can learn by watching us." The family then heads to the peat bogs and spend the day with Seathan doing the heavy dirty work of cutting. Catherine and her *clanns*, except for young Anna, spend their day carrying the wet slabs to the moor for drying. Anna watches and chats incessantly.

101

While cutting peat, Seathan can't get out of his mind that all these reoccurring daily struggles make it difficult for him to leave his family who need him so much. Nevertheless, as each season passes he becomes more and more restless. Lach and Catherine have never made him feel guilty for his yearnings, but he is aware of how much of his labour is of value to his family. Nonetheless, he continues to desire new adventures. At one time he believed he could be a warrior for his clan. However, with the changes in the life of the clansmen that is no longer a reality. Lately he has thought there is another option for him. He could join one of the military regiments of Great Britain. Highland clansmen are greatly valued by the English for their aggressive fighting style. Seathan, who has been well-trained in warrior ways in the use of the Highland sword, knows this. It is his own dedication to the well-being of his family that keeps him here and until things change, he will stay.

The next day Seathan then turns his focus to his farm chores. Soon the family will go to the peat bogs for more cutting and hauling. Now he and Iain will plant the summer crops. He had planted kale in early April and today they will plant cabbage seeds. After several hours of work, Seathan glances over at his *brathair*, "Iain, you are doing a good job. You make a good farmer." Seathan appreciates the hard work of Iain. Although he does not have his own strength, he does have commitment. "Each of the Maclean *clanns* are dedicated to family," Seathan remarks to himself. Suddenly thoughts of Anna intrude his thinking, "I am not at all sure about little Anna. She is different and she lives in her own world." Seathan then reminds himself, "Right now her sweetness and joy make up for her lack of focus."

While Seathan is reminiscing about Anna, she appears with Catherine and Caitriona. They are headed to the meadows to check on the livestock. There is enough grass in the closer meadows now but later Seathan will move the cattle into the moorlands and the hills. This will mean staying with them in a *shieling* (a little hut) built for such a task. Later in the summer it will be Iain's job to hike to the summer meadow and bring Seathan food. A couple times during the summer and autumn Iain will also take over for Seathan so that he can go home, be with his family and sleep in his own bed.

The beginning of May finds the moor and the meadows covered with yellow flowers and Anna cannot contain herself, running ahead of her *mathair* and Caitriona. Catherine calls out, "Anna slow down.

Don't leave our sight. We don't want *Black Donald* or a faerie stealing you away from us."

"No, *mathair*, I just want to pick more flowers," answers the effervescent Anna. "I will not lose sight of you."

Catherine and Caitriona continue into the meadows with Anna running ahead of them until they spot the livestock. They find their *torrach* cow who will soon be giving birth. They will soon lead her back to the *byre*, where the birth can be supervised. She is very large and birth is imminent. Catherine then decides to lead her back now instead of waiting. Catherine knows from her many years of experience that birthing is not always easy for a cow. She has supervised and aided the birth of many calves through the years.

24
La Bealltainn (Beltane)

Tomorrow is May 1st and everyone is preparing for the *La Bealltainn*. This is a very special celebration for the Highlanders and everyone is hopeful with the promise of summer. The May Day rituals will ensure the success of the growing season as well as the health of the cattle and the clansmen. Lach and Catherine are discussing their preparation needs. Catherine asks, "Lach, are you ready for *La Bealltainn* tomorrow?"

"Aye," responds Lach. "Seathan has helped me hunt hares for the feast and we now have 5 hares to add to the fire."

"Good," Catherine says, "I will prepare them for the feast. The *clanns* and I will get up at sunrise tomorrow for the final preparations." And with that she goes inside to instruct the *clanns*. Iain, now 12, and Caitriona, 10, are excited about their roles in the upcoming festival.

The morning cannot come soon enough for them. Although life remains difficult, the *clanns* bring a brightness into the ever-lurking threat of hunger or eviction. The most serious concern of Catherine is about Seathan, now almost 19 years old. He has remained at home helping on the farm. With Lach working for the laird in order to earn rent money, Seathan had felt unspoken pressure to stay. He knows that his *athair* works hard. He sees his *athair* return to the *bothie* every night after a long day of back breaking work managing the laird's large estate. Lach often talks of abandoning his farm but he has not yet had the courage to do this. Farming and estate work are all he knows and despite all the struggles of his life, he loves the Highlands.

Little Anna, 5, reveals her unbounded spirit by dancing around the fire. "Today," she exclaims, "I am going into the meadows and I will pick yellow May flowers which I will put in my hair." Iain and Caitriona roll their eyes; they know that they cannot contain Anna. From the time she could speak, she sang and from the time she could walk, she danced. She brought the most joy to dismal days.

She then sings a little ditty, *"It's May, it's May, the merry month of May. Our Highland rain doth bring the flowers. And I will put them in my hair."* Anna's long hair is curly and dark brown. Through the years Catherine has never forgotten to dye Anna's hair. As Catherine predicted at her birth, Anna has bright blue eyes and pale skin. Anna, however, even at 5, is questioning the annoying secret ritual of her hair dyeing.

For several months Lach has been storing kindling and drying it in his *bothie*. Two special pieces are put aside and will be used to light the bonfire by his ancestor's method. Lach calls out to Catherine, "Catherine, I am leaving now to help my kinfolk build the bonfire for the festival. I will take Seathan with me and we will both carry some of the dry wood to add to the pile." The bonfire, located on the top of a small knoll, is a hike from the Macleans' *bothie*. This spot has been chosen for centuries so that the bonfires can be seen by all the clan's folk of the glen as well as the village of Inivea.

Many clansmen have already gathered around two large piles of wood when Lach and Seathan arrive. Before they add their contribution to the pile, Lach sets aside the wood sticks he will use to start the fire. After many years of practice, Lach is a master of the ancient method of creating fire by friction. He is selected by the clan members every year for the honored responsibility. He was taught by his *athair* to choose the exact type of wood to start the fire and now is passing on this knowledge to Seathan.

While Lach and Seathan are on the hill summit starting the bonfire, the other *clanns* venture out onto the moor to collect yellow flowers for the traditional May festivities. Opening their door, they hold out their hands and collect the dew of the first May morning and spread the wetness on their faces. This custom, believed by the Highlanders, will insure them beauty and youthfulness until they perform the ritual again next May. Anna then skips alongside Iain and Caitriona until they reach the moor where the flowers grow abundantly. Their *co-oghas* and other *clanns* from Inivea are already there busily collecting the flowers. The flowers will be used to make wreaths and bouquets to decorate doors, *byres* and cattle. Some of the *clanns* will make necklaces and hair decorations so that they will look more festive. This part of the *La Bealltainn* ritual is a favorite of all the *clanns*.

Meanwhile in their *bothies* all the women of the clans have doused the fire. This is one of the few times during the year when the fires will be extinguished. Later each woman will take a lit torch from the bonfires, bring them back to their *bothies* and relight their fire. Presently, however, the women gather all types of raw meat; hare, chicken and lamb as well as their stored cheese, eggs, butter, oats and milk. While the meat is being roasted on the bonfire, the women will make a *caudle* by mixing together eggs, butter, oats and milk. Some of the mixture will be saved as a warm liquid which will be drunk later by the clans folk. The remaining *caudle* will be cooked on the bonfire, producing an oatmeal cake called *bannoch Bealltainn*. Each person will take a *bannoch Bealltainn* and offer it bit by bit to the faeries *(aos si)*, as well as to wildlife to pacify them so that they will not harm their livestock.

As the women and *clanns*, outside their *bothies* peer into the distance, they observe a scene that always amazes and fills them with awe. The enormous bonfires, piercing the landscape and sky with their heaven-seeking flames of red, yellow and orange, are their annual promise of protection from harm and disease. Catherine sees Lach in the distance making his way back and she waves to him. Catherine then shares with her *clanns*, "Your *athair* is on his way back to us. You have decorated well the livestock, our doors and yourselves with the yellow flowers of May. I am sure that your *athair* will be greatly pleased with the sights that greet him as he returns."

"Oh *mathair*," shouts Anna, "I am so happy. When will we bring our cattle to the magic bonfires?"

"That will happen soon, Anna, when your *athair* returns," says Catherine.

As soon as Lach and Seathan arrive the *clanns* greet them with much excitement. "*Athair*, when will the cattle be led to the bonfires?" they all shout in anticipation.

"The bonfires are ready and I am going now to get our cows," responds Lach to his restless audience. "Seathan, let's go." The two then enter the *byre*. The cattle seem to know what is coming and greet them with the loudest of moos. Once out of the *byre* the cattle are almost prancing to be out in the fresh air and sunshine. Lach calls to Seathan, "Hold them steady! The ropes need to be taut to control the cows' movement up the hill."

Once up on the hill of the bonfires, the farmers make their annual trek with their cattle between the burning mounds of timber safely. Some of the young calves balk at such an undertaking, causing a great commotion. It is of utmost importance to keep the cows under control and the nearby Highlanders rally quickly to assist the affected farmers. Although some distance from the dancing, sputtering and extremely hot flames, most of the cows move quickly to avoid the intense heat. It is not a long walk and the cattle soon are on the other side of it and the farmers will quickly lead them to the grazing meadows.

When the last cow is on its way to the green meadows, the women hike up the slope to the bonfires. The fire, once blazing and strong, is beginning to die down. This is good for it is now time for the women folk to cook on the embers. Catherine meets up with Isobel from the village, "Isobel, how are your *clanns*? I hope they are well!" Isobel responds, "Roderick is now working with Iain in the shop. Roderick appears to be well-suited to the trade, already having the interest as well as the brawny build of his *athair*. And Donald still likes to play and help his *mathair* in the *byre*. I am not sure what his future will be."

"And your *clanns*, have they come through the winter in good health and growing bigger?" asks Isobel.

"Seathan turns 19 next month. He is yearning to leave home and join the British regiment. Alas, he is a such great help to Lach and me and, sadly, I will not be able to hold him back much longer. When Seathan leaves us, Iain will have to take his place and help more on the farm. Caitriona has become a good dyer and spinner of wool and we will soon ask her if she would like to learn to weave."

While walking slowly with Isobel to the bonfire, Catherine continues, "Anna does not seem to have a care in the world. She is always out on the moor collecting herbs and berries. She seems to have a special relationship with the livestock, especially pregnant ones. She brings much joy and sunshine into our desolate lives, especially during the winter months. Nonetheless, she continues to be a mystery to us."

Suddenly the two women realize that their chatter has slowed their pace. They abruptly stop their conversation, speed up and soon reach the other women who are already cooking on the fire. Their *clanns,* who have followed behind, soon reach the gathering of other *clanns* and join hands with them. *Mathairs* look up from their cooking and watch their *clanns* dancing and singing as they release their pent-up energy from winter.

Once the cows are busy feeding in the meadow the menfolk join their *beans* around the fires. When the food is cooked and the offering of *bannoch bealltainn* is made, everyone sits down to enjoy a feast of cheese, bread and roasted meats. An abundance of ale for the adults and *caudle* for others adds to a feeling of relief after another year of winter confinement and food deprivation. Now they are ready to once again begin the annual chores of spring and summer.

25
Life of the Campbell Family in Inivea

Iain Campbell and his family have become used to life in the village of Inivea since they moved there five years ago. Not much is different from their old village of Ballygown, except it is smaller.

The family attends Inivea's winter *ceilidhs* where they are able to socialize with other clansmen. At the *ceilidhs* Roderick and Donald listen to the tales and poetry of the bard and learn more about clan life and their ancient history on the Isle of Mull. They learn about the Battle of Culloden and the valiant effort of Bonnie Prince Charlie to take back his Stuart throne from the Protestant Rulers. Donald is particularly interested in this history. He wants to know more and he will ask his *athair* later.

Roderick spends every day with his *athair* learning the trade of blacksmithing. Iain believes that his oldest *mac* will have to leave Inivea someday and take up his trade in a larger city or town, perhaps in the Lowlands of Scotland. There are several unfavorable circumstances in the Highlands which will make it difficult for Roderick to profit from the blacksmithing trade; a shrinking population and the scarcity of new iron. Iain is already feeling the effects of these conditions.

About five years ago in Scotland, an inventor named James Small converted the all-wood plows of antiquity to plows made with cast iron moldboards and shares. This was a wonderful innovation for the croft farmers. However, it is impossible for a Highland blacksmith to get the iron needed to make these new plows as the British placed restrictions on the making of iron. This policy forces Iain to stick to what he knows best: repairs of outdated tools for the farmers, household items and hunting equipment. It also deprives the farmers of equipment that would make their work easier and more productive. Without the work from new innovations, Iain is unable to increase his income and it keeps his family barely out of poverty .

Isobel, on the other hand, sits in her *bothie* contemplating some news she has just realized. She is *torrach* (pregnant). Her outer body does not yet reveal any changes as a result of her condition, but other symptoms don't deceive. She has had nausea which has been difficult to hide. She knows of Iain's troubles and she doesn't want to put another burden on him but knows that soon she must. She will tell him tonight when Roderick and Donald are outside. She remembers the night of passion with Iain and smiles at the memory. Due to their demanding lifestyle as of late, lovemaking has been a rare occurrence. Through the years, since Donald's birth, such a rare event did not lead to another *bairn*. So Isobel was unprepared and surprised when she found herself *torrach*. But once the initial shock wore off, she hoped in her heart of hearts that she will give birth to a *nighean*.

Roderick and Donald leave the *bothie* after their meal. In the summer they have a few hours before they go to bed to be outside, enjoying the fresh air of their Isle. They join some of their friends in the village to play. They cavort around the village; running to see who can run the fastest by tagging each other to prove it. Meanwhile inside Isobel and Iain take advantage of their absence to socialize around their fire.

Isobel begins the conversation, "Iain, I have some news for you." She pauses and is silent for a moment. Iain impatiently interrupts, "Well, Isobel what is the news? I hope it is good."

"Iain, I hope it will be good news for you," responds Isobel. "I am *torrach*, about 3 months. I wanted to be sure before I told you," adds Isobel.

Iain is stunned! For a while he is speechless. "I am not upset, Isobel, just shocked," answers Iain. "It has been eight years since you gave birth to our last *bairn*. It will take me awhile to get used to the idea. How are you feeling?"

"I was dismayed when I found out, but I have had a couple of months to get used to the idea. I have been nauseous, but much less so than it was with our first," explains Isobel. "I love our two *macs* but have always missed having a *nighean* to share the womanly tasks of life," she continues.

Iain takes many minutes to absorb Isobel's news. It is a difficult announcement for him, but he wants to say the right thing to Isobel. Finally, he speaks, "I am happy, Isobel, and I know that if it is a *nighean*, this will be a gift to you. Shall we tell our *macs*?" questions Iain.

Catherine quickly responds, "I think it is better to wait until I show more to make sure that all is well." I might tell my friend, Catherine Maclean, at our service on Sunday."

Iain, being supportive, replies, "It will be good to have a friend to share your condition."

26
Terror Fills the Maclean Family

It is a beautiful summer day in August in the Highlands and the red-purple heather fills the landscape of the moor. Catherine and her youngest *clanns* venture out of their *bothie* in midmorning. Catherine explains to her *clanns*, "I have to tend the garden and also bring more peat to the stack beside our *bothie*."

Iain and Caitriona reply, "*Mathair*, would this be a good time to look for berries? May we go into the moor to look for them?"

"That will be good, but you need to take Anna with you and make sure that she stays near you," answers Catherine.

Iain and Caitriona would rather be on their own. Anna, an adventurous *clann,* is difficult to control but they know that they have to help their *mathair*. When their *athair* had gone to work for the laird, they had promised him that they would work hard and help her. Iain calls to Anna, "Anna, we are going hiking in the moor to look for berries. *Mathair* wants you to join us. Stay near us." Anna is joyful with the prospect of hiking on the moor with her two older siblings.

Anna responds, "Don't worry I will be able to keep up with you. Maybe, I can pick some berries too."

Iain reminds Anna, "Today, we are not going to pick any roots or herbs. We will find them more plentiful in the woods and we will wait until then."

The three *clanns* wave goodbye to their *mathair* saying that they will return by mid-afternoon when the sun is lower. From earliest years the Highland *clanns* are taught how to rely on the sun to tell time.

As they are about to depart Catherine reminds them, "Watch over Anna. Anna, stay close to Iain and Caitriona. Do not be troublesome to them. They have important work to do. Watch them so you will learn to do the same."

Iain and Caitriona love gathering berries because it gets them out onto the moor. Berries are a special treat added to their usual food.

Summertime in the Highlands is a time of beauty with all of nature surrounding them. On the moor, where they are spending the morning, the landscape is like a moving puzzle of flyers and creepers. The *clanns'* favorites are the butterflies. They come in a variety of colors of green, copper, brown, yellow and blue with various patterns of spots and stripes. They sometimes briefly alight on the abundant wild flowers and then gayly flitter about, finding nectar and places to lay their eggs. To the delight of the *clanns* they sometimes land on them. They stay just long enough to give the *clanns* a thrill.

Anna chases the butterflies. "Look, look," she excitedly yells as an orange and brown butterfly lands on her hand. Anna runs ahead to find more butterflies and wild flowers. She practically dances in the purple heather which covers everything. The earth looks as if it was painted with a broad brush of red-purple with some green, making its own patterns in between. "This is the home of the faeries," Anna explains. She is caught up in the beauty and mystery of it all as only a young spirited child can do. Anna's imagination is filled with the faeries and mythical characters of her birthplace.

Meanwhile as Anna prances and dances about, Iain and Caitriona are busy looking for berries. Like Anna they would like to be running carefree on the moor, enjoying the flowers and sunshine, but the work they do is serious business and they don't want to let their *mathair* down. Today the bright August sun has ripened the blueberries on a myriad of small bushes. These will be good for eating and dyeing the wool. There is also an abundance of sweet blackberries.

Iain advises Caitriona, "Caty, put the blueberries in my basket and the blackberries in yours. That way they will stay separate." "Yes, that is a good idea and our *mathair* will be pleased that we thought of it," responds Caitriona.

Lost in picking berries for several hours, Iain suddenly realizes that for some time he has not heard Anna's joyful exclamations about everything she was seeing and hearing. With alarm Iain calls out, "Anna, where are you?" No response. Then he calls to Caitriona, "Caty, can you see or hear Anna?" "No, I cannot," responds Caitriona nervously.

Together Iain and Caitriona begin yelling for Anna, "Anna, Anna, where are you?" Their shouts go on for several minutes. They see other *clanns* on the moor as they move forward and ask them, "Have you seen our *siuir*, Anna?"

114

Many indicate they saw her earlier but not recently.

Getting worried, Iain and Caitriona continue to shout Anna's name. "Anna, Anna, Anna!!" Still there is no response and they are terrified to return to their *mathair* without her. They had promised their *mathair* that they would look after her. Finally, they both realize it is hopeless; she is nowhere to be seen. Iain tells Caty, "I am afraid *mathair* will be very angry with us, but it is more important that she knows what has happened as quickly as possible."

"Aye," responds Caty, "We must hurry back."

With their buckets of berries in hand they run back to their *mathair*. For several hours they had been on the trail through the moor. It will take them at least a half an hour to get back. They run while making sure that they do not fall and spill all the berries. On the way they forget about their own panic and focus only on the whereabouts of their *siuir*.

As they reach the *bothie*, their *mathair* is laying some peat slabs on the pile beside the door. "*Mathair, mathair*," both *clanns* with anguish in their voices yell. "Anna wandered away while we were picking berries and she is lost. We called and called but she never answered us. We didn't know what to do so we came home as quickly as we could."

Catherine is overwhelmed and filled with horror. At first, she, herself, is not sure what to do but she tries to reassure her young *clanns*, "Do not be afraid. We will find her. Knowing how willful Anna is, I should not have put her in your trust. It is like her to get lost in her own mind and lose track of everyone around her. I am sure that she just ventured a little further into the moor than you and she could not hear your calls. I will gather our kinfolk and we will search for her. Perhaps some of the other clansmen will form a search party. I will ask your *seanmhair* to watch over you while we are all searching."

"But *mathair*, can I go with you to help search for Anna," questions Iain. "No Iain, it is best if you stay here. You and your *seanmhair* can tell the news to your *athair* when he returns home from the laird. He will want to join in the hunt. That is if Anna has not been found," Catherine responds with urgency.

At that Catherine hurries to Jannet to ask her to watch over Iain and Caitriona. Jannet is very concerned and rushes over. Catherine hastily travels on to the *bothies* of her *siuirs*; Molly, Lilli and Marta. It is of good fortune that their *fears* are home for a brief rest at high noon before they return to their chores. Micheal, the *fear* of Marta, volunteers to run to the *bothies* of Lach's *brathairs*, Seumus and Tomas. Along the way both Catherine and Micheal meet other clansmen. They greet them with the story of little Anna. All volunteer to become part of the search party.

27
The Search

Apprehension for the well-being of Anna fills the minds of clansmen as they gather in front of Catherine and Lach's *bothie*. They all have long sticks to push back and forth through the high growth of the moor in case little Anna has fallen and is hurt. In their belts they carry a *dirk* for protection. From the beginning of the trail they plan to travel in fours, one on the trail and the others spreading on either side. They use this formation in case Anna doubled back when she found herself alone. Two of the clansmen have dogs and Catherine hands them several pieces of Anna's clothing so that they can search by scent. Catherine has moments of panic but remains hopeful due to the cooperation of many folk in the glen.

Before she starts out Catherine reassures her *clanns,* "It is still early in the afternoon and it is good that you came back immediately to tell me of Anna being lost. We still have a lot of daylight to search for her. Wherever she is the sunlight will keep her warm."

The search starts with the two clansmen with the dogs leading the way. Catherine is not far behind them. The echo of everyone calling "Anna, Anna, Anna," can be heard by all those left behind.

The red-purple heather usually looked upon by the clansmen as beautiful is now a hinderance in the search for Anna. It has grown to about three feet high and Anna is no taller than that. If she is in the midst of the heather, she will not be seen by the searchers until they are almost upon her. They are relying on their shouts and the dogs to find her. On the moor after about a half an hour there is still no trace of Anna. Catherine becomes more concerned as the search continues. She and her kinfolk are particularly worried because of her red hair. Could her absence be an omen? Perhaps a witch or the *Black Donald* has snatched her in the hopes of using her for their own bad deeds. Everyone is thinking this but do not utter their misgivings aloud.

Meanwhile the searchers trudge on continuously calling her name.

Catherine begins to realize that the dogs are not helpful at all in scenting her little Anna. They are enjoying their outing on the moor but that is all. Several hours pass by and there is still no sign of Anna. Catherine wonders how her little *nighean* could escape from being sighted by these skillful clansmen. "Where could Anna have wandered," Catherine ponders. "The moor is big and wide and yet Anna is only a little one with little legs. She could not have travelled that far, or could she?"

Thoughts of where Anna has wandered constantly runs through her mind. She first thinks of the woods, but they would be too far away. What other locations would be near enough for a her little *nighean*? Catherine suddenly has a thought which makes sense. Anna has a close relationship with animals. Could she have wandered to the nearby winter pasture where their cow, who recently birthed twins, is pastured for the summer? Anna really loves that cow and her two little calves. Catherine thinks that if Anna reached one of the clearings on a rise she could have looked afar and recognized the meadow was not that far away.

Catherine stops in her tracks and shares her hunch with those around her. They all quickly agree that they must follow her lead and focus some of the searchers on the meadow. As soon as other searchers catch up with her, Catherine explains the change in plan. Four kinfolks will go with Catherine to the meadow while the others continue on the way through the moor. If Anna is not found by sunset, everyone will return to their *bothies* and resume the search in the morning. The thought that Anna might not be found by sunset horrifies Catherine. She knows, however, that for everyone to get back before dark they must turn back by sunset.

Catherine and four of her kinfolks then leave the searchers and start toward the meadow. They travel five abreast switching their sticks back and forth through the high grass and heather. It will take them about a half hour to reach the meadows, but they are hopeful that they will be able to see Anna wandering in the meadow before they reach her by foot. Catherine prays that her premonition is right. It might mean her *nighean's* well-being or even her life.

"Swish, swish, swish," echo the sticks of the searchers through the moor. Besides that sound, the occasional rustle of animals in the growth on the moor and the songs of birds, there are no other sounds. The travelers remain silent, focused on the goal of reaching the meadow and finding Anna alive and well. While trekking to the meadow Catherine finds herself constantly pushing aside bad thoughts and trying to replace them with thoughts of hope and reunion with her youngest. She feels guilty for her carelessness in taking care of little Anna. It has become extremely difficult for her to attend to all the chores of the farm, the *bothie* and her *clanns* with Lach working for the laird.

Suddenly in front of her Catherine spies a somewhat rare bush of white heather. Her heart is in her throat knowing that this is a sign of good luck. Does this foretell the safe return of her *nighean*? She passes by the lucky heather and it renews her hope of finding Anna. Catherine's step takes on a renewed energy and soon the group reaches a clearing, making the travel a lot easier. The distance to the meadow has narrowed and they begin to view the forms of livestock, but they have not spotted the small figure of Anna. However, seeing the animals pushes the searchers forward in anticipation. All of them have revived hope and believe in Catherine's premonition of the location of Anna. Reaching the meadow they keep their search formation. They switch their sticks back and forth while their eyes pierce the meadow.

Many of the animals have been taken to the more distant grazing summer meadow, but a smaller group of livestock remains in the closer winter meadow. They are generally the ones who have recently given birth, the very young or those who are older. The meadow is large and the cattle, sheep and goats are scattered in different groupings throughout. The searchers decide that each of them will focus on a different corner of the meadow while Catherine will hike straight through the middle to the very top of the hill. If anyone finds Anna they will shout it out as loud as they can.

While the searchers use their sticks to locate a small Anna, they also call out her name. Catherine, knowing that Anna will recognize her voice, repeatedly calls, "Anna, Anna, Anna, are you here?" For a while the voices of the other searchers can be heard. They fade as they move further away from Catherine. She is trying to remain hopeful, but it is not easy as seconds creep into long minutes. Suddenly Catherine spies a grey object in the grass ahead. She rushes to get closer. When she gets near she is able to see it as a grey woven shawl. Many of the *clanns'* shawls look the same, but this gives Catherine hope that it belongs to Anna. She moves forward with cautious anticipation. All the while calling, "Anna, Anna, Anna, it's your *mathair* looking for you. Are you here?"

A few long moments later a wee voice responds from a group of trees. Catherine first spots a large black Highland cow with two calves under the trees. Then up jumps Anna exclaiming, "*Mathair, mathair,* I am over here with our cow and her calves. I got tired from the long hike and have been sleeping. I was missing them and decided to hike to the meadow to visit."

Catherine responds to Anna in a grateful but stern voice, "Anna, we all have been very worried about you. Clansmen from our glen formed a search party and have been looking on the moor since the sun was at its highest! I am very happy that I found you, but you have caused a great amount of anguish."

Anna is contrite and responds quietly, "I am very sorry *mathair.* I did not mean to make you worry. All day I have been chasing the butterflies and just forgot what I was supposed to be doing. The moor is such a magical place and the faeries appear to be calling to me. I will take care the next time."

Catherine mutters to herself, "There will be no next time for a long long time!" Catherine, with Anna in tow, heads towards the glen and their *bothie*. On the way she calls out to the others, "I have found Anna and she is well!"

Anna, having felt no negative consequences from her unexpected excursion, chatters away. "*Mathair*, I had such a wonderful time, but I am ready to go home."

After about fifteen minutes of calling to the searchers, they meet up and return to their *bothies*. The word is sent to the rest of the searchers who return hours later and are extremely happy to see the lost *clann*. Despite everyone's joy, they caution Anna that she should be a lot more careful about excursions on the moor.

Later in the evening Lach returns, having missed the drama of the day. He hears the whole story from Catherine and his other *clanns*. He is not too pleased but also knows that if he were around more, this probably would not have happened. He heads to bed with a heavy heart.

Lach awakens the family early the next morning before he is to leave for work. Lach, with a warrior's training, can be a very frightening figure of fury when provoked. He has strong opinions about the events of yesterday. He gathers everyone around the fire still smoldering from the evening.

First, he addresses Catherine, "I know it is difficult for you to handle all of the chores of our household, especially because I am no longer around to share in the daily tasks. However, I hope you have learned a lesson from the events of yesterday. Anna is not old enough to be responsible for her own well-being. She cannot be left in the sole care of the younger *clanns*." Lach is controlling his anger with contained civility. However, he is worried about the reactions of the other clansmen who were taken away from their daily chores.

Catherine responds, "Aye, Lach, I am now very aware of my bad choice with Anna. Iain and Caty are very responsible, but the task of collecting berries and also watching Anna was a bigger job than is appropriate for their ages."

As Catherine turns to address Iain and Caitriona, Lach interrupts her, "I have something first to say. I realize that it is difficult to watch over Anna but that should have been your primary duty. Your carelessness caused great difficulty and panic in our glen. Everyone spent the day hunting for Anna, when in fact they had many chores of their own to do. The life of a farmer requires that everyone take responsibility. I hope you learned a lesson from yesterday!"

"Aye, *athair*," Iain and Caitriona humbly respond. "We are very sorry and we will not be so careless in the future."

And to Anna who has remained quiet and subdued, Lach says the following, "Anna, even though you are only five years old, I hope you understand how your disobedience upset our glen. I realize that you are an exuberant child who enjoys all the good things that our Isle of Mull has to offer, but in our glen, obedience is the first rule of life. We cannot survive if everyone decides to do as they please. I am not sure if you understand the importance of following the instructions of your *mathair* and *athair*, but you must obey our rules." Anna who is a little overwhelmed with this stern command of her *athair* can only respond with, "Aye, *athair*, I understand."

With that Lach takes leave for his daily work for the laird. He hopes that all have heard his message regarding the seriousness of the situation. After Lach leaves the Maclean family is quiet. If Lach could see them now he would know without a doubt that his family heard and took in his words. Iain, who is a serious and conscientious twelve-year-old, feels particularly bad. He will make sure that he will never again let down his *athair* and his *mathair*.

28

Rut Raises Suspicions About Anna

Meanwhile, in another Maclean household, Rut is talking to Tomas about the happenings of yesterday. She is angry that Anna's escapade took all the clansmen away from their daily chores. Rut emphasizes, "Tomas, we lost so much time when you could have instead tended to our farm. We are behind and it is already the middle of August. Peat needs to be stacked for winter and our thatched roof needs repair."

Tomas responds, "Aye, Rut, we are behind but I will just have to work harder to catch up. It will not be an impossible task to do that. I will go out now and get to my chores." His two *clanns* follow, leaving Rut still stewing about the events of yesterday.

In her mind Rut has proof that Anna is indeed a witch. Her thoughts continue with her reasoning, "Who or what did Anna meet while hiking in the meadows? Did she encounter the many evil creatures roaming the hills and woods? Beings that would love to entice a young witch and make a deal with her into wrong doings. It could even have been the *Black Donald* himself. By wandering away Anna has inflicted her first spell on the glen. For a day she led them away from their work and chores and there are not many folks who have such powers, except a witch." All day the question of what to do about Anna circles in her conscience. Should she first tell Tomas and see what he says? Or should she spread the news to some of the other Campbells in the glen. After all they would want to know so that they can protect themselves and their *clanns* from future harm. She is worried about her own *clanns* playing with Anna. She doesn't want Anna to inflict any bad on them. She decides that she will first tell Tomas and see his reaction. It will be a long day, but she has a lot to do before Tomas returns at sunset.

Rut bundles up the clothes of her *clanns*. She will take them to the river to wash them because it is a good day for drying them on trees in the sun. They will dry quickly and the summer sunshine and breezes will add a sweetness to them. Rut likes her time at the river. Often there are other women gathered there. She has a favorite spot where she has good access to the river. It is also a perfect spot to overhear the gossip of the other *beans* and *clanns*. Today she will listen and pick up any tidbits that the women might be sharing about Anna and yesterday's incident.

Much to Rut's disappointment the only women at the river are Catherine Maclean and Isobel Campbell. They are good friends and are chatting away about their *clanns*. Anna is at the river with her *mathair*. Rut briefly greets them but then makes her way to her own special place on the river's edge. Today there will be no gossip. Both Catherine and Isobel are careful about what they say in Rut's presence. They know and understand her reputation of spreading false rumors around the glen.

Soon after Catherine, with Anna and Isobel, leave the river's edge, Rut is left alone to finish her washing. She continues to mull over Anna and the old beliefs that a person with red hair is a witch. Rut also has a deep resentment regarding the Macleans even though she is married to one. It was not so long ago that the Campbells and the Macleans were enemies. Although the conflict between the clans no longer exists, Rut grew up hearing many tales of the warfare between them.

Rut's bitterness runs deeper though. She is also jealous of Catherine Maclean and her beautiful *nighean*. In her mind Tomas is an ineffective *fear*. He does not have the ambition of Lach. She believes that Tomas is lazy and should be working harder to provide for his family. Her *clanns* are very affectionate but this does not impress Rut who admires ambition and drive. In her mind they are slow and clumsy and cannot compare to the multitalented *clanns* of Catherine and Lach. Rut's washing is done and she returns to her *bothie*. Her *clanns* are at the farm with their *athair*.

Rut hangs the clean clothes on the nearby trees. Her young *clanns*, Lucas (6) and Deirdre (5), return from the farm with their *athair*. They each carry a basket filled with vegetables and oats. Tomas reports on the day and announces to Rut, "It was a good day. The *clanns* and I harvested a lot. Tonight we can have some fresh kale and potatoes along with our usual meal. It will be a hearty fare."

Rut prepares the meal and after Tomas gives the blessing, they all sit around the fire to eat.

After her *clanns* have gone to sleep, Rut shares with Tomas her concerns about Anna. Tomas listens to her story intently, "Rut, I do not agree with you about little Anna. She is only five years old. It could have happened to our *nighean*, Deirdre, who is the same age. Unfortunately, Anna was left to the care of her *brathair* and *siuir* who were not old enough to watch over such a lively *clann*. Anna is free spirited and she often gets caught up in her own imagination. I don't want you to spread this rumor about Anna. She is our *banta* (niece) after all and such a tale will do my *brathair* and his family great harm. The other clansmen and their *beans* have let the incident go and I want you to do the same." At that the conversation ends for Tomas. However, Rut holds onto her theory in her heart and will continue to collect evidence against Anna.

29
The New Pastor

The summer has ended and September brings cooler and rainier weather on the Isle of Mull. Today the sky is grey and overcast. It is not raining but there is a cold heavy mist coming from the ocean, making it advisable to be dressed in warmer clothes. All the farmers and villagers have finished the repairs on their thatched roofs. The peat squares have been cut, dried and stacked, ready for the glen's unpleasant winter.

Seathan is still in the summer pasture with the Maclean's livestock. He will return with the animals in late October. Lach continues to leave daily to work for the laird. Iain Campbell and his *mac*, Roderick, have been busy all summer in their blacksmith shop, making repairs for the farmers. Their work will slow down in the winter, not good news for one who survives from day to day.

Today is the first Sabbath in September and the clan members are eagerly expecting a new pastor. The parishioners were not sorry to say goodbye to their old pastor, Pastor Douglas, who treated them as if they were ignorant barbarians. They tolerated him because they did not believe that they had any choice. Pastor Douglas frequently insinuated that any troubles that befell them; death, illness, crop failure, storms, hunger and poverty were their own fault for not following the commandments of God. Many still held onto their ancient beliefs and did not believe him. Most blamed their misfortunes on the curses of witches or the *Black Donald*.

The clansmen could not help but notice how different in appearance their new pastor was to the bulky, paunchy and bald Pastor Douglas whose soft form was very distasteful to the hardy muscular Highlanders. Their bodies reflect their life of hard work and a sparse diet. Pastor Robertson, on the other hand reminds them of one who has spent his youth in a classroom. However, he was not soft and mushy from too much learning. He was in his late twenties, slim and fit of figure. His eyes were blue and he had fair ruddy skin with sandy brown thinning hair. In personality he had a serious side but also enjoyed a good laugh. He related to the youth of the clan. However, he was also able to interact with the older folks in his flock.

Pastor Robertson had met the villagers several weeks before he moved to Inivea. He had called a meeting to evaluate whether this *kirk* would be a good fit for him as the villagers had no choice in the matter. Luckily, they had liked him and they assumed the feeling was mutual since it was announced that he would be the new pastor.

The Pastor, having heard about the strict and judgmental nature of the former pastor, decided to give his first sermon as a message of love. He focused on the love of God for his people as well as the need to love one another. Most could accept the love of one another sermon at least in their own village and glen. However, they had doubts regarding the love of God. Why would a loving God inflict so much hardship on them? Poverty, starvation, illness and early death were their life experiences. The clansmen found more comfort in blaming evil beings for the cause of their troubles and so secretly they kept their ancient beliefs.

Pastor Robertson's initial Sabbath with his new congregation was also Donald Campbell's first experience with this new pastor. The pastor made a point to talk to the youth as well as the adults, bringing in his own life experiences of hardship as well as better times. He recounted how the love of his family and neighbors brought him through the early deaths of a brother and a sister from typhoid. He remembered that his older deceased brother had been his protector and his hero. His sister, a year younger at 10 years old, was sweet and funny. He misses them both.

Pastor Robertson had related his story with such detail and emotion that when Donald glanced at his family and other members of the congregation, he noticed their eyes filled with moisture. Pastor Robertson also stated that his life was not just filled with misery. He related the good times he had at school, playing with classmates and times at home being with his family and other visiting kin. The sermon ended on a positive note with Pastor Robertson confirming how happy he was to be able to minister to the residents of Inivea. At the *kirk's* door Donald, with the rest of his family and congregants, shook hands with the new pastor.

30
Donald and the Pastor

After listening to Pastor Robertson's first sermon, all the Inivea folk were pleased with their new minister. Donald spends the long days by the fire with his *mathair* recalling their clan history. At the winter *ceilidhs* Donald had listened to the stories, songs and poems of the Bard. Donald became interested in Highland clan history with its battles and warriors. He learned of the conflicts between the Campbells and the Macleans. His *parantans* expressed openly and passionately their feelings about the abandonment of the Campbell chiefs. Their conversation made a great impression on the mind of an 8-year-old.

One weekday afternoon in late September Donald decides to visit his new pastor. Young *clanns* of the village are usually not so bold as to make a visit to their pastor by themselves. Donald, however, is driven by a thirst to know more, especially about God and the stories of the Bible.

He nears the cottage of the pastor. The start of autumn is seen by Donald in the remaining faded flowers; most around the cottage have already gone to seed or have died. Behind the cottage in the distant landscape the heather is still in full bloom, red-purple with green foliage. The beauty of his village's surroundings is one of wonder to young Donald. Donald uses the old iron knocker to bang on the heavy wooden door. The housekeeper comes to the door and speaks, "What brings a young *clann* to the door of the pastor?" Donald replies, "I want to speak to Pastor Robertson. Will he talk with me?" "Wait here at the door and I will check with the pastor," says the housekeeper.

While waiting at the open door, Donald peers by it and sees a large dark somber room. Donald remarks to himself, "This is a big and scary place." Waiting outside in the September sunshine feels like a long time and even the friendliness of the pastor does not ease his fear. The only comforting sight for him is the fireplace with several burning logs which cast some dancing light and eases the gloomy effect of the room. Before he can continue looking over the room, the gruff and very large-bodied housekeeper returns and ushers Donald in.

Pastor Robertson does not look bothered with the arrival of young Donald. "Hello Donald," the pastor speaks in a friendly manner to the young *clann*. Pastor Robertson dismisses the housekeeper who is following him and then leads Donald into the large room. After sitting down at the large oak table with large chairs, the pastor inquires, "What brings you here today?" Donald's feet dangle loosely and that is all he seems to be able to think about. He knows that he must be polite to his pastor but right at this moment he only wants to leap up and leave this imposing room. Donald's fear takes over and he is left without words.

The pastor, mindful of the feelings of a young *clann*, says, "Donald, sit here and gather your thoughts and I will ask the housekeeper to prepare some tea." At that Pastor Robertson leaves the large room through a door at the far end, leaving young Donald immersed in his own thoughts. The pastor has made him feel welcomed, so when he returns he will be able to tell him about his yearning to know more about the stories of the Bible. Donald might also slip in the idea that he would like to learn how to read and he knows that the pastor knows how.

Pastor Robertson soon returns, "The housekeeper will soon bring us some tea. While we are waiting Donald can you tell me about this unexpected visit to your pastor?" Donald reacts with a nervous twitch of his dangling legs and arms. Pastor Robertson notices but does not comment on it. Donald answers, "Pastor Robertson, I came here to learn more about the Bible stories." Then Donald makes a bold comment, "Pastor Robertson, I also want to learn how to read."

Pastor Robertson responds to the inquisitive Donald, "Does your *mathair* and *athair* know about this visit?"

"No, they think that I am out playing," answers Donald.

"And why did you not tell them that you were coming here?" queries the pastor.

"I am not sure," replies Donald. "Perhaps that they would think it too bold of me to come here on my own."

The pastor squints his eyes and his brow and forehead take on deep furrows. He does not want to discourage an inquisitive *clann*, but also knows that there are traditions among the clan folk that he is not totally familiar with. While thinking out his position he watches an uneasy Donald looking sheepish and clenching his restless hands. "Donald, before I give you an answer you must tell your *mathair* and *athair* about this visit. Depending on their reaction, I will then make a decision." Donald, not knowing if he will do what the pastor requests, decides to take his leave before the tea is served.

"Are you not going to have the tea that the housekeeper is preparing?" questions Pastor Robertson.

"If you don't mind, I have too much to do and my *mathair* will worry about me if I am gone too long. I will think about telling my *mathair* and *athair*," Donald responds. At that Donald hastily exits the room and out the big wooden door.

31
The Festival of Samhain

"From goulies and ghosties
And long-legged beasties
And things that go bump in the night,
Good Lord deliver us!"

Not knowing what his *parantans* will think about his visit to the pastor and his reason for it, Donald does not tell them. Donald doesn't want to chance upsetting them. Pastor Robertson, who has left Donald's choice in his own hands, has not questioned him. For the time being Donald decides that he will do nothing. It is nearing the end of the month and the great festival of *Samhain* will be celebrated after sunset on October 31st and through the end of the next day, concluding at sunset. All of Inivea are focused on this important celebration.

Donald, who has always celebrated this festival with his family, is questioning his *athair*, "*Athair*, tell me again why we have the *Samhain*?"

Iain responds to his youngest *mac*, "It is the end of the 'lighter half' of the year and the beginning of the 'darker half.' It is also time for us to celebrate our harvest."

"*Athair*, why do young men wear costumes of white and blacken their faces?" questions Donald. He has heard the answer before, but its meaning is still confusing.

"This is done to please the *Aos Si* (the spirits and faeries) who can come into our world during this time. We make peace with them so that we and our livestock can survive the winter," explains his Iain. "But why *athair* do the spirits and faeries need to be pleased?" questions Donald.

"This tradition goes back for centuries and centuries," replies Iain. "There must have been a time when the *Aos Si* came into our world and did great harm to our people. From that time on our clans believed that we must make peace with the spirits every year," explains Iain. "We leave food and drink outside our *bothies* for them in hopes of receiving their protection. I am sure that this might be difficult for you to understand but it is what we accept. We also believe that the souls of our dead visit our *bothies* and seek our hospitality. Thus, we have our feasts, keeping a place for them around our fire and invite them to come and sit with us while we all enjoy our harvest."

"*Athair*, can I see all these spirits and the souls of the dead?" questions Donald.

Iain responds, "There may be clansmen who have seen them, but I never have." At this point Donald has all the explanation that he wants and he leaves his *athair* to help his *mathair* with food preparation.

In another family the Macleans are looking forward to the return of Seathan from the summer pastures with their livestock. It is the time when the clansmen slaughter their livestock for the winter. Lach mentions to his family, "I will be able to sell two of our cows this year since one of our cows had twins. That will give us more money for rent. Perhaps this year the money I make working for the laird and the money I get for the cows will give us enough to pay our rent." Silently Lach thinks, "Provided that the laird does not raise our rent again."

Lach has taken a few days off from his work to help with the festival preparations. Two bonfires will be built and Lach will bring firewood to the location. As in the past, Lach will start the fires. First he must go to the summer pastures to tell Seathan that it is time to bring the livestock back for winter. This is a long trek and Iain will accompany him. As they walk they discuss the festival. Iain is excited that he will join Seathan in the ritual of *mumming* and *guising* (custom of disguising oneself in costume with painted faces or masks). Iain has his verses memorized and in costume he will go from *bothie* to *bothie* in exchange for food. Iain has stopped asking the why of this ritual because no one knows.

In the *bothie*, Catherine and Caitriona are preparing for the celebration. They have gathered the largest turnips on which they will carve faces. A candle will be placed in each one to make them into lanterns. Anna watches as her *mathair* and *siuir* start the carving. Catherine puts a candle in one and using a stick, lights the candle so that Anna can see its magic. "Ooh," Anna exclaims. "Light them all for me."

134

"Not yet Anna. They will be lit on *Samhain* which is several days and nights away," replies her *mathair*. Caitriona likes to carve creatures that hold a prominent place in folklore. She first sculpts a likeness of the Unicorn with its cloven hooves, the tail of a lion and a perfect spiraled horn in the middle of its forehead. Two other creatures carved by Caitriona from her knowledge of the Highland folktales are a kelpie (a water creature) and a black cat. Anna with her great imagination concocts a myriad of stories about each creature in the carvings. Catherine notices her *nighean's* attachment to the carvings and she believes that Anna will keep her stories in her memory for many years, repeating them frequently to all who will listen.

Lach, Iain and Seathan meanwhile have arrived back in time for the celebrations. Lach lights the bonfire and the cattle of the clan are led between them to the winter meadow. Here Lach chooses the cow that will be slaughtered and the two that he will sell. Once back at their *bothie* Seathan and Iain prepare themselves for an evening of *mumming* (young males wearing masks and costumes) and *guising* (young males visiting homes in costume). At dusk they leave their *bothie* for the long night ahead of them.

Catherine then gathers everyone else for their feast of beef, kale, turnips, potatoes, cheese and bread. An empty space is left for the spirits and the carved turnips glow around them. The night is without rest as the youth, chosen as the *mummers* and *guisers*, knock at their door to receive their food and recite their verses. Catherine, looking around at her happy family thinks about how it has been a good day and night of fun and light spirits. She is glad everyone has had a good day.

32
December Light

It is the day of the Winter Solstice, the shortest day and longest night of the year. Isobel is at home preparing for the birth of her *bairn*. At the Sunday services last week she had alerted Jannet Mackinnon that the birth was imminent. Jannet is known as the best midwife around and her *nighean*, Marta, is an experienced assistant. The only problem is that Jannet lives in the glen four miles away from the village. Isobel is to tell Iain the minute her water comes so he can get her in time. Otherwise Isobel might have to rely on another midwife in the village and she does not want to. Isobel feels safer with Jannet, the *mathair* of her good friend, Catherine.

As Isobel wakes up early on this morning she remembers it is the day of the *Winter Solstice*. She makes her way to the cupboard to start the porridge, but as she crosses the room her water breaks. With surprise, she calls to a sleeping Iain.

"Iain, my water has come." Iain rises quickly hearing the anxiety in Isobel's voice. You must travel immediately to Jannet and tell her that she is needed." Iain pulls on his breeches, followed by his *plaid* and tartan secured at his shoulder with an iron pin. Lastly he puts on his shoes and bonnet.

Before he rushes out the door he assures Isobel, "I will be back soon with Jannet and Marta." Roderick, who has woken up, rises from his bed as he hears his *mathair* anxiously call him, "Roderick go to Sine and tell her that she is needed."

"Aye *mathair*," Roderick reassures her.

In good weather it takes Iain about an hour of climbing uphill to the hidden glen of the farmers. However, today the path is icy and slippery and Iain has to watch his footing. It is good that Isobel's water broke in early morning because there will be enough daylight for the travelers. He is grateful for the stones on the trail which break through the ice, making his trek less treacherous. From time to time he is distracted by the white-tailed eagles with their magnificent aerial displays of courting.

After a little while Iain finally reaches Jannet. Knowing that Isobel's time was near, she had packed her supplies a few days before so that she could leave quickly when the time came. Iain's arrival did not surprise her. When did Isobel's water break?" inquires Jannet.

"It happened this morning. I rushed to you immediately after it happened," replies Iain. "Roderick has gone to fetch Sine. Although she does not have your experience, she will help Isobel cope until we arrive."

"It is good that you thought of a backup," reassures Jannet.

While she dons her cloak Iain leaves her and goes over to Marta's. Marta is also prepared and comes quickly. They both eat a mixture of oats and water, a birthing ritual. In her pockets Marta stores the other protective objects for the *bairn's* birth except for rowan berry juice which Jannet is carefully carrying.

Jannet and Marta, one on each side of Iain, link their arms in his and head out. They make their way back down the hill to the village of Inivea. It is slow going and the trio is a comical sight.

When the group arrives at the *bothie* of Iain and Isobel, Isobel is already in heavy labour. Both Roderick and Donald have gone into the *byre* so that their *mathair's* sounds will not be as frightening. Without their *athair* present they have become more alarmed. This is Roderick's and Donald's first witnessing of childbirth. Their *athair* and *mathair* had tried to prepare them but it did little to help them with the reality.

Jannet and Marta quickly take over. Jannet first gives Isobel the rowan berry juice and then encourages Isobel to get up out of her boxed bed and walk around the fire. Soon Isobel is on her hands and knees crawling. After an hour of crawling Isobel emits one more loud curdling sound. Jannet sits Isobel on a low stool and determines that the time has come for the *bairn* to be born. Jannet and Marta are there ready to begin the job of guiding the little *bairn* through the birth opening. When the *bairn* emerges, they notice immediately that she is a *nighean*. The *bairn* gives out some loud cries. They clean her and quickly administer the protective rites. Meanwhile Sine waits for Isobel's afterbirth. As soon as it appears she wraps it in a cloth and hands it to Jannet who will bring it to the designated hole where a rowan tree will be planted in the spring.

Isobel is cleaned by Sine who then hands her *bairn* to her. Isobel looks down at her. She is very sweet and Isobel is ecstatic to finally have her little *nighean*. Isobel then sweetly calls her, "Eilidh, you are a light in my world and for this I have given you the name for light." By the time the birthing and the rituals have been finished the sun is already going down. Jannet and Marta will spend the night with Isobel and Iain.

PART IV
Three Years Later (1793)

33
The *Hogmanay* Celebration

It is December 31, 1793 and the farmers and villagers of Inivea are looking forward to the festivities of *Hogmanay*. During the darkest months of the year Highlanders greatly anticipate any event that disrupts the gloominess and isolation of winter. In the Maclean household Catherine calls to all her *clanns*, "Today is the day we must clean our *bothie*. Seathan and Iain, go into the *byre* and clean out the area as well as you can. Caitriona and Anna, you can help me clean out our living space. We want to be ready for the celebration of *Hogmanay*."

Seathan and Iain quietly whisper their dislike for the worst chore in the *bothie*, "Ugh." Obediently, however, they amble into the *byre*. The stench of both animal and human feces and urine fill their youthful lungs. They take their shovels and pile the waste into buckets which they will dispose of in the woods. No more words of complaint or disgust are spoken by the two. They work fast to rid the *byre* of the smelly excrements as best they can.

In the meantime Caitriona and Anna under Catherine's supervision sweep the floor and remove any clothes left around on the beds. They pick up droppings of food on the floor as well as sweeping up the ash debris around the fire. Using old rags they remove soot from the kettle, pots and storage cabinet. Their job is much easier than that of their *brathairs* and they quickly finish their cleaning. After the cleaning is done Catherine gathers all her *clanns*. They sit around the fire to hear Catherine's instructions. There is really no need for this. They all know the ritual of *Hogmanay* by heart, but Catherine instructs them anyway. She ends by confirming Iain's role, "Iain, you will be our *first-footer*."

Anna asks her annual question, "*Mathair*, what is a *first-footer* and why can't it be me or Caitriona?" Catherine patiently responds to Anna, "Anna, '*first-footing*' has been the tradition of *Hogmanay* for many years on our Isle of Mull. She continues, "As you know a *first-footer* is a dark-haired young man. It is his job to present a gift of a black bun and recite verses. And most importantly he must be the first person to enter a *bothie* after midnight. If all this is followed, the *bothie* will be bestowed with good luck for the next year. We will also have a young dark-haired man from the glen visit us. I will have food and drink to offer him."

"I understand, *Mathair*. I just wish that I could be a *first-footer*," responds Anna.

"Anna, as you know, a girl or someone with fair hair visiting the *bothies* on *Hogmanay* is bad luck." Catherine smiles to herself because she knows that this annual inquiry of Anna is her childish way of questioning the tradition of her clan and she doesn't mind.

In the village Iain and Isobel Campbell are also making *Hogmanay* preparations. Once again Roderick is chosen to be the *first-footer* from their household. He knows the routine and will be ready to visit at midnight to the other village homes with the required gifts. The village will be overrun with several dark-haired young men on an identical mission.

Despite the excitement of the villagers, Isobel does not share in their gaiety. She is worried about Eilidh who had become sickly and frail within her first month of life. Despite Isobel's careful attention, her health has not improved. Isobel has an unspoken fear and wonders if Eilidh was switched at birth by the faeries. She had appeared healthy and strong right after her birth, but soon became weak after not taking to nursing well. Due to her delicate physique and the frigid weather both Isobel and Iain decided that she would not be baptized right away. It would not be until February that they brought Eilidh to the *kirk* for her baptism.

After the late-night *Hogmanay* celebration, the family has slept in. Eilidh, unable to sleep, awakens her *mathair*. Although she is a sickly child, she is bright and has many words for her feelings and needs. "*Mathair,* I am hot and wet"

Isobel arises quickly and goes over to her ill *bairn*. "My sweet Eilidh, I will get a cloth and dip it in cool water." After getting the wet cloth she passes it over Eilidh's face and brow.

"I feel better, *Mathair*," reports Eilidh.

Isobel then changes Eilidh's wet clothes and replaces the wet straw mat with a dry one. To comfort Eilidh Isobel sings a lullaby as she continues to kneel beside her, wiping her face and singing, *"Dear little*

Eilidh your mathair is near. She will cool your face so have no fear. You will soon feel better and sleep with great peace. Rest easy my clann, your fever will cease. " Isobel repeats the lullaby several times and then hums the melody to her. Eilidh, cooler and peaceful, dozes off again. Despite Isobel's thoughts that Eilidh has been switched by the faeries, she loves her *nighean* and has a strong maternal attachment to her. Isobel is worried about her sweet *nighean* but knows she can only wait and see what God has in store for her.

34
Caitriona Meets the Village Weaver

It is now spring in Inivea and the beginning of chores for the new year. Lach and Catherine Maclean are in the middle of a conversation about Caitriona. "It is time to consider the future of Caitriona. She has shown great skill in dyeing and spinning."

"Aye," Lach responds. "I have seen she notices the patterns and colors of the different clans' tartans."

"Lach, I have not brought this up to Caitriona because I wanted your opinion first." Catherine then shares, "Now that she is 13 years old, I have been thinking that she could become an apprentice to our village weaver and learn the trade."

Lach thinks and then adds, "She would be staying in Inivea while learning this trade. Would you not miss her help around here?"

"Aye, Lach, I will miss Caitriona, but I believe that she needs a trade," responds Catherine. "Anna has been following Caitriona while she does her chores. At 8 years old it is important for Anna to start having responsibilities."

"I agree, Catherine. Up till now Anna has played more than worked," contends Lach.

"I will talk to Caitriona in the morning when you have gone to work," declares Catherine. The *clanns* loudly enter the *bothie*; hungry from their work. Happy that they are on the same page about their *nighean*, they end their conversation quickly so that Catherine can finish making their meal.

The next morning when she is alone with Caitriona, Catherine discusses the conversation that she had with Lach, "Caitriona, your *athair* and I believe it would be good for you to learn a trade. You show skill in making dyes and spinning wool. You also have a good eye for patterns and colors around you. I believe that the village weaver, Flora McDonald, would be willing to take you on as an apprentice and teach you the techniques of weaving. She has several looms and has had apprentices in the past."

"*Mathair*, what would happen to you without my help? I don't want to leave you," a disturbed Caitriona replies.

"Caitriona, I will have Anna to help me. Seathan and Iain are still with us. Your *athair* and I believe it is important for you to learn a trade," states Catherine.

"*Mathair*, do you know what Flora is like? Can I ever return to here to live with you and my *athair* again?" Caitriona appeals to her *mathair's* sympathies. Catherine responds to her *nighean's* fears with reassurance, "Caitriona, she treats her workers with respect and I am sure that she would not be against visits to your family, especially during our festivals. Caitriona, let's visit her tomorrow, so you can meet each other with an apprenticeship in mind. We will find out if she can take you on as an apprentice. If she agrees, we can then discuss the arrangements with her."

"*Mathair*, I would like to learn how to weave," Caitriona reassures Catherine. "I am just not very happy with the thought of leaving you and my family."

Catherine then responds, "The good news is that the village is only four miles away from our glen. We will be able to talk every Sabbath and during your visits here . It is fortunate that there is a weaver in Inivea. Highlanders come from faraway for the services of Flora McDonald. She is well known for her talents in weaving cloths and tartans. So, is it the plan to visit her tomorrow?"

Caitriona takes a moment to respond thoughtfully, "Yes, *Mathair*, that is the plan."

Caitriona leaves the conversation with mixed feelings. Throughout her life she has been her *mathair's* support and little Anna has been under her care since she was a wee *bairn*. She will miss the routine of her life and the glen. All these thoughts weave in and out of Caitriona's head as she moves through her day and awaits her visit to the shop of Flora McDonald.

The next morning it is cold and foggy. Finally it is time to go and she asks Iain to look out for Anna and calls to Caitriona, "The fog has lifted. It is time for us to make our trek to the village."

"I am ready, *Mathair*," says Caty.

Before they set out Anna calls out, "*Mathair*, why can't I go with you and Caty?" Catherine reassures her youngest *nighean*, "Anna, it is important for you to stay and help Iain with the animals. Caitriona and I must do this errand by ourselves. We will be back by midafternoon." At this, Catherine and Caitriona take their leave and make their way on the rough path to the village.

Catherine and Caitriona hike in silence. They both understand that today might mean great changes in the Maclean family. Soon they reach the shop of Flora McDonald which is located a few doors away from the blacksmith's shop of Iain Campbell. Catherine uses the iron knocker on Flora's door. Flora, herself, opens the door to her visitors. "Come in Catherine and Caitriona," motions Flora. They enter a large room filled with four looms and several piles of woven cloth in different colors. Some of the cloths have bright patterns and Caitriona is immediately attracted to them.

Caitriona goes over to the cloths, touching and admiring them. "I love the patterns and colors of your cloths," shares Caitriona.

Flora responds, "Caitriona, these are the *plaids* of several clans that live in this area. Are you interested in learning how to weave cloths like these?"

"Aye, Flora, I would like to learn," agrees Catriona.

"Lately my business has been brisk and to fill orders I have employed the services of two weavers to help me fill them. Flora then introduces them to her weavers, "Giorsail and Mairi, this is Catherine and her *nighean*, Caitriona. Caitriona is interested in becoming a weaver." Both weavers respond with a positive greeting, "Hello and welcome."

"Let's sit here on the stools near the fireplace," instructs Flora, "and I will explain everything." The three make their way to the warm burning embers of the fireplace. "Catherine, are you aware of what an indenture to a master means?"

Catherine replies, "I have heard that there are such arrangements when a person wants to learn a trade, but I do not know more."

Flora states, "I will explain it to you and if you agree to the arrangement, Caitriona would sign a contract." Flora continues, "Caitriona will be committing to five years of service. During this time she will live with me and work six days a week. I will also require, as is the law, a fee of 10 pounds which Lach can pay me in installments. If Caitriona is a good learner and becomes proficient as a weaver, I will pay her a small wage in a couple of years. Does this sound agreeable to both of you?" Flora questions.

"Aye, Flora. However, since neither I nor Caitriona know how to read, I would like, with your permission, to take the contract to Lach.

Since he also does not know how to read, I am sure that he would like our pastor to review it. Will you agree to that?"

"Aye, Catherine, that will be fine," agrees Flora. At that Catherine and Caitriona depart from the shop of Flora, saying their farewells to the weavers and Flora.

On the way back to their *bothie*, Catherine and Caitriona discuss Flora's terms. Caitriona begins, "*Mathair*, I did not know that there would be a contract that I would have to sign. I will feel like a captive."

"Caitriona, I can understand your concerns but this is the way it is done," Catherine reassures her. "Remember, she will be giving you a lot of her time and expertise. In doing this it will take away from her own earning time. She will also be giving you the secrets of her trade. It is a lot for her to do this. The contract will help to create trust and commitment for both of you."

"I guess it makes sense, but it will take me time to get used to the arrangement."

Later that day after Lach arrives home the contract is shown to him. Knowing his misgivings about letting go of Caitriona, Catherine carefully explains her conversation with Flora to Lach. Lach interrupts, "Why do we need a written and signed contract? Can't Flora just have our handshake that Caitriona will remain loyal to her and the apprenticeship? A handshake is all that ever has been required among our clan."

Catherine replies to Lach trying to ease his apprehensions, "Lach, this is the traditional contract of an apprenticeship. It protects our *nighean* as well as Flora. Do you need more time to think about it?"

"I will think through dinner and sleep on it," Lach replies. "In the morning I will have an answer for you."

Catherine notices that Lach is restless through the meal. Knowing that her *fear* needs time to adjust to what would be such a major change in their family, Catherine remains silent. Mentally she decides, "I will not pressure Lach anymore tonight. He will mull over it and let her know what he decides when he is ready."

Lach wakes up at his usual hour. Catherine and Caitriona are already preparing an early meal before Lach leaves. Lach speaks first, "Catherine, you arrange a time with Pastor Robertson so he can read the contract to us. If I agree to the terms, we will all sign it and then Caitriona will pack up and head to Flora's."

After the service, Pastor Robertson walks with them over to his manse. On the way Pastor Robertson asks, "What is the contract about?" After Catherine explains, Pastor Robertson replies, "So, Caitriona wants to become a weaver like Flora."

"Aye, Caitriona agrees that it would be a good choice for her," answers Catherine. They reach the pastor's home and the housekeeper opens the door. The pastor invites them in and shows them to the large wooden table in the middle of the front room.

"Come sit here." He beckons the housekeeper to prepare some tea. "Mrs. MacDougall, I am sure that my guests would like some tea while they wait for me." The housekeeper rushes off and Lach hands the pastor the contract.

The group sits quietly and respectfully while the pastor takes time to review the contract. Meanwhile the housekeeper comes back with a tray of tea and biscuits for the group. Unaware of the housekeeper's return, Pastor Robertson with a furrowed brow carefully examines the details of the written words before him. He feels a great responsibility to make sure that he understands to what the Macleans are committing their *nighean*. Then he reviews the contract with the Macleans. Catherine explains that there are no surprises because the terms are exactly what Flora had stated.

Lach then speaks up, "I don't like the fact that Caitriona must serve Flora for five years. It seems like a long time to be in service."

Catherine then reminds Lach, "Flora will be spending a lot of time with Caitriona, teaching her valuable skills for earning money. After she is finished with her apprenticeship Flora will pay her for her work."

"Lach," pipes in Pastor Robertson. "I understand your apprehension; however, this is the way of all apprenticeships and Caitriona will be close by. You will be able to visit her and she will be able to come to the holiday celebrations."

Lach takes time to finish his tea and biscuits while Pastor Robertson and the family wait patiently for his final decision. Lach finally speaks, "All right, if Caitriona agrees to its terms, we will sign the contract."

As the Macleans leave Pastor Robertson's manse they meet Donald who has come for his weekly bible and reading lesson. They are unaware of the arrangement that Donald has made with Pastor Robertson. Earlier in the year Donald found the courage to talk to his *parantans* about his desire to learn to read. At first Isobel and Iain were wary about Donald's yearnings, but then decided it would be of no harm to him. On every Sabbath Donald visits the manse in the afternoon to have his lessons.

"Hello Donald," Catherine speaks. "Are you visiting the pastor today?"

"Aye," Donald briefly responds and the housekeeper who expects him comes to the door and invites him in not giving Donald the chance to add anything to his response.

Several days later after the Maclean's visit to Pastor Robertson, Caitriona puts her clothes in a large cloth satchel and after hugging her *brathairs* and *siuir* farewell, she leaves her beloved home with her *mathair*. They wistfully make their way to Flora McDonald's shop where Caitriona will begin her new life.

35
A Light is Extinguished

Isobel Campbell wakes up in her bed with a start, disturbed by the continuous coughing of Eilidh. Her coughs have become more frequent and deeper and often keep Isobel awake most of the night. This night, however, Isobel had managed to go into a deep sleep. Although Isobel has tried many approaches to help Eilidh: fresh air, lots of rest, herbs and rocking, nothing has worked. Isobel and Iain worry that Eilidh cannot survive much longer. She has no appetite, sleeps fitfully, has frequent fevers, coughs incessantly and is losing weight. Despite being three and a half years old, it is easy for Isobel to carry her around the *bothie* while trying to comfort her. Isobel goes over to Eilidh's bed, picks her up and heads to the door. When she looks out there is a breathtaking sky. Its hue is a dark red-pink with some streaks of a lighter pink and gold. Isobel reminds herself of the farmer's ancient ditty known throughout the Isle: *'Red sky at morning, farmers take warning. Red sky at night, farmer's delight.'*

Isobel is worried because many of the crops in the first of July are still young and vulnerable. The animals are also out in the meadows and could be in danger. Animals have been known to take a lightning strike or be harmed by an unexpected snow or hail storm. Iain and her *clanns* are still sleeping. She will wake them and warn them of an upcoming storm. First, she points out the stunning sky to Eilidh. "Oh *mathair*," exclaims Eilidh in a feeble voice, using what energy she has to muster some enthusiasm. "The sky is pretty."

Despite her illness, Eilidh has an appreciation of life around her. She is very fond of her *brathairs* and they of her. They give her special care, taking her outside so that she can feel the sunshine and warm weather. They sing folk tunes to her and when Eilidh has the energy, she joins in.

Today before the expected storm, they take Eilidh out of the *bothie* and sit with her on a stool. Although the sky has faded somewhat, subtle pink hues are still scattered throughout the sky. Roderick and Donald sing her favorite tune:

Blow Away the Morning Dew

There was a farmer's son,
Kept sheep all on the hill;
And he walk'd out one May morning
To see what he could kill.

Eilidh rocks in their arms as they sing the chorus.

And sing blow away the morning dew
The dew, and the dew.
Blow away the morning dew,
how sweet the winds do blow.

He looked high, he looked low,
He cast an under look;
And there he saw a pretty maid
Beside the watery brook.

And sing blow away the morning dew
The dew, and the dew.
Blow away the morning dew,
How sweet the winds do blow.

For a few moments Roderick and Donald forget about their *siuir's* illness and enjoy a carefree moment with her. Eilidh is also very happy until she begins an incessant coughing spell. She gulps in air between the coughs, trying to reestablish a stable breath. Roderick then comments, "We must take her in and lie her on her bed so that she can rest."

They bring Eilidh in, but Isobel quickly notices how distressed her *nighean* is. "Roderick, bring Eilidh to me quickly," Isobel cries. The situation is serious because Eilidh cannot catch her breath due to her non-stop coughing. Isobel places Eilidh on her chest and gently pats her back. After several minutes Eilidh brings up some dark green mucus, stops coughing and her breathing, although shallow, resumes its natural rhythm. Isobel knows that these episodes take a lot out of Eilidh and that perhaps her *brathairs* should not take her out of doors. It may be too stimulating for her. Roderick and Donald might not notice when Eilidh's fragile body cannot tolerate it.

"*Mathair*," exclaims Eilidh, "I hurt," and she points to her chest.

"It is probably because you coughed so much," Isobel responds.

"We will have to limit your time outside and what you do because it makes you cough more."

"But *mathair*, I want to be with my *brathairs*," Eilidh responds.

"I know Eilidh but your body cannot handle the fits of coughing," explains Isobel. Eilidh does not have the energy to make her plea anymore so she requests to be put back into her bed.

Several hours pass by and Eilidh sleeps. The red sky holds true to its warning and in the early afternoon the storm begins. It is a thunder and lightning storm, a common summer occurrence on the Isle.

The slanting rain pounds on the roof of their *bothie*. Isobel worries that some of their planted crops will not survive the damaging rain and wind. After the storm has stopped they will go to their garden to check on it. They do not have a large one, but nevertheless, storms such as this affect their wellbeing. Fortunately, most of the crops are cold weather and could be replanted before the Highland winter arrived.

Eilidh sleeps through the storm, exhausted from the morning coughing spell. Isobel is well aware of the future for her *nighean* and she decides that she must have a serious talk with her *macs,* warning them that their *siuir* might not live much longer. This breaks Isobel's heart. She will paint a picture of a better place for their *siuir* where she will no longer have pain and she will be surrounded by flowers, meadows and music. There will be others who have died before her to keep her company. This will be the heaven that she hears about in her *kirk*.

Meanwhile the storm subsides and the family goes out to look at the damage to their garden. To their surprise it looks as if the crops weathered the storm. The potatoes will need some extra fertilizer to help with the drainage. Roderick and Donald will be able to collect the compost from the pasture. The potato mounds, which Roderick built up when the first green leaves appeared, were washed down from the rain and will have to be rebuilt with new soil. They will not know until August whether their cabbage crop survived the extra rain. It could mean mildew or rot. Later Roderick treks to the pasture where the Campbell's livestock stay. He is pleased to see that they are all alive and well.

A week passes and Eilidh's condition worsens with fever and more intense coughing spells. Isobel finds a secluded and private moment to talk to her *macs* about Eilidh's illness and her future. "Roderick and Donald, come outside with me while Eilidh is sleeping," requests their *mathair*.

"Aye *Mathair*," they both respond in unison. There are several stools located outside and all three sit down.

Isobel begins, "You are aware that Eilidh's health is not good. I think that soon Eilidh will be joining other kin who have died and reside in heaven. In that place Eilidh will have no more coughs or pain. She will be surrounded by flowers, heather-filled meadows and the music that she loves. Her company will be our Lord and others who love her; kinfolk who have died before her. All we can do right now is give her as much comfort as we can."

Roderick interrupts his *mathair*, "I don't want Eilidh to die. I love her and want her with us always."

"Aye, I do too," adds Donald. "I love her so much."

"We all love her so very much and do not want her to leave us," agrees Isobel. "But she is in so much discomfort and pain that I do not believe her frail body can handle much more. Someday we might all awaken and Eilidh does not. Or perhaps she will have a coughing fit and no matter what we do, we will not be able to stop her coughing so that she can catch her breath. It will be easier if she never wakes up, but we are not in charge of this. It will be God's will." Tears fill the eyes of all three. They do not cry out loud, but the sobs fill their hearts. It is finally out in the open that Eilidh's death will be soon and they can no longer deny it.

Over the next few days life goes on in the Campbell *bothie*, but there is always a sadness that permeates the dwelling. They hide it from Eilidh, but she knows.

One evening she says to her *mathair*, "I have a lot of pain." These are the last words that Isobel hears from her *nighean*. Eilidh dies in her sleep and does not wake up with the rest of her family.

Isobel is the first to know and when she finds her beloved *nighean*, she quietly picks her up in her arms, cradling her small body with a deep sorrow. Silently she lets her tears drop on Eilidh's bedclothes. They are quickly absorbed into her *nighean's* woven gown. She sits on the bed for a long time. The others are asleep and are unaware Isobel's immense grief. She is grateful for the alone time with her sweet little Eilidh. Knowing that she needs to be a strength for the rest of her family, she composes herself and lowers Eilidh into her bed.

Iain is the first to wake up when he hears Isobel's soft whimpers. He goes over to Eilidh's bed where Isobel is still sitting. He sits down beside her and takes Eilidh up in his burly but gentle arms. Isobel puts her arm around Iain's waist as he holds their young *nighean.* They spend several moments in this embrace of grieving which is broken when they hear Roderick speak out, "What is wrong with Eilidh?"

Isobel answers her oldest *mac,* "Eilidh has finally gone to the place where she will feel no more pain and be with her ancestors who died before her."

Roderick quickly joins his *mathair* and *athair* at the bedside of Eilidh. He kneels before his *siuir* and his grieving *parantans.* They are all silent while Iain continues to hold the body of Eilidh. Soon Donald wakes up and joins the family at the bedside of his deceased *siuir.* Finally Iain places his *nighean* on top of her bed covers. There will be many things to do now before she is buried.

Immediately Roderick is sent to the glen to tell Catherine Maclean the news. Several hours later Catherine arrives with Jannet and Marta who help Isobel wash Eilidh's body. Then they wrap the *winding sheet* around her tiny emaciated body.

As soon as the word of Eilidh's death is given to him by Iain, the bell ringer stands in the village's center ringing his bell to announce that there has been a death. Along with the bell ringing he also calls out the name of Eilidh. Her death spreads quickly throughout the village and glen. For several days the body is waked. Roderick and Donald watch over Eilidh around-the-clock on those days to keep her spirit from falling to the devil. Dughall, Iain's cousin, is sent to Ballygown to let Isobel's and his family know. The Ballygown relatives travel to Inivea to pay their last respects.

After several days of visits the women carry the wrapped body outside and hand it to Iain, Roderick and Donald. Pastor Robertson makes his way to the *bothie* of Isobel and Iain. He joins the procession of men, women and children while Iain and his *macs* carry the sheeted corpse of Eilidh to the cemetery beside the *kirk.* Earlier in the week volunteer men had prepared a grave where Eilidh was to be buried.

The procession reaches the cemetery. Men, the pastor and Iain with Roderick and Donald stand in silence as they gather around the gravesite. Women are forbidden to enter the cemetery, but a small group respectfully stand outside the grounds. Lurking behind these grieving women stands Rut, unnoticed, but taking it all in.

Then Eilidh's sheeted body is lowered into the grave. The pastor, although yearning to say something to honor Eilidh, is aware of Scottish law which says that the pastor must remain silent with the others. Iain who has attended other burials before is, nonetheless, deeply affected by this custom. He would like to hear some words of remembrance and the lack of it is dark and sad. He tries to console himself by remembering, "The life of dear Eilidh will be celebrated after the funeral with dancing, singing and food at the *aite cruinneachaidh*." Iain inwardly trembles, knowing that no celebration can relieve him and Isobel of the enormous grief they are feeling.

While Eilidh is being carried and buried some women have stayed behind at Isobel's *bothie* preparing the *Dredgy* (after-funeral feast) of whisky and butter and cheese with oat bread. Soon Jannet announces to Isobel, "I will go to the *aite cruinneachaidh* to ready it for the celebration."

"Aye, Marta should join you. I have enough help here," replies Isobel.

Jannet and Marta reach their destination. On the way they share with each other the sadness they feel with the death of Eilidh. "She was a sweet little *bairn* and her family was devoted to her, even her two *brathairs,*" Marta speaks first.

"There is going to be a big empty hole in that home as they grieve the death of such an adored *bairn,* adds Jannet. "I don't know how Isobel is going to recover from such a loss." It is going to be difficult for her—her only *nighean!*"

They soon reach the *aite cruinneachaidh* and open the heavy crude door. A blast of stale hot air greets them as they enter. Immediately Jannet states, "This room will not be good for the celebration of Eilidh's life."

"It is too hot and airless," adds Marta. "We will have to carry some tables and benches outside."

"Let's hurry," Jannet urges. "We do not have too much time before the women are here looking for places to put the food and drink."

They begin taking out the tables first. Sine and another villager suddenly appear from the village. When they reach Jannet and Marta, Sine announces, "We thought you might need some help here and I guess I was not wrong."

Quickly they all pitch in to carry tables and benches outside.

The women soon appear with food and then the mourners arrive from the cemetery. Iain and his *macs* lead the pack, followed by Lach and his family. Catherine had stayed to help Isobel and as soon as she spots Lach and her family she joins them.

For the rest of the afternoon the villagers and farmers together celebrate the life of Eilidh with dancing, song and food. While they consume a fair amount of whisky, all are able to participate in a customary funeral of celebration. At the end of the day Isobel and Iain return to their *bothie* with heavy hearts.

36
Rut Makes Her Case

After witnessing the mourners at the funeral of Eilidh, Rut knows that the mood in the village is ripe for planting the seeds of Anna's witch-craft. She is also convinced that Anna put a spell on Eilidh to cause her illness and eventual death. Rut is now going to let the clansmen of Inivea know the truth. She must go about her case carefully so that the folks will believe her. The Macleans are well respected in this area and Catherine is a good friend of Isobel; probably her best friend and confidant. In plotting her attack, Rut must decide who she will weave into her web of destruction first. She has convinced herself that this is being done to protect the folks of Inivea and for no other reason.

Rut summarizes in her mind the case against Anna:

- She is a red-head and all clansmen know that
  all red-heads are witches.

- Anna, when she was 5 years old, disappeared. All the clansmen
  abandoned their chores for a day in order to search for her.

- The *bairn*, Eilidh, became very ill within a month of her birth.
  She never was a well *bairn* and died at just 3-1/2 years old.

And perhaps, if she searches, she might be able to find other deeds which could be connected to the spells of the witch, namely Anna.

Rut believes that these arguments will be all the evidence needed to convince everyone that Anna is a witch. She will point out that Anna has just begun to cast evil deeds on their village and glen. Rut knows that witches are no longer burned at a stake, but they are ostracized and no longer allowed to participate in village life. Anna will also not want to come to *kirk* services where all the gossip will be directed at her.

Rut reviews her plan of action. This time she will not tell Tomas what she is doing. She mulls over in her mind to whom she will first reveal the evidence. She will sleep on it, as the disclosure will make

161

significant changes in her life. She will gain the respect of her clansmen and will probably be consulted on other matters in the village.

Rut wakes up with a start. All through the night her mind has been busy in her dreams. She is feeling empowered and yet there is a darkness in her soul.

Rut, after much thought, makes the decision to start with Sine, the village midwife. She believes that as a midwife Sine has seen many births and is more able than most to see the connection of Anna and witchery. Sine has most likely delivered *bairns* who were later switched at birth. For a long time Rut has suspected that Sine Campbell would be an ally to her cause. To insure this allegiance Rut has befriended Sine by bringing her oats and other foods to supplement her meager garden. Sine is single and has no *fear* to help her in times of need. In the early afternoon Rut will walk to Inivea to speak with Sine.

Although busy all morning long, Rut's dark mood grows and she ruminates on telling Sine her suspicions about Anna. She recalls that this is not the first time she has told folks about her suspicions of other village women. She is also reminded that it will be the first time, however, that she has accused someone of being a witch.

"Tomas, I am hiking to the village to visit Sine. Watch over our *clanns*. They can join you and help you with the chores," Rut announces.

Tomas responds, "What is your business with Sine?"

"I am just making a social visit and will bring her some cheese and bread," Rut answers. She then dons her *kertch* and cloak to make the four-mile trek down the hilly path to the village. She is hoping that Sine is in her *bothie* or in her garden. She was not aware of anyone in the village needing the services of a midwife right now.

After an hour of travel Rut arrives at the door of Sine's *bothie*. She knocks on the big wooden door and there is no answer. "Hello Sine, it is your friend, Rut. I have brought some bread and cheese for you."

Again there is no answer. Rut waits impatiently for couple of minutes. "She must be in her garden. I will go and check there," Rut thinks. She then goes behind Sine's *bothie* and is reminded that it is a small garden, one that a single woman who has no relatives can handle on her own. Overlooking the garden Rut quickly notices that Sine is not there. "I will go once more to her *bothie*. Perhaps she returned while I was in the back at her garden," Rut thinks to herself.

There is no one around to question the whereabouts of Sine, but hoping she might return, Rut waits at Sine's home for several more minutes. Still no one appears. Disappointed that her important mission has been flaunted, Rut treks back to the glen. She will return again soon.

37

Seathan Makes His Decision

Being alone is no stranger to Seathan Maclean. In the summer pastures, often by himself, Seathan has time to think and sort out his plans. At 21 years old he is becoming more and more restless for change and adventure. He cannot deny his dreams of travel much longer. While he guards the Maclean livestock he looks over the vista. Now at the end of summer, Seathan believes that there is no greater beauty than his Highlands. The sky above him is bright blue with billowing white clouds traveling across its vast terrain. He has looked at the sky scene frequently throughout his life, but today it takes on new meanings. Seathan feels more intensely the vastness of the world. This sky will be the same sky whether he is far away in another land or right here on his Isle. This thought makes his dream of leaving easier to bear and also fills him with a nervous anticipation.

The sun is at its highest and Seathan takes a break. He treks up to an incline which overlooks the pasture and his livestock. His day's meal is stored in a leather knapsack swung on his shoulder with a coarse piece of rope. Later he will hike to a spring and fill his wooden bowl with water. Hopefully his *brathair,* Iain, will arrive the next day to replenish his food. There are times when Iain stays overnight so that Seathan can trek down the path to his *bothie* to have a hot meal around fire and sit with his family. It is also nice to get clean clothes and rest in his own bed. Seathan welcomes those times of comfort but it will not happen this time. The beginning of the harvest is in full swing and Iain will be needed on the farm.

While resting and eating, Seathan overlooks the meadows. His livestock are busy eating the grass. Although it is the end of the summer there are still many flowers dotting the landscape; yellows, whites, reds and purples create a colorful canvas of color. When he leaves, Seathan will miss this beauty. As if implanting them in his forever memory, Seathan takes time to admire the abundant yellows of the meadow; buttercups, toadflaxes, dandelions and the kidney vetches. His eye also is drawn to the red and white clovers among all the green pasture and yellow wildflowers. Most of all, however, he will never forget the beauty of the bluebells of the woodlands in spring and the red-purple heather of the autumn.

At twilight Seathan leaves his livestock for the evening and hikes back to his *shieling* where he will sleep, protected from the cooler night air and the elements. Before he retires he sits outside and stares at the dark sky of the night. A partial moon makes it possible for him to see the numerous bright stars. While staring at them he smiles as he has a flashback to Anna and her persistent comments about the magic of the night sky.

He recalls the time when he witnessed a gigantic display of shooting stars filling the sky for hours. He remembers huddling outside his *shieling*, terrified that the world was coming to an end. Seathan did not have memory of any other time when he was so frightened. Later he shared his experience with his *athair* who assured him that he had viewed the same phenomenon years ago when he was very young and it had put fear in him also. Lach explained that he doesn't know what causes this strange event, but he was confident that the world would not come to an end.

Seathan sleeps fitfully through the night. Dreams of leaving his beloved home cause him to toss and turn. He wants to move on to new adventures and new lands but still has some apprehensions about it all. Here in the Highlands, surrounded by his family and kinfolk, he feels secure.

Iain arrives the next morning laden with dry clothes and food. He greets Seathan, "How are you? I have brought you porridge, bread, eggs and cheese as well as some cooked kale and cabbage and your favorite treat of blueberries and blackberries." The fresh provisions will not last long but Seathan appreciates the delightful refreshment they will give him, if only for a few days.

Seathan answers his *brathair*, "These are good, and I will enjoy the fresh ones the most. And how are you my *brathair*? Is everything all right at our home and farm?"

Iain replies to Seathan's questions, "The harvest season has now begun and we are very busy. *Athair* is hopeful that the harvest will be abundant enough to last through the winter. In between helping on the farm Anna uses her free time to collect herbs so that she can go to Beitris in the village to learn about healing."

"I was wondering if she has continued with that interest," responds Seathan.

"Aye, she has," Iain answers.

"I will miss not having a trip back to our glen at this time, but I know that it is important for you to continue with the harvesting," Seathan states. "I will see you in a couple of weeks."

And with that Iain starts down the path to his glen. He looks back one last time and sees Seathan deep in thought. Iain waves to him but Seathan does not notice. He wonders what is on Seathan's mind. Someday he will be taking Seathan's place here watching over the livestock in the summer. For now, though, he will return to the farm and help with the harvest.

38
A Chance Encounter

It is a lovely autumn afternoon. However, it makes Sine Campbell sad. Sine had been busy with several births during the summer. Widowed and now 30 years old, living in this small isolated village has been extremely difficult for her. Her role as a midwife in the village has filled an empty space in her life. She is not sure why it is in autumn that she feels particularly lonely. Perhaps it is because it reminds her of when her *fear*, John, died of smallpox. She went into a deep dark place barely surviving her grief. If it weren't for neighbors she would probably have followed him into the grave. Eventually she came out of her darkness and thanks to Jannet McKinnon, she learned how to be a midwife.

Not wanting to revisit that memory she decides, "I need to go out for a hike through the moor. The weather this afternoon is warm and the beauty of the heather will lift my spirits." She has begun to use a walk to change her mood recently and it helps take her loneliness away, at least momentarily. Donning her cape and bonnet, Sine opens her door and goes out into the sunshine.

Taking in a deep breath she inhales the brisk cool air. She looks beyond the village onto the moor and admires the tall red-purple heather overtaking the landscape. Pulling her cloak closer around, she begins her hike. Sine never tells anyone that she is out on a walk, which is a bit risky in case there is a midwife emergency. Today, however, Sine is less anxious because there are no imminent births in the village.

Beyond the moor are the hills covered with meadows and more heather. And in the distance are the craggy mountains, stark and austere even in the summer and autumn months. Sine believes in the monsters that lurk in the cliffs and caves of these mountains, but she never lets those fears deter her from her wanderings. However, they come to mind right now, "I hope the monsters of our Isle stay where they belong." She knows that they don't venture out until the dark of the night. Nonetheless, the tales of monsters told to her by her *mathair* often to come into her mind when she is alone on the moor.

Meanwhile Pastor Robertson is also on the path through the moor. There are several trails but today he decides to follow this one because it is the most spectacular at this time of year. The vistas extend as far as the eye can see. Closest are the meadows covered with red-purple heather. The butterflies and dragonflies that have not migrated flutter their wings close by in search of food. Sometimes he wanders off to climb one of the hills so that he can see the beach and ocean, but not today. He reflects, "It is beautiful here but sometimes I miss my family and the big city."

Deep in reverie he is startled by a lone figure of a woman in front of him. She walks more slowly than he does and he slows his pace in order to observe her. "What is she doing out on the moor all by herself," he wonders. After several minutes he quickens his pace. His line of work gives him familiarity with everyone in the village, but he is unable to determine the identity of this woman from behind.

He is suddenly upon her, "Uh hum," he softly stammers as not to frighten her.

Despite his subtle warning, Sine makes a sudden vocalization showing that she was startled by the unexpected hiker. "Why Pastor Robertson, I did not expect to see another walker here right now."

"Yes, it is a little late to be so far away from the village," responds the pastor. "Do you think that we should turn around and head back home?"

"I was just thinking about heading back before I got lost in my thoughts," answers Sine.

Pastor Robertson suggests, "May I accompany you back to the village then?"

Right from the day that she had met Pastor Robertson, preaching his first sermon, she was intrigued. She never imagined that she would have the opportunity to be alone with him. It was not the custom of single women and men to be alone with each other. At this moment Sine had no other choice, "Yes, that would be nice. It is time to head back to the village before it gets dark."

Pastor Robertson then queries, "What are you doing out here on the moor by yourself?"

"I know it seems strange but I often hike on the moor, especially when I am not busy. It is so beautiful," replies Sine. "The dark winter months will be coming soon and I don't want to miss any lovely days before that happens."

"You are not worried about being alone?" responds Pastor Robertson.

"Not usually," answers Sine. "Once in a while I think about the monsters that live in the cliffs, but then I put it out of my mind. I know this moor well and do not take unknown trails," continues Sine.

Pastor Robertson is silent for a while. He then remarks, "I also like coming out on the trails on the moor to be alone and think. Sometimes I hike up the hill and look over the landscape. Far away I can see the ocean and when the wind is right I can smell the salt air."

"I don't usually stray from the trail but a couple of times I did hike up the hill close by," adds Sine. "I did not go high enough to see the ocean."

"It is nice to have someone to talk to about something other than *kirk* business," Pastor Robertson reflects.

They talk casually with each other as they hike along the trail back to the village. "What do you do in the winter when you can no longer hike on the moor," queries Pastor Robertson.

Sine responds, "Sometimes there are midwifery duties. At other times I visit friends and relatives. And you, Pastor Robertson, do you have any hobbies which take up the dark hours of winter?" asks Sine.

"I have several books that I like to read," responds the Pastor. "I also spend many hours preparing my sermon for Sundays. These keep me somewhat busy. But I do miss having someone to talk to at night as well as share my meal with."

"Aye, I also miss the evening company in my *bothie* of someone to share my thoughts with," agrees Sine.

As they near the village and to avoid gossip, they jointly decide that Sine will go ahead and enter the village alone. Before she leaves his side, Pastor Robertson shares, "I have enjoyed our hike together."

"Aye," responds Sine.

After a short hike back Sine arrives at her *bothie*. She goes in and comes out with a blanket. She sits outside on a stool with the blanket on her lap to watch the sunset. Before the darkness sets in she observes the return of Pastor Robertson. He briefly looks over at her before he enters the manse. She smiles and surprises herself with a feeling of wanting to see him again.

Left with warm memories of her encounter with Pastor Robertson, Sine is eager to attend services each Sunday at the *kirk*. She wants to hike with him into the moor again soon, but autumn is quickly passing and she has not heard from him. She will have to be patient and hope that he will contact her again or that he will attend the village *ceilidhs*.

39

Rut Maclean Meets with Sine Campbell

Without being able to talk to anyone, Rut Maclean has been stewing in her blackness all summer long. It is now the end of September and she feels an urgency to talk with Sine. Her suspicions concerning Anna have not ebbed and she must find a way to make another visit. She finally decides that she will tell Tomas that she needs to visit Flora so that she can weave her yarn into cloth. After all her *clanns* will need new warm clothes for the cold months. Tomas is too stupid to doubt her and will accept this.

In her *bothie* Sine Campbell is busy taking stock of her supplies. A lot of births this summer have strained her resources. A knock on her door surprises her; there are no births expected right now. She opens her door and is startled to see Rut. True they are distant Campbell cousins but that is where the relationship generally ended, nothing more. There had been a couple of occasions throughout the years when Rut came for a visit bearing a small gift of food. Although Sine depended on the villagers' bartering for her midwifery services, she also relied on kinfolk making additional gifts of food as well as helping her with chores.

Despite Rut's occasional food gifts, Sine had no special love for her. Sine was not an ignorant woman. She had heard tales about Rut spreading nasty gossip about some women in the village. Sine guesses, "Perhaps Rut is making a visit to give her some of the harvest from her farm." Just as that thought crosses her mind, she notices that Rut's hands are empty. Sine politely invites Rut in to sit at the fire.

Sine speaks first, "What brings you here this afternoon? I would imagine that you have many chores waiting for you on the farm."

Rut responds to Sine's query, "I had to make a trip to the weaver. I must sew new clothes for my two *clanns* for the cold months. They are growing so fast that it is difficult to keep suitable clothes for them. Since I had not made a visit to you in a while, I decided to stop by and make sure that all is well with you." In her haste to deceive Tomas and gather her spun yarn for Flora, she had forgotten to pack cheese and bread for Sine.

"Well, Rut, that is nice of you," replies Sine. "I have had several births this summer and that has kept me busy. How are you and your family?"

"Lucas is 9 years old now and although he has grown through the summer, he needs to grow more to be of sufficient help to his athair. Deidre is 8 years old and helps me in the *bothie*."

"Rut, I have some hot tea. Would you like a bowl?" inquires Sine.

"That would be nice," responds Rut. Rut adjusts herself on the stool. Sine passes tea to her.

The moment that Rut has waited for is here and she begins, "Sine, I am making this visit to you not just for conversation. I have some knowledge about a threat to the safety of our village and glen."

Sine discreetly tightens her stomach muscles and clinches her hands in anxious anticipation of Rut's revelations. Up to now Sine has been able to avoid Rut's dark rumors and she wants it to remain that way. "Why, oh why, did she invite Rut to sit and have tea with her?" she wonders.

Sine sits quietly while Rut goes on with her revelations, "Sine, I have knowledge of the presence of a witch in Inivea. I am sure you understand how dangerous witches are and I want you to be safe." Sine does not respond. She does not want to encourage Rut to disclose her suspicions. However, Rut does not need any motivation from Sine to continue her revelations. "You know the youngest *nighean* of Catherine and Lach Maclean, I am sure. Her name is Anna."

"Aye, I know Anna well. She is a delightful girl and brings much joy to her family and others," responds Sine.

"Sine, there is so much that you don't know about Anna," pushes Rut. "Do you know that Anna was born a red-head and that Catherine dyes her hair every month so that folks will not know? And you must know what being a red-head means?" Rut inquires of Sine.

Sine is too shocked to reply. Sine does not know whether she should believe Rut. Sine finally speaks, "How do you know this about Anna?"

Rut replies, "I was part of a *coinneamh* when the family was trying to decide what to do about Anna when she was first born. I was convinced at the time that Anna was indeed a witch, but the kinfolk

174

wanted to hide her red hair from the rest of Inivea. Their argument was that she was only a wee *bairn* and not to make false witness against her. So, I went along with them, knowing that I would be watching her carefully."

Sine then adds, "But Rut, there is still no proof that she is a witch. She has performed no harm on our village or glen."

"Sine, I did not come to this conclusion until I had evidence," responds Rut. "The first harm she did to our clan was when she became lost in the winter pasture of our glen. Twenty clansmen including my *fear*, Tomas, joined in the hunt to find her. They had to spend the day searching and were unable to tend to their own chores. Only a witch could have the power to cause such havoc among the farmers. Perhaps while lost she was also approached by witches or the *Black Donald* who enlisted her to carry out future bad deeds."

"The villagers did hear about the situation of a lost child several years ago," responds Sine. "But no one suspected a child of getting lost intentionally in order to lure the farmers away from their chores. Any active five-year-old could get lost without evil intentions. I can't accept that this proves that Anna is a witch, even if she had the fate of being born with red hair."

Rut protests, "Yes, but I have heard of no other child having the power to force twenty farmers to take time from their chores to search." She forcefully continues, "But this is not the only evidence that I have implicating Anna in witchery. Recently the youngest *nighean* of Isobel and Iain Campbell died suspiciously from an unknown illness. She became ill about a month after her birth. Catherine Maclean and Isobel Campbell are good friends and Catherine brought Anna frequently to visit Eilidh. It was soon after Catherine's visit with Anna in the first month of her life that Eilidh became ill. So, you tell me, was it not the witchcraft of Anna that caused the illness and death of Eilidh? I can see no other cause. This is all the evidence I need to prove that Anna is a witch. Sine, you now have all the proof you need."

Sine is silent. The evidence that Rut presents does not convince her of Anna being a witch. She knows enough not to debate Rut's conclusions with her. Instead she nods her head, "Rut, I hear what you are saying about Anna and I will take your evidence into consideration."

At that Rut rises and bids Sine farewell. "Sine, I hope you take what

I have said seriously and find ways to keep yourself safe. It will also be a noble deed to our kinfolk if you spread the word of Anna and her witchcraft."

On her way back to her *bothie* Rut believes she has found an ally in Sine. She reminds herself, "I will keep this a secret from Tomas. He will know soon enough when the truth is spread throughout Inivea. Rut is pleased and reminds herself that she can sleep better tonight, thinking that Sine will now spread the truth about Anna."

40
Sine is Troubled

Sine is having a difficult time with the recent claims of Rut. She has known Anna since she was born and has watched her. She has always been a happy child, believing in the magic of butterflies, flowers, birds, summer skies, rainbows and the glistening ocean. She has heard Catherine talk about her youngest *nighean's* interest in herbs of healing, not the black magic of witches. Catherine has even shared that Anna wants to be a healer like Beitris.

In the silence of her *bothie*, Sine ponders on her relationship with Catherine, Isobel and their families. She feels uncomfortable questioning her allegiance to them and would not want to betray them. Her ever-present loneliness increases; she feels lost and isolated. If John were still alive she would be able to talk to him about everything she had just been told. She doesn't even have close kinfolk to talk to.

Of all the clans folk she feels closest to Isobel, Catherine and Jannet. When the previous midwife of the village died, Sine was newly widowed. Catherine's *mathair*, Jannet, took Sine under her wing and taught her the art of midwifery. This was a real risk for Jannet because Sine was young and had not borne a *bairn* herself. The help they had given her, emotionally and physically, had made life bearable after her husband's death.

Sine questions why Rut chose her to share the dark secrets about young Anna. She wonders if Rut has told others of Anna's condition. After thinking about the situation throughout the evening, Sine concludes that Rut is counting on her to spread the frightening news to others in the village.

Sine does not want to believe Rut's evil accusation. On the other hand if Anna is indeed a red-head, Rut might not be so far off. After all, festivals are celebrated throughout the year to ward off evil. With every birth, rituals are performed to protect newborns from faeries. In death, ceremonies are held to prevent the deceased's spirit from falling to *Black Donald*. How can she ignore her ancestors' beliefs?

Confused, Sine eats her meal and retires with a heavy heart to her bed. Sleep does not come easy. She tosses and turns throughout the night. In one terrible nightmare a frightening monster visits her and sews up her mouth so that she is unable to speak.

Sine arises early in the morning, the awful dream lingering. Is this perhaps an omen? With a start she realizes the message of her dream is guiding her to the right decision. She will not spread Rut's accusations about Anna, but she will share with Catherine what Rut has told her. On the next Sabbath day she will discreetly invite Catherine to her *bothie* under the guise that she needs her advice about a household matter. At that time she will gently ask Catherine about the information that Rut has shared.

After the Sabbath Catherine came to visit Sine. "Come in Catherine and sit down by my fire," motions Sine. Sine offers Catherine some brewed tea before speaking, "Catherine, you and your family have always been kind to me, especially since the death of my *fear*. I would never want to betray you or anyone in your family. However, I must tell you something that Rut recently shared with me." After seeing Catherine's startled look she takes a quick sip of tea but realizes she can't put it off any longer. "Rut is trying to build a case for Anna being a witch. She told me her proof includes Anna being born with red hair which you dye monthly. Other proof she gave relates to the time that Anna got lost and lured twenty farmers away from their farms to search for her. Finally, she also blames Anna for the illness and death of Eilidh."

Catherine is shocked. She responds, "I always knew that Rut had some vendetta against my family, but I can't believe how far she has gone. It is true that Anna was born a red-head and within a week we met with our kinfolk to decide what to do. My *siuir*, Lili, came up with the idea of dyeing Anna's red hair a dark brown. Throughout the years we have always feared that Anna's secret would be discovered. Except for the time when she got lost in the heather, Anna has always been under a watchful eye. On the day she became lost, her *brathair* and *siuir* were charged with watching her. They were careless and lost sight of her. Fortunately, before any harm was done to her, I found her in the winter pasture sleeping with the cows.

Sine, with her lingering concerns questions Catherine, "I know that you want to protect your young *nighean*, but what about the belief that red-heads are witches?"

178

"My answer to you, Sine," responds Catherine, "is this. Of all the folks that have been labelled as being witches throughout the years, how many were red-heads? My brother-in-law, Seumus, has traveled to other villages where there are red-heads and none of them have been found to perform witchcraft."

"This is true. I have never known any red-headed witches," replies Sine. "But what about the evil deeds that Rut claims regarding Anna?"

"As I mentioned before, Sine, getting lost at five years old could happen to any adventurous *clann.* That incident is due more to my unwise decision. As for blaming a young *clann* for the illness and death of Isobel's *nighean,* that does not make sense to me. Of course you can make your own decisions, but I beg you to examine the absurdity of it all. Have you ever known of any young *clann* being accused of witch craft in our community?"

"Catherine, I want to trust you. You have all been very kind to me. But it is difficult for me to forget our ancient beliefs."

"Sine," replies Catherine, "Before you decide I want you to consider one other idea. Anna has long been intrigued by our Highland plants. In fact, she has been collecting herbs for many years trying to figure out their qualities. Perhaps this is the characteristic of a white witch, a healer."

"Anna has never shown the dark qualities of evil. In fact she has always been just the opposite; joyful, happy and giving. She cares about the wellbeing of her family and kinfolk. She suffered so when she watched the decline and death of Eilidh. Her sadness permeated her whole being and she was sad for several months. I am sure that Rut will be spreading the dark rumors about Anna without your help. If you believe that our community needs to be protected from Anna and her supposed witchery, that is your choice. I believe that someday Anna, if she is allowed to be, will be treasured as a healer in our community."

"Catherine, it is true our world is changing and many of our old beliefs are being tested. I also have witnessed the goodness of Anna and I want to put my trust in you and in Anna. I will keep Rut's evil gossip to myself. However, I will not be surprised if she spreads her ideas about the witch Anna to others. She does not have a good reputation in these parts."

"Thank you, Sine," a relieved Catherine says. "I appreciate that you believe in the goodness of Anna and not the evil insinuations of Rut.

I will inform my *siuirs* and my *mathair* about Rut's accusations so that they will be prepared. Lach will talk to his *brathairs* and we will all need to keep a closer eye on Anna. I do pray that these nasty rumors will go no further. I do not have too much hope of this, knowing Rut's destructive disposition. Thank you for coming to me first." And with that Catherine finishes her tea and collects her things. She will have a long walk back to think about the conversation.

41
Catherine's Plan

As Catherine leaves Sine, she is not at peace. She shivers with the thought of a destructive Rut traveling around the community telling all who will listen that Anna is a red-headed witch. She does not know how many will believe Rut, but she also knows that people are always looking for the causes of calamities.

With a heavy heart Catherine proceeds up the hill to her *bothie* in the glen. Thoughts roam around in her mind as to her plan of action. She decides that number one on her agenda is to share today's revelations with Lach. After she talks with him she will speak to Anna about the reasons behind dyeing her hair.

It is now midafternoon and Iain and Anna are outside on the farm harvesting the ripened crops. Catherine believes that it has been a good growing season for all the farmers which will work in favor of Anna. With a full larder the farmers will not be so apt to pounce on Rut's predictions that Anna is a witch. Besides, no one except Rut had accused Anna of witchery when she got lost on the moor. Silently Catherine also reminds herself, "I have never heard anyone blame Anna for the illness and death of Eilidh. Hopefully, Lach and I will be able to convince all of Anna's good spirit."

Lach arrives home in time for the evening's meal with his *bean* and *clanns*. Iain and Anna always time their return to be at home when Lach arrives. It is not only the sun's movement towards the west but also their hunger which makes their return in the late afternoon a routine event.

Lach greets his family, "How is everybody today?"

Right away Iain speaks up, "*Athair*, I have some bad news about our cabbage. Some of the crop has black rot. I have gotten rid of those heads by burning them."

"You are right, this is not good news," responds Lach. "Keep a check on them to make sure that you found all the bad cabbage."

Catherine's confidence of a good harvest a few minutes ago has just been weakened by Iain's report of the condition of the cabbage crop. She thinks to herself, "Hopefully, the black rot is a small and isolated situation. The news of Rut and Sine will not be good for the mood of Lach, but I must tell him tonight so it can be dealt with before Rut spreads more gossip."

"Aye," Iain gives assurance to his *athair*. Iain is aware that every lost crop means less food for the family.

Catherine calls her family to their meal. Lach gives the blessing after which they sit and eat quietly, with only Catherine knowing the news that no one else is aware of.

After they eat, Iain and Anna go out again before the sun sets. Outside the sun is a brilliant orange color with the sky reflecting its brilliance. "Look Iain," exclaims Anna. "It will be a beautiful day tomorrow. This must be what heaven looks like."

"We are lucky to live in such a beautiful place," acknowledges Iain. And trying to join Anna with her bright mood, he spontaneously suggests, "Let's take a hike into the moor before it turns dark."

"Aye," answers Anna.

Meanwhile, Lach and Catherine finally have some moments alone. Catherine speaks first, "Lach, I have some upsetting news. As we always feared Rut has betrayed our family."

"Catherine, what is it? What has happened?" Lach anxiously questions.

"On Sunday after the service, Sine invited me to visit her to talk over a personal matter. Today I made the visit. It didn't take Sine long to tell me that Rut had recently come to her with some disturbing information." Catherine continues, "I could see by her demeanor that she was anxious and out of sorts."

Catherine goes on, "Sine informed me that Rut had told her about Anna's red hair and how I dye it every month to fool all of Inivea. According to Sine, Rut also shared that Anna is a witch because she vanished in the heather that one time." "Only a witch," Rut announced to Sine, "would arrange to be lost, causing twenty farmers to waste a day searching for her."

"Only someone filled with treacherous thinking would accuse a young *clann* of using witchcraft," laments Lach.

"That is not all," Catherine adds. "Rut told Sine that Eilidh's illness and death was caused by an evil spell cast on her by Anna. We need to quickly decide on our plan of action to counteract Rut's claims.

Sine has assured me that she will not spread Rut's falsehoods. She trusts us and although has some concerns regarding Anna's red hair, she has always observed Anna to be a loving, joyful and caring young *clann*."

Lach paces back and forth, "Rut has betrayed us, Anna and our clan. I will spread the news to my *brathairs*, including Tomas. He must know what his *bean* is up to. I do not think that he will be very happy. She must be reported to the rest of our Maclean clan."

As Catherine is about to reply, Iain and Anna burst in. Anna excitedly begins to share her experience with the beauty of the sunset, "*Mathair* and *athair*, the sun and sky tonight are so beautiful." Both stop suddenly noticing the somberness of their *parantans*. Iain speaks first, "What is wrong? Has someone died?"

It is difficult to keep secrets in the *bothie*, but they are not ready to share the news of Rut's betrayal. Catherine responds, "When it is time to share news, we will do that. Right now your *athair* and I want to be alone because we have more to discuss. Both of you go outside and watch the evening descend on our glen."

Iain and Anna obediently go out. It is twilight and the sun is quickly setting below the horizon. Both Iain and Anna sit on the stools outside. Anna, who is intrigued by the tales of the monsters of the Highlands, asks, "Iain, have you ever seen the *Black Donald* or the *Clootie* or any of the monsters or faeries that live in the caves in our mountains."

Iain answers Anna, "No, I have never seen any of these creatures. I only have heard about the evil things that they have done to our clansmen and to our farms. Why do you ask, Anna?"

"I am curious and a little afraid," replies Anna. "I have heard so many stories about their evil deeds, but yet I have never seen one."

Inside Catherine and Lach continue their discussion. Catherine states, "Lach, you will go to your *brathairs* and I will go to my *siuirs* to explain to them what is going on. We need to pursue this plan of action as soon as possible."

Incensed, Lach speaks, "I don't know what should be done with Rut. Right now I want her to be expelled from our clan., but I know that we cannot do that. It is up to Tomas to decide on how he wants to handle her."

"And then there are our *clanns*, especially Anna. We need to explain the whole story to them," adds Catherine.

A little later Anna and Iain come inside for the night. They know enough not to question their *athair* and *mathair* about their need for privacy. Their *parantans* will share the news when they are ready. Yet it is still difficult for them to be kept in the dark about the current worries of their *mathair* and *athair*. Catherine speaks to both of them, "Iain and Anna, tonight is too early to talk to you about our concerns, but you will not have to wait too long. You have worked hard tending to our crops. Tomorrow there will be more work. The sun will rise early enough so go to your beds now."

After their *clanns* go to bed, Catherine and Lach decide to go outside. Catherine dons her cloak and *kertch* and Lach puts on his *plaid*. Catherine starts the conversation, "Lach, I am wondering if it would be better to tell all our kinfolk at the same time in a *coinneamh* about Rut's betrayal. This event should also include Tomas and Rut. It will probably come as a surprise to them. I am hoping that the rest of the Macleans will stand behind us and Anna. What do you think?"

Lach responds, "Catherine, I do think it is a good idea to inform everyone at the same time. However, I am unsure about Tomas and what his reaction will be if he is not forewarned."

"Aye, Lach, it might be difficult for Tomas to hear this news about his *bean*. On the other hand, he might get support from the other kinfolk. I will leave it up to you as to whether you share the news with your *brathair* before the *coinneamh*."

A plan is finally made but it does not relieve either of the situation weighing on them. They come inside and Lach retires to his bed. After she cleans up from the meal and checks the fire, Catherine joins Lach. Lach comforts a troubled Catherine by briefly taking her in his arms and kissing her. Catherine responds by bringing her body closer to her distraught *fear*. As they embrace Catherine can feel Lach's tension diminish. They snuggle for several minutes before they finally turn away ready to fall asleep.

42

Catherine Shares the Truth with Her *Clanns*

Several days later Lach Maclean did as he promised Catherine and arranged a *coinneamh*. So as not to interfere with the end of the summer harvest, the *coinneamh* was scheduled just after the sun had set. Lach then shares with Catherine, "I did not tell Tomas and Rut about the purpose of the *coinneamh*. Perhaps the surprise will startle them into being honest. We cannot assume that Tomas is innocent of Rut's vile deeds. Right at this point we can endure no lies. We have to know what and to whom Rut has already shared her accusations regarding Anna."

Catherine adds to the conversation, "I still don't understand how anyone can accuse an 8-year-old *clann* of casting evil spells and performing magic."

Catherine now has the difficult chore of telling Iain and Anna the whole story, a story that she has wanted to keep hidden from them for several more years. That evening after dinner Catherine gathers both of her *clanns* around the fire. Lach, who is easily aroused to fits of anxiety and anger, keeps away from Catherine's time with her *clanns*.

"Iain and Anna, come over and sit," invites Catherine. "I know that you have been wondering what has been troubling your *parantans*."

"Aye, *mathair*," Iain agrees.

"Anna, you have always questioned why I dye your red hair every month. I have not given you a good and honest answer, except to tell you that you needed to fit in with the rest of our kinfolk."

"Aye, *mathair*," agrees Anna. "I have not understood why you say that, but because you are my *mathair*, I accept it."

Catherine continues, "When you were born with red hair we were reminded of our clans' centuries' old beliefs that a red-head is born a witch. We did not want you to be shunned by our clansmen who believe in witches. We did not want them to think that you were born a black witch who would cast evil spells. Soon after your birth we met with our kinfolk and we all agreed that it would be best to hide the fact that you are a red-head."

185

"*Mathair*, I am not afraid of being shunned by our clan. I want to have the hair that I was born with," Anna reassures her *mathair*.

"You don't understand the whole of this terrible damning of red-heads," responds Catherine. "I do not mean to alarm you, but in the past it was very dangerous to be labelled a witch. Thousands of men and women were hung or burned at the stake if they were thought to be one. This practice had gone on for centuries until recently when it became illegal."

"However, Anna, a law does not abolish long-held beliefs," adds Catherine. "Any person believed by the clan to be a witch is shunned by them. They are so ridiculed that they do not feel welcomed in the village, at the *kirk*, *ceilidhs* or our annual festivals. Anna, we did not want this to be your fate. Thus, from the time you were baptized I dyed your hair. Our kinfolk supported the decision and everyone agreed to watch over you. In our midst, however, there has been a traitor."

"This brings us to what happened recently and why your *athair* and I have been so distressed," continues Catherine. "Recently Rut, your *piuthar-mathar,* has begun to make accusations about the fact that you are a red-head and therefore a witch. We are not sure how many she has told. We do know that she brought her accusations to the midwife, Sine. Sine has told us of this betrayal and she further explained that Rut wanted her to spread the allegations.

"Your *athair* has arranged a *coinneamh* with all our kinfolk to address Rut's betrayal." Catherine, generally a calm and patient woman, becomes more agitated as she shares with Anna and Iain the purpose of the *coinneamh*. Catherine, disclosing the challenges they are facing, then says, "At the *coinneamh* we will demand that the spreading of rumors about you being a witch stop. We hope that the rest of the kinfolk do not believe that you are a witch."

"But *Mathair,* I am not a witch," asserts Anna when Catherine has finished. "I would never cast evil spells on anyone."

"We understand that, Anna," shares Catherine. "The rest of the clan must believe the same so that you are safe. Right now I do not think it wise to stop dyeing your hair. Let's hear what our kinfolk says at the *coinneamh.*"

Iain, who has been silent during the whole conversation, adds his thoughts, "*Mathair*, this is unfair for Anna. There is no one who is as loving and kind as Anna. I will always protect Anna. Of that she can be confident."

43
Revelations

On this first morning in September the Macleans wake up to a blustery cold autumn day. It has been a week since Rut's accusations and the family is still troubled. Lach decided late last night that he could not work for the laird today and he hopes that his absence will not upset him too much. He is worried that the laird may find out about Rut's accusations.

The rest of the family is also uneasy this morning. Catherine, Iain and Anna try to go about their daily chores. Once finished Anna asks, "*Mathair*, I would like to go to the river."

"Anna, I would rather you not go there by yourself," replies Catherine. "I have some clothes to wash and you can join me. Hopefully Rut will not be there. I don't know if I can disguise my feelings." Catherine can see that Anna is troubled. She believes that she has given Anna a lot more information than she usually would, but she is worried that Anna is in real danger of being ostracized.

Iain tends the crops. The focus helps him cope with the angst he feels regarding the upcoming *coinneamh*. He knows in his heart that his *siuir* is not a witch, but he also knows how his clansmen feel about red hair. He will protect Anna no matter what.

The day passes slowly with everyone immersed in their thoughts about the *coinneamh*. What if the kinfolk join with Rut and agree with her? It is a thought too terrible to dwell on.

Finally, it is time for Catherine and Lach to depart for the *coinneamh*. They don their outer garments and say goodbye to Iain and Anna just before sunset. Lach carries a lit torch down the rocky path. They reach the *aite cruinneachaidh*. Upon entering, Catherine knows right away that she must quickly stoke the fire and add the additional peat that she and Lach have brought so the room will be comfortable and warm.

Both Catherine and Lach remember the *coinneamh* that Lach had organized eight years ago when Anna was born. "Lach, I am very wary of how our kinfolk will accept this claim by Rut. Do you think that it will make them doubt their own acceptance of the innocence of Anna as they were willing to do eight years ago?"

"Aye, I am also fearful as to whether they will continue to believe in the innocence of Anna. I pray that they will not buy into Rut's accusations," adds Lach. "Despite my apprehension, I feel ready to face our kinfolk."

"I hope they will be our allies and not our adversaries," continues Catherine.

"We must keep our hope and positive energy so that we will be able to confront Rut," Lach keeps the focus. Our Anna is worth fighting for."

Soon the kinfolk begin to arrive and settle around the fire. Lach, sensing it is finally time, begins "Thank you all for coming. As you know our *nighean*, Anna, was born more than eight years ago. I called you together at that time to help Catherine and me decide what would be best way to disguise her red hair. We were worried that she would be called a witch and wanted to protect her. Everyone agreed that dyeing her red hair and keeping a watch over her was the best plan." Lach continues, "Until recently, this remedy worked perfectly. Anna has become a happy and caring *clann* and she brings joy to all those around her. Unfortunately, someone in our glen has been spreading the rumor that Anna has been casting evil spells on our community of Inivea. That person is here tonight. I would like that person to speak up and share his or her concerns," adds Lach.

There is silence in the room until Seumus speaks up, "Lach and Catherine, are you sure about this accusation? I would not want one of our kin to be falsely condemned."

"Nor would I," Lach reassures his *brathair*.

Micheal, the *fear* of Marta, who had also had questions about Anna in the beginning, shares his thoughts, "I am still not convinced that Anna is not a witch, although I have not seen any evil spells that she might have cast on our community. I also would like to raise the question as to whether an eight-year-old should be accused of witchcraft. As far as I know no *clann* has ever been condemned as a witch. Although I am angry and dismayed that someone here would betray our trust, I would still like to hear the thoughts of the person who has been spreading the accusations."

Lili then speaks up, "I don't think any of our kinfolk should share witch rumors about our young Anna. I am surprised and shocked that anyone in our clan would take it upon themselves to report such damming accusations. I have seen no evidence that Anna has cast evil spells on anyone. I would also like to hear from the kinfolk who has done this. To me this is the evil person and not the *clann*, Anna."

Lach then adds the question to the dialogue, "Does anyone else have further thoughts on this serious matter of betrayal?"

"I would like to talk about my experiences with Anna," interjects Jannet. "I know Anna well. I was the midwife at her birthing. I agreed on the dyeing of her red hair so that she would not be labelled as a witch. She has been under my care many times and not once have I observed Anna to have the evil qualities of a black witch. Rather she has been a loving and caring *clann* ready to help others. I can attest to the fact that she is curious, always ready to explore the world around her. This curiosity sometimes gets her into trouble, like the time she got lost on the moor when she was 5 years old. Sometimes she would prefer to play and explore the woods and moor around her rather than work and help her *mathair*. These are not the characteristics of a witch, but rather the qualities of an inquisitive, playful and happy *clann*."

Suddenly Rut speaks, "I am the one who has been telling others about the witch, Anna."

Tomas looks incredulous and interrupts Rut, "You what? I have warned you in the past not to spread such unfounded rumors. Who have you told and what did you say?"

Defiantly Rut responds to her *fear*, "I have proof that Anna is a witch and that's what I told Sine. I wanted her to share the evidence of Anna's witchcraft with others so that they will be on their guard."

Tomas then demands from Rut, "What convinces you that Anna is a witch?"

Rut quickly responds while everyone sits in silence, stunned by the drama that is being played out in front of them,

"I am sure all of you remember the time that Anna got lost and many clansmen spent the day away from their chores. That is one proof of Anna's witchery, but it was not until I had evidence of another evil spell that I was convinced of her witchcraft. Eilidh was born strong and healthy to Isobel and Iain. Catherine, who is a good friend of her *parantans*, brought Anna to visit Eilidh and soon after Eilidh became ill. Poor Eilidh spent three difficult years being very ill until Anna cast another evil spell and she died."

It is at this point that Catherine interrupts Rut, "Rut, you are so wrong about the visit of Anna and me to Isobel and Iain. The first time that we saw Eilidh was at her baptism. It was a difficult winter of much snow and consequently we had delayed our visit due to the treacherous hike to the village. You have intentionally forgotten that her baptism was also delayed until February because of this weather and Eilidh's weakened condition. So, Rut, you have come to a wicked and wrong conclusion about Anna."

Rut was defensive, "I still believe that young Anna is a witch and the rest of our community should be warned."

Tomas interjects at this point, "Rut, I am alarmed by your accusations and very angry that you have inflicted this betrayal upon our clan. You will spread this evil about Anna no more. You will make a visit to Sine and any others and tell them the truth so that they will no longer think of her as evil. Your malicious thinking and betrayal have caused great humiliation for me and for our *clanns*. I no longer trust you to be loyal to the family and I think we will be making changes about our life here in Inivea." At this, Tomas demands that Rut leave the *coinneamh* with him.

Outside the *aite cruinneachaidh,* Tomas who is generally a non-confrontive man, verbally attacks Rut with rage, "Rut, you are an evil vindictive woman!! I repeat that I have lost my trust in you."

Rut is without words. She has never seen her *fear* so enraged. However, so committed to her beliefs, she does not apologize to Tomas.

Tomas continues, "You are not fit to be my *bean* or the *mathair* of our *clanns*.

After the departure of Tomas and Rut, the rest confirm their allegiance to Catherine and Lach. Seumus speaks up, "I am very angry with the maliciousness of Rut and the distrust of Anna and our family which she might have created in Inivea. Hopefully Sine was true to her word and she did not tell anyone else except Catherine about Rut's claims."

Catherine then states, "I think that Sine came to me as soon as Rut told her about Anna and I also trust that Rut has not had the opportunity to spread more rumors."

All the women gathered there agree with Catherine's assessment of the situation. "I know Sine well and I believe her to be loyal to our family," Jannet adds.

The annoying grumbles of the men present at the *coinneamh* can be heard in the undertones while all get ready to leave. Seumus shares the final thoughts, "We will continue to watch over Anna. As of now there is no proof that Anna is a witch and if Rut makes any more wicked accusations, we will defend Anna by stating that Rut is out of her mind. Meanwhile there are other things to be concerned about in our glen." At that final comment they all rise and silently leave the *coinneamh*.

On the path home Catherine shares, "In case Rut found time to spread her gossip about Anna, I am more convinced than ever that I must continue to dye Anna's hair. It is obvious that everyone was shocked by the events of today."

Lach replies, "I am sure that there will be more conversation about it in the days ahead."

Catherine states, "I wonder what Tomas meant by his final comment to Rut that he would be making changes to his family's life in Inivea?" Casting aside the question of Tomas's intention, Lach and Catherine become silent as they follow the rest of the clan until everyone reaches their *bothies*.

44

Rut and Thomas Maclean

The accusations of Rut Maclean have caused great disturbance in the household. The next day Tomas has a talk with her, "Rut, for your own purpose you jumped to conclusions. I don't understand why you didn't share your concerns with me before spreading these horrific rumors about Anna. Catherine has proven that she and Anna did not make a visit to Isobel until well after the time when Eilidh became ill. I expect you to visit those folks that you told these unfounded falsehoods and reveal your misjudgments about Anna. Hopefully these evil rumors will be forgotten in time."

Rut answers, "Tomas, I cannot understand why you and the rest of our kinfolk do not see that Anna is a red-headed witch. Why do you not fear the evil that Anna will cast on our community? I cannot forget this omen of Anna's birth even though she is only a child."

Tomas responds, "Rut, aye, we are all aware of the ancient beliefs. However, I have not witnessed any evidence which proves that Anna is casting evil spells. I am sure you know that it is a crime to accuse a person of practicing magic and if you didn't, I am telling you now. It is a sad that I no longer have confidence that you will stop spreading these rumors about Anna."

Tomas decides now is the time to tell Rut why he thinks they should move.

"The laird has told me that he is going to raise the rent again this year. We are already behind and he may tell us that we have to vacate the farm. Luke and Deidre are too young to help out so that I can seek labour elsewhere. I have been considering a move to the community of Tobermory where there are more ways to earn a living. "

Your recent actions have made the decision easier for me. Right now, I am sure we have much dishonor with the other clansmen. I am unable to find a way to explain your behavior to them, especially to Lach and Catherine. Before I decide to move our family for sure, I will be traveling to Tobermory to explore work opportunities."

Rut is stunned and questions, "Tomas, what kind of work opportunities would you get there?"

"I am not sure yet, but I know that they have fishing, kelp harvesting and farming opportunities. In the spring, before planting, I will make the trip to Tobermory."

"It will be good to get out of this village," decides Rut. "In Tobermory Anna's spells will no longer be able to reach us."

"I hope when we move to a new village you will forget about witches," implores Tomas. "Your wicked gossip is putting a black stain on our family."

45
A Foreboding

In the other Macleans' *bothies* there has been much conversation about Rut and her accusations. There is sympathy for the burden that Rut has created for Tomas. They are unaware of his newest plans about moving away from Inivea. Catherine and Lach, in particular, remain apprehensive about Rut. When they returned from the *coinneamh,* Anna and Iain were, of course, very anxious to hear what had happened. Catherine had told them that it was late and she would talk to them in the morning. Waiting is not easy for the *clanns* of Catherine and Lach. It has given more time for anger to fester in the mind and spirit of young Iain. Although only fourteen, the betrayal of Rut has brought out his warrior spirit.

While alone waiting for the return of their *parantans,* Iain announces to Anna, "I would like to take my sword and put it into the heart of Rut!"

A startled Anna responds, "Iain, you must not do that! We must wait until our *mathair* and *athair* return. I am sure they will tell us what we must do."

The next morning Iain and Anna awaken early eager for their conversation with their *mathair.* However, they know that they must wait until their *mathair* calls them, so they go out to the fields and continue harvesting crops. While Iain and Anna are busy in the fields, Catherine and Lach have a conversation.

Catherine speaks, "Lach, I am unsure about our next steps regarding these latest revelations. I know that first I must explain to Anna what happened at the *coinneamh* and that I must continue to dye her hair. Also, we must stay out of the presence of Rut."

Lach then responds, "Catherine, I think for now it is best that we wait and see. Tomas, I am sure, has taken some action regarding Rut."

"You are right Lach," agrees Catherine. As Lach leaves, he hopes the Laird has not found out about why he was absent. Catherine also is thinking of the future. She hopes that Tomas can find a way to control Rut. But for now, she must push these thoughts to the back of her mind and begin her day's chores.

Anna and Iain spend the early hours of the morning filling numerous baskets with potatoes, turnips, kale and oats to be stored for the winter. As they work Iain continues to murmur his disdain for Rut.

Soon they both hear the call of their *mathair*, "Iain and Anna, bring your filled baskets and come here." They rush home. Anna hopes her *mathair* will help Iain deal with his anger.

Catherine greets them at the door and after they have taken care of the baskets, invites them to sit around the fire. The *clanns* wait impatiently for her first words. "Anna and Iain, I first want to assure you that things went well last night. Rut will no longer gossip about Anna and Tomas will make sure of that.

Anna replies, "This is good *mathair*, but what did the others say about Rut's rumors?" Before Catherine could reply, Iain, who has been filled with rage since he found out about Rut's lies, sputters, "*Mathair*, I would like to take my sword and pierce Rut's heart."

Catherine is alarmed but calm, "Iain, I know you are very angry about what Rut has done. The rest of our kinfolk, however, said that they do not see any evidence that Anna is practicing witchcraft. Your *athair* and I will not allow you to do something that you will regret. Although Rut has betrayed our family, Macleans do not retaliate in the way that you are suggesting. The best way that you can support your *siuir* is to remain her protective big *brathair*. She will keep you busy in that role." Iain leaves in a huff. In his mind the situation has not been resolved and he wonders if there is something he can do to stop the wildfire of Rut's accusations.

All through the rest of September and October Iain remains quiet. Tomas has not yet announced to his kinfolk that he plans on moving his family to Tobermory to seek new work.

For her part Rut understands that Tomas remains very angry with her. She carries out his orders immediately and visits Sine to explain that she had misjudged young Anna. Thanks to Sine's quick thinking, Rut had not had the opportunity to share her gossip with anyone else.

46
Seathan and Iain

The usual celebratory mood of anticipating the return of Seathan from the summer pasture and upcoming *Samhain Festival* is overshadowed by the uneasiness created by Rut. On the morning of October 31st, Iain volunteers to fetch Seathan and the cows from the summer pasture. Iain wants Seathan all to himself so he can tell him about Rut and Anna. In the morning he sets out in a dense fog. At first the going is difficult. He takes his time so as not to get lost in the growth of the summer. When the fog lifts and Iain spots Seathan close by.

"Seathan, I'm here" Iain calls out.

Seathan, hearing his *brathair's* voice, answers, "The cows and I are ready to return home. "It has been a long summer," he adds. Together they herd the cows and lead them back home.

On the way Iain speaks, "Seathan, I volunteered to fetch you from the summer pasture. I want to share with you what has happened."

"Iain, our *athair* has already told me about the betrayal of Rut and how upset everyone is. Do you have something more to add?"

"Our *athair* does not know I am so angry with the betrayal of Rut that I would like to stab her with my *dirk*. I have never felt that way before."

"Iain, I know how angry you are because I feel the same, but we must control ourselves. I don't like hearing you consider such a violent act. Is this something that you have been truly contemplating as a plan?"

"Aye, I have," replies Iain.

"Iain, you are now 14 years old and just beginning your journey of manhood. There will be much more appropriate ways for you to use warrior skills later in your life. Does our *mathair* know how angry you are?"

"Aye, she told me that she and *athair* are horrified and will stop me. I know that I cannot go against my *parantans'* orders no matter how much rage I feel."

"I agree, Iain," warned Seathan. "It will soon be winter and harboring these angry feelings will be very difficult for you. Wait awhile. Situations often find their own way of working out." Seathan knows that soon he will no longer be Iain's confidant. He hopes that before he leaves to join the Army, Iain will understand that taking Rut's punishment upon himself is a futile endeavor.

As they trek back to the glen Iain looks across the valley and contemplates what Seathan has said. He can see the bonfires are lit and the flames are reaching skyward. As they descend the hill they are joined by the other families with their cows. Iain slows his pace so that he can take up the rear and guide any laggards. They join the others in a line to guide the animals between the two bonfires. Once through the passage of the two bonfires Seathan and Iain prod the cows to the winter pasture. They meet Lach at the winter pasture who is waiting to choose two cows to sell and one to slaughter.

While Lach remains in the winter pasture, Seathan and Iain take leave and head back to their *bothie*. While examining his cattle, Tomas unexpectedly appears. At first Lach feels cool towards Tomas as the betrayal of Rut lingers. Tomas breaks the silence, "Lach, I want you to know of my decision before I tell the rest. I know that you and Catherine must be very angry about Rut's betrayal of Anna and I don't blame you. I am very angry with her also. I do not want Rut to be involved in any more vicious lies about Anna."

"It has also become very difficult to support my family here. The laird has assured me that he is going to raise my rent and I am already behind. So, I have made a decision to take my family away from Inivea." My thought is to explore the opportunities in Tobermory. Recently, the British Fisheries Society have been enlarging the town by building a small pier, a Customs House and an Inn. I hope to go there in the spring. I have been thinking about a move for quite a while now and Rut's difficulties have quickly pointed me in this direction."

Lach is taken by surprise, "Of course, Tomas, we do not want Rut to spread any more falsehoods about Anna, but we also will be sad to see you move out of our glen. The Macleans are a close family and we do not like to lose one of our own."

"I know that Lach," responds Tomas. "But I must make changes for the good of my family."

"If there is any way we can help, you let us know. Meanwhile, I know the rest of our kinfolk will agree to help you with a move if that is your decision."

Seathan and Iain soon arrive home and they greet their *mathair* and Anna as well as Caitriona who has come up from the village to join the celebration. Seathan has missed his family this summer and is happy to see them. However, he silently decides that he will wait until the next day before he shares his news with them.

Lach returns soon after his meeting with Tomas and now that all are home, Catherine invites them to the fire, "Come and sit." She then asks the souls of the dead to join them, "Come our dead ones, a place is set for you also." Catherine has prepared a feast. They all are grateful for such an abundant harvest.

Much later at midnight there is a parade of young men coming to their *bothie* disguised in costumes, reciting verses in exchange for food. Iain has left already to join in the ritual.

The next day Seathan finds a chance to talk to his *parantans*, "*Mathair* and *athair*, as you know, I have been eager to become a warrior and join the Highland regiment of the British Army. I am now 21 years old and have made the decision to travel to Tobermory in the spring and sign up with the 5th Duke of Argyll as an enlistee."

Catherine and Lach exchange a knowing glance. They are not surprised by Seathan's announcement. They had been anticipating it for a couple of years now. They are, however, grateful that he had stayed as long as he did.

Catherine supports his decision, "Seathan, we have been expecting this announcement from you for a while now. Although we will miss you very much, we feel that it is important for you to follow your dreams. We know you would not be happy here if you stayed."

"*Mathair*, I know that you understand, but I also know the hardships you face. To make life easier I will try to send you some money as I receive it to ease your burdens."

"Thank you, Seathan," respond both Catherine and Lach. "Take care of yourself first," adds Lach. "We will be all right."

Not quite finished, Seathan shares, "I have one more concern. Iain is very angry, and I am particularly worried about him."

"We are mindful of this, Seathan," replies Lach.

"I think that Iain misses your guidance, *athair*," asserts Seathan. "When I was Iain's age you spent so much time with me, sharing stories and teaching me."

"This is true, Seathan," answers Lach. "I hope to cut down on my work with the laird so that I can spend more time with him."

"In addition, Rut will soon no longer be a problem for him," shares Lach. "Tomas has just told me that he hopes to move his family to Tobermory in the spring. This will remove Rut from spying on Anna." Hearing this news, both Catherine and Seathan sigh in relief.

"I will share this news immediately with our other *clanns* so that they will also have peace," announces Catherine. True to his word Tomas shares his decision with his other kin about exploring work options in Tobermory in hopes that he can move his family there. The word spreads quickly throughout Inivea. Most are not sad when they think about Rut leaving their community.

With the help of his kinfolk, Tomas and Rut moved to Tobermory in the spring as promised. Six months later, Seathan left.

47
The Marriage

Since the business with Rut, Sine has been withdrawn. She felt that it was partially her fault that Tomas and Rut had to leave Inivea. She has been spending a lot of time alone. One day someone unexpectedly knocks on her door. Sine, not knowing who was there, opens the door to the figure of Pastor Robertson. "May I come in?" he asks.

Startled by this surprise visit, Sine is tempted to speak with him outside, but it is now winter and instead she invites him in, "Aye, come over and sit by the fire. What brings you here?" The pastor responds, "Sine, I know this is highly unusual, but I find that I can think of no other way to get to know you better. Will you come over to my home after the next Sabbath and have lunch with me? My housekeeper makes a very nice meal."

Nervous and thrilled at the same time Sine answers, "But, Pastor Robertson, what will your other parishioners say?"

"Sine, I am not sure but I believe it is important for us to get to know each other better." Pastor Robertson then adds, "I hope you agree. My housekeeper will be there to chaperone us, so you have nothing to fear."

"I also want to know you more," Sine answers. "So as not to raise suspicions I will come to your home about an hour after the service ends."

Lunch at Pastor Robertson's manse on that cold winter afternoon begins their courtship. The housekeeper makes the lovely lunch as the pastor had promised. She has also agreed to keep their secret. Through the winter the pastor and Sine have frequent get-togethers at the manse.

One spring day Pastor Robertson asks Sine, "Let's hike in the moor this afternoon. It is a beautiful warm spring day."

"Aye, I will leave at noon and meet you," Sine happily agrees to the suggestion. "I will pack a bundle of cheese and bread which we can have before we return back," adds Sine.

Thus begins a ritual of hiking together on the moor through the spring months. On these walks they exchange sweet words of the love they have for one another. One beautiful day as the pair were nearing the village, their romantic idyllic time together was turned into sorrow when they hear the toll of the bell from the village. Since there were no imminent births or current celebrations in Inivea, this could only mean one thing; someone has died. Both Sine and the pastor know immediately the meaning. So as not to cause gossip, Pastor Robertson leaves Sine and heads quickly to the village. Sine lingers for a while, wondering about the person whose death was just announced.

Word of Sine's mentor and friend's death has already spread through the village by the time Sine arrives back. In the past few months Jannet had become frail and sickly. Caught up in her own love life Sine realizes now that she had not paid enough attention to the demise of her beloved Jannet. A great sadness permeates her being for this great loss in her life. The reality also sets in that she will be solely responsible for the midwifery role in the village. Without her mentor this is a huge responsibility. In the past she always had Jannet to rely on if there were problems.

Jannet was a prominent and well-loved woman in the glen and in the village. There will be great mourning and after an enormous funeral celebration. Sine feeling alone and abandoned slowly walks to her *bothie*. The late afternoon shadows deepen her feelings of emptiness and despair.

After the funeral of Jannet, Sine and Pastor Robertson continue their secret hikes through the moor. These romantic meetings lift Sine's spirits. Then one afternoon on their hike Pastor Robertson suddenly stops. Hidden in the growth of the meadows, Pastor Robertson proposes, "Sine, will you marry me?"

"Aye, John Robertson, I will," responds an adoring Sine.

One Sabbath day after preaching Pastor Robertson finally shares that he and Sine are going to wed. Unlike the usual reverent atmosphere of silence and prayer, the parishioners begin to clap with this not so unexpected announcement. Unbeknownst to them the parishioners had been observing their developing friendship and courtship. They wonder why it took them so long to declare their plans to wed. On the way out after the service each parishioner lovingly greets them.

Pastor Lindsay, from Dervaig, is asked to marry the couple and on a beautiful August Saturday all the parishioners come in their best clothes to witness the wedding of Pastor John Robertson and Sine Campbell. Pastor Robertson's *parantans* and siblings had travelled from Edinburg to see their *mac* and *brathair* marry at last. At the end of the ceremony Pastor Robertson's *siuir,* accompanied by a fiddler, sings "*Auld Lang Syne*" in Gaelic, her wedding gift to the newlyweds. The villagers and farmers are thrilled to hear their favorite hymn sung in their native tongue. After the ceremony a huge feast prepared by the congregation is waiting outside for the couple and the wedding guests. While feasting the fiddler plays many of the Highlanders favorite Scottish folk tunes.

The Maclean family is gathered in a small group, chatting about the ceremony and listening to the music, when Sine comes over to them. "Sine, we are so happy for you and Pastor Robertson," declares Catherine. She embraces Sine with a loving hug.

"Thank you, Catherine, I am so glad that you could be here to share in my joy, but there is one person missing," adds Sine. "I so wish that Jannet, my teacher and dear friend, was around to share the joy of my wedding."

Anna then joins in the conversation, "Aye we all miss her very much, but she is not missing your celebration. I know that she is happily looking down from heaven watching and cheering. She is with us and with you."

"Aye," all agree with Anna and glance upward at the heavens.

48

Anna, the Healer and the Witch

On a warm late August morning with a brilliant red sunrise, Anna, now 13 years old, calls to her *mathair*, "I am going to the village for my training with Beitris."

"Be careful Anna, it looks as if it might storm in the afternoon. The red skies in the morning today were beautiful but warn of us of a storm." Anna, who is well acquainted with the frequent storms of the Isle, does not fear them.

"I will be careful. After my training with Beitris, I want to visit Isobel and see how she is doing with her *torrach* time. I will also stop in and spend time with Caitriona and if a storm arises and becomes too violent, I will stay with her and Flora until the storm ends, or overnight if need be. Do not worry about me *Mathair*."

With that Anna dons her protective cloak and *snood* (head covering of a maiden) gathers the sack full of herbs that she had collected through the summer months and takes off. The trip to the village takes Anna about an hour. She walks in a leisurely manner admiring the beauty of her glen. It is the season of the heather which casts a magical red-purple glow on the landscape. She admires the flocks of birds around her. The butterflies are abundant and make her trek to the village one of delight.

In this small village the *bothies* are close together. Anna passes by some villagers who are outside their homes visiting and watching their *clanns* chasing each other in a game of tag. Some stop and wave to Anna.

Anna arrives at Beitris's *bothie* and knocks on her door. Beitris smiles as she greets Anna, but her smiles do not hide her aged face and body. She has a mass of grey hair which she ties back with a rag. Her face is lined and sallow and her eyes have deep shadows. Anna remarks to herself, "Beitris appears more stooped over than ever. I wonder if she is ailing?"

Despite her fragile appearance Beitris is happy to see young Anna.

Anna is a quick learner and she is glad to pass on her secrets to such a gifted and avid student. "How are you Anna," Beitris greets her.

"I am ready to learn more about herbs," responds Anna. "During the summer I have been collecting."

"Come over to my fire, show me what you have found and I will explain their uses," invites Beitris.

Anna eagerly joins her at the fire where Beitris offers Anna a bowl of herbal tea and some cheese and bread. Once settled by the fire Anna pulls out her sack and begins to show Beitris each plant that she has found. Beitris holds out her hand and asks, "May I?" Anna hands over the sack to Beitris.

"I am going to separate your herbs into categories of healing so that it will help you to learn them more easily." While Anna drinks and eats, Beitris is busy taking out each plant and arranging them into piles.

When she finishes she puts one pile on her lap and comments, "This is good Anna. You have found some of the most beneficial herbs for curing digestive issues." She holds up the *blaeberry*, "This herb soothes ordinary stomach discomforts." She also adds, "It's other healing qualities are the curing of throat and mouth infections and helping to improve eyesight." Beitris then proceeds to hold up two other plants, "*Common Centaury, and Tormentil* are other plants that also help with stomach issues."

Anna, excited to learn more, questions Beitris, "My *athair* is suffering a severe darkness. Do you have any plants that can help with this condition?"

"Anna, your *athair's* issues are very prevalent. I believe it has to do with the fear of eviction and loss of work. You have brought a few of the plants which I have given to help those symptoms." Beitris then holds up *Scots Oregano,* and *Common Valerian.* "However, I must remind you that these herbs generally do not completely eliminate the darkness you talk about, but they help."

"The *Common Valerian* is a potent plant and should not be given by a young novice such as you. If your *athair* agrees, it could be administered by me. He would need to visit me weekly. If you collect this plant I will not charge him much for this service. You can administer the *Scots Oregano* by yourself though with no danger. It has a spicy flavor and could be added to some of his food. Another plant for helping with the symptoms you described is the *Roseroot* which is growing high on the sea cliffs of our Isle. Before you leave I will show you what this plant looks like. Due to its location you must be very careful when you attempt to find it and harvest it. I would suggest you bring your *brathair*, Iain, to help you with this task."

"Beitris, you have two other piles. What are those plants used for?" questions Anna.

"Well the plants in this smaller pile, as far as I know, have no medicinal uses," responds Beitris. "In the other pile are plants that help with a variety of infections. This one is the *Frog Berry* which is good for infections of the urinary tract. This other plant, the *Crowberry,* is good for reducing cold and coughs. You are familiar with garlic which we all use to make some of our food taste better. It has been known for a long time that this plant also has general health giving and medicinal properties."

Beitris then ends her session, "Anna, you have made a good start in collecting some healing plants. It takes a healer a long time to learn her trade. I warn you not to become bold in the practice. I will let you know when you are ready. You may, however, with my supervision carry out the recommendations I have given you for your *athair*. The most important advice is to urge him to come to me for the administration of the *Common Valerian.* Continue to search in the fields and woodlands. Keep the plants separated in their own sacks and you will then be able to learn their names and qualities. Return to me when you have new plants." Beitris then goes over to her cupboard and selects the *Roseroot* herb. "Anna, here is the *Roseroot* which I have warned you is very difficult to reach. Remember, don't climb the sea cliffs without Iain's help."

Anna responds, "I appreciate your instruction and will return to learn more soon. I will also ask my *mathair* to recommend to my *athair* about coming to you for the *Common Valerian.* My *athair* will listen to her more than to his young *nighean*. As Anna opens the door she notices and remarks to Beitris, "It has begun to rain. I will stay overnight with Caitriona, if the storm becomes bad. Goodbye."

"Goodbye, Anna," Beitris says, quickly closing the door so that the rain does not get into her home.

The path to Flora's shop is already muddy and slippery. Anna rushes and quickly arrives at the big wooden door of Flora's shop and knocks. Flora comes to the door immediately and welcomes her.

Caitriona, hard at work at her loom, sees her *siuir*, "Oh, Anna, it is so nice of you to come for a visit. I have been yearning to be with my family. I have missed services at our *kirk* because there has been so much work. Now that I am the only apprentice the work takes us much time."

Before she speaks Anna notices the beautiful *plaids* scattered over the tables in the room. Caitriona is weaving a Maclean *plaid.* The dyed red and green yarn makes a beautiful pattern and when finished the material will be returned to the owners so that a tartan can be sewn.

Anna feels pride for her older *siuir* and she responds lovingly, "Caitriona, we have missed you too. We hope that you will be able to take a day off soon to visit us."

Catriona aware that Flora is listening chooses her words carefully, "I think once winter comes our work will slow down and I will be able to come to a few festivals."

Flora jumps in, "Aye, Caitriona, I am sure that our work will slow down and you will be able to enjoy all those visits that you have been missing. For now let us all enjoy an afternoon tea together."

The three then sit near the fire and use the time for catch up. Anna then has a surprise for her *siuir,* "Caitriona, I almost forgot. Here in my sack is a new petticoat that our *mathair* made for you from the cloth you had woven."

"Oh, this is so pretty. Tell our *mathair* how much I love it," admires Caitriona.

"May I see it?" interjects Flora. "Aye, this is a beautiful petticoat and the fabric is so finely woven." Then Flora speaks directly to her worker, "Caitriona, you have been my best apprentice and I am so pleased that you are now my full-time employee."

It is now late afternoon and the storm has not abated. Anna realizes that it is best if she remains with her host for the night. There is always an extra bed in the shop and Flora's cupboard is well stocked with provisions for a hearty meal. Caitriona continues weaving while Flora and Anna prepare the food. Flora begins a conversation with news, "Isobel will be delivering another *bairn* in October."

Flora continues, "I believe that Isobel never completely recovered from the death of her little *nighean,* Eilidh. She loves her macs deeply but knew she would never have the same relationship that your *mathair* has with you."

The prospect of having a new *bairn* in their community is always big news. Flora adds, "It was a surprise to Isobel that she was *torrach* again. It has been five years since the death of Eilidh and Isobel is now older."

"I will be visiting her tomorrow in the morn to see how she is doing," adds Anna. "My *mathair* is eager for any news I can return with." And with that Flora calls everyone to sit as she dishes out the prepared meal onto their wooden plates. They all eat quietly as they listen to the raging storm outside. Anna remarks, "I didn't realize how hungry I was. Thank you, Flora, for your hospitality."

Flora quickly replies, "Anna, you are always welcome to visit your *siuir* at my shop."

Soon after the meal is finished all, especially Anna, realize how sleepy they are. The decision had already been made for Anna to stay overnight at Flora's shop and Anna is the first to announce her sleep needs, "Flora, I have had a busy day and I am ready to retire. Will you show me my bed?"

"I will grab some bed quilts from the cupboard. Your bed is over here away from the looms," instructs Flora.

Gratefully, Anna follows Flora to her bed and after undressing, plops wearily down upon the cozy quilts.

Anna has a troubled sleep with nightmares about the unborn *bairn* of Isobel. Anna can remember only parts of her dream, but what she can recollect is disturbing. In her dreams she sees a newborn *bairn* being snatched by a monster and when she awakens the next morning, Anna believes her dream to be an omen. She quickly decides to skip her visit to Isobel. Instead she will rush home and tell her *mathair* about her dream. She knows that her *mathair* will understand. The accusations when Eilidh died have never left her. She keeps her thoughts and fears to herself and says a hasty goodbye to Caitriona and Flora, thanking them for their hospitality.

The storm, which ceased sometime in the early morning, has left the village looking and feeling cleansed. There is still a morning mist hovering over the *bothies* and shops. Anna looks over to the stone *kirk* and she notices the simplicity of the humble structure. Beside it is the graveyard. She remembers her *seanmhair* dying after declining in health and she has an aching in her heart for her. There was a great sadness in all of Inivea when she died. With the memories of both her *seanmhair* and Eilidh coming to the surface, Anna decides to go to the fence and the locked gate to look over the tombstones. She yearns to go inside and touch the tombstones, but she knows that women are not allowed inside. She is agile enough to climb over the fence but she thinks better of it. She does not need anyone else condemning her and accusing her of black magic.

She lingers for a while with her memories. She thinks of when she cuddled in her *seanmhair's* lap while she told her folk tales and sang her lullabies. She remembers holding her *seanmhair's* bony and calloused hand as they traipsed through the moor and woodland, searching for herbs. Her *seanmhair* was more like a *mathair* to her. She was always with her when Catherine was busy in the garden. Anna's list of her *seanmhair's* blessings in her life could go on and on. Someday she might ask Donald, who has begun learning to read and write, to record some of her memories.

While standing at the graveyard Anna also recalled the sweetness and bravery of little Eilidh. Despite her illness she was always cheerful and had a smile. It was as if she had been sent to this world to help folks remember that there were good things in life to be thankful for. How she wishes that Eilidh had lived. They would have been good friends and have fun playing on the moor. She would have shown Eilidh what she had discovered in her glen; the birds, the butterflies and the plants. Eilidh would be her little *siuir*. Suddenly Anna comes back to her reality and realizes that the village is beginning to buzz with activity. With a certain heaviness of heart, she makes her way back home.

49
Seathan Comes Home

Anna arrives back at her *bothie*, somewhat downhearted. Each day she realizes more and more how her red hair has affected her life. When she opens the heavy wooden door, ready to tell her *mathair* how she is feeling, her *mathair* is nowhere to be found. She wonders, "Perhaps she was kneeling in the garden and I missed her." Anna quickly goes outside and scans the garden. After several minutes of looking and calling she realizes that Catherine is not close by. "Maybe she has gone to the river to wash clothes," Anna reflects on.

She decides to head back inside, wondering what she will do until her *mathair* returns. She looks over the room and spots enough shallow dishes of milk to make butter. The cream has been settling to the top for a few days and is perfect for churning. She takes a wooden skimmer hanging on a nail by the cupboard and skims the cream. She then pours the cream into the wooden churner, a lengthy and laborious task, but perfect for her mood right now. The monotonous motion gives her something to focus on instead of the curse of her red hair. One day she is going to abandon dyeing her hair and not worry about being called a witch. Right now though she does not feel courageous enough.

After a while Anna hears the telling sound of a pop which means that the butter is coming. She takes off the lid and with a small flat board she scrapes down the sides and the lid to prevent waste. When the butter is fully come, the buttermilk which has been formed is poured off. As Anna is pouring off the butter milk, she hears the door opening. It is her *mathair*. "Hi Anna," she exclaims. "It is good to have you home."

"I spent the night with Caitriona and Flora so as not to come home in the storm," replies Anna.

"That is what your *athair* and I believed." Catherine comes over to the churn.

"Where have you been, *mathair*?" queries Anna. I have been waiting for you for a while now."

Catherine answers, "I took a walk into the moor. The rain last night has left the meadows with a freshness of sweet smells and bright colors."

She then motions that she wants to assist Anna with the final steps of churning. She takes some fresh spring water and pours it into the churn. Anna plunges the churn with the new fresh water for a minute or two. The steps are repeated several times until the fluid poured from the churn has no more milkiness.

While working they chat. Catherine speaks first, "Tell me about your visits."

Anna then lifts the butter out of the churn, places it on a wooden slab and responds to her *mathair*, "I had a very nice visit with Caitriona and Flora. My *siuir* is so clever. She weaves beautiful *plaid* cloths."

"Aye, I have seen her work and Flora is very happy with her," adds Catherine. At this point Catherine salts the butter. After years of experience Catherine knows just how much salt to add which will please the family.

As Anna takes a moist cloth and presses all the moisture from the butter she continues, "Caitriona has such a large work load right now that she must work long hours. She misses her visits with us."

"Aye, we have been missing her also," replies Catherine.

"Flora says that in the winter the work will slow down and Caitriona will be able to come home and attend services," adds Anna.

"We look forward to that time. I am glad she is doing so well," agrees Catherine.

Catherine and Anna leave the butter to give it time to dry and become firm. Later Catherine and Anna will flatten the butter with boards, making it into rolls for use by the family.

"*Mathair*, I did not visit Isobel and her family," reports Anna.

"And why is that Anna?" questions Catherine. "*Mathair*, do you not remember Rut's accusations?"

"Aye, Anna, of course I remember," answers Catherine.

"Even though Rut has left our glen, I do not want anyone accusing me of witchcraft with the unborn *bairn* of Isobel. I will stay away from this *bairn* until at least after its baptism."

"I do not like to hear this Anna, but I know that you are right," acknowledges Catherine. "You were wise to think of this plan."

"It makes me sad but it comes from feeling threatened for much of my life."

Catherine is silent. She knows how much her young *nighean* has

212

suffered through no fault of her own. While they are sitting quietly they hear some commotion outside. Catherine rises and go towards the door, she opens it and is startled by the sight in front of her. Anna joins her. There stands Seathan, weary but glowing, holding the hand of a young lady. Seathan speaks first, "*Mathair*, Anna, this is Rose, my *bean*."

Dumbstruck both Catherine and Anna rush closer to and embrace them. "We are so happy to see you and this unexpected visit is beyond our dreams," exclaims Catherine. Catherine quickly motions to them, "Sit down by the fire and tell us all."

Seathan recounts his life up to this point, "After I enlisted I traveled to Edinburgh to join my regiment. I spent a year in the barracks of my regiment, training to be a Highland soldier in the British Army. The training was grueling, but thanks to the warrior training by my *athair* and my rugged life here, I had the stamina for it. We were then sent overseas to Flanders to fight the French. We joined the contingents of Hanover; the Dutch, Hessian, Austrian and Prussian. In the long run we were unable to defeat the French. I was then sent to Holland and once again our British army was defeated. We were evacuated and in 1796 I returned to Edinburgh with the rest of my regiment."

"Since then our regiment has been in Edinburgh. I met Rose there while enjoying some of my leave in a pub where she was waiting on tables. It was not the easiest environment for a young lassie such as Rose, but I could see she could handle it. That was one of the things that caught my attention. It took me several times to get her to notice me."

While Seathan is recounting his tale, Anna has a chance to look over her new *piuthar-cheile* (sister-in-law). When Seathan and Rose entered Anna noticed right away, "My, she is tall, taller than most of the Macleans, even the menfolk," she ponders. "In fact she is several inches taller than Seathan. She definitely does not resemble the figures of my clansmen who are short and muscular. She has more delicate features and her skin is fair and freckled." The most startling feature for Anna was Rose's straight chestnut-colored hair, a dark red-brown hue. Anna questions silently, "Another red-head in our family?" Anna continues her mindful observations of Rose, "She has large brown eyes somewhat piercing, but trustworthy nonetheless." Anna believes that Seathan has made a good choice for his mate.

While Anna was thinking, Seathan had been sharing his tale, "After a while Rose brought me to her home where I met her family. They lived in the most unpleasant environment in the slums. The living conditions are horrendous; crowded, filthy and very poor. Her *parantans* shared with me that they had left their croft farm hoping for a better life. They found work in one of the many factories in Edinburgh and continued to raise their family. Rose, the oldest, was forced to find work where she could and most of her income went to help her family."

Rose then interjects, "I did the best I could to help my family but it was very difficult. I did not like seeing my family in these conditions and was troubled by them. We thought about moving to North America, but we have not been able to raise enough money to pay for our passage. Seathan and I have talked about someday moving to North America, but he believed that he had to fulfill his obligations to the British Army."

Seathan continues, "We decided several months ago to get married in a small parish in Edinburgh. I sent a post to you. I can tell by your astonishment when we arrived with Rose that you did not receive it. The Army had given me a couple of weeks of leave to visit my family. We left Edinburgh and traveled to get passage on a small boat to Tobermory. There I rented a horse and cart which brought us here to Inivea. We arrived in Inivea just about an hour ago. We quickly travelled up the trail to visit you."

Catherine lovingly acknowledges her *mac* and his new *bean*, "We are so ecstatic that you made this trip. Your *athair* will be delighted. And perhaps you can visit Iain at the summer pasture before you leave. He would not be happy if he misses you."

"It must have been a long and tiring trip and I am sure that you are hungry," Catherine invites the young couple to have some tea with bread and cheese. "Later I will fix a large feast when Lach comes back. He will want to catch up with all your news. Anna, perhaps you can alert all our kinfolk about this unexpected and joyous visit. Let them know that we will plan a *ceilidh* very soon for the new couple so that they can all meet them."

Anna finishes the refreshment, leaves them and then makes her way to each of her kinfolk in the glen. As she traipses to each *bothie* she resumes her thoughts about Rose, "I wonder how our kin will accept Rose, the red-head. Will she be treated suspiciously and given a lukewarm reception by everyone? Anna decides to keep her thoughts and fears to herself. She will tell all of the arrival of Seathan and his new *bean* and let her kinfolk have their own opinions.

50
Seathan Tells the Truth

Lach soon arrives home and he happily greets his eldest *mac* and the lassie by his side. Seathan quickly introduces his *athair* to his first *bean mhic* (daughter-in-law). Lach is overjoyed by this unexpected visit. Soon they all gather around the fire with the festive meal that Catherine and Anna have prepared for their expanded family. Lach gratefully gives the blessing. While they eat, Lach asks Seathan, "Fill me in on what you have already told the others and share with me all that has happened since you met Rose." After Seathan shares about his life before he met Rose, he continues with the rest of his story, "*Athair*, initially Rose was going to join me in the Army after we married which is often done. I shared with Rose and her family the life of hardship of an infantry man while on campaign. I told them that we were often forced to sleep in the open with only our blankets and greatcoats for warmth. Conditions of army life were just as horrendous for the *beans* who were forced to wash, cook and more. Only 6 *beans* would be chosen by ballot to accompany their *fears.*"

"After sharing the reality of army life with my *ann an laghs* (in-laws), I decided that I would not take the risk of either needing to leave Rose behind or exposing her to the conditions of army life. So I made a decision to desert the army. Rose's family agreed and hid us until we were married, bringing us to now. After our visit here, we will travel to Tobermory and wait for passage on a ship to North America where we hope to build a better life. We have saved some money for passage and, if not enough, I will work in Tobermory or on the ship,"

While everyone is shocked, Lach is particularly stunned. In the tradition of the Highland clans desertion is a shameful and dangerous decision. Lach is the first to speak, "Seathan, I am dismayed by your careless decision to desert your Highland regiment."

Seathan speaks directly to his *athair*, "I feared that might be your response, but I have to do what is best for Rose and our marriage. If

215

it were me alone I would not make such a decision, but I cannot expose Rose to army life. I have seen many die, including the *beans,* and I don't want that to be her fate."

"I hope that you will come to understand," Seathan continues. "Life for a soldier in the British Army is a much crueler and hopeless life than it was for you here. Our clan battles were mostly fought on Scottish soil and your ancestors were always able to return home after battle. The only way to leave the British Army is through death or desertion. It is a lifelong commitment. I hope that someday you will accept Rose's and my choice." There was great uneasiness in the Lach household.

Catherine, the peacemaker, encourages Lach to sleep on it and when he leaves she whispers to Seathan and Rose, "Let's go outside and look at the sunset."

Once outside Catherine adds support to Seathan and Rose's decision, "Rose, I am glad that Seathan has found you. Seathan, I am very sad that you and Rose must leave our Isle, but I do understand that the conditions here are dire or you would not be doing this. You must find a better life for yourselves and I hope that will be in North America. I am sure that deciding to desert must have been very difficult for you, but I also realize that you are making the choice that you believe you must. Perhaps someday we will all be together somewhere in North America." All, including the younger *clanns,* Iain and Anna, who had decided to follow the others outside, were silent during Catherine's comments.

Seathan ended the evening's conversation by sharing, *"Mathair,* I am happy that you are not angry with me and that you have welcomed Rose into our family." After this comment, they remain outside for a while watching the sunset until it got dark and then they went inside to their beds, hopeful that they would have a brighter tomorrow.

The next morning Rose and Seathan wake up early to set out to the summer pastures to visit Iain. They are glad to be out before the others. Seathan is eager to see Iain again after such a long absence and to introduce his Rose to him. Before Seathan and Rose depart for the summer meadows, he picks up the sack of refreshment that his *mathair* had packed for them. The bundle also contains supplies to replenish his *brathair's* food supply. As they open the heavy wooden door they observe the early morning dew which has covered the meadows. Before they begin their trek, they take in several deep breaths of the fresh Highland air.

After several hours of hiking Seathan spots Iain in the distant meadow, tending the livestock. Excitedly he points out the far away figure of his *brathair* to Rose. He knows that if he calls Iain right now his voice will be lost due to the distance and the wind. He waits until they are closer and then yells, "Iain, it is Seathan, your *brathair*."

At first Iain, who is focused on his cattle, does not hear Seathan's call. Seathan shouts again, "Iain, it is Seathan come from far away to visit you."

Iain hears this, stops what he is doing and begins to run toward Seathan and Rose. "*Brathair, brathair*, is it really you?" exclaims Iain. "I can't believe it is you!" Iain and Seathan finally reach other and embrace. As they head up the hill Iain immediately inquires, "And who is this that you have brought with you after such a long absence?"

Seathan answers, "Iain, this is my new *bean,* Rose. Throughout our long journey she has told me of her eagerness to meet you."

"Hello, Rose," Iain extends his warmth to his new *piuthar-cheile* with an embrace.

Rose replies, "Hello, Iain. I am so happy to meet you after such a long time of hearing about your family." Seathan then encourages them to proceed up the hill to the *shieling*.

Once they reach there they sit on the ground in front of it. Seathan takes out the meal packed by his *mathair.* After everyone eats, it is then that Iain asks to hear Seathan and Rose's story. Once again Seathan relates his experiences in the Highland Regiment and the meeting of Rose and their marriage. Seathan saves the most difficult part of his tale to the end. "The life in the British Army for a *bean* is so ghastly and often leads to illness or death. I did not want to inflict this upon my Rose. So, I have deserted the army. After this Rose and I will travel to Tobermory and eventually board a ship for North America."

"I understand, Seathan, I am sure it was a difficult choice," responds Iain with great empathy. "I will miss you. How did our *athair* receive this news?"

Seathan answers with great sadness, "He was not pleased and probably is ashamed of my choice. A clan warrior who had fought in battles for the chief would not have made my choice, but Highland life has changed. I did not want to lose Rose to such hardship and am willing to take the risk of traveling to a new country. I do not see good things for the Highlands of our Isle."

"Nor do I," responds Iain. "Perhaps someday I will also travel to a new country for better opportunities." With the story told, Seathan, Rose and Iain spend several hours together with mixed feelings. Finally, Seathan and Rose must say goodbye to Iain. They extend their final embraces to each other and Seathan and Rose proceed back down the hill to the glen.

51

Anna Shares Her Secret

As Catherine is digging up some potatoes, she notices Seathan and Rose walking down the mountain trail after their visit with Iain. She watches as Lach meets up with them. He had mentioned asking Seathan to go hunting with him for rabbits for the wedding feast. After a few moments she can see Seathan agreeing and giving Rose a quick kiss as he heads to the woods with his *athair*. Rose heads down the mountain by herself to the *bothie*, waving to Catherine as she goes by.

Anna looks up with excitement when Rose enters. She has been wanting to talk to her new *piuthar-cheile*. She cannot contain herself as she says, "Rose, it is a long trek from the summer pasture to our *bothie*. Would you like some tea?"

Rose responds, "That would be nice and we can sit and chat and get to know one another better." Anna prepares the hot tea with the kettle of boiling water. She also brings over some bread and fresh blueberry jam.

"Thank you," murmurs Rose softly.

Anna begins the conversation, "How was your visit with Iain?"

"It was nice to see two *brathairs* who have not seen each other in a long time renew their *brathair* connection," responds Rose. "I think Iain has missed his *brathair* greatly."

Anna replies, "Aye, you are right, Rose. It is very lonely up in the summer pasture tending the livestock for months. We accept it as the life of a farmer, but it is more difficult for Iain because he is the last *mac*."

"Iain mentioned," Rose adds, "that he would someday like to leave the Isle and travel to North America as Seathan and I are doing. The opportunities for work here are diminishing and emigrating might be the only way for the Highlanders to survive," continues Rose.

"Aye, I know, my *athair* is very worried about our future. I know that he will want to stay here on his beloved Isle of Mull unless it gets very bad for us," explains Anna.

"Rose, while we are alone, I want to ask to you about your

red-toned hair. Have you ever received any negative accusations about having red hair?"

"What do you mean? I am not sure I understand," replies Rose.

"Since we are now related I will tell you our hidden secret," begins Anna. "I was born with red hair, not your darker hue but a bright red. Since I was born my *mathair* has been dyeing my hair this brown shade that you see now."

"And why is that?" queries Rose.

Anna replies, "Have you not heard of the ancient belief that folks born with red hair are black witches who cast evil spells? Even though it has been outlawed to accuse someone of witchcraft, there are some folks here on our isle that still do. Several years ago one of my kinfolk falsely implicated me in the death of a *bairn*. My *mathair* was able to show that I could not have done so. Thus I continue to keep my red hair hidden from the rest of the community. Only my kinfolk know the secret."

"Anna, this is terrible," exclaims Rose. "I can understand why you want to keep your red hair hidden. As for me I have heard snide remarks infrequently. However, if a stranger says something I take no mind of them. To tell you the truth, Anna, the folks of Edinburgh live so poorly that they do not have the time or energy to focus on my red hair. Additionally, I am not as much a rarity in Edinburgh as you are here in Inivea.

"This is good to hear, Rose," responds Anna. What was it like to live in such wretched conditions?"

"Our home is crowded but my parents have jobs. My *mathair* works as a weaver in a large factory and my *athair* now works as a bartender in a small local pub."

Anna thinks about this for a second and then knowing that she needs to address the red hair dilemma shares with Rose, "There is another problem. Generally, I stay away from celebrations where the *torrach mathairs* will be. I do not want to be charged with causing a *bairn* being born sickly and developing an illness. Fortunately, the woman who accused me of witchcraft no longer lives here. However, I do not know how many others continue to keep the same beliefs. We should talk to my *parantans* about this. Since you are being introduced to our community, perhaps it is the *torrach mathairs* who need to stay away if they are fearful."

"Yes, I believe that your *mathair* and *athair* should be consulted before a decision is made," agrees Rose.

Just as Anna and Rose pause, Catherine opens the front door, armed with produce from their farm. She unloads the crops on a small cabinet. She then gives a sigh of relief and motions to Anna and Rose that she will join them around the fire.

Anna welcomes her *mathair,* "Aye, come and rest before we begin to prepare the evening meal." After a short interlude of silence while Catherine settles herself, Anna begins, "I told Rose about my red hair. I hope you don't mind."

Catherine responds, "Anna, I am surprised that you took it upon yourself to tell this to Rose. I would have expected that you would have waited until I was alone with Rose and Seathan so that I could share this news with them. We have just met Rose and we don't know how she would have reacted."

"Perhaps you are right, *Mathair.* I believed that since Seathan trusted Rose enough to make her his *bean* that I could also share our family secret with her. Rose has reddish hair so I thought she might have encountered some of the same accusations that I have here. She told me that she has had only an occasional comment. The people of Edinburgh are so poor that their survival takes all their energy."

"At this, Rose interjects, "Catherine, like you, I also believe that important family information should be shared by the *parantans.* What I understand from Anna is that she has kept her secret for such a long time that she wanted to share with someone she believed would accept the truth of her misfortune. I also hope that you do not think me disrespectful in telling you this."

After a minute Catherine responds, "No, Rose, I do not think you are being disrespectful. Now that I have had a few moments to think things over I can share that Anna, throughout her life, has had a great deal of stress keeping her secret from others." Then she addresses Anna, "I do realize you have always been afraid that people would find out you have red hair and the threat of being labeled a witch cannot be an easy burden to bear.

"I am sorry, *Mathair,* that I did not give you the chance to share with Rose first," Anna addresses Catherine.

Catherine reassures Anna, "It is alright, Anna."

Anna then speaks, "I also shared my secret with Rose because I thought there might be a problem with the *torrach mathairs* coming to Seathan and Rose's marriage celebration. There are now two red-heads in the family and certainly Rose cannot miss her own wedding celebration."

"Aye, Anna, "Now we have a predicament because Isobel and Sine are both *torrach*. We have not informed them of Rose's hair color. Since Rose and Seathan are the reason for the celebration, I do not believe that Rose can stay away. We will see what each of them decides."

The next morning Catherine and Lach set out to the village to visit Isobel and Sine. They first go to Isobel and Iain. Lach knocks and Isobel opens the door. Isobel, now large with *bairn*, greets Catherine and Lach, "Come in." She is always very happy to see her good friends. She invites them to sit at the fire. "What brings you here?"

Catherine responds, "Isobel, as you know tonight there will be a big celebration for the marriage of Seathan and his new bride, Rose. What you don't know is that Rose has red hair. It is not the bright red of Anna's but rather a darker red-brown. Her hair color is definitely red though."

"Catherine and Lach, I have no fear of Anna and Rose. I do not believe that either of them will cast an evil spell on my unborn *bairn*. We would not miss coming to the celebration of this marriage but thank you for telling me of your concerns." Catherine and Lach are relieved and are grateful for her acceptance. They also assure her that they will be glad to see the Campbell family at the party to introduce Rose.

Catherine and Lach depart and then head to the home of Pastor Robertson and Sine. The housekeeper greets them at the door. "Good morning. I will check with the pastor and Mrs. Robertson to see if they are ready for visitors." The housekeeper invites them into the front room of the manse. As usual there is a fire in the room which gives some warmth to the dark cold room. Catherine and Lach sit at the large table in the middle of the room.

Shortly Sine and Pastor Robertson enter the room. Sine speaks first, "What brings you here this early in the morning?"

"Pastor Robertson and Sine, it is so good to see you and we hope that you don't mind our unexpected visit," Lach speaks first, "As you know the celebration of Seathan and his new bride, Rose, is tonight after sundown. But what you are probably unaware of is the fact that along with Anna, Rose is also a red-head. Her hair is more of a dark red brown than Anna's bright red hair, but it is red nevertheless."

Sine speaks, "Pastor Robertson and I have talked often about the clan's ancient beliefs about witches. I have told him about Anna's red hair and your reasons for dyeing her hair since she was baptized. Although Pastor Robertson understands your choice, he does not believe that Anna is a witch. He also does not believe that black witches exist."

Pastor Robertson then adds to the conversation, "I do not know the future of our *bairn* and whether he or she will be born healthy and live a healthy life. What I do know is that it is not red-haired witches that cast evil spells on us. Many times I do not know what causes our difficulties. We do not like seeing a *bairn*, a *clann* or a young person die before they have had a chance to live out their life. The harsh life that we live here is often the cause and we need to accept what we do not understand and place our faith in our God."

Sine then adds, "I know that when Rut came to me years ago when Eilidh got sick and died, I was confused and had some inclination to trust our ancient beliefs. But that has changed since I wed Pastor Robertson. He has been able to calmly and logically explain the falseness of these old thoughts. I am not afraid of Anna or Rose and we will be there to join in the joy of the newlyweds. We are eager to meet Rose and to welcome her into your family."

Catherine responds, "I am sure that you know that they will be emigrating to North America soon. You will know Rose for only a short time."

"No matter how little time we have with Seathan and Rose as a newlywed couple, we will feel blessed by those moments," Pastor Robertson closes the conversation.

At this Catherine and Lach signal their departure, thanking Sine and Pastor Robertson for their trust and belief in them.

Just as they are about to leave, Pastor Robertson advises, "I hope that this time with Rose will also help you and Anna face her red hair dilemma and that someday Anna will feel the courage to return her hair to its natural state."

"Aye," is Catherine's last comment to the pastor as they open the door and go out to journey back to the glen and their farm. Before they reach the trail, Catherine mentions to Lach, "Shall we visit with Caitriona before we head back?"

Lach answers, "It is getting late and we have to stop at the *aite cruinneachaidh* to stoke the fire and add more peat. You still need to collect heather and thistle to decorate for the celebration."

"Aye, you are right. Caitriona will join us tonight at the party and we will have time to socialize with her then," Catherine responds. Then Catherine adds, "I feel so much relief after our visit with the Campbells and the Robertsons. This will be good news for Anna and Rose. I am sure that Rose will be eager for her introduction to the rest of the Inivea community. However, I have concerns about Anna who has had such a trepidation about interacting with her kinfolk since Rut accused her of witchery."

When they arrive back, everyone is gathered around the fire and are eagerly awaiting the news. Late August has begun to show signs of the autumn and it is cooler and damper as of late. The fire is a welcomed warmth and comfort to the hikers. Lach speaks first, "We bring good news from the village. Isobel, Sine and Pastor Robertson have no fear of red-haired witches. They are eager to meet the new member of our family."

52
The Wedding Celebration of Rose and Seathan

While Catherine and Lach were in the village, Anna and Rose were busy preparing food for the celebration. They skinned the several hares which Seathan and Lach had hunted down the day before. Preparing the hares for cooking is a laborious job and it is good that Anna and Rose began early.

Seeing that the food is being handled by Anna and Rose, Catherine states, "I am going now into the meadows to gather heather and thistle to decorate for the wedding. Lach, go get some large pots and bring them to the *aite cruinneachaidh* so I can fill them with bouquets."

Catherine then declares, "I don't have much time to collect everything I need for the celebration. I will be back as soon as I can to dress for the wedding."

Meanwhile in the bothie, Anna and Rose slowly cook the cut-up hares with vegetables and herbs in a large iron pot. Anna is happy to have company while preparing the food. She misses her older *siuir*, Caitriona, and having Rose here makes her feel as if she has another big *siuir*. She is sorry that Rose and Seathan will be leaving so soon after the wedding celebration. An hour later the hare is ready and is dished out into a large wooden bowl. Anna becomes worried that her *mathair* has not returned. "I hope my *mathair* returns soon," Anna frets to Rose.

"I am sure that she will be here shortly," comforts Rose. "She is probably setting up the bouquets in their pots."

No sooner had Rose declared her confidence the door opens. "I know I am late," declares Catherine. "We must dress quickly."

The rest of the family have already donned their clean Sabbath clothes. Seathan and Lach, carefully placing their Maclean tartans across their shoulders, are ready to depart. Anna, however, remains seated on her bed. "Hurry up Anna," calls Catherine.

Rose then intervenes, "I will stay with Anna until she is ready to join the festival."

"Don't stay too long. Remember this gathering is a celebration of your wedding, Rose," reminds Catherine. Catherine is reluctant to leave. Thinking of all the details that still need to be done, Catherine nods her head towards Rose.

"We will be there soon, Catherine. Do not be concerned," encourages Rose. All depart out the door, leaving Anna and Rose to sort out the situation.

Rose silently sits next to Anna on her bed, waiting for Anna to have the first words. After several moments Anna finally breaks the eerie silence. Not even Rose can change the ominous sense of doom that Anna feels. "Rose, I so appreciate your staying behind for a while, but I do not think I can find the courage to go to your wedding celebration. I am so afraid that something will happen to the *bairns* and I will be blamed."

Rose comforts Anna, "I understand your concern, Anna. Remember, I also have red hair and I could be blamed for any misfortune that could happen to the newborns."

"But you are leaving soon after with Seathan to travel to new lands," reminds Anna.

"Aye, I know, but blaming me for anything will then eliminate you as the cause of any evil spells," continues Rose.

Once again Anna sits in contemplative silence. She is troubled, but Rose's words comfort her and make sense. "All right, Rose, I will trust your wisdom and go to your wedding feast. I do not want to miss my last chance to honor you and Seathan."

At these words Rose rises and sits by the fire, waiting for Anna to finish her dressing. Rose knows that Anna is taking a big chance and hopes that her advice will not have negative consequences for her.

Soon Anna is ready and they hike down the path to the *aite cruinneachaidh*. Anna is composed and quiet. Rose knows that there are stirrings of doubt in Anna's heart. Rose is proud of her *piuthar-cheile* and sad that she and Seathan will be leaving soon. They reach the festivity location and from a distance they can view all the kinfolk carrying items of food into the large *aite cruinneachaidh*. Rose spots Seathan from afar and is more relaxed after she sees him. Convenience and not love is often what drives folks to marry. But in this case Rose is able to remind herself that she and Seathan love each other.

Seathan speeds up the path to greet his beloved and his *siuir*.

Seathan reaches them and gives his *bean* a great hug and a kiss. On the cheek of his *siuir* he also places a brotherly kiss. Both are glad to see Seathan and his exuberant mood as he accompanies them. Inside the room Anna joyfully announces, "Look Rose, my *mathair* has filled many buckets with red-purple heather and she hasn't forgotten the lucky white heather in the smaller vase over there."

Catherine soon joins them and Rose compliments her on the beautiful decorations for her wedding celebration. "Catherine, I am so happy that you have also included a bouquet of the purple thistle of Scotland," responds Rose. "A celebration would not be complete for me unless it included this national symbol of our Scotland."

"Aye, *mathair,* all the heather is beautiful, but the purple thistle really adds something special to our celebration. We will dry some thistle in a book and bring it to our new land, always to be reminded of our beautiful Scotland," adds Rose.

The sight of the room decorated so thoughtfully and beautifully by Catherine and her kinfolk lifts the spirits of Anna and gives her hope. It isn't long before the benches fill with her kin and other folks from the village and farms. The fiddler begins playing a folk song which Seathan has requested for his *bean, "My Love is Like a Red Red Rose."* While it was playing Seathan softly sings the words to Rose:

"O, my luve is like a red, red rose,
That's newly sprung in June;
O, my luve is like a melodie
That's sweetly played in tune.
As fair art thou, my bonnie lass,
So deep in luve am I;
And I will luve thee still, my dear,
till a' the seas gang dry,
And I will luve thee still, my dear,
Till a' seas gang dry.
Till a' the seas gang dry, my dear;
And the rocks melt wi' the sun;
And I will luve thee still, my dear,
While the sands of life shall run.
But fare thee weel, my only luve!
O, fare thee weel awhile!
And I will come agian, my luve,

Tho' 'twere ten thousand miles.
Tho' 'twere ten thousand mile, my luve,
Tho' 'twere ten thousand mile,
And I will come again, my luve,
Tho' 'twere ten thousand mile."

The fiddler keeps playing and all at the festivity join in the singing. Some folks rise to dance to the tune and it is a joyful time. Anna spots the Campbells across the room. She notices Donald, now sixteen years old, and feels a slight flutter in her heart. Quickly she shifts her gaze to others in the room and notices Sine, large with *bairn*, sitting with the Pastor. Seathan and Rose are in the middle of the dancing couples. Both have flushed cheeks from the excitement and their love. Anna notices that there are no folks reacting to the small amount of Rose's red-brown hair revealing itself from the exposed areas of her lacy *kertch*. The dim lighting also lends to keeping Rose's red hair unnoticed. Anna is happy about this but does wonder how they would react to the new bride if they knew she had red hair.

Caitriona, who has been able to take time off from her weaving, takes some moments to chat with Seathan and Rose. "I wish I could have spent more time with you this week." My work has been very demanding and I was unable to leave. I am so happy for both of you but wish you could stay longer. It is difficult to say good-bye and I am sad, knowing that you will be leaving our Isle forever and traveling across the ocean to a new land."

Seathan give his *siuir* a warm brotherly hug and whispers, "I will miss you and will forever keep you in my heart."

Then Rose adds, "Caitriona, I am so sorry that we have to leave before I have had the chance to spend time with you. Seathan has told me much about you and I know that we would have been best *siuirs* and friends." With those thoughts Rose gives her a loving hug. The newlyweds then depart to greet the others attending their celebration.

The Highland whisky and ale are the favorite drinks of any *ceilidh* and this celebration is no exception to the custom. It helps to make all the attendees unusually joyful and uninhibited. The dancing and singing accompanied by the fiddle become louder and more boisterous lasting into the early morning. When all the food and drink are gone, the celebration begins to ebb and folks depart. Soon the last strains of the fiddle fade and as people leave they extend their last farewells to Seathan and Rose.

53
Plans to Leave

Anna is the first to rise later in the morning. It was a celebratory group that left the wedding festivities in the early hours just before dawn. During the evening she had forgotten about her troubles. She hopes that this is a good omen for the well-being of the unborn *bairns* of Isobel and Sine. Meanwhile she goes out into the morning air. The fog has vanished and there is the appearance of sun behind some thin clouds. The coolness of the evening has not yet lifted. She reenters the *bothie* to grab her shawl from her bed, tiptoeing carefully so as not to awaken the rest of her family.

Once outside again Anna begins to silently make some plans. First, she will arrange a time to talk to her *mathair* about the recommendations of Beitris for the frequent dark moods of her *athair*. Then she will talk to Seathan and Rose about their plans to travel to Tobermory. If possible, she would like to travel there with them. Saying goodbye to Seathan again will be heart-wrenching but she wants to extend her time with him and Rose as much as possible. Anna realizes what a great loss their departure will be for her. She tries to hold back the tears that begin to well up in her eyes and she realizes that this is one of the first times that she has cried. She has never felt as lonely and vulnerable as she does now. She hadn't realized how much she was missing Caitriona until Rose came into her life and took on the Caitriona's big *siuir* role.

Anna wipes the tears from her eyes quickly. She does not want to explain the reason for her sadness right now. She sits on the stool and waits for the first signs of family getting up. In the distance she observes a few people slowly emerging out their doors. Her reverie is suddenly disrupted by the emergence of Rose. Rose joins Anna on the stool next to her. They quietly whisper about last night's festivities. Rose remarks, "I was so touched by Seathan's song to me, '*My Love is Like a Red Red Rose.*' And then to have everyone join him in the singing and dancing of the song. I have never have felt such a display of affection and joy."

"Aye, I agree," responds Anna. "It was wonderful to be a part of this honoring of you. You and Seathan must feel so lucky to have found each other. I am proud of him and he will always remain that way deep in my heart whether near or far."

"Aye, Anna," acknowledges Rose. "I am indeed a lucky *bean* and Seathan will always be my everlasting love."

Anna tries to keep her emotions under control. "Rose, I have been thinking that I would like to travel with you and Seathan to Tobermory to say one last goodbye."

"That would be wonderful, Anna! Perhaps your *athair* will also travel with us."

"Good, I will share this idea with my *mathair* and then, if she agrees, she can talk to my *athair*. When do you think you will be leaving?"

"Seathan and I have not made it definite yet. We must travel before the weather changes significantly."

The rest of the family soon rises. Seathan and Rose decide to take a hike and Lach sets out to visit his *brathair* Seumus. He and Seumus will have lots to say about the festivities last night and Seathan's decision to desert. In his heart Lach still hasn't resolved this choice of Seathan. It will help him to talk to Seumus who always seems to put things into perspective. Seumus has generally had a more positive and calmer demeanor than his younger *brathair*. Anna is happy that she will be left alone with her *mathair* so that she can share the things that are on her mind.

As soon as everyone leaves Anna addresses her, "*Mathair*, can we sit here for a while? I want to talk some things over with you."

"Of course," replies her *mathair*. "What is on your mind?"

"I want to talk to you about *athair*. He frequently appears to be lost in worried thoughts. When I was with Beitris she told me about this plant, *Common Valerian*. It is a potent herb which has helped some folks in the village with their dark moods. Beitris told me that I do not have enough training to administer it, but she would be glad to do it if my *athair* comes to her shop once a week. If I collect the herb myself, she will charge very little for her help."

"Anna, I am not sure about this. I will think about it for a while and then decide whether I will share it with him."

"You know best, *mathair*," replies Anna.

"Were there other things you want to talk over with me?" continues

230

Catherine.

"Aye, *mathair*," responds Anna. "As you know I have missed Caitriona." Anna goes on, "Already Rose is like a *siuir* to me. I will miss her and Seathan so much when they leave, knowing that I will never see them again. I would like to travel to Tobermory with them to say my final goodbye. Can you inquire whether my *athair* will be traveling with them to Tobermory and if I can join him?"

"Aye, I will do that," Catherine says, "I am not sure if he has gotten over the fact of Seathan's desertion yet. He is making a visit to Seumus to discuss things and I will observe his mood when he returns."

"Thank you, *mathair*." Anna is pleased.

Seathan and Rose return from their hike and they have decided about their departure. Anna and Catherine are still sitting after finishing their conversation. Seathan speaks first, "On our hike, Rose and I have talked about our timing for leaving Inivea. We have decided to spend another week with everyone. Then we will travel to Tobermory and board the first ship sailing to North America. While waiting for a ship, we will stay with kinfolk. Maybe I can seek kelping work in Tobermory and Rose might be able to work at the inn or the tavern. Don't worry *mathair,* it will all work out. Many before us have taken this path. Hopefully *athair* will travel with us to Tobermory and he might find out more about the next ship. Then he could bring the news back to you."

"Are you worried about the Army learning your whereabouts and arresting you for desertion?" questions a concerned Catherine.

"*Mathair,* I am not. There are many people entering Tobermory every day looking for work. None of the troops that might recognize me will be stationed in Tobermory and they do not know Rose. The Duke is mainly concerned with getting rent from his tenants and signing up new recruits for the Army. He would not know who I am. When I enlisted in the Army I was only with the Duke for a short while. I believe my identity would be a mystery to him."

Anna remains silent during this conversation. A week more spent with the family will give the issue time to resolve itself. Perhaps Rose has already shared with Seathan about her interest in accompanying them to Tobermory. She knows that Seathan will only bring up the issue with his *athair* if Anna asks him. It is time to prepare the food for tonight and they all go inside and begin to make the meal. For now, it is time, no matter how short, to be a family.

54

The Departing

The week passes quickly. After his visit to Seumus, Lach's attitude to Seathan has become more positive. He does not share the conversation with anyone, but Anna is happy to observe her *athair's* mood change. She also can see Seathan's great relief. This is good news because she is sure that Seathan and Rose do not want to spend their last days here under a dark cloud of despair.

Seathan spends the week helping the family harvest crops. Rose, on the other hand, spends her time churning butter, mending clothes and sewing a new petticoat for Anna. Several visits are made to Seathan's kinfolk. Rose and Seathan will keep these moments in their hearts, knowing that they will never see them again.

The day finally arrives. They will make an early start with Lach and Anna traveling with them. Due to the rugged trail it will take them several hours. Taking a packed sack filled with food for the journey they set out. Catherine will follow them down into the village to say her last goodbyes. As they leave their glen many stop their labour for a moment for a final wave of farewell.

"Godspeed my dear kinfolk. Perhaps someday we will see you again," shouts Seathan followed by Rose's wave. Rose adds, "It was good to meet Seathan's family. God bless you and may he bestow on you good health."

They move along quickly down the path to the village. The wind is blowing gustily and the salt air fills their lungs. The red-purple heather and end of summer colors fill their sight and hearts. Both Rose and Seathan take in the views so as to remember them when they are far away. They have mixed feelings about leaving their beloved Highlands but believe in the promises of new opportunities. They trust in the gifts of youth, life and love and pray that it will be a safe passage across the seas.

They first reach the home of Sine and Pastor Robertson. As they come near the door they hear screams and moaning. Anna speaks first, "I wonder if Sine is in labour?"

Catherine concurs, "I believe you have heard it right."

"Perhaps we should leave without making our presence known," adds Rose. Just then the housekeeper opens the door. Seeing the group, she announces that she is in pursuit of the midwife to help in the birth. Catherine regrets that Marta stayed back in the glen. However, Sine has been training a new midwife, Elizabeth, and as she lives in the village, she will be able come immediately. The housekeeper waits no longer and runs to fetch Elizabeth.

The family moves on to Flora's shop. They knock on her door and Caitriona answers and gestures to the stools outside. She is so happy to see Seathan and Rose. Except for Iain, who is still tending the livestock in the summer meadows, she is able, for a final time to be with all her family. After several minutes of chatting, Caitriona speaks, "What if you find no ship waiting to sail? What will you do then?"

Seathan explains, "Rose and I are aware that there will surely not be a ship for us when we arrive in Tobermory. We will find labour in Tobermory and wait. If after a year there is no news, then we might go to a bigger city, such as Glasgow, where ships sail more frequently."

"I will still have concern for your well-being," adds Caitriona. "Do you think the British Army will catch up with you and arrest you for being a deserter?"

Seathan answers, "No, I am not worried. There will be many new residents and strangers in Tobermory and we will be faceless and nameless among the crowds. We will send a post to let our families know what happens, although it may take time to reach everyone. Do not be afraid, but we must leave now." At that the young couple embrace Caitriona.

Next the family moves on to the Campbells. They knock on the door and Donald opens it. He greets them with much familiarity and affection. "Hello Seathan and Rose, have you come here to say goodbye?"

"Aye," responds Seathan. "We will be traveling to Tobermory today. How is your *mathair*? We were just at the pastor's house and Sine is in the middle of giving birth to a new *bairn*."

"We were unable to say our final farewells," adds Rose. "But she has other more important things to attend to right now."

"*Mathair*," he calls into the *bothie,* "Seathan and Rose with the rest of the family are here. I will go to our shop and fetch my *athair* and Roderick."

Isobel comes out immediately. She is heavy with *bairn* but still has another month or so before she will give birth. "Good morning," greets Isobel. "I fear that you have come to say your farewells to us."

"That is why we are here, Isobel," responds Seathan. "We come to you with our goodbyes. We must leave to seek a better life for ourselves, but we feel sad. We will miss everyone on our beautiful Isle."

As Seathan utters his final words, Donald returns with his *athair* and Roderick. They rush to Seathan and Rose with an embrace. They also extend their hand of welcome to Catherine and the other Macleans. Lach speaks, "Seathan and Rose have come to give you their final farewells, but we cannot tarry too long. While they say goodbye, I will go and fetch the horse and cart so that we can begin our journey."

When Lach returns, Catherine hugs her *mac* and Rose before they board the two-seated cart. Catherine weeps silently as she says her final goodbye; she knows that she will never see them again. Seathan and Rose then climb aboard as they wave. Seathan does not show the grief that he is feeling on the inside, but Rose expresses the grief for both of them as the tears well up in her eyes. She knows their lives will never be the same. The thought of never seeing any family again weighs heavily on her heart.

55
The Trek and the Reunion

The group's plan is to first hike on the well-traveled route to Dervaig which will take them about one and a half hours. Once they reach there they will have another three more hours before they reach Tobermory. The going will be slow on the rough terrain but if all goes well they should be in Tobermory when the sun is at its highest.

Once there they will seek out Tomas and Rut to see what they know about ships to North America. Anna is not very happy about seeing Rut. She knows that it is something she will have to do if she wants to say goodbye to Seathan and Rose. They will be tired when they finally get there. Hopefully Tomas will have some suggestions about where they can stay.

"*Athair*," Anna asks, "How do you think Rose and I will be treated when we see Rut?"

"I believe as kinfolk we will be received with a welcoming hospitality," replies Lach. Anna gets lost in her own reverie and reminds herself that it has been five years since Tomas and Rut left Inivea. She wonders if they have changed and how Lucas and Deidre are doing. She must not waste too much energy thinking about it, she reminds herself. At least this time there is another red-head who will provide support to her.

The trail to Dervaig is filled with natural beauty. A narrow path just barely accommodates the horse and cart and two hikers. If they meet others on the twisting path, one of the hikers has to step aside and allow the others to pass by. Anna's *athair* has told her that when he was a wee *clann* the trail would not be safe to travel. At that time the Isle was filled with warring clans who would attack enemy clans.

Anna does not have to think about these dangers now. She enjoys the sights and sounds beside her as well as the lake waters as she travels. She spies the white-tailed eagles and other birds along the way. When all the travelers are silent the woods are filled with a cacophony of bird sounds. Anna likes it when there is the silence but also enjoys the easy conversation as they hike. "Seathan, when you passed through Tobermory on your way here, what was the town like?" queries Anna.

"It was much different than when I joined the British Army five years ago. At that time Tobermory was filled with farmers trying to eke out a living and were paying rents to the Duke; the same Duke that I signed up with for military service."

Quickly moving he continues, "However, about a year ago the British Fisheries came to Tobermory and built up the village with wooden structures in order to lure clansmen to abandon their farms and become fishermen. There are still many struggling farms on the hills surrounding Tobermory. Some of these farmers have taken up harvesting kelp which is even more demanding. This is what your uncle Tomas is doing. What the future of Tobermory holds is unknown. It does have a good port which enables ships to collect passengers and sail them to distant ports."

"I am eager to see Tobermory but not eager to say goodbye to you and Rose," admits Anna.

"We know that, Anna, and we will also miss our families here in Scotland," chimes in Rose. "We have to believe that there are better opportunities for us in North America. Tobermory has a post office now which will give us a way to let you know where we are going. Perhaps someday you and your family will join us wherever we go."

Anna is silent and not quick to respond. She does not know if her family could ever leave their beloved home and sail to ports unknown. The circumstances of life on Mull would have to get a lot more desperate for that to happen.

They reach Dervaig and Rose and Seathan climb out of the cart. Lach and Anna take their turn sitting in the cart while Seathan and Rose now walk. Anna is happy for the change. Instead of needing to focus on keeping up with the horse and cart, she will now be able to look around her and take in the beauty of the land.

The travelers trade seats once more as they come close to Tobermory. Anna is again walking and begins to see the ocean on one side and farmlands on the other. Anna gives a shout of glee as she notices these changes, "We must be on the outskirts of the town."

"You are right!" agree the rest of the travelers shouting out together. Lach then adds, "Another half hour and we will be there. I can tell by the sun above us. It is nearing being at its highest point of the day."

"I will remember to keep my eye on it," adds Anna.

The rest of the journey passes uneventfully. They soon see the buildings of Tobermory and Anna is dumbstruck. She has never seen such a sight. A group of wooden buildings occupy the center of town. If one looks slightly beyond the structures, there is the sea with its broad bay and harbor surrounding the town of Tobermory. The houses are more elegant than anything she has ever experienced before. The village of Inivea has the *kirk* and the manse of Pastor Robinson, but they are humble in comparison. In the middle of the row of houses is a grander structure.

Anna shouts to Seathan, "What is that larger building right in the center of the smaller homes?"

Seathan answers Anna quickly, "That is a hotel where travelers can have a room for a small fee. Rut works there now as a maid. We will stop there first and speak to her. She will be able to guide us with information about lodging and food."

"Seathan, I knew that we were coming to Rut's town when I asked to join you," adds Anna. "I guess I believed that I would be able to forget about the past and what Rut accused me of, but I am afraid that is not so. You will have to visit her yourselves. I will stay here outside."

"If that is what you want," replies Rose. "I understand why you are feeling the way you do." At that the rest of the travelers leave Anna alone and make their way to the small inn.

While they are inside visiting Rut, Anna looks around her. She is still amazed at the modern village of Tobermory. She wonders how it must be to live in such a clean town. She wants to wander and explore but must wait for the return of her family and keep an eye on the horse. Her legs are jumpy with restlessness and she gets out of the cart. Once out, she lovingly embraces the horse.

Several minutes later the group emerge from the hotel. Seathan speaks, "Rut asked about you, Anna."

"Why does she care?" replies Anna.

"I am not sure. She graciously received all of us. Perhaps she is now sorry for the way she treated you," suggests Seathan.

"Maybe, but I am still not ready to see her," says Anna.

Seathan unloads their items and then jumps into the cart, takes the reins and declares, "Wait here while I bring the horse and cart back to the owner."

While waiting for Seathan, Lach informs Anna of his plans, "I have rented a small room for the night, Anna. We will return to Inivea in the morning." Turning to the small group, Lach says, "Meanwhile we will look for Tomas down by the bay where he is working. Later we will hike to their *bothie* and call on Lucas and Deidre. Seathan and Rose will stay with them until they find other means of housing. With worry in his eyes, Lach continues, "Rut had the disappointing news that there have been no ships leaving Tobermory for several years."

From the hotel the group walks down to the bay to find Tomas. Through a dense cloud of acrid smoke, they peer at the bay. The shore of the bay is crowded. As they draw closer their eyes begin to smart from the smoke. Knee-deep in sea water and far from the shore, a large group of farmers use their sickles to cut the seaweed. Another group piles the weed into a nearby kiln built of loose stones from the beach. *Clanns*, women and a few men are at the kiln, stirring the harvested weed constantly with long irons.

The travelers stop a short distance from the kelpers. They are not sure if they will be able to spot Tomas in this motley group of harvesters. The bitter smoke makes their search more difficult. Anna speaks, "*Athair*, how will we find Tomas in this huge group? He will not hear us through this crowd."

"I know, Anna," acknowledges Lach. "Perhaps we will return to his *bothie* and wait for him to return at the end of the day."

Then Rose adds, "This smoke is terrible. Seathan, I would not like you to take on this type of labour." Seathan, who does not know what he will do to support Rose and himself, just nods in agreement.

They stay awhile hoping to spot Tomas. The sun has long passed being its highest point. They decide that they must move on. Just as they are leaving Anna, who is sick of the smoke and waiting, spots him coming up from the bay. "There is Tomas," shouts Anna. "Tomas, Tomas," Anna calls out. At first Tomas does not hear her but draws closer.

"Anna, I see you," Tomas calls out assuredly. Tomas, who has greatly missed his family, gains a new energy and rushes to his family. He embraces his family and then stops in front of Rose saying, "And who is this young lassie?"

Seathan speaks, "Tomas, this is my new *bean*, Rose."

"I am so happy to meet you, Rose," responds Tomas.

"And I you," replies Rose.

With the introduction over the group begins the hike to Tomas and Rut's . The troop chatter as they walk. Tomas shares more about his work.

Anna speaks up, "Tomas, the smoke is awful. My eyes are already hurting, and I have only been here a short while."

"Aye, Anna, I don't mind the hard work, but I am also worried about my eyes. Every night after work I put a cool wet cloth to my eyes to stop the burning."

It is still daylight when the group arrives at Tomas and Rut's *bothie*. Deidre and Lucas are sitting around their fire with a bowl of tea when Tomas enters. They are very excited and happy to see their kinfolk. It has been a long time since they have enjoyed their company. Lucas, the oldest, speaks first, "*brathair-athar* Lach, Seathan and Anna, it is so good to see you. And who is this?" he asks, pointing to Rose.

"This is my *bean*, Rose," Seathan explains. "We met in Edinburgh where I was stationed. We have decided that it was best for our future to leave the British Army and to immigrate to new lands." Seathan has decided not to use the word "*deserted*" when explaining his situation. It might leave Lucas and Deidre confused. Lach remains silent during this part of the conversation and for this Seathan is grateful.

"What about your life here?" questions Seathan.

Lucas shares, "We have a small farm and Deidre and I tend to it while our *parantans* work in town. Farming keeps us busy."

"I also help my *mathair* inside; cleaning, churning the butter and mending our clothes. Sometimes I help cook our meals," adds Deidre.

After getting these updates from the family, Lach and Anna make plans to depart. Anna is happy to leave before Rut comes back home.

Just as they are about to leave, Tomas shares a ray of hope, "A businessman, a John Sinclair, has just built the *Ledaig Distillery*. This distillery will produce malt scotch whisky and is now looking for men to work there. I will apply for a job. I would be so happy to leave the kelping work."

Anna and Lach moan as they say goodbye to Seathan and Rose. After several minutes of embracing, they wish them good luck in their travels. Tears well up in the eyes of Seathan and Rose as they bid their final farewells. It is a very difficult goodbye.

56
Return to Inivea

Anna had a fitful night, crying silent tears in the unfamiliar bed of the hotel. She cannot get Seathan and Rose out of her mind. When she wakens she briefly dwells on the agonizing pain of loss. Her heart hurts with great sadness. She takes time to regain her composure by taking several deep breaths. Noticing that her *athair* is also awake, Anna speaks, "*Athair,* shall we get up and get ready to travel?" "

"Aye, let's hurry. I want to have an early start," replies Lach. In silence they pack their goods and are soon ready to leave. Anna is pleased that she has not laid her eyes on Rut.

Once on the path Anna thinks about her life in Inivea. Anna shares her thoughts with Lach. "*Athair,* why don't we do what Seathan and Rose are doing?"

"Why do you say that?" responds Lach.

"*Athair,* I mean why don't we leave this island and sail to new lands?"

"Anna, why would you want to do that?" questions Lach.

"It is because our life here is so difficult," pleads Anna.

"Aye, I agree with what you are saying, Anna, but we know what we have here on our Isle. We have our little farm, our *bothie* and our livestock. All of this has kept many generations of our ancestors alive."

"I know this, *Athair,* but perhaps life would be better in a new land. The laird continues to raise our rent. And what do we get for it?"

"Anna, your *mathair* and I are getting older. It is not so easy to start all over again in a new country. We do not know what we would be getting into. Here we have our farm, our *kirk* and our kinfolk. Life is difficult, but so far we have survived. Sometimes nature does not make it easy for us and we have almost starved, but we have managed to live through it. I do not see moving to a new land as an answer."

"Aye, *athair,* I see your point but I do not see that it will become better," adds Anna. She then becomes quiet, knowing that her *athair* has always been set in his ways and has a lot of fears of the unknown. She recalls that he would continue to believe in the actions of monsters and the Black Donald no matter where they made their home.

All around Anna is seeing a change in the scenery. The ocean and open pasture land of Tobermory are left behind. The landscape now on one side of Anna is the dense woods and beyond the forest are the mountains. On the other side she and Lach are now passing by a beautiful still lake. The sounds of the birds have become more abundant. The pathway is narrow, rough and exceptionally twisty. Anna reminds herself that she must pay attention to her steps so that she will not fall.

After a couple of hours, the sun is beginning to get higher in the sky. It is warm for an August morning and Anna and Lach take off their outer covering and place them in their traveling bag. They resume their pace after Lach remarks, "Our travels are going smoothly and we are making good time. Soon we will stop and eat our lunch." No sooner had Lach spoken these words, his body suddenly feels the thrust of someone jumping on him.

Startled by the assault, Lach hears one of the men shouting, "Give us your money and your weapons or your life."

Lach attempts to grab his *dirk*, but his response is not quick enough. The bandit that attacked Lach defends himself by thrusting his own readied *dirk* into Lach's side and arm. Lach keeps fighting the two robbers but the wounds have caused him to lose much of the advantage that his experience and training usually give him.

Meanwhile, the bandits have forgotten Anna. Anna, seeing this, sneaks away into the woods. She quickly spots a large heavy branch on the forest's floor. She picks it up and heads out to the path. She creeps behind and with a violent thrust of the branch hits one of the bandits over the head. The other robber, seeing what has happened to his accomplice, quickly flees.

Anna notices that the bandit that she hit is not going anywhere fast. She quickly goes over to her passed out *athair* who is bleeding heavily from his wounds. Anna knows that she needs to stop the bleeding as soon as possible. She removes one of her petticoats and rips a piece off. Folding it sufficiently to cover her athair's wound, she adds pressure. She rips another strip of cloth and winds it tightly above the wound on his arm. Using one hand she maintains the pressure on Lach's side and using her other hand she takes out the food from her satchel. She fills the now empty satchel with Lach's outer wrap and uses it as a pillow to support his head. As he begins to regain consciousness, he groans loudly. Anna rips another strip of cloth, dips it in the drinking water and puts it to Lach's lips. She wets a remaining fragment of her petticoat to wipe his face.

As she tends her *athair*, Anna hears the disabled robber becoming conscious. She leaves Lach and moves over to the bandit. Before he is fully conscious Anna rips another petticoat and ties the robber's hands as well as his feet. Then she returns to her *athair* and continues to administer some water to his lips. Lach becomes more and more aware of his surroundings and through his groans he speaks at last. In a barely audible voice he inquires, "How are you Anna? Are you hurt?" Anna answers her *athair's* queries, "No, my *athair* I have not been hurt. I found a large tree branch and whacked the head of one of the robbers with it. It knocked him out. The other robber fled when he saw what happened."

"I have tied the bandit's hands and feet," adds Anna. "He appears to be just barely a man. How are you feeling, *Athair*? That is quite a stab wound and you have lost a lot of blood."

Lach weakly responds to his youngest *nighean*, "I am very weak, Anna, and we must stay here for the night. Perhaps in the morning I will be able to travel to Dervaig. Your *mathair* will be very worried about us but I need to get stronger for travel." Lach then closes his eyes and drifts off, leaving Anna alone to make all of the decisions.

The second robber has awakened. He briefly struggles and then realizes that his hands and feet are tied. "Let me go," he screams.

"I will let you go after you tell me something about yourself. I have the tree branch here beside me and I will not be afraid to use it if you try to escape. Tell me now. What is your name and why are you robbing folks instead of doing more honorable labour?" questions Anna. "Where is your village?"

"Let me go. I do not have to answer your questions," asserts the robber.

"So you think," threatens Anna. "I will thrust my *athair's dirk* into you as your robbing friend did to him if you don't answer me."

The young lad remains quiet for a while as if mulling over the demands of Anna. He certainly does not like the fact that this young lassie is in control. Anna returns to take care of her *athair* and to ask again how he is feeling. Her *athair* is resting with his eyes closed. She examines his wounds and they have stopped bleeding. Anna then searches for Lach's traveling bag. Finding it where it was thrown aside during the attack, she removes her *athair's plaid* and covers him to keep him comfortable. Anna knows that it is important to keep him warm.

Anna eyes the robber and notices that he is trying to get his hands free of the cloth ties which, in reality, are not very secure. She will not let on to that fact but will instead continue to distract him by conversation. "What is your name lad?"

Finally the lad cooperates, "I am Finlay McKinnon from Tobermory."

"And why have you decided to be a bandit?" queries Anna. "As you can probably see now, it is a very dangerous occupation. I am warning you that you do not try to attack my *athair* and me again. If I suspect that you have these intentions, I will use this *dirk* to stab you. Then I will gladly dump your dead body into the forest where you will be devoured by the hungry vultures and beasts."

"I felt desperate to help my family. My *athair* moved us from Salen to Tobermory in hopes that we would be better off economically. I believed I could make easy and quick money by becoming a robber. I had no intention of ever killing or severely hurting another person. I can see now that my fellow robber did not share that thought."

"I can see that you are young and foolish," responds Anna. "Life is very difficult here especially for young lads. Do you think there is anything else you can do to help your family?"

"I do not know the answer. I guess that I will probably have to join my *athair* kelping."

Anna then mentions, "Have you thought of joining the Highland army? You could send your pay home to your family. It is a difficult life also, but this choice might help your family more. Have you been trained as a Highland warrior?"

"Aye, when we lived in Salen on our farm my *athair* was able to teach me. Perhaps, if you release me, I can go to the Duke in Tobermory and enlist in the Highland Army."

"I do not wish to keep you as a prisoner any longer, but I am not sure that I can trust you," responds Anna to this pitiful prisoner.

"Here I will give you my *dirk* and some coins that I have from my

246

recent robbery," offers Finlay. Anna is not sure that she should mention a soldier's hardships to this young lad. However, it is more honorable than being a robber. Maybe not less dangerous, but more virtuous.

Then Anna has a brilliant idea. "Finlay McKinnon, I have thought of a way that you can help us and also earn my trust."

"And what is that lassie?" questions Finlay.

"If I release you, can you prove your worthiness by traveling to Dervaig and getting someone to cart my *athair* back to the shelter of the village? There is a *kirk* and a hotel in Dervaig and the folks will be able to guide you to the townsfolk who will be willing to help us. Dervaig is not that far away."

"Lassie, why do you trust me to carry out that task?" Finlay asks.

"I do not see you as a bad lad. I believe that you will prove yourself. What do you think, Finlay? Can I trust you with this important mission?" Anna asks.

"If I were in your place, lassie, I would think this to be unwise. However, I would like you to trust me. If you release me I will make haste to travel to Dervaig and make the townsfolk aware of your situation. I also hope that you will not betray me, because I want a new start. You can expect help to arrive."

Anna does not know what her *athair* would say if he knew that she was releasing the prisoner. However, he is asleep right now and she wants help to come as soon as possible. After she makes sure that Finlay's *dirk* is not within his reach, she carefully unties his feet first. When he doesn't run she carefully unties his hands. Finlay, still feeling the effects of the blow, rises unsteadily. It takes a few minutes for his body to adjust and then he turns to Anna. "Remember to expect help by sunset," he reminds her as he leaves.

Anna watches her *athair*. Gradually Lach awakens from his sleep and he murmurs that he is in a lot of pain. Anna draws closer to him. "*Athair*, I released the prisoner. The cloth ties were not strong enough to keep him immobile for very long. He has promised to seek help for us in Dervaig." Unexpectedly Lach agrees with her choice of actions, "I do hope that he follows through with our request. Meanwhile all we can do is rest here. I do not have enough strength to walk to Dervaig." Anna and Lach share the packed food and water while they wait. Anna never lets her *athair's dirk* leave her side.

The afternoon drags on. Lach is in a lot of pain while Anna is anxious and wary. The sun gets lower and lower in the sky. Anna can't let go of her worries. Did she do the right thing? She questions her decision to free the prisoner. But she does not question her decision to accompany her *athair* on this trip. What if she had not been around when Lach was attacked. Would he be dead or lying on the path, badly wounded? She will not allow herself to fall asleep even though the boredom of the slowly passing time encourages such a reaction.

She and Lach are startled when they hear voices and a whinnying from afar. They wait anxiously in anticipation and soon spot Finlay running. Behind him is a horse and cart and several townsfolks. They hear their rescuers crying out, assuring Anna and Lach that they have come to help. The group finally reaches Anna and Lach. "I am Lach and this is my *nighean*. Thank you for coming to help us out. We were attacked by two bandits. They ran and left us here to perish. Finlay came along and agreed to lead you back to us," explains Lach.

They load Lach into the horse-drawn cart. After collecting their goods Anna climbs in and sits beside her *athair*. Placing his head on her lap, she silently thinks that she has never felt as close to her *athair* as she does right now. She notices Finlay and motions to him, "Finlay, thank you for getting help. I have one more favor to ask. Would you make the trip to Inivea and find my *mathair*, Catherine Maclean? She will be out in our garden or in our *bothie*. Introduce yourself as a friend and tell my *mathair* that we will be staying at Dervaig until Lach feels well enough to walk. Will you do this for us?"

Finlay responds with a positive nod, "Aye, Lassie, I will carry the message to your *mathair*. I will need your name also so that your *mathair* will believe me."

"My name is Anna, Anna Maclean. You can also mention that her *fear* and *nighean* traveled successfully to Tobermory to say goodbye to her *mac*, Seathan and his *bean,* Rose. With that information she will trust that what you say is true."

The folks of Dervaig watched as Anna and Lach entered the outskirts of the small village. Lach recalls that there is a small inn. He asks the driver to park in front of the inn. "Driver, what is the name of this inn?" The driver responds, "*Bellachroy*, a very old inn, since 1608." Lach is carried by the stretcher into the inn. Anna follows with their bags and Finlay takes off for Inivea.

Finlay at last arrives in Inivea and travels up the path to the glen and nears the *bothie*. Catherine, who is tending to her garden, is startled to see a disheveled stranger coming up the path towards her. Her *fear* and *clanns* are not around to protect her.

When the lad gets nearer Catherine notices his youth. He is slight of figure and does not appear to carry any arms. He looks earnest to get her attention and suddenly calls out, "Catherine, I come here with news about Lach and Anna."

"What news and why are they not here?" questions Catherine. Finlay responds, "Catherine Maclean, your *fear* and Anna were ambushed by bandits outside of Dervaig."

"Oh no," screams Catherine, a piercing cry which could be heard throughout parts of the glen.

"Anna was not hurt but your *fear* was wounded with two stab wounds in his side and arm," continues Finlay. "Your *fear* is alive but in great pain. He was transported by a horse and cart to the village of Dervaig. He will stay in a room in the inn called *Bellachroy*. Even though Anna was able to stop the bleeding, he has lost a lot of blood and is weak right now. He will not be able to travel back to Inivea for a couple of days," says Finlay finishing his summary.

Catherine questions Finlay, "Where are you from?"

To cover his role Finlay lies, "I was returning home to Tobermory from Dervaig where I was visiting some kin when I came upon your family. Anna asked me to return to Dervaig and get some folks who would agree to rescue Anna and your *fear*. They came with a cart and drove your kin back to the hotel for the night."

It was growing dark and Catherine suggests, "Let's go to the *bothie* of Seumus, Lach's *brathair*. There you will be fed and you can stay the night. In the morning Seumus will borrow a horse and cart. You can ride back with him to Dervaig where he will leave you and then he will bring Lach and Anna back to Inivea."

Meanwhile Anna and Lach are spending another restless night at the hotel. Lach continues to be in a lot of pain and Anna, sleeping near him, hears his moaning all night long. In the morning Anna will look for *Lus na fala* (yarrow) to help heal his wounds.

The morning finally arrives, and Anna asks Lach, *"Athair,* how are you feeling?"

Lach responds, "A little better than last night but I am still in a lot of pain."

"Here, have some bread, cheese and water. You need to build up your strength," asserts Anna.

"I wish I was back in Inivea with Catherine," Lach adds.

Anna reassures her *athair,* "While you eat and rest I will go into the fields and see if I can find some *Lus na fala* to help heal your wounds. I will be back in a while."

While Anna is out in the fields a few of the villagers come with bowls of hot porridge, milk and fresh berries for Lach and Anna. Lach is grateful for the meal, "I appreciate your kindness."

Anna returns shortly with bunches of *Lus no fala* found in the fields near the hotel. She asks the proprietor, "Can you give me a bowl of hot water so that I can make a compress of these herbs for my *athair's* wounds?"

"Aye," replies the innkeeper. "Wait here and I will return shortly. I hope that he is better."

"Aye," responds Anna. "He is well as can be expected."

The old gentleman, stooped and slow-moving, ambles off to a back room. After several minutes he returns with a bowl of steaming water. He has placed a cloth around the bowl so that it can be carried.

"Thank you for your kindness," says Anna to the aging innkeeper.

As soon she returns to their room Anna sees Lach eating. "This is a good sign, my *athair.*" Anna prepares the herbs and while they are brewing, they both sit on their beds and finish the meal brought by the generous villagers. Once the solution cools sufficiently, Anna soaks a rag and makes a compress. She then applies it to Lach's wounds. Lach is grateful for his young *nighean's* knowledge of healing herbs and for her loving attention.

Meanwhile back in the glen of Inivea, Seumus borrows a cart and horse. He and Finlay quickly leave and arrive in Dervaig just as Anna is applying the compress to Lach's wounds. Seumus leaves Finlay outside to mind the horse and cart. He enters the hotel and asks the proprietor about the whereabouts of Lach and Anna. Before going to their room Seumus settles the bill.

Seumus knocks at the large crude door while at the same time announcing his presence, "Lach and Anna, it is me, Seumus."

Anna opens the door and embraces her *brathair-athar,* "I am so happy to see you."

Lach calls from his bed, "Seumus, it is good to see you. I am ready to go back home."

"Lach, I have borrowed a horse and cart and if you are ready, we will leave immediately," adds Seumus.

While Seumus helps Lach out of his bed and out to the cart, Anna gathers their goods and follows. As they are nearing the cart they spot Finlay. Anna is the first to greet him, "Thank you, Finlay. You have done a good job at helping us out. I wish you luck in Tobermory."

"Goodbye, Anna," responds Finlay. To Lach he says, "I hope you will feel better soon." Finlay bids them a final goodbye as he takes off for Tobermory.

Anna has one final word for Finlay, "If you meet my *brathair,* Seathan and his *bean,* Rose, let them know that you met us on the road back to Inivea. Don't tell them the whole story because they will worry about us."

After an uncomfortable trip for Lach, they finally arrive back in Inivea. Catherine who is out in the garden sees them immediately and greets them with tears in her eyes, "Oh, Lach, I am so happy to see you and so sorry that you were wounded."

Lach is helped out of the cart by Seumus and assisted into his *bothie* . He is placed on his bed and Catherine comes in and sits beside him. "I need to sleep awhile," Lach pleas.

"Of course, Lach, sleep as long as you like," adds Catherine.

While Lach is sleeping, Anna updates her *mathair* of the events of the past few days. She does not share the whole truth about Finlay. Anna tells her about saying goodbye to Seathan and Rose and that there are no ships that have left Tobermory for several years. "Seathan and Rose will stay with Rut and Tomas. They hope they can earn some money and find a place of their own," shares Anna.

Catherine then updates Anna on the news of Inivea, "While you were gone Sine gave birth to a little *mac.* Both Pastor Robertson and Sine are delighted with their little *bairn* and they named him Adhamh from the bible. I gave Adhamh his protective rites of birth. Isobel Campbell has also given birth to another *mac* and she named him Alexander. Although Isobel wanted a *nighean,* she is happy that this *bairn* is healthy and strong.

PART VI
A New Century Unfolds

57
1803

It is now February and as is the custom among the clansmen, Inivea is having a winter *ceilidh* to break up the darkness of the winter and despair and give the crofters and villagers time to socialize and have fun.

Donald Campbell helps his *mathair* with the youngest *clann* as well as the chores of the *bothie* and farm. Now in his 20s, he is frustrated and yearning to establish his own livelihood and independence. He is proud that he has learned to read in Gaelic and takes time daily to read the bible. He also meets with Pastor Robertson weekly to discuss the meaning of its verses, particularly the Old Testament. However, being able to read in Gaelic serves no practical value for him in Inivea.

Roderick continues to work with his *athair* in the blacksmith shop. Roderick has the luck of having a trade handed to him. Donald often feels the sting of disadvantage and struggles to find his way. Roderick is busy with his *athair* and does not have the inclination to listen to the troubles of his younger *brathair*. Donald's *mathair* is the only one that he can confide in. Isobel is sympathetic to Donald's plight but does not have answers for him.

Anna Maclean is now 18 years old. During the years since her visit to Tobermory, Anna had struggled with returning her hair to its natural red color. She and her *mathair* decided that the beginning of the new century would be the right time to transform. They discuss whether it will be better to dye her hair red or wait until it grows out naturally. "*Mathair*, I am now ready to return my hair to its natural color," shares Anna. "There are two choices; let it grow out naturally or dye it red over the brown shade," answers Catherine.

"It will take a long time but I would rather I let my red hair grow out naturally. I can wear my *snood* to cover up my hair as it grows out. I can also cut my hair so that it will not take as long. What do you think my *mathair*?" questions Anna.

Catherine responds, "I think it will work. Have you thought about how you will handle those folks who will be questioning the sudden appearance of your red hair?"

"I guess I could either ignore the questions or make up a tale about wanting to blend in. I will have time to decide," replies Anna.

Now Anna has a mass of red wavy hair. Her *snood* covers up most of this vibrant mass. At the *ceilidh* Anna is looking forward to what might be of life changing importance. She has been casting her eyes at Donald. For the last three years he has been the focus of her yearnings. Now that the occasion has arrived, Anna wants some input, "*Mathair*, I think that young Donald Campbell is a very handsome young man. What do you think?"

"I agree with you, Anna," responds Catherine. Catherine has been aware of Anna's current interest in Donald. Hesitantly Anna questions her *mathair*, "How do I let Donald know how I feel?"

Catherine shares how she met Lach. "Anna, when I met your *athair*, I was a little older than you are now. I was at a winter *ceilidh*. That is where your *athair* and I made our first acquaintance. I was sitting across the room from him. It was crowded and I never thought he would notice me, but I had a plan. My plan was to join the other young kinfolk in some of our Highland country dances. Every time I passed by him I would smile and hoped he would notice. That first year Lach did not acknowledge me but I never gave up. A year later he did and asked me to dance. A year after that first dance we were married."

Anna, encouraged, continues, "There is also the issue of my red hair. I have heard folks whispering when I pass by them as I travel to the village to have my lessons with Beitris. No one has been bold enough to accuse me of practicing black witchcraft. Do you think that Donald will dislike me because of my red hair?"

"I am not sure, Anna, but I don't think that he will have a problem with it," answers Catherine. "Donald and his family have been our good friends ever since they settled here. They have known about your red hair since the death of Eilidh and they do not blame you for that. I believe you are safe with them and with Donald."

"We shall see," responds Anna. Although she has let her red hair grow out, the stigma has never left her.

The night of the *ceilidh* arrives and Anna dresses in her finest

Sunday wear and dons her *snood*. She does not regret her decision of returning to her natural hair color. She continues to believe that her success in treating folks with herbal medicine will develop trust. Her reputation of helping her *athair* when he was wounded is well known around Inivea.

The family leaves their *bothie* and halfway to their destination, a sudden snow storm begins. The path in front of them is soon covered with snow making their trek to the *ceilidh* difficult. Familiar with the violence of winter storms, Lach quickly instructs his family to turn around and head back. The wind begins to howl and blow forcefully. The snow is blinding and not only is it difficult to see the pathway, but it is also difficult to stand up. Anna and Iain hold onto each other while Lach takes the arm of Catherine. The icy-cold air also makes it difficult to catch one's breath. All know that they must get back to their *bothie* as soon as possible. They look behind them and spot other kinfolk making their way back. Anna is glad that they are not the only ones returning.

58

News from Pastor Robertson

On a lovely spring day Donald Campbell is making his weekly trip to Pastor Robertson's home. He decides that it would be good for Alexander to make the short trek with him so that Alexander and Adhamh can have some playtime together. Donald has loved watching the *clann* of Sine and Pastor Robertson grow from being an active *bairn* into an inquisitive 5 years old. He notices that Adhamh is very bright. He is able to speak both Gaelic and English and has begun to read in both these languages. Donald compares Adhamh to his younger *brathair*, Alexander, and is aware that Adhamh is much more serious and less playful than his own *brathair*. Alexander, it appears, brings out the playfulness of young Adhamh.

Donald also enjoys his time with Pastor Robertson and he relates to the difficulties that the early Israelites had in their lives. It reminds him of the challenges that the Highland clans have had throughout the centuries. The comparison helps Donald to deal with adverse conditions in his own life.

Donald hands over the active Alexander to Sine. Adhamh is very happy to have playtime with his good friend, Alexander. The housekeeper leads Donald to Pastor Robertson's office. Pastor Robertson is expecting Donald and his Gaelic bible lies open on his desk. "Pastor Robertson, what story shall I read today?"

"I believe that the story of Job would be a good story to read," responds Pastor Robertson. Donald begins Job's story. He has read it before but it has been awhile. Donald always has questions when reading the Bible stories and today is no exception.

Donald stops at the passage, 'And the Lord said unto Satan, Behold, he is in thine hand; but save his life.' "Why would the Lord give Job to Satan?" queries Donald.

"This Old Testament story is one of the most difficult Bible stories for Christians to understand," replies Pastor Robertson. "Continue on and perhaps you may gain some insight into the meaning of the

Lord's choice."

So Donald continues to read as he questions within himself the why of each evil that Satan has cast upon Job. Finally, Donald reads the words of Job's wife and Job's response to her. 'Then said his wife unto him. Dost thou still retain thine integrity? Curse God and die.' Job responds, 'But he said unto her; Thou speakest as one of the foolish women speaketh. What? Shall we receive good at the hand of God, and shall we not receive evil?' The Bible concludes the tale saying "In all this Job did not sin with his lips. Throughout his troubles Job loved and trusted God. In the end God rewarded Job for his righteousness. He bestowed upon Job more than he had before."

Donald then questions Pastor Robertson, "Do you think that God has made a pact with the Devil to give the clans all that they have endured through the ages?"

Pastor Robertson attempts to sooth Donald's confusion. "Donald, sometimes we cannot know God's intentions. I think that the story of Job tells us that it is important to continue to trust and love God no matter what troubles befall us. I know that this is difficult for a young man, eager to make his way in the world, to understand. I believe that someday you may discover new horizons."

With that Donald rises and replies to the Pastor, "Pastor Robertson, it is difficult to accept what you are saying, but I will continue to learn and try to understand."

On the next Sabbath, Pastor Robertson announces to his members that he has been called to another *kirk* outside of Edinburgh. He also shares that for the past thirteen years he has come to love and admire the folks of Inivea. He shares that Sine has mixed feelings about leaving her village, but she feels better knowing that Elizabeth has been trained to be a midwife. He wishes God's blessings on the crofters and Inivea's village residents. He and his family will not leave until the new Pastor arrives in a month. Meanwhile, Donald is stunned. He had no inkling that the Pastor would be leaving Inivea.

Outside their *kirk* when their Sabbath service is over, Donald is not the only one that has been shaken by Pastor Robertson's announcement. The clansmen feel betrayed by him and cannot remove themselves from their anger and dismay. They had rejoiced in the marriage of one of their own to the Pastor. They had shared in Sine's and the Pastor's delight with the birth of their *mac*, Adhamh. With all this history they cannot understand why their Pastor would leave them.

Donald, meanwhile, is pondering over the last Bible lesson he had with Pastor Robertson. Is this why Pastor Robertson had him read the story of Job?

Back in the *bothies* of the Campbells and the Macleans, all are astir. They are not as upset at the fact that their pastor is moving to a new *kirk* as they are of the timing of his departure. Through the years they have relied on his leadership and guidance.

Up to now the residents of Inivea have felt exempted from the ongoing tragedy of the many Highlanders. Seumus and Lach decide that it is time to hold a *coinneamh* to talk about the recent events. Before Seumus leaves, Lach shares "Seumus, I just received word from Tobermory that Seathan and Rose have sailed to Prince Edward Island, Canada aboard the ship, *Rambler*. The note is dated May 1803. I hope that they have a safe passage. They have had to wait five years for a ship."

Lach continues, "I have begun to envision also taking my family to North America. Although our laird has not informed us that he is going to do the same as the other landowners on Mull, he might soon be tempted to make the same choice. I hear that there is a bigger profit in raising sheep and selling their wool than supporting a bunch of croft farmers. The past loyalty of the chiefs and lairds to their tenants is quickly disappearing in favor of more money."

Seumus adds, "I share your fears about our future. Right away we need a *coinneamh* to discuss our concerns with everyone. I will alert our *brathairs* and their *beans* and you can alert Catherine's *siuirs* and their *fears*."

Lach adds, "I can also go to the village and invite others, such as Iain Campbell and his family. I think that the next full moon will give our kinfolk enough notice."

And with that they leave to start telling the others.

59
Goodbyes

It will not be easy to move a family and household goods to Edinburgh from Inivea. During the month while everyone is waiting for the new Pastor to arrive, Pastor Robertson and Sine prepare for their move. The housekeeper who has a *nighean* in the village will stay and live with her and her family. They will have to leave a lot behind and take only those goods which they will need in their new home. They will also bring along some personal belongings that they treasure; books, hand-made quilts and favorite toys of Adhamh. They will leave most of the furniture for the new Pastor of Inivea. They know that they will find their new manse in Edinburgh to be adequately furnished for them.

Their plan is to rent a horse & cart and hire two villagers, Malcolm and James Campbell, to accompany them to Craignure where the Pastor will find a ferry or hire some fishermen to transport them across the Firth of Lorn to Oban. In Oban they will hire a coach to transport them to Edinburgh. The whole journey will be arduous and take about a month.

The villagers and the farmers have had time to forgive their Pastor for leaving them. They plan a farewell party for him and Sine. In the center of the village in front of the *kirk*, the villagers set up several large wooden tables and the parishioners bring the food to share. Anna and Catherine have gathered bouquets of May flowers and placed them in large wooden containers on the tables. Although there is a slight chill in the air, the weather has cooperated with a sunshiny afternoon.

Once everyone is gathered the Pastor speaks to the crowd first, "My parishioners, it is with great sadness that I must say my final goodbye to all of you. My life here in Inivea has been rich with friendships. And I know Sine is grateful for the special kinship that she has felt from everyone. We both will miss you greatly. I will keep in my memory the beauty of this Isle and the strength I have witnessed from each of you to make a meaningful life here. Life is not easy on this rugged landscape, but you have all managed to maintain deep connections with your family and land."

"Sine and I are headed to a new and bigger Parish, but it is here that I gained in my ability to be a Pastor. All of you have been good and loyal teachers. I know you are concerned that a new Pastor has not arrived and I promised to stay here until then. I do not know the reason why one has not come but I am hoping that there will be one soon. Meanwhile I must leave to fulfill my commitment to my new Parish. I wish all of you God's blessing and courage as you face all of the changes in the Highlands."

After the Pastor's goodbye, Caitriona presents her gift to Sine. "Sine, I hope this blanket will always remind you of your home. May it also help you to remember all the lives that you helped bring forth into this village. Many of those that you helped birth are here saying goodbye to you. Best wishes for a good life in your new home. We wish your son, Adhamh, health and wisdom in his youth and adulthood. May God shower all of you with many blessings."

At the conclusion everyone cheers, "Aye, aye, aye and God bless you." The Parishioners then sing "Auld Lang Syne" as their final goodbye to their beloved Pastor and his family.

60
An Alarmed Community

Several days later the folks of Inivea gather together for the *coinneamh*. The clansmen had been informed earlier about the purpose of it and came armed with observations, thoughts and questions. Seumus begins first, "Lach and I decided to call this time together to start sharing our concerns about what is happening on our Isle and in the rest of the Highlands. All of you have probably heard of the terrible changes that are being inflicted on many clansmen. Here in Inivea we have remained safe thus far, but I believe that our destiny will soon be affected."

"Aye, aye, aye," shout many of the attendees of the *coinneamh*.

"We are at the mercy of our laird," shout others.

One of the villagers, Morgan, stands up and bellows, "My rent goes up every year and I can no longer pay what the laird claims is due him. He states that his own expenses go up each year and thus the rent must follow. I ask him what expenses and he tells me that improving his estate requires more money. We don't benefit from his estate improvements so why should we have to pay for them? We struggle on our small allotment of land each year."

Lach interjects, "Aye, to raise enough cash each year to pay my own rent I work on his estate. When I started 18 years ago, the laird appeared to be sympathetic and willing to help me out. However, as the years have gone by, the laird has become more and more greedy."

"It is difficult for the *beans* and *clanns* also," adds Lili. "My *fear*, Brian, leaves me early every day so that he can go to the sea and harvest kelp. The earnings from this trade are small but we must have these extra wages to pay our rent. My *clanns* and I do the best we can. The laird does not account for our hard times. He cares not. It is not like the time of our ancestors when the chiefs took care of their clansmen."

"Aye, aye, aye," a chorus of *beans* scream. At these exclamations of despair some of the clansmen shout out, "What are we to do? We have no money to make changes in our lives."

Lach then adds, "I fear that we might be forced soon to make changes against our will. I believe that a time of our eviction is coming closer and closer. Our greedy landlord will soon recognize the benefits of raising sheep for wool and meat. Are there any of you that believe we will be spared the fate of so many other Highlanders who have been forced to leave their farms and *bothies*?"

Lach gives himself a minute to get control of his emotions and then turns calmly to his clansmen. "Now is the time for us to decide what we will do. We have seen too many folks passing through our farms and village, dislocated by eviction and lack of work. Some have been forced to relocate to the rocky lands near the ocean so that they can earn money through kelping. Others have emigrated to the lowlands. And a few have boarded ships to faraway lands. What choice shall we plan for?"

"We are poor and have little to make changes," add some of the clansmen.

"That is why we have to start planning right now to help ourselves," adds Seumus. "Families must begin to plan and stick together to save money so that they will be able to make the changes that are best for their families. I, myself, and my grown *macs* have been talking about our options. My *macs* will work in the kelping industry and contribute to the pot. My *brathair's mac*, Seathan, and his *bean* have just sailed from Tobermory to Prince Edward Island in North America. We will be saving to join them someday."

"That is easy for you to say, Seumus," shout many from the crowd. "We do not have grown *macs*. We only have *nigheans*."

"Our *nigheans* are strong women. We will figure out ways to add to our pots," adds Lili.

"The road ahead of us is not easy, I know," adds Lach and Seumus together. "This is a beginning. Unless we have more to add, we can depart and begin discussing solutions in our own families. We will have more *coinneamhs* to share our progress," closes Seumus.

61
Crisis in Inivea

There are lots of rumblings throughout the village of Inivea when news gets out about the recent *coinneamh*. Some of the villagers are angry that they were not invited. However, the Macleans and the Campbells are not selfish with what was discussed in their *coinneamh* and soon the plans are shared and adopted by the rest of the villagers. Before everyone can focus on making plans for their future, there is a crisis in Inivea.

Several *bairns* and *clanns* in the village are ill with small pox, as well as several adults. Anna and Beitris have been very busy visiting affected *bothies* with herbs which lessen some of their symptoms.

Anna makes a visit to Marta's to check on Michael. She brings more herbs for Michael. She looks at Michael who is lying on his bed. She gives him a dose of *Lus nan laoch* (roseroot) and asks him how he is feeling.

Michael responds with a groan.

Anna comforts Michael by wetting a cloth in a nearby bowl and putting it on his forehead. "Michael," she says, "the herbal mixture should help you feel better."

Michael, unable to respond, turns his head and body away from her and closes his eyes.

Anna leaves Michael and joins Marta at the fire. Anna whispers, "Michael does not appear to be improving."

"Aye, Anna, nothing seems to help him" responds Marta. "Lately he has had little energy, sleeps a lot and eats very little. I worry that he is more than just run down. He is now seventy-three years old and I don't know what God has in store for him."

Soon after Anna's visit, Marta breathlessly appears at Catherine's *bothie*, pleading for their help. Anna and Catherine can see that she is quite distressed. Marta cries out, "My Micheal is suffering so and has taken a turn for the worse. Please come with me right away." Anna quickly retrieves her satchel of herbs and then she and

267

Catherine don their cloaks and follow Marta.

When they enter her *bothie*, Micheal is groaning. Anna pulls a stool over to his bed. She places a cool hand on Micheal's forehead which is very hot. He is able to murmur that his head and back are hurting. Marta adds, "He woke up this morning in agony and complained of a severe headache."

"I have brought some *Lus-Marsalaidh* (Scots Oregano) which might lessen his pain," consoles Anna.

Despite the diligent and loving ongoing care from Marta, Anna and Catherine, Micheal dies within a month. He was unable to fight off the small pox which afflicted him. Marta is grief-stricken. The only thing that Marta is grateful for is that Michael will never have to experience a relocation to a new land across the seas.

As is the custom, Micheal is prepared for his burial by the *siuirs* of Marta. Marta's *bothie* is silent as Marta, Lili, Molly and Catherine wash Micheal's scarred body and then wrap him with *winding sheets.* Word has spread around the village, first by the tolls of the bell ringer and later by word of mouth.

Catherine consoles Marta and then says, "We must go now to prepare the food." Seeing Marta distressed, she assures her, "We will return soon. Anna will remain to assist you."

"Aye," responds Marta as her eyes fill up with tears. Soon Marta's young kinfolk arrive to watch over the body. In low hushed tones familiar bible verses are spoken and hymns are sung. Over the next several days folks come solemnly to pay their respects. After everyone has viewed the body, the women wrap Micheal in a burial sheet.

"The time has come to carry my *fear* to the men for the funeral procession," states Marta.

"Aye," reply all the women.

Waiting kinsmen hike the body up so that they can carry Micheal to the churchyard. Lach is in charge of announcing the stops along the path to the village to rest and switch the pall bearers.

Soon Lach announces, "Here is the first *cairn* (a mound of stones built as a memorial). We will rest the body on it and the new kinsmen will carry the body to the next stop." Each of the kinsmen, carrying the body of Micheal, scoops up a stone and throws it to the side of the road as a token.

Pastor Lindsay, recruited from Dervaig, meets the procession at the churchyard. The men of the crofts and the village enter the gateway. At the gravesite Pastor Lindsay reads verses from the Gaelic bible and several hymns are sung by the attendees. The women, including Marta, listen at their customary places outside the fence and join in the service when the hymns are sung. Meanwhile the *siuirs* of Marta stay back at their *bothies* preparing the after-funeral feast.

62
A New Year, 1804

The previous year was a terrible year for the clans of Inivea and for all of Mull. Sickness and poor crop yields resulted in near starvation for many of the islanders. There was little energy among the clansmen to focus on escaping the Highlands in pursuit of better opportunities across the seas. In February the residents of Inivea need relief from the gloom and desperation. Thus, the word was spread through the crofts and the village that the date was set for a February *ceilidh*.

Anna is excited as she shares again with Catherine. "*Mathair*, as you know I will be 19 years old this month and I continue to desire a more grown-up relationship with Donald. When I am dancing I will smile more intensely at him and I will invite him to dance the reel with me. Do you still think that this is a good plan?"

Catherine replies thoughtfully to Anna, "I still believe that you are ready to consider a relationship with Donald. However, these are difficult times. I have talked to Isobel who reports that it is a particularly troubling time for Donald. There is no labour or land to establish a farming livelihood and a home."

After her conversation with her *mathair,* Anna, not discouraged, is ready to make her interests known to Donald. She is anxious about carrying out her plan, but considers that the time has come. The night arrives and Anna combs her beautiful long red hair and puts on her Sunday petticoat. Just before she leaves she stuffs her hair under her *snood.*

It is still winter on the Isle and it is difficult to take a breath in the frosty air filled with the icy crystals of winter. The snow has held off and the family makes its way down the path to the *ceilidh.* They finally arrive and open the large wooden door of the *aite cruinneachaidh.* Many of the clan families have already assembled. The fiddler is playing familiar Scottish tunes and several folks have formed dance lines of a reel. Anna looks over to the area where the

Campbells are usually gathered and she spots Donald who is not looking her way; instead he is entertaining his young *brathair*, Alexander.

The Macleans relax on the benches at first, welcoming the warmth of the large fire after their long trek in the bitter cold. The *ceilidh* is an appreciated distraction to the sufferings of the past year. Caitriona appears at the door and she spots her family. Anna knows that Caitriona is grateful for time with her family. She moves closer to her *mathair* so that Caitriona can sit with them. Anna has missed her older *siuir* and she grasps her cold hand with a display of affection. Caitriona holds onto to Anna's hand tightly, indicating that she also has missed her *siuir*.

Anna speaks first, "Caitriona, will you join me in the dance?"

"You go first, Anna," responds Caitriona. "I want to warm up and spend more time with my *parantans* and Iain"

Anna nods and makes her way to the dancing group. She finds her way at the head of the reel. Across from her is one of the village youths. The music is intoxicating and soon Anna is lost in the world of music and dance. She momentarily forgets that her mission tonight was to engage Donald enough so that he would recognize her interest in him. The music stops before the fiddler starts another dance tune. Anna wakes up from her dreaming and looks over at Donald. She finally catches his eye. She gives him an intense smile and motions him to join her in the next dance.

Donald sees Anna's invitation, hands his *brathair* over to Isobel and makes his way over to Anna. Anna's heart flutters with anticipation of the attention of Donald. "Hello, Donald," she utters breathlessly. Anna wonders if Donald notices her lack of composure. "Hello, Anna, it is good to see you!" answers Donald.

The dancing, the music and the hubbub of the *ceilidh* do not leave room for much conversation. Anna hopes that Donald got her message of interest. Donald dances several reels and then excuses himself to go back to his family. Anna could have danced the reels with Donald all night, but she knows that dancing is not Donald's prime attraction at the *ceilidhs*. After Donald departs, Anna remarks to herself that she is honored that Donald spent as much time dancing with her as he did. Time will tell if he feels the same way about her as she does about him.

Finally, the evening of socialization is ending. Anna is happy with Donald's response to her. She again looks over at the Campbells before she and her family leave the *ceilidh*. She notices that Donald is not sitting with his family. She wanted to wave a last evening goodbye to him. Just as she was giving up hope of making this last connection with him, Donald appears at her side. Anna blushes when she notices him beside her. Her cheeks are almost as red as her hair. Donald takes her aside momentarily and quickly requests permission to call on her. Anna replies, "Aye, aye, Donald. Come when the weather improves and we can sit outside on the stools." At that encouragement from Anna, Donald quickly leaves her and returns to his family.

63
Anna and Donald

Spring is in the air. It is Anna's favorite time of year. She decides to hike down to the village and visit Beitris who lately has been under the weather. Sometimes she wonders to herself how she can leave the beauty of her island. The thought of all the changes brings tears to her eyes, but not given into raw emotions, she quickly wipes her tears away. She instead focuses her thoughts on what is in store for her and soon arrives at the *bothie* of her mentor. Working with Beitris and learning the skills of herbs and healing has helped Anna gain confidence in her own abilities.

Beitris greets her at the door. She does not look well. In fact, she looks worse than just last week. Feebly Beitris ushers Anna in, "Good afternoon, Anna. Come in. I am happy to see you." Anna carefully enters through the big oak door of the shop. She is cautious not because she is afraid, but more out of concern for the spectacle that she sees before her. Anna decides to wait before she shares her impression until Beitris speaks first. "I have a pot of hot water for some tea," announces Beitris. "The spring air still has a chill in it and the hot tea, I am sure, will warm your insides and my fire will warm the rest of you," adds Beitris.

"Let me help you with the tea, Beitris," comforts Anna. "You sit, and I will make our tea."

Beitris, who is quite fragile and in ill health, does not protest. She sits on one of the stools around the fire.

Then Anna decides to speak, "Beitris, I am concerned about your frail appearance. I am noticing a decline in your condition since last week. Are you ill?"

Beitris answers matter-of-factly to Anna's inquiry. "Anna, I am not well. I feel tired and weak. I do not think I have much time left. I have come to terms with my demise. You have been a good student which has helped you become a gifted healer. I think it is time you take over. Folks have come to trust you due to your innate ability to make the

275

right decisions about ailments and herbs. I have also come to trust you."

Anna exclaims, "Beitris, I still need you by my side."

"I know that you count on me to continue to mentor you, Anna," responds Beitris. "However, I have taught you all I know. You have been a good student and I do not have the well-being to continue."

"I still worry that without you by my side folks will suddenly turn against me, accusing me of witchcraft because of my red hair," adds Anna, defending her position.

"Anna, this will always be a reality for you, but I believe you should not desert your God-given gifts out of fear."

"You are right, Beitris," agrees Anna, "but I will miss you."

"You are a healer and some folks consider us as white witches," explains Beitris. "Embrace your gifts and your role as a healer. God will be by your side."

Several days after visiting Beitris, Donald makes a visit to Anna. Anna had just donned her *snood* and is ready for a hike in the woods.

"Good morning, Anna," shouts Donald from a distance.

Startled, Anna turns around and sees Donald on the path from the village. She blushes. "Hello Donald."

Donald comes closer. "I have come to call on you as I promised at the *ceilidh*."

"I am happy to see you but I am ready to go into the woods to find plants for my practice," shares Anna. "But, if you would like, you can join me. It is a perfect morning to walk in the woods. The woods will be filled with our Isle's beautiful spring flowers. Outside my *bothie* I have been listening to the birds returning to our Isle."

"I would love to join you on your search, Anna," replies Donald.

Anna shouts to her *mathair*, "*Mathair*, Donald has come to call and will join me on my search for healing plants." Anna knows well that the custom is to have a caller remain within earshot of the family. However, she also realizes that Donald has long been a friend of the family and will be trusted.

"I am ready, Donald. We can leave now." They are both silent as they proceed towards the woods.

Donald speaks first, "Anna, I am so happy that we at last can be together to talk and share our thoughts."

"Aye, as am I," replies Anna.

"I have long had my eyes on you Anna but held back due to my own situation. Anna, it is difficult for me to consider a relationship because I have no way right now of providing for a family. I can't find any labour except to go to Tobermory and work in the kelping industry. This would take me away from my home and you. Other options are even worse. I could go to a large city in the Lowlands and find work in the factories or become an apprentice in a trade."

"Aye, Donald, the situation here is difficult," responds Anna to his feelings of hopelessness. "For me the idea of relocating to Tobermory sounds like the best option for you and for our future together. There you could work and save. Many in Inivea are wondering when our laird will decide to force us off our farms so that he can enclose our farmland. My family is saving extra cash as best we can and waiting for word of the next ship that will take us to faraway lands."

"Aye, Anna, my family is also working towards that goal. We hold no hope of a future of remaining in Inivea. Compared to your family, we are new residents here. We left our ancestral home in Ballygown so that my *athair* could support his family. For many years he has been able to do what he set out to do. The blacksmith trade has been good to us but my family, like yours, is worried about our future."

"Donald, you could live in Tobermory and work in the kelping industry. Every month or so you could travel back to Inivea and we could continue to see each other, planning our future together. We can soon marry even though we will be unable to live together. I will continue to be a healer, saving any earnings I receive from my services. Then, if the situation looks good and you find temporary housing for us, I can move there to be with you."

Donald responds, "This plan sounds good Anna and it makes me happy." At that Donald takes Anna's hand. While they walk and hold hands Anna is silent but content. Along the way she stops and picks the plants that will help with her healing work.

64

A Conversation with the Laird

Lach continues to work for his laird, saving as much cash as he can for a passage on a ship to North America. Lach decides to ask him about his intentions towards the farmers. One day he gets his courage to confront him. "Laird, I am hearing tales of other lairds evicting farmers from their farms in the Highlands. Do you have such plans?"

"Do not worry, Lach, I have not considered such horrible plans for my faithful farmers of Inivea. You can be assured of that."

Lach replies, "Good day then, I am at peace with your answers." Lach leaves his laird but in truth has not been calmed by his response. While hiking on the path back to his *bothie*, Lach is reminded about his laird's treatment. Despite his recent reassurances that he appreciated the farmers' loyalty, Lach has not seen how this has been imparted to his "faithful servants." Although he had given him work, he had paid him minimal wages for back-breaking work. Raised rents, almost annually, have also caused all of his tenants to suffer excessive hardships.

He returns without his usual enjoyment of the spring beauty of Inivea. Instead his thoughts focus on speculating about the laird and his plans for his renters. He arrives and finds Catherine preparing the soil for spring planting. The setting sun is almost fading into the horizon and dusk is beginning to set in. The evening spring air has become cold and Lach calls to Catherine to come inside. Catherine is glad for the evening's interruption of her work. She takes the kettle of hot water and prepares several bowls of herbal tea. Anna and Iain will be returning soon for the night. Lach sits down and shares his thoughts with Catherine. "Catherine, I spoke to the laird about his intentions regarding the farmers."

Catherine sits besides Lach and responds to his comment, "What did he have to say?"

"He said that he has never considered such a terrible fate for his

279

faithful tenants. Catherine, I do not trust our laird," discloses Lach. "Our laird has not been the kindest or most sympathetic landlord to our people. He satisfies his own selfish needs without a care to the hardships and poverty of the crofters. Every time I have asked for an increase in my own wages he would complain about his own economic difficulties, while making sure that he hired servants to maintain his estate, inside and out. Meanwhile, he raises our rent almost annually because of his own economic difficulties."

"Sadly, I agree with all you have shared, Lach," acknowledges Catherine. "Unfortunately, our lairds have not adopted the role of the former Highland chiefs. The wool of sheep will be a lot more profitable for the lairds than the rent of their tenants. I see our future, if we remain much longer on Mull, to be extremely difficult with no work or home and extreme poverty. We just have to hope that a ship will arrive at Tobermory in time to sail us across the seas. If we are lucky the ship will come soon with the destination of Prince Edward Island. But no matter where it takes us, we will sail. The new lands have to be a better situation than our future here."

Just as Catherine finishes her thoughts, Iain and Anna open the door and join them around the fire. Anna speaks up first, "Why are you talking about a ship and our future here on Mull? Have you heard any recent news?" Lach responds to Anna's questioning, "I discussed the possibilities of eviction with our landlord today. He said that he was not planning on it, but I don't trust him. He has shown himself to be greedy and lacking in compassion. We must keep up with our plan to save for our escape."

Iain then shares, "As you all know I was planning on joining the Highland Branch of the British Army, but after hearing what Seathan went through I have changed my mind. Instead I would like to go to Tobermory and stay with my uncle, Tomas. In this way I will work and earn money which I will save to pay for my passage on a ship to North America. I hope that Anna and my *mathair* will be able to take care of the animals and the farm while I am gone. I will return in late Autumn to help out around here."

Anna then pipes in, "You may have noticed that Donald Campbell and I have developed an affection for each other. Like you, Iain, he is also planning to relocate to Tobermory this summer to seek any available work so that we can save for our wedding and eventual passage abroad. Donald will be sharing this with his family very soon.

It would be good if you can travel back and forth to Tobermory together."

Catherine then adds, "This sounds like a very good idea. Hopefully we can plan for a more positive future."

Lach gives his amen to the situation. A disheartened mood has never left Lach. However, with the news of Iain's and Donald's plans to work in Tobermory in order to save for a passage on a ship, the mood of Lach appears brighter. He never did take to the idea of taking an herb to lift his spirits.

65

The Passing of Beitris

Iain and Donald are soon ready to leave Inivea for Tobermory. Due to the current unrest on their Isle, both families are relieved that their *macs* will be traveling together on the dangerous road to Tobermory. Both Donald and Iain have been trained in warrior ways and carry their *dirks* and swords. Donald arrives at the Maclean bothie for departure. While Iain says his goodbyes to his *parantans,* Anna visits with Donald. Anna's last words to Donald are whispered in his ear, "Take care of yourself, Donald. I will miss you but I know your parting is for our future."

Donald speaks lovingly back, "I will miss you also, Anna. Thinking about our future together will give me the energy to work hard. I will return when I feel the cool breezes coming off the ocean, reminding me that the cold weather is not far off. Iain and I will travel together and keep each other company through the long spring and summer. I believe that we should not abandon our work to return here until our kelping is finished for the season."

"Aye, Donald, I will miss you greatly but your decision to remain in Tobermory sounds like a good idea," replies Anna. Iain emerges with Catherine and Lach behind him. Anna gives her *brathair* and Donald a final goodbye hug.

After Donald and Iain leave for Tobermory, Anna decides to go into the village. She carries her cloth satchel of plants and makes her way down the pathway. The weather is grey, misty and very windy, typical of an early spring day. The breeze comes off the ocean and her nostrils are filled with the salty brisk air of sea mists. Anna is used to this early spring weather, but she is also eager for the warmer summer months to arrive. In the summer months she will have more to do on the Maclean's farm and the warm weather will bring fewer illnesses to the farmers and villagers. It will give her time to help her *mathair* with the chores of the household and farm. When she reaches the village, she will first stop in on Beitris and get an update on the healing needs

283

of the villagers. Then she will visit Caitriona and the Campbells so she can update them on Iain and Donald's departure to Tobermory.

As she nears the village she first passes the former home of Pastor Robertson. She sighs with a sadness. During this time of confusion and unrest, Anna misses his guiding presence. The Heads of the Church of Scotland have not seen fit to give Inivea a new Pastor. If they want any spiritual guidance the villagers and farmers have to travel to Dervaig; about an hour and a half away by foot. In the summer and spring months they are too busy working their farms. The rest of the year the weather is too unpredictable to make the journey. So the villagers and farmers basically go without their Sunday worship.

Anna then passes by the cemetery and memories of little Eilidh permeate her being. She still has not been able to let go of the accusations of Rut about black witchery. Anna fears that without the religious guidance of the pastor, the villagers and farmers might return to their old folklore of witches and monsters. Then she passes by the old stone *kirk*, deserted and dark. The grounds are unkempt and weedy. Folks have given up on ever having any religious services again in their home of Inivea. Anna wishes that someone would watch over and keep the old *kirk* and graveyard in good repair.

When Anna sights the shop of her mentor Beitris, she buries her thoughts and focuses on seeing her. Beitris has been a very special friend and advisor in her young life. She has gained much insight and knowledge of the world from Beitris. Beitris had lived with her family in Edinburgh where she had training from the knowledgeable herbalists of the city. When she was in her mid-twenties, Beitris decided to move to the Isle of Mull where her ancestors had originated. She never married but instead devoted her life to the folks of Inivea. She was well respected in the village as well as in the glen by the croft farmers. Although alone in the village without family, she never appeared to be lonely. She was always busy trying to help folks with her herbal and healing skills.

Anna reaches the shop and knocks on the old large wooden door. When there is no response she calls out, "Beitris, Beitris, it is Anna. Are you home?" There is still no response. Perhaps she is on an emergency visit to someone in the village. However, Beitris had pretty much retired from her occupation, leaving the work to Anna. Anna decides, nonetheless, to open the door and peer in to see if there is any sign of Beitris. Doors are never locked in Inivea. What Anna sees shocks her. There on the floor of her shop is Beitris. Anna quickly closes the door and runs to the Campbells. She is cautious because she does not want to be suspected again of being responsible for another death.

When she reaches the Campbells, little Alexander is playing outside. Anna asks him the whereabouts of his *mathair,* "Alexander, is your *mathair* inside?'

"Aye," responds Alexander. "She is getting ready to go to the garden. My *athair* and Roderick are in the shop."

Anna goes up to the door and knocks. Isobel comes quickly to the door. She is not expecting Anna but is happy to see her. "Anna, what brings you here so early," questions Isobel.

"Isobel, I am in the village to visit Beitris and make any calls needed for my herbal remedies. When I knocked on the door of Beitris's shop, there was no answer. I carefully opened the door and saw her looking lifeless on the floor. I came to you immediately to check on her. I believe that I still have to be cautious around death, if that indeed is the condition of Beitris."

"I will grab my shawl and come immediately," responds Isobel. They both hurry over to Beitris's shop. Isobel enters first and spots Beitris's lifeless body on the floor. She checks Beitris for signs of life. "She has no life left in her," Isobel says. Together they look at Beitris's body and notice a large bump on her head. "It looks as if she fell and hit her head on the cabinet."

Then Anna notices some herbal oil which she could identify immediately by its pungent earthy odor as *Common Valerian.* There is also a half-filled bowl of herbal tea still warm. A sniff of the tea leads Anna to believe that it is a potent mixture. Beitris knew the dangers of this herb if not taken in small doses. She wonders if Beitris was ailing so much that she decided to mix a strong concoction of the tea. She drank it and feeling dizzy and disoriented, she fell. Anna will not share this thought with anyone. She would not like to spoil Beitris's lifelong reputation of being a gifted healer and caregiver.

Isobel finds a blanket and places it over Beitris's body. She will gather folks in the village to provide an appropriate wake and funeral for her. Some folks in the village did know of Beitris's family in Edinburgh and a messenger will be sent to inform them of Beitris's passing.

Anna is relieved that Isobel will take care of the wake and funeral needs of Beitris. Isobel will put the word out to the villagers while Anna will inform the croft farmers. Before she leaves she inquires if Isobel knows of any ailments in the village needing her herbal healing. Isobel indicates that there are several folks who are not feeling well. "Thank you so much, Isobel, for taking care of the funeral arrangements. I will visit my *siuir*, Caitriona, and then the folks who are sick to see if there is anything I can do.

Quickly Anna heads to the shop of Flora McDonald to inform them of the recent passing of Beitris. Anna knocks on the door of the shop and is greeted as the door opens by Caitriona. "It is so good to see you, Anna," greets Caitriona. "And I you," responds Anna.

Once inside Anna and Caitriona give each other a warm, embracing hug. Flora comes out, "Anna, it is so good to see you. What brings you to the village?"

"I came to visit Beitris who was not feeling well last week," replies Anna. "But the bad news is that when I knocked at her door there was no answer. I looked in and Beitris was on the floor. I ran to Isobel and told her what I had found. She quickly went with me to Beitris's shop and found that she was dead. She will prepare for her wake and funeral and alert the villagers about her passing. I was going to visit some folks who are ailing, but I think instead I will return to the glen and give the sad news to the farmers. I will wait until after the funeral to tend to the ailing villagers."

Beitris was a beloved person who always gave comfort during dark times. With great sadness the folks of Inivea honored her with a beautiful burial and service. The minister from Dervaig came to perform the ceremony.

Because Beitris was without living relatives in Inivea, the customary burial traditions were organized by the Campbells. Anna and Catherine helped with food preparations. Beitris was buried in the cemetery alongside her several deceased ancestors. After the service the folks of Inivea celebrated her life with food, music and dancing.

PART VII
Three Years Later—1807

66
Donald and Iain Return to Tobermory

As they promised, Donald Campbell and Iain Maclean made the trek to Tobermory and kelping every spring. They return in the late summer to spend the winter with their families. Their hope is that the extra cash will eventually be enough to help transport their families away from Mull and across the ocean to a new life. Each spring they have hoped that they will hear news of a ship.

Another spring has come and Donald treks from the village to the Maclean's to collect Iain and say goodbye to Anna before they leave for Tobermory. Anna worries about her *brathair* and Donald. They return at the end of each summer, looking thin and pale. Both Donald and Iain complain about aching legs and arms. Their eyes are always blood-shot and half-closed.

Anna hopes that this is their final season of kelping. Their earnings are minuscule and what they do earn is not a good trade for the weakened state of their health. When they are not in the ocean kelping, their eating and sleep time is spent in a wet, crudely-erected hut near the bay. They subsist mainly on oatmeal and water, except for the weekly visits to Tomas and Rut's who feed them well and give them some extra produce from their small croft farm.

Rut continues to work as a maid at the hotel and Tomas has been able to leave kelping to work in the local distillery. Lucas and Deidre continue to maintain the crops and livestock of the farm. The generosity of Tomas and Rut has made the existence of Donald and Iain somewhat improved, compared to most other kelpers working alongside of them.

Before he leaves, Anna and Donald embrace and whisper sweet thoughts. Anna adds, "Donald, I hope that this is Iain's and your last year as kelpers. None of my herbs can make up for the cruel conditions of kelping. You and Iain need a long lazy summer to return to your good health." Anna knows that her wish is an unrealistic dream. But at least their legs and arms could find relief away from the cold ocean waters. Their eyes would also have a chance to heal by spending time away from the acrid smoky conditions. Anna then hands Donald and Iain packages of *Vetch* (Wild Liquorice) which will help keep their appetites satisfied on their long journey to Tobermory. While Anna is saying her goodbyes and reflecting on her concerns, Catherine comes out from the *bothie* to hand them satchels of food and bid them farewell. "Iain and Donald, please take care of yourselves and have a safe journey to Tobermory. Give my blessings to our kinfolk." Donald and Iain depart, glancing back one more time before they disappear into a curve in the path which hides them from view.

Anna then announces, "*Mathair*, I will take my satchel of herbs to our kinfolk. I will stay with Marta for a while. I know that she gets lonely without Micheal. I am hoping that the rest of our kinfolk are feeling well. I will be back before the sun goes down."

67

Torquil Becomes Ill

Anna first visits Lili and Brian. Much to her dismay she finds the whole family in bad shape. Brian had been well enough until today. He was nursing the family but now he, himself, is also suffering from a severe sore throat. Anna first brings Lili and Brian some water and then prepares her herbal concoction. Before she is able to administer the mixture to them, she hears great moaning coming from a bed nearby. She quickly goes over to the bed and finds a very hot Torquil (25 years old).

Anna knows that Torquil must be cooled down. "Brian, help me fill some buckets with cold water from the outside. Torquil is burning up," announces Anna. She and Brian then go outside and fill buckets. When the tub is sufficiently filled, Anna takes several kettles of hot water and adds them to the tub.

"Brian, quickly get Torquil into the tub," insists Anna. Torquil groans more as he sinks into the cool water. He shivers and cries. "We cannot leave him in the water too long. Feel his head, Brian," advises Anna. Is it cooler?"

"Aye," replies Brian

"I will gather some cloths and you wrap Torquil up until he is dry," instructs Anna.

Brian carries Torquil back to his bed. Torquil's moaning has stopped. He has cooled down but he continues to complain of a very sore throat. Anna quickly administers her herbal mixture to the family. Anna is particularly concerned about Torquil.

Anna stays around for an additional hour nursing the family. Throughout her stay Torquil continued to moan. To Anna's relief he had at least stayed cool. While there she checks on Niel (23 years old) who also was not feeling well. He does not appear to be as ill as Torquil, however. She gives him the herbal medicine and checks his head for fever. He is slightly warm so she places a cool wet cloth on his forehead. She advises Lili and Brian to do the same for both their *macs* throughout the night.

Although Lili is still feeling quite sick, she rises and sits beside her *mac*. She takes a damp cool cloth and wipes Torquil's forehead while Brian does the same for Niel. She comforts her *mac*. "Torquil, you will feel better soon. Anna's herbs will give you relief."

Before she leaves Anna cooks some porridge for the family. She promises Lili, "I will let the rest of our kinfolk know about your family's condition. I will return in the morning to check on you."

Feeling that she has done all that she can right now, Anna leaves and rushes to the *bothie* of Seumus and Moire. She knocks on the door and then lets herself in. She finds the family preparing their evening meal. Moire speaks, "What is wrong, Anna. You look as if someone has died."

"I have come to let you know that Lili and her family are ill. Torquil is the sickest. I have just come from spending time with them, but I am worried," Anna replies.

Moire assures her, "We will help them with food and their care."

"I am going to Marta now to let her know," Anna replies. "I will spend some time with her and return to Lili and Brian's in the morning."

With the news of the illnesses of Lili's family, Marta is very concerned. "I will go over tomorrow and bring them some food." Anna then spends some time with Marta. While visiting, she and Marta talk about the hardship of the difficult winter. More folks than usual are ill. They are hoping for warm weather and sunshine. Anna thanks Marta for her promise to look over the well-being of Lili and her family and then departs.

Anna arrives back at her *bothie* just as the sun is setting. "Lili and her family are quite ill," reports Anna to her *mathair*. "I fear for Torquil. His head and body were burning with fever. I prepared a cool tub of water to cool him off and with Brian's help we got him into the tub. It cooled him down but swallowing is very painful. He doesn't eat except for tiny amounts of broth. Before I left I made the family some porridge. I will return in the morning."

During the month Anna continues to check on the status of Lili and her family. After several weeks most of the family have recovered, but Torquil continues to have bouts of fever and coughing and remains very weak. Lili and Brian hope that warm weather and summer sunshine will help him recover.

68

The Laird Looks Out
for His Own Pocketbook

The festival of La Bealltainn had always been a renewing celebration. This year, however, this hope had instead become a huge cause of dismay for the farmers of Inivea. A cold and wet summer left many vegetables rotting in the fields and several unseasonal hail storms left crops damaged and broken.

After the previous punishing winter the clansmen became more and more discouraged. As May went into June, June into July and finally August there was no letup of the poor weather. Everyone was fearful knowing they would be facing another wretched winter. Lach complains to Catherine, "How will we feed our family? With the meager crops this summer we will not have enough food."

Catherine responds, "We will survive. We will have to ration our food. We no longer have *bairns* to keep alive."

Lach also fears that the laird will soon announce that he and the rest of the farmers must leave their *bothies* and farms with no word of a ship arriving in Tobermory.

One late day Lach sees his laird approaching him. He gets a lump in his throat fearing the worst. The laird nears him, "Good evening, Lach. I have come to you to tell you that I have to make changes here. As you must know, maintaining property of this size drains my pocketbook. I now must manage the crofts of my tenants differently. I have delayed making my decision for as long as possible."

"I hope that this is not what I fear," adds Lach.

"I am afraid it is," announces the laird.

"But you promised me several years ago that you would never evict me and the other crofters from their homes and farms," states Lach.

"I know that I made that promise, Lach, but nothing in life stays the same and circumstances have forced me to renege on my promise."

Lach bows his head momentarily to control his anger. "Laird,

I don't believe that you can imagine what this might mean to me, my family and my kinfolk. We have been a loyal tenant for many years and now you turn against us."

The laird then replies, "I must look out for my family and heirs, as you must look out for yours. I will give you and the other crofters six months to evacuate your farm. There is land near the ocean. You can farm that land and build another home. Since you have time you will be able to transport all your goods there. This is a better proposal than most other lairds offer their tenants. Meanwhile I will begin to arrange for the purchase of sheep and I will enclose the property where the crofts and *bothies* are. The villagers can stay, if they wish."

Lach then replies, "It is the middle of August and six months away will bring us into the dark of winter. It will not be a good time to establish a new croft or build a new *bothie*."

"You are right about that," responds the laird. "It will also be a bad time to transport sheep and establish them in new enclosures. I will give you a year then, but will show no mercy if you and your kin have not left." Lach reports that he will share the news with the other crofters but perhaps the laird, himself, should also appear and inform them and the villagers about the evictions."

"I will see that I get to the glen and to the village to announce my decision," agrees the laird.

Lach treks back with a heavy heart. He will have to give Catherine and Anna the bad news. If only there was word of a ship planning on coming to Tobermory this summer. But alas there has been no such word. He takes his time to make the trek, trying to delay his announcement for as long as he can. The sun is setting when Lach arrives. He opens the heavy wooden door which feels heavier than usual.

Catherine and Anna are sitting on their stools around the fire. Anna has been telling her *mathair* about her visits, "Except for Lili and her family I found our other kinfolk well. Seumus and his family are sad that their oldest and only mac, Calum, who emigrated to Glasgow, has not been heard from for over a year. They pray that that he was able to find Lili and Brian's oldest *macs* there. Marta is lonely and continues to mourn the death of Micheal."

Lach reluctantly joins Catherine and Anna at the fire. "I have bad news," he shares. The laird has told me that all of the glen has to leave their *bothies* and crofts by the end of next August or there will be sad consequences for all who do not follow his orders."

"He plans to burn down all the standing buildings and enclose the land for the sheep which he will import. Contrary to his promise to me, he has decided to follow in the footsteps of the other lairds who have already evicted their poor tenant crofters. The villagers will be allowed to stay but I imagine many of them will not want to."

"He informed me that we are free to relocate to the ocean. Hah, does he not know that the soil there is sandy and rocky and not fertile enough to grow? I am sure he knows but does not care. I told the laird that I will tell my kinfolk. He assured me that he will also inform the farmers and villagers about his decision."

Catherine then speaks, "We knew that this was coming. We have all been saving our extra cash. I believe that we have enough, if only a ship would arrive needing passengers. I know that Donald and Iain will travel back to Inivea to inform us immediately if they hear of one. Meanwhile, we will plan how we will dismantle our home and what to do in case a ship does not arrive in time."

"In the morning I will visit our kinfolk and inform them of the laird's decision," says Lach.

As promised the laird had called a meeting at the *kirk* for all the villagers and crofters. He announced his plans to evict them from their homes and land. He explained that his expenses were getting too high and that he was going to enclose their land and use it for raising sheep. The villagers could stay in Inivea if they wished but they would still be the laird's tenants. He concluded that those in the glen had a year to leave his land and their *bothies*.

There was much talk in Inivea following the visit of the laird. Seumus and Lach meet outside Lach's *bothie* a few days later. Sitting on the stools, Seumus speaks to Lach, "Well, the time has come. We have a year to make plans. I hope a ship comes in before next August."

"I will sell most of my livestock this autumn when the drovers come through," responds Lach.

"Aye, that is a good plan. Right now, however, I am going to the village to bring my *dirk* for sharpening. Do you have anything that you want me to give to Iain?" questions Seumus.

"Aye," replies Lach. "My *dirk* could also use sharpening. I will not bother with my farm tools. It will be the last season of use."

"Aye," agrees Seumus.

"Wait a moment while I get my weapon for you." He leaves Seumus.

While Seumus waits for Lach, he thinks about his trek to the village, "Perhaps there will be clansmen gathered lamenting about the recent news." As soon as Lach returns, Seumus places the two *dirks* under his belt and takes off for the village. Before he descends out of sight, he looks back at Lach and utters, "I will return before dark."

Lach waves an agreement to his *brathair*.

Seumus treks down the well-worn path to the village. Despite a difficult winter and a poor growing season this summer, he is despondent at the need to leave his beloved Mull. It is the land of his ancestors and he wanted it to be the land of his *clanns*. It is not to be. He cannot keep his mind from reviewing his life and all the changes the years have brought; good & bad. The sight of the village and the folks milling around awakens him from his reverie.

He waves to several of his clansmen and then heads right away to the blacksmith's shop. He knocks and then enters. Iain and Roderick are busy making repairs. Farm tools, household items and weapons are lying about. Both look up as Seumus enters. Iain speaks, "Good afternoon, Seumus."

"Iain, Roderick, how are you?"

"Busy, but disturbed by the laird's decision," answers Iain. "What brings you here?"

"I have my *dirk* as well as Lach's to be sharpened." Do you think you can sharpen them while I wait outside?"

"Aye," responds Iain. "It should not take too long. I will send Roderick out to fetch you when they are ready."

Seumus agrees, "That is perfect." With that he leaves and crosses to the grassy area in the middle of the village where he sees some of his kinsmen gathered. Several Campbells, Malcolm, James and Dughall along with Morgan MacKinnon, are talking together. As he gets closer Seumus can see from their voices and faces that they are angry.

Dughall, the elder clansmen, is speaking when Seumus approaches, "I know the situation is very difficult, but we need to face reality and make plans now and through the winter."

"Aye, we know that," Malcolm and James utter unanimously.

Seumus does not say anything during this discussion. He knows that it is going to be a time of difficult choices and he has no easy answers for them.

Morgan cries out in anger, "Where is God?" Why is he not helping us?" "Aye," they all agree.

The anger of the gathering continues until Roderick arrives to tell Seumus that his work is ready. Seumus, who has hardly been recognized during the meeting of his kinfolk, says his goodbyes.

He quickly gathers the sharpened weapons and returns to the home of Lach. He shares what happened at the gathering, "I met several of our kinfolk and they are angry and bewildered. I had no answers for them. They will need time to face the realities of their situation and make decisions." At that Seumus departs knowing that there will be a lot of conversations and plans to be made by all during the year.

69
The Return of Donald

Anna's hands are full caring for all the ill folks. She misses the support of Beitris. It was not only tending to the sick in the community but also conferring with her about the best herbs to use for the various ailments.

The stress on Anna is at times almost too much to bear but she sticks to her mission hoping that she, herself, will not succumb. Throughout her young life Anna has known illnesses common to folks in the Highlands but these lasted no longer than a week or two. She feels fortunate that she has avoided some of the fatal diseases such as small pox, diphtheria and consumption.

Despite knowing that they will all need to leave by next summer, they still have to face winter. With heavy hearts the farmers carry on with their usual chores of harvesting the crops that had made it through the wet growing season. Panic and fear are evident as they meet and debate where they will go if their ship does not come in. Some mention Glasgow and others think the longer trek to Edinburgh is better. Except for farming few have other skills which could provide income for their family. What they have heard is that these large cities have deplorable conditions for living. The only work available is in dark factories. The older folks have little hope of finding a better life.

One day in August as Catherine and Anna are tending their crops they hear a voice from the distance, "Anna, *mathair.*" At once Catherine and Anna look up from their chores. In the distance they spot two figures. They recognize that it is Iain and Donald. Donald seems to be hunched over and limping with Iain supporting him. Anna moves closer, "What has happened," she calls out. "Why are you here before the autumn weather has begun?" Anna adds. "Do you have news about a ship?" There is no answer. The two figures continue to walk towards Anna but with great effort, especially from Donald.

Finally, Anna and Iain and Donald meet up with each other. Donald raises his head and peers at Anna with red bloodshot eyes and a hopeless stare. Iain speaks for the two, "Donald has been feeling ill all summer. He finally admitted to me that he could no longer carry on with the kelping and had to return to you and his family."

"Oh, my poor dear," Anna speaks out while embracing Donald at the same time. He can barely remain upright. The trek from Tobermory was the last straw. Anna observes this and supports him on his other side. They make their way to Catherine, who has been waiting. She calls to Donald and her *mac*, "It is so good to see you but not under these circumstances." Once they reach her they all sit on the outside stools. It is only then that Iain recounts their time in Tobermory.

"Right from the start Donald was weak and ill. When I suggested that we return before we even got to Tobermory, Donald insisted on continuing. He said to me that as soon as he could rest for a while with Tomas and Rut he would feel better. When Tomas and Rut arrived back in the evening, they gave us some food and Donald felt better. That next morning Donald and I made the decision that we would set out to the bay early, find our make-do hut and begin kelping. Donald kept saying that he needed to save cash for Anna and himself so that they could sail to North America to begin their life together." Iain then responded to Anna's question, "No, there has been no word of a ship."

"Due to his weakened condition, Donald worked like a man on his last legs. I continually badgered him to return back to Inivea. He was as stubborn as our young calves who balk at walking between the bonfires at the *La Bealltainn* festival. One day, however, Donald collapsed; his legs buckling under him. I was standing beside him but was not quick enough to catch him before he went head first into the salty ocean. If the circumstances of his fall were not so desperate, it would have been a comical sight. I raised him out of the water and brought him to the shore. Fortunately, it was a warm and sunshiny day. When he dried off, I supported him as we made our way back to the hotel. I rented a room for a couple of days after I informed Rut of the situation. The next day Rut came with some food. With the care that Tomas and Rut have given to Donald and myself, I can forgive her for how she betrayed you. I will never be able to forget but I do forgive her."

"I do also, Iain, but will never be able to feel safe with her," responds Anna.

"When Donald became a little stronger we decided to hike back to Inivea. It was a rough trek and it took longer than usual. Donald needs a lot of care and rest and maybe some of your herbs will help him. In a couple of days I will go back to Tobermory. I will inquire of our kinfolk and maybe one of their *macs* will go back with me and take Donald's place in Tobermory."

It took the rest of the summer for Donald to recuperate. Anna gave him a daily dose of *Lus nan laoch* (Roseroot). "Donald," Anna inquires, "how long have you been feeling this weak?"

Donald replies, "I was feeling somewhat tired before I left in the spring. I thought I just needed some time to feel better. Instead, working in the cold ocean, I got worse. I tried to push my way through my weakened state believing that I would soon regain my strength. It did not happen. Finally one day I just could not continue to hold myself erect."

Through the rest of the summer Donald spent most of his time resting and being carefully tended by Anna. Sometimes he would also trek to the village to be with his family. There they talked endlessly about the laird's decision to evict his tenants from the crofts. Although Iain and Roderick were blacksmiths, they knew that once the crofters were gone they would not have enough work to sustain them. They could migrate to one of the larger cities of Scotland where their skills would be needed. Iain commented, however, to his *macs* one day, "I don't want to relocate our family to Glasgow or Edinburgh when the eviction happens." Then speaking directly to Donald, "I want us to join you and Anna. It will be difficult to start all over again. But I would rather take the chance on making a new life in a new land with my family than remaining here in Scotland."

Donald responds to his *athair*, "I am happy that you will be joining Anna and me, but surprised. I did not think that you would want to leave Scotland."

"Once we heard about the laird's decision, your *mathair* and I had many discussions and finally decided that we also would like to emigrate. Roderick will come with us and, of course, Alexander. Have you talked to Anna about a wedding?" adds Iain.

"We have talked some but believe that we should hold off until we felt more secure. However, now that the laird has made his decision, it appears that Anna and I should decide. Perhaps this September will be a good time. There is no sense in building our own *bothie*. We will stay together at the Macleans' until the time to depart arrives. I hope that a ship will come soon so that we won't have to figure out a temporary residence. I realize that we are safe here in the village, but Anna would not desert her family. They also want to emigrate to new lands. We will all go together."

One day soon after he had a conversation with his *athair*, Donald treks to the glen to see Anna. He meets Anna out in the garden, harvesting some fresh vegetables. "Anna," Donald begins, "I think it is time for us to marry. I am feeling much better and I believe September will be a good time. What do you think?"

Anna had been waiting for this formal proposal from Donald for a long time, but she knew any earlier timing would have not been right. "Aye, aye, Donald," Anna responds quickly. "I think that will be a good time. And when a ship arrives we will be ready to emigrate to new lands together as a married couple."

Thus, the last weeks of August were filled making wedding plans. The first thing to decide was the date. They needed to ask the pastor in Dervaig to perform the ceremony. He would tell them his schedule and what was a good date. The pastor promptly came up with September 26, 1807, a Saturday. Anna was very happy that the pastor had time in the month of September for her marriage to Donald. She recited an old rhyme to her mathair:

"Married when the year is new, he'll be loving, kind, and true.
When February birds do mate, you wed, nor dread your fate.
If you wed when March winds blow, joy and sorrow you will know.
Marry in April when you can, Joy for Maiden and for Man.
Marry in the month of May, and you'll surely, rue the day.
Marry when June roses grow, over land and sea you'll go.
Those who in July do wed, must labour for their daily bread.
Whoever wed in August be, many a change is sure to see.
Marry in September's shrine, your living will be rich and fine.
If in October you do marry, love will come but riches tarry.
If you wed in bleak November, only joys will come, remember.
When December snows fall fast, marry and true love will last."

Anna seeks confirmation, "*Mathair*, due to the circumstances I believe that my marriage to Donald should be subdued but a happy one. We will have some food, music, and dancing. Everyone will be invited but we will have a simple ceremony. Our wedding will probably be the last one in the Inivea as we know it. There will be some sadness even though we will try to make it as happy an occasion as it can be. I know that all will understand."

"Aye, Anna, your words are true, but I believe that folks will not let you down and they will want to make sure that your wedding will be a memorable one," adds Catherine.

70
The Wedding

While Anna is pleased about the wedding plans she continues to be very concerned about Torquil's condition. The sore throat is gone but new symptoms have developed. She is troubled that his symptoms resemble those of Eilidh who just wasted away and eventually died. She was blamed for Eilidh's death and she hopes that the kinfolk will not accuse her of black witchcraft again. She will talk to her *mathair* about her concerns. Maybe she will know something else to try.

Today, however, she can only help Lili and Brian with his care. The first task is to cool him down and then put him in some clean dry cloths. When Torquil is back in his bed, Anna asks Lili, "Do you have some warm broth that I can give Torquil?"

"Aye, I will get it," replies Lili. "We have been trying to feed him, but he refuses, saying that he cannot stomach a morsel."

"I will try again," replies Anna. "He is losing too much weight." Anna then puts a wooden spoon filled with the broth to Torquil's lips. Torquil takes a couple of sips and then motions Anna to stop. Anna then recommends to Lili, "Let Torquil take small doses of broth but frequently."

"That we will do," answer Lili and Brian in unison. Anna stays a while and then departs, knowing that there is nothing else she can do.

She returns home and her *mathair* is out in the garden harvesting root vegetables. Anna watches her awhile. From her worried countenance she believes that Catherine is thinking about Lach. She knows that Catherine broods about the stress that her *fear* is undergoing as he continues to work for the laird. It is taking great restraint for Lach to hold his tongue. However, he silently keeps on so he can accumulate as much cash as possible for the future. Holding in his real emotions is taking its toll, filling him with despair and depression.

Anna greets her *mathair*, "Torquil has become sicker. I am very worried about him. Lili and her family are holding their heads up hoping for recovery, but it doesn't look that way to me. Torquil's symptoms look a lot like those of Eilidh. I don't like focusing on my own well-being in such a time of need, but I am worried that if anything happens to him, I will be accused of black magic."

Catherine then interjects, "Anna, your fears are even more unfounded now and were baseless then. Remember, it was proven by me that you had no connection to the death of Eilidh. I don't know why God decided to take Eilidh from us at such an early age, but it was not your fault. You are not a Black Witch!" Catherine then adds emphatically, "You are a healer and have helped many with symptoms of illness. You cannot be expected to save folks from every ailment. Remind yourself that you have helped relieve the discomfort of many. It is important, if you want to live a fulfilled life with Donald, that you let go of these fears or they will accompany you to North America and your grave."

"I hear what you say, *mathair*," murmurs Anna. "I am afraid, however, that God will decide to take Torquil from us as he took Eilidh."

"That may be, my dear Anna, but you will not be responsible for whatever happens to him," comforts Catherine. "You have done your best to help relieve his symptoms. That is what you have been trained to do. Sometimes we must give up our fate to the decision of God. It is too bad that a new pastor has never been assigned to our *kirk*. Donald might help you with your doubts. You and he will be together after you are married and you will have time during the dark season to listen to the bible's passages."

Anna responds, "*Mathair*, I hope that will help me but I still have my doubts."

Several days later Lili comes running to the Maclean's *bothie*. Tears are streaming down her face. "Catherine, Catherine," she screams out. "My Torquil passed away during the night. When I did not see him stir this morning I went over to his bed and he was not breathing and his eyes were closed. I think he died sometime during the night. He has been having more and more trouble with his breathing." Catherine moves closer to Lili and embraces her *siuir* lovingly and compassionately. "I am so sorry, Lili. Anna and I will come over at once." Catherine and Anna then gather their shawls and follow Lili.

Brian and Niel are sitting beside Torquil. Both are quietly weeping. Brian speaks to Lili as she enters with Catherine and Anna, "I don't understand why God should take him from us. He was always such a caring and helpful *mac,* especially when his older *brathairs* left for Glasgow to seek work. I believed that I could not lose another and now I have lost Torquil. Next May when we must leave, we will go to Glasgow to find our two *macs.* I cannot bear to be without them too."

At that point Lili and Catherine move to take care of Torquil's body while Anna extends comfort to Niel and Brian. Throughout the morning Torquil's body is prepared for burial. Anna then departs to spread the word of Torquil's passing. After alerting kin, she hikes to the village to inform her betrothed and the other Campbells. She visits the shop of Flora and shares the sad news with Caitriona. Her last stop is to inform the bell ringer of Torquil's passing. His bell outside the *kirk* will let the villagers know that there has been a death. Soon all the villagers will know and Torquil will be waked for several days. Niel, Donald and Roderick keep watch over his body until all the visitors have paid their respects. Then Lili, Catherine and Anna carry Torquil's wrapped body to the men. The men travel down the path with the body to the cemetery where Torquil is buried next to the ancestors of Brian.

Not long after Torquil's burial, Iain and Malcolm, the *mac* of another farmer, return from kelping in Tobermory. As they enter the glen Anna sees her *brathair* first in the distance. "Iain," she shouts in vain. They do not hear her at first. But Anna's call has alerted her *mathair* and she opens door. She moves near Anna and blends her calling voice with her *nighean's.* Together they shout out, "Iain, welcome home." Finally Iain and his companion hear the welcome and their pace picks up, energized by the familiar voices.

"*Mathair,* Anna," Iain calls as they reach each other and embrace. Malcolm adds a perfunctory hello. It is not that he is rude, only eager to return to his own family.

"How are you, Iain?" questions Catherine. With a summer that has been filled with mainly disappointments and the tragedy of Torquil's death, she is eager for the warm embrace and news from her *mac.* Before they embrace Catherine takes a moment to look at him and sees that he is wan and thin. He has a dark beard and mustache which hides some of the deep furrows of his face. It doesn't hide the fact, however, that the work in Tobermory has taken its toll on him.

Iain responds, "I am well, *mathair,* but very happy to be back in Inivea and to be with you and my family. How is everything here in our glen? What's the news around here?"

At that Catherine fills him in on the sad news about the passing of Torquil and the plans for Anna and Donald's wedding. Malcolm, eager to see his own family, bids Iain farewell, "Goodbye, Iain. See you soon"

After Malcolm's departure Catherine suggests, "Let's go inside and I will fix some tea for us."

"Aye, I would love that and maybe some fresh bread and cheese," says Iain. "Do you have any fresh berries?"

Catherine replies, "No fresh ones but I have some blueberry jam that you can put on your bread."

"Oh, I would love that. I am famished after our long trek from Tobermory," replies Iain.

Iain puts his satchel of clothes near his bed. He motions to his *mathair*, "The clothes in my bundle are filthy. Kelping and the ocean have made them unfit for wearing."

Catherine enlists the help of Anna with serving tea while Iain sits on the stool by the fire, "Anna, carry over the bowls for the tea and I will bring the hot water. You can then help me bring the food."

Soon all are sitting by the fire and Iain, hungry and tired, is silent for several minutes while he gratefully eats. Catherine and Anna who are aware of his exhaustion leave him alone.

After finishing his meal, Iain states, "I need to go to my bed and rest for a short while. Later, you can update me on more news. I am sorry to hear about the death of my *co-ogha*."

While Iain is resting Catherine looks through Iain's satchel, "Anna, Iain is right. These clothes are a bunch of rags. In fact, after they are washed, that is what they can be used for." Iain's satchel is then placed outside and Anna and Catherine spend the rest of the afternoon out in the garden, harvesting turnips and digging up potatoes.

Iain sleeps for a while and when he wakes, Catherine invites him outside to sit on the stool with Anna and herself. Catherine asks Iain to talk about his summer, "Tell me more about your time in Tobermory."

With a downcast look Iain shares, "There is not much to tell you. It was the same as last year and the other years. It is gruesome and exhausting work and difficult for everyone. I will be relieved when I don't have to do it anymore. Tomas and Rut and their *clanns* were very good to us and helped us endure another summer in

Tobermory."

Anna expresses her concern about the conditions of Iain's work, "I am sorry that the work in Tobermory is so difficult and I will also be glad when you do not have to return." She then decides to share with Iain how she felt after Torquil died, "I did all I could to help Torquil when he was very ill. I went to Lili and Brian's every day to care for him, but all the time I was very afraid that he was going to die. I saw that Torquil's symptoms were very similar to Eilidh's. When Torquil died my old fears about being labelled as a Black Witch came up again. I can't shake it."

Iain comforts distressed Anna, "You must not be afraid, Anna. Times have changed. We are now in the 19th century and those old-fashioned beliefs have subsided. Instead of thinking of you as an evil witch, folks now look on you as a healer. You cannot expect yourself to cure everyone. Someday we will be far from here and the old black witch label will soon be forgotten."

During the next weeks Anna tries to forget her fears about being labelled a witch and focusses instead on her wedding needs. Caitriona has woven her a white shawl and veil. Anna visits her to get her wedding shawl and veil, "Oh, Caitriona," she exclaims as she tosses the shawl over her shoulders and dons the veil. "These are so lovely, and I will feel so beautiful on my wedding day," Anna adds.

The wedding day arrives at last but there is a pall throughout the glen. The bright and celebratory mood that Anna and Catherine have hoped for is lacking. Dark clouds, rain and cold winds from the ocean mirror the dark moods of the kinsmen and clansmen. Once again, like the past three years, it has not been a good growing season. Drought one year and years with too much rain killed many of their crops, leaving the farmers with a depleted supply of vegetables for the rest of the year. With this in mind Anna and Donald had planned a humble wedding.

That afternoon God bestowed a blessing upon the betrothed couple. Lach is pleased that the sun has replaced the gloomy and wet weather of the morn. This is the first wedding ceremony of his *clanns* that he will witness and he is very happy. Lach will honor this important event by donning his newest and best Maclean *plaid*.

Anna and the rest of the family, dressed in their best wedding clothes, are careful not to soil their dress as they traipse to the village along a path of rocks, puddles and wet grass. Anna in her white shawl has attached a sprig of white heather for good luck. She carries her white lacy veil which she will don in front of the entrance to the *kirk*. They finally reach it and Caitriona meets them outside. They enter together leaving Anna and her *athair* at the entrance so that they can proceed down the aisle together.

Before Anna and Lach enter, Anna whispers, "*Athair*, I am so happy for this day." Lach then loops his arm into Anna's and they enter. Ahead of them is Donald in a beautiful *plaid* Campbell tartan which Caitriona had woven for him throughout the summer. On each side of the aisle sit the Campbells, the Macleans, the McKinnons as well as other kin and friends.

Candles on the altar and the sunlight entering the narrow windows brighten what would otherwise be a gloomy and dank sanctuary. The candles flicker creating shadows on the awaiting groom and the pastor. While Anna approaches the altar, she thinks to herself, "Life is so unpredictable right now on our Isle, but I feel less fear knowing that I will be facing the future with Donald."

When Anna reaches the altar, Lach removes his arm and he gives her a slight nudge towards Donald. He then turns around and goes to the pew to take his place beside Catherine. Anna and Donald hold hands while they recite their vows to each other:

"I, Donald, take thee, Anna, to be my wedded wife,
to have and to hold from this day forward, for better
for worse, for richer for poorer, for fairer or fouler,
in sickness and in health, to love and to cherish, till
death us depart, according to God's holy ordinance;
and thereunto I plight thee my troth."
"I, Anna, take thee, Donald, to be my wedded husband,
to have and to hold from this day forward, for better
for worse, for richer or poorer, in sickness and in health'
to be bonny and buxom at bed and at board, to love and to
cherish, till death us depart, according to God's holy
ordinance; and thereunto I plight thee my troth."

Anna and Donald then kiss, turn to face their family and friends, and lead them all out of the *kirk* to the *aite cruinneachaidh*. Earlier Catherine and her *siuirs* had gathered bunches of red-purple heather and placed them in large wooden vases. One special arrangement of white heather for good luck was placed in a prominent corner space.

Family and friends brought dishes of chicken, vegetables, cheeses, bread, butter and jams and placed them on the large wooden table near the wall. Each family has their own wooden cups which they will use to freely ladle ale and whisky from the large vats provided by the Macleans and Campbells.

Soon the wedding party and guests arrive and they are greeted by the fiddler's music. The celebration quickly turns into a cacophony of the fiddler's music, singing, dancing, eating, drinking and laughter. Whenever there is a pause, family and guests congratulate the newlyweds. Caitriona and Iain share their happiness for the newlyweds. Caitriona endearingly embraces them, "Anna and Donald, you are a beautiful couple and God will be with you as you share your life together."

Iain also makes a point of speaking to his youngest *siuir* and Donald, "Congratulations, I am very happy for both of you."

The festivities last into the wee hours of the morning with clan members not leaving until all the ale and whisky had been drunk.

Before Catherine and Lach depart, Catherine imparts an ancient Gaelic blessing on the couple:

"May the roads rise with you
And the wind be always at your back
And may the Lord
Hold you in the hollow of His hand.
May God be with you and bless you;
May you see your children's children.
May you be poor in misfortune,
Rich in blessings
May you know nothing but happiness
From this day forward."

After all have left, Anna and Donald wearily head back to the Maclean's *bothie* to start their life together. The early dawn gives them just enough light to make their way along the path. Anna loops her arm into Donald's. Exhausted, their words are few except when Anna remarks to Donald, "I have great joy that we are together as husband and wife at last."

Donald hugs his bride and responds, "Aye, Anna, our life together has just begun and I love you."

They reach the *bothie* together and quietly open the door. Quickly they remove their wedding attire and slip into their night shirts. In bed, they quietly kiss and hug each other, too exhausted for any nuptial endearments.

71
The Final Days

The wedding of Anna and Donald was the last celebration and happy event in Inivea. Autumn's focus of the farmers is on surviving the winter. As is the custom the crofters and villagers celebrate the festival of Samhain, but it is at a greatly subdued level. No one forgets, however, to please the souls of the dead by setting a place for them around their fires. Anna and Donald share with Lach and Catherine as they sit around the fire after eating, "It is a difficult time for all of us as we make decisions as to where and when we are going to locate."

Lach responds: "Aye, and so many of our decisions can't be made until we hear about a ship or are forced out of our farm and *bothie*. Of course those of us who have decided to leave our Isle are hoping that the news of a ship will happen before the end of August. We all know that if we do not receive good news, we will have to make a makeshift home somewhere until a ship arrives."

"It will be a long winter of not knowing, while we also must face meager food supplies," adds Anna.

Since their wedding Anna and Donald are boarding with the Macleans. As suggested by Catherine, Donald spends time each late afternoon with Anna, reviewing passages from the Gaelic Bible. Anna's first question to Donald is, "Donald, I want to know why God gave me this red hair. Surely God must have known the ancient belief of red-heads."

Donald responds, "Anna, I don't think that we will find that answer. Maybe the Bible, however, will help you come to terms with the circumstances of your birth. Perhaps it is more how you accept what God has given to you rather than the why of it. Just like our clan must now accept the circumstances of our life and move on to find solutions."

Anna then questions, "Donald, where is that mentioned in our Bible?"

"Anna, I am not trained as a Pastor," answers Donald. "It will take time to explore the Bible. Maybe I can read each night some of the stories and passages that Pastor Robertson had me read and in these you might find your answer." One of the first stories that Donald shares with Anna is the story of Job.

Anna speaks, "Donald, I don't understand. Why would God inflict such pain upon Job?"

"Anna, it is very difficult to understand this story of Job. Perhaps it shows us that no matter what happens, it is important not to give up our faith and trust in God," replies Donald.

"Such trust and faith are very hard for me to accept right now," adds Anna.

"Aye, Anna, life is very difficult for all of us in Inivea and for folks throughout our Isle. I hope that someday we will have a more hopeful and brighter future."

Anna reflects to herself, "I don't understand why God doesn't help us more in these difficult times."

Soon after the *Samhain* some cattle drovers come through the glen inquiring as to whether any of the crofters want them to drive their cattle to the mainland of Scotland. Lach meets the drovers outside and says, "I am ready to sell some of my livestock."

"Man, we are buying cows only," answers one of the drovers, a large and burly fellow.

Lach has dealt with him in the past and he reminds himself, "This one is definitely the boss and there will be no point in arguing with him to trade any of my other livestock. I have four cows to sell," adds Lach.

"Let me look them over," demands the head drover. "I will judge which cows I want."

"They are out in the pasture. We can go there and you can look them over," suggests Lach.

The boss drover then adds, "Let's hurry, I don't have any time to waste."

Lach and the boss rush to the pasture. Lach picks out his four cows, "These are mine," he says.

The drover looks them over, "This one is too skinny. She does not look as if she can make the long trip to the lowlands. I will take these three. They are not worth the full price. I will give you only half of what I usually give for larger and more hardy cows. I am taking a chance on these three," the boss drover adds arrogantly, knowing that this crofter is at his mercy.

Lach begrudgingly agrees, "Take them then."

The drover gives him the small change and leaves with the cows and his men to visit the other farmers.

Lach hopes that he is doing the right thing for his family. He goes inside and talks to Catherine and the rest, "I had to accept a small amount of cash for three of our cows. The boss drover made a difficult trade for me, but I knew that I had little choice. We do not have enough to feed our cows throughout the winter and the money will help pay our rent. We will slaughter the rest of our livestock throughout the year as we need them," adds Lach.

Catherine responds, "You did what you could, Lach. We will manage."

And thus, it is that the cold dark winter is passing in the Maclean *bothie* . Anna and Donald make frequent trips to the village to visit family. Donald misses his young *brathair*, Alexander and teaching him the way of the world. "Alexander, how are you?" Donald greets his young *brathair*.

Alexander responds "I miss you greatly. Roderick is too busy with our *athair* in the blacksmith shop to entertain me."

Donald asks, "Do you help your *mathair* with the feeding of the livestock and chores?"

"Aye," replies Alexander. "But sometimes I still want to have you here."

"You must remember, Alexander, to help out and forget about being entertained. That time is long gone when you were a little *bairn*. Now you are big and ready to help your *mathair*. At nine, almost ten, it is time for you to give up childish ways." Donald knows that Anna and he have a new life to forge and Alexander will have to get used to the separation of his older *brathair*.

In the Maclean *bothie* during the cold bleak days and nights there is also a lot of conversation about the future. Lach often speaks up first, "I wonder if our ship will come this year. It is now 1808 and it feels as if we have been waiting a long time. We must leave our *bothie* by the end of August and it is already February."

"If we have to move to temporary homes, it will be best to locate to Tobermory where I hope a ship will come soon," offers Catherine.

"It is such a time of confusion and not knowing," adds Anna.

Donald is quiet during the whole exchange. Then he speaks up, "In July, Iain and I will travel to Tobermory to see if there is any news. We will go to the post office and the hotel. They might have received notice."

July comes at last to the glen and Iain and Donald make plans to travel to Tobermory. They wait for a pleasant day, hoping that the often-unpredictable weather of their Isle will remain travel worthy for their journey. "Let's go, Iain," Donald beckons to his *brathair-ceile.*

"Aye, I am ready," responds Iain.

Anna cautions as they leave, "Take care of yourselves and come back soon."

The duo hike in silence hoping to make good time but also on the lookout for bandits who might be lurking behind rocks and trees. There have been several robber encounters on this trek to Tobermory since the experience that Lach and Anna had faced several years ago. Mostly the clansmen have been prepared for these and armed with their *dirks* and swords, they have been able to fend off the bandits. However, there have been several injuries and one fatality. The Isle has become more dangerous since the lairds began evicting the crofters from their farms. The dispossessed have been desperate for their own survival. Every movement of animals and birds alert the travelers and with hands on their weapons, Donald and Iain are prepared.

With good fortune they arrived safely at Tobermory. The sun, just as they had hoped, is at its highest point. Donald and Iain agree that they have made good time. Their first stop is at the hotel. There they meet Rut and tell her of their mission. "Hello Rut," they greet her.

"Donald and Iain, it is good to see you," responds Rut. "Both of you are looking so much more robust and healthier, since the last time I saw you. What brings you to Tobermory?"

"We are here to find out if there is any word of a ship taking passengers to North America," adds Donald.

"I have not heard of such a happening," replies Rut. "The post office always has the latest news and they have not posted any ship news in the village."

"Thank you, Rut. We will walk to the post office now," reports Donald. "Is there a room here at the hotel for an overnight?"

"Yes, you will be taken care of," responds Rut.

Donald and Iain, downhearted, traipse to the post office. Since

Rut did not know of a potential ship arriving they are not too hopeful. They enter the modest wooden building of the post office. The postmaster greets them, "Hello, and what can I do for you?"

Iain responds this time, "We want to know if there is word of a ship coming to Tobermory to take passengers to North America."

"No, not yet," answers the postmaster. ""But if you can stay in Tobermory for a few days, I expect mail from the mainland soon.

"We will do that and hopefully there will be good news," answers Donald.

Two days pass and there is no new mail. Rut and Tomas invite Donald and Iain to eat the evening meal with them. When they are all sitting around the fire, Donald announces his marriage to Anna. Donald is not sure how Rut will receive this news, but she has mellowed since those days in Inivea. In her work as a maid at the hotel she has met many travelers, some of them were red-heads. Tomas has made sure that Rut let go of her old beliefs and superstitions. Rut was not one to be warm and affectionate but she did congratulate Donald. Donald was secretly glad that he told the truth to Rut.

Iain asks Rut and Tomas, "Will you be joining the Campbells and the Macleans on the ship to sail to North America?"

"No, Iain, our life is good here," Tomas answers. Both Rut and I have good work and someday Deidre hopes to join her *mathair* at the hotel and Luke has already joined me at the distillery. We will stay here."

On the third day at Tobermory, Donald and Iain once again traipse to the post office. The postmaster happily greets them. "I have good news. The mail from the mainland has arrived and there is a ship arriving here soon, the beginning of August. The ship is the Clarendon and it will be taking on passengers to sail to Prince Edward Island in Canada."

Donald and Iain are ecstatic, "That is the place where our kinfolk, Seathan and Rose, sailed to several years ago. We will travel back to Inivea and alert everyone." Armed with their weapons and some food that Deidre had packed for them the previous evening, they waste no time and quickly begin hiking home.

They arrive safely in the late afternoon and Anna is the first to greet them. She first embraces Donald and then Iain. "I was worried about you. Why did it take you all this time to return?" she questions.

317

Lach, who has returned from his labour with the laird, comes out and also greets the two with an embrace. "Do you have any news for us?"

"Aye, *athair*, there will be a ship traveling to Prince Edward Island at the beginning of August," says Iain.

Catherine emerges and overhears the conversation. "Aye, this is wonderful news," interjects Catherine.

Lach then adds, "Iain, I know you are tired but everyone will be waiting for your news. Visit the rest of the farmers and share what you have found out. Donald, tomorrow you can go to the village and tell the villagers the good news."

In unison both Iain and Donald agree to Lach's request, "Aye." Iain takes off immediately while Donald joins Anna. They embrace and kiss each for many moments while also express joy for the good news. Anna lovingly whispers to Donald, "I am so happy to have you back safe. I missed you so much."

"Aye, my dear Anna, I have also missed you. At times I was quite discouraged thinking that a ship would not come to Tobermory. The postmaster, however, advised us to stay, saying that in three days he was expecting mail from the mainland. Hoping for the best we stayed and waited."

The following day Donald and Anna trek down to the village to alert everyone about the good news. Donald first visits his family. "I have good news," he announces. Isobel and Iain are very attentive as he tells his family about the Clarendon and its expected arrival time. Isobel and Iain agree to tell the other villagers.

Meanwhile Anna knocks on Flora's shop and Caitriona opens the door. "Caitriona, I have good news. A ship sailing to Prince Edward Island will be arriving in Tobermory the beginning of August. We must all get ready to leave Inivea soon."

Caitriona says, "Anna, this is good news. I will let Flora know. As you know she will not be leaving with us. She will go to Glasgow and find a shopkeeper whom she hopes will hire her for her weaving skills."

Now that the kinfolk has a ship and a date, the rest of the time before departure is spent saying goodbyes to the kinfolk and other friends who have decided to stay behind. Most have decided to travel to Scotland's mainland and try their hand at surviving in the bigger cities. Seumus and Moire Maclean and their family, as well as Lili and

Brian and their *mac*, Niel, will move to Glasgow. They know that they will live in poverty with work in factories. They are hoping, however, that this will pave the way for their *clanns* to develop better skills and eventually move out of poverty. They will take their chances because they do not want to leave their homeland. Others will move to the less desirable farmlands of Mull near the ocean, hoping to eke out a survivable living. Still others will move to Tobermory and take up the kelping trade or perhaps someday become fishermen. It is a difficult decision, but many do not want to travel into the unknown.

The last week before departure arrives. Lach calls to Catherine and his *clanns* along with Donald, "It is time to make our final packing decisions. Pack those items and clothes that you will be able to carry to Tobermory. Seumus will borrow a horse and cart to help us transport our items but remember storage of the ship will be limited. You must choose carefully those items that you believe will help you on board the ship and in a new land."

Anna makes sure that she packs some of her healing plants. Catherine selects her wooden spindle and several wooden bowls. Lach's items include his prize possession, a Maclean tartan. Donald packs his Campbell tartan. All the men will travel with their *dirk* and sword. Warm clothes for all, blankets and much food items will also be stuffed carefully into their satchels. It is a small load of items compared to what they will be leaving behind.

Lastly, Lach invites those who will not be leaving the village to take the remaining livestock, farm equipment and household items.

The day of bidding farewell arrives and the Campbells, as well as the other families planning to travel to Tobermory, gather at the Maclean *bothie*. Lach and his family, including Marta, Molly and Roibeart await the arrival of all the travelers. Lach then announces to the group, "I close this door forevermore. I give this blessing for our journey":

'Bless to me, O God,
The earth beneath my foot.
Bless to me, O God,
The path whereon I go;
Bless to me, O God,
The thing of my desire;
Thou Evermore of evermore,

Bless Thou to me my rest.
Bless to me the thing
Whereon is set my mind,
Bless to me the thing
Whereon is set my love;
Bless to me the thing
Whereon is set my hope;
O Thou King of kings,
Bless Thou to me mine eye!'

At that the group say "Amen" and then sing "Auld Lang Syne." At the ending there are tears in every eye. *"Tioraidh* (goodbye) our dear Inivea and our dear kinfolk and clansmen. At that final utterance the group departs for Tobermory.

Anna remarks to Donald, "It is a sad time when we must leave our beautiful island. But life as we had known it will never be the same. I am glad we are beginning this new phase of our life together."

"Aye, Anna," responds Donald. "It is another beginning for us and our families.
It is good that we are all going together to our new home."

72
Hope for New Beginnings

The travelers are a sight as they enter Tobermory. Small *bairns* are crying and the younger *clanns*, filled with energy, scamper throughout the crowd. Some have never seen a town like this before and they are surprised by the many sights. There in the bay is a very large sailing vessel with four white gigantic masts, ready to take them across the seas. Such a sight none of them have ever viewed. Whispers of amazement and disbelief spread throughout the crowd.

The folks from different parts of Mull find spots near the bay to camp out and wait for the boarding of the ship. Other travelers, mainly from Perth County, have traveled at least a week to seek passage to North America. Tobermory explodes with strangers desiring a better life of new beginnings.

The mood of these strangers all packed together is mixed with hopefulness and fear. Anna overhears a young *bean* near her, "Peter, I worry so much about our future. How will we survive in a new land where we are without our kin?"

Peter McFarlane answers, "Janet, we are young and we will work hard. We have been told that there are opportunities of work and land on Prince Edward Island. We have nothing here. On our journey here we have met many others who agree that we will work together to form a Gaelic community. We will support each other for our mutual survival."

"I pray every day to our Lord for a safe passage and the survival that you speak of," responds Janet McFarlane.

Overhearing this conversation confirms Anna's feelings. She reflects, "Like this young woman I am also afraid and I do not want to leave. But I also believe that we have no other choice." She has shared these thoughts with Donald who has reassured her in the same way that Peter has given hope to his young *bean*. At that point she introduces herself to the young couple, "Hello, I am Anna Campbell from Mull. Would you like some bread and cheese?"

Janet replies, "Yes, that is so kind of you. I am Janet McFarlane and this is my *fear,* Peter McFarlane. We have traveled from Caplia, Perth. It was a long and difficult journey and we had to leave family behind. They might decide to join us in a couple of years, but they saved their money for our passage.

Anna is feeling positive now that she has made a new acquaintance. It gives her some hope for her new life.

Others from Mull and Perth are making new acquaintances. They generally get to know one another by sharing food. Those from Perth do not have as much food because they have traveled a long distance. The folks from Mull, having traveled a shorter distance, have some to share. Anna views this as proof of Peter's comment that in their new land they will form a Gaelic community and help each other to create new beginnings.

Several days after their arrival they are told that the ship will be leaving on August 6th. When Tomas and his family visit, the Macleans let them know.

On the day they are leaving, Lach, who is usually quite stoic, embraces his younger *brathair,* "Tomas, I wish you were joining us. I know that you and Rut have a good life here which is a good reason to stay, but I will miss you."

"Aye, I am very sad to say this a final goodbye to you and all my family," replies Tomas. "I wish you were just several hours away instead of across the ocean. You will be making a new life for yourselves. Good luck and I wish you safe passage," Tomas adds with tear-filled eyes.

All hug each other before they depart to board the ship. Anna speaks to Luke and Deidre, "I will miss seeing you get married someday and having *clanns* of your own. Be good to your *mathair* and *athair!*"

Gathering all their belongings the Macleans and the Campbells head to the ship. As they go up the gangplank Anna cries to Donald, "It is too difficult to leave and sail across the sea to the unknown. I don't want to go!"

Donald whispers back, "We have each other and with family we will all survive together. I trust in the Lord who will guide us."

Catherine overhears this exchange between her *nighean* and Donald and she adds, "Anna, try not to be afraid. There is nothing for us in Mull. There is much promise for us in a new land. We have each other."

Anna adds, "I know all these things, *mathair,* but I am so very sad. It is hard to say goodbye to my home and land."

"Aye," Catherine agrees, "It is very difficult for all of us."

They reach the top of the gangplank and are greeted by a sailor. He introduces himself, "I am the master of this ship, The Clarendon, and I need to collect information from everyone to put into our passenger log. Please give me your first name, your surname, your age, your occupation and your place of origin. I will also put you into family groups."

Lach responds first, "I am Lachlann Maclean, age 60, labourer from Mull, Argyle." The master then proceeds to take the information from the rest of the Macleans, followed by the Campbells behind them. Anna and Donald present themselves as *fear* and *bean* for the passenger log.

It takes all day to board and record 192 passengers. Meanwhile Anna and Donald with the rest of their families make their way down the steep stairs to steerage where they will be spending long weeks of travel.

Anna is horrified when she sees the condition of the living quarters. She speaks out rather loudly, "There are no bunks for sleep. The living space is filthy and cold. There is a stink of urine and feces already. It is airless and I am sure it will be much worse when all the passengers arrive here. I fear what living here for 6 weeks or more will be like."

Isobel Campbell, almost silent throughout much of the trek and while waiting to board, cries out in anguish, "How will my young *clann* endure these decrepit conditions?"

Hearing his *mathair's* cries of despair, Alexander Campbell, now 9 years old, tries to console her, "*Mathair,* I am strong. Do not worry about me."

Iain joins Isobel, Alexander and Roderick and gives them reassuring hugs, saying, "Do not be afraid. We have many blankets to keep us warm. We will huddle together for protection. Anna has brought many herbs to help us with symptoms if we ail. Our Lord will take care of us."

Securing their spaces for the journey with their bundles, the Macleans and the Campbells decide to go to the deck for fresh air and to say a final goodbye to their beloved Scotland. On the deck they look over to the village and beyond it to the farmlands and the hills. The meadows are covered with red-purple heather and thistle. Summer flowers, pink, red and yellow dot the hillsides.

They and other passengers are finally aboard and logged in. All the passengers are now standing on the deck to say goodbye to the crowd and their homeland. They hear sad wails from below. The Macleans quickly spot Tomas and his family in front, tearful and waving. The ship horn blasts alerting all that it is time to sail. As the ship pulls out from the harbor the strains of "Auld Lang Syne," fill the air. The village and the green hills are quickly lost in the distance.

Author's Notes

This tale was written to reflect the life of the Western Highlanders of Scotland after the Battle of Culloden in 1746. To the best of my ability I have tried to make this life as accurate as possible. However, it comes from a twentieth century woman who has never lived in Scotland and has never visited the Highlands. All descriptions of the landscape, flora and fauna were derived from research. The lifestyle of the clansmen was also gathered from many resources. I wanted to portray their celebrations and the struggles of survival on a somewhat infertile land with difficult weather patterns for farming. I have included also some of the illnesses that the clansmen suffered from. Despite living basically in a primitive fashion and near starvation some of the time, it is reported that due to their simple diet, they had better health than many of the Scottish Lowlanders.

Two of the folks described, Donald and Anna Campbell, were the Scottish ancestors of my mother. The only information I had regarding these folks were the fact that they were born in 1782 and 1785, respectively. I chose to write a tale about these ancestors, descendants of the Western Highland clans of Scotland, because the history during that era of the 18th and 19th Centuries was interesting and fateful. The timing of the birth of these ancestors makes it clear that their direct ancestors were part of the life-changing upheaval to the clans that had been occurring in that part of Scotland, namely the Battle of Culloden and the Highland Clearances.

Many Scotsmen believe that the lairds, many being chieftains of the old clans of the Highlands, became selfish and vicious to their subjects. The lairds decided that raising sheep for their meat and wool would be a better financial decision for their pocketbooks. Thus, they began evicting the croft farmers from their *bothies* and small rig farms, replacing them with enclosures to raise their sheep. Some English Lords also took part in this feudal system of land ownership, evicting tenant farmers when it became more profitable to raise sheep and developing sporting estates, stocking deer for hunting.

There was often no place for these crofters whose ancestors had built their *bothies* and farmed their small plots for centuries. Since there is very little arable farmland on the Western Highlands, the farmers found it necessary to emigrate to the big cities of Scotland, the lowlands and the faraway lands of North America and Australia.

My ancestors affected by the Highland Clearances decided to relocate to North America. They sailed from Tobermory on the Isle of Mull in the Western Highlands of Scotland on August 6, 1808 on the Clarendon to Prince Edward Island, Canada. I believe that I can assume that economics drove them to leave the land of their birth. Donald Campbell declared on the ship's log that he was a labourer who was unable to find work.

I have developed a tale of the Campbell and the Maclean families who are also listed on the Clarendon's ship's log. Anna and Donald Campbell are listed separately, and I made a leap, developing a kinship between Anna and Donald with one of the Maclean families and one of the Campbell families. Since families often emigrated together this relationship could be a strong possibility.

Many of the records of the Highlanders in the 18th and 19th centuries were destroyed during the Clearances. The only way I was able to trace my family was through the log of the Clarendon. I was lucky that this ship kept such a good log. Many ships during this time period did not keep any passenger logs. Out of the 192 passengers, 92 were from the Isle of Mull, whereas most of the other passengers on this ship were from Perth, Scotland.

In summary I plan to write another historical novel tracing my ancestor's emigration aboard the Clarendon in 1808 to Prince Edward Island. This new novel, as with the one I have just written, will use as much written documentation as is available. The life of my ancestors will, however, be developed in the same manner as "Anna, The Witch of Mull." I hope you enjoy this tale as much as I have had writing it.

Glossary

Gaelic	English
aite cruinneachaidh	meeting place
ann an laghs	in-laws
athair	father
Aos Si	the spirits and faeries
bairn	baby
ban-ogha	granddaughter
banta	niece
bean	wife
bean mhic	daughter-in-law
Black Donald	devil
bothie	black house
brathair	brother
brathair-athar	uncle
byre	animal shed
cairn	a mound of stones built as a memorial
caudle	a ceremonial cake or drink
ceilidh	social gathering
clann	child
Clootie	devil
coinneamh	meeting
co-oghas	cousins
dirk	dagger
Dredgy	after-funeral feast
fear	husband
guising	young males visiting homes in disguise
kertch	cap of a married women
kirk	church
mac	son
mathair	mother
mumming	young males wearing costumes & masks
nighean	daughter
ogha	grandchild
parantans	parents
piuthar-cheile	sister-in-law

327

Glossary

Gaelic	English
piuthar-mathair	aunt
plaid	men's garment blanket
seanair	grandfather
seanmhair	grandmother
seantuismithheoiris	grandparents
shellycoat	bogeyman
shieling	a little hut
siuir	sister
snood	head covering of a maiden
tioraidh	goodbye
torrach	pregnant

About the Author

Virginia Altmann, a psychotherapist by vocation and a graduate of Boston University School of Social Work, grew up in a suburb of Boston, Jamaica Plain. She did not begin writing until her mid-70s after she retired. Her mother grew up in the foster care system of Boston in the early 20th Century and Virginia was able to obtain information of her mother's early life through the records obtained at Boston Social Services. These records also contained background information about her mother's matrilineality. From this research Virginia was able to understand her mother's life in the foster care system. It was not an easy life for her mother or her grandmother.

Wanting to honor her mother and make a written record of her mother's story as well as her ancestry, Virginia's first book, *Searching for a Four Leaf Clover*, accomplished what she set out to do. However, she became intrigued by her Mother's Scottish ancestry, especially those ancestors from the Isle of Mull in the Western Highlands of Scotland. These ancestors, poor croft farmers, were part of the emigration of the Highlanders due to the Clearances and lack of labour.

Always curious about cultures and history of earlier generations, Virginia wrote her first novel. This required much research in order to discover just how her Highland ancestors might have lived and why they eventually felt the need to leave their homeland and sail to the new land of Prince Edward Island. The dates and people of her ancestry were obtained by researching on the Ancestry.com site.

Virginia is planning on writing a sequel to this novel, reflecting the life of the early settlers on Prince Edward Island. Despite the desire to find a less hostile life in a new land, the new immigrants would face many challenges in their new home.